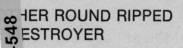

**...HER ROUND RIPPED
...ESTROYER**

...w the waterline and water began to thun-
d... ...gh the jagged hole. Prince ordered half
s... ...en twelve knots, but it was hopeless.
N... ...ould halt the onrush of water toward the
e... ...ms.

Suddenly an exploding shell sent shrapnel through the wide-open bridge. A metallic shard smashed into Prince's shoulder, knocking him to his knees in the slippery pool of blood under his feet. Despairingly, he called for the assistant gunnery officer. But he didn't answer. A scared rating came on the phone.

"Sir?"

"Who's left back there?"

"Just two of us. All the rest are dead . . . ."

Here's what the critics said:

"The author writes of the chaos and confusion, of the sound and fury of war at sea with an intimate knowledge that is utterly convincing."

Publishers Weekly

". . . has a completely authentic ring, highlighted by Captain Bassett's salty familiarity with the turbulent seas of 1942."

The New York Times Book Review

"Somewhere near the top of war novels are the books of James Bassett. (He) puts new swash and buckle into the old warfare-seafaring life . . . . Always there is the Hemingway-vintage search for the essence of manhood."

New Orleans *Times*

Commander Prince, USN

BY JAMES BASSETT

MANOR
BOOKS
INC.

A MANOR BOOK 1974

Manor Books Inc.
329 Fifth Avenue
New York, New York 10016

Library of Congress Catalog Card Number: 77-154089

FOR MY OFFICER-COMRADES OF HUT 15,
HEADQUARTERS, COMMANDER SOUTH PACIFIC,
SOME LIVING, SOME NOW DEAD,
WITH WHOM I SERVED DURING THOSE CRUCIAL
MONTHS OF 1942–43

CONTENTS

THAT FIRST YEAR of the Pacific War was difficult, critical and, in many ways, impossible for the Allies, already enmeshed in a tremendous European effort. Those who fought in the Southwest and South Pacific, often faced with hopeless odds, were gallant men.

This is their saga, told as a novel, although based on certain historical facts. All characters portrayed herein are fictional, except for the admirals and generals of the time, who are clearly identified by their true names.

There was an actual incident involving the capture of an American destroyer in drydock by the Japanese during the Allied evacuation of the Netherlands East Indies. But the circumstances of that seizure and the subsequent career of the former U.S. vessel were entirely different from the account given in this story.

Cowards die many times before their deaths;
The valiant never taste of death but once.
Of all the wonders that I yet have heard,
It seems to me most strange that men should fear,
Seeing that death, a necessary end,
Will come when it will come.

—SHAKESPEARE, *Julius Caesar*, II, ii

PROLOGUE

I

"Proceed on Duty Assigned"

SOMEWHERE BEYOND the dark Celebes Sea, the first light of
dawn was a pale, probing finger, gingerly testing the night sky,
as a surgeon might explore a clotted wound. Its uncertain reflection penetrated the dirt-smeared portside windows of the lumbering aircraft, lending ghostly substance to the men asleep on the
bucket seats that extended longitudinally down the fifty-foot
cabin. Forward in the boxlike compartment were a pair of fi-
bered fuel tanks, designed to give the transport a 3,000-mile
cruising range, instead of its normal 2,000, and a small mountain of baggage stenciled with the code name of their destination: Cutlass, for Balikpapan, Dutch Borneo. The gear was
secured with heavy rope against the plane's unpredictable gyra-
tions; the passengers slept untrammeled by safety belts, their
hands clutching the tubular rails of the seats, even in sleep.

There were six of them: two officers of commander's rank,
a chief yeoman and three minor deck ratings. All wore grimy
khakis. Rivulets of sweat furrowed their unshaven faces as they
slumbered, for the plane had descended to within a few hundred
feet of the fetid Borneo jungle, as a precautionary measure

against any stray Japanese Zeros once the sun rose. The cabin temperature was in the high nineties.

The elder of the two officers, a man in his late thirties, lay sprawled face up across several metal seats. His left arm still shielded his eyes from the naked cabin lights which had, in fact, been extinguished ever since the craft started its taxi run down the tarmac at Manila airport. All that was visible of his face was a bulbous potato of a nose, a flaring red mustache shaped to artillery specifications, a wide-open mouth from which issued snores loud enough to be audible over the roar of the twin Hornet engines, and a beard that flowed down over his barrel chest like a child's bib. In the quickening dawn, the burn scars that had impelled him to grow the mustache and the beard a year earlier glistened whitely beneath the tangle of rufous hair.

It came as no surprise to strangers that the man's nickname was Beaver. None of his peers ever called him anything else, particularly since his real name, Algernon Monk, struck them as being so utterly incongruous. He was the permanent British liaison officer between the Royal Navy remnants in the Far East and that ragtag assemblage of antique ships known rather pretentiously as the United States Asiatic Fleet.

Across from the Beaver, the second commander was already coming awake. His right hand groped automatically into a breast pocket for the silver case in which he kept his Luckies. With casual disregard for the nearby auxiliary tanks, he ignited his first cigarette of the new day off the thin flame of a gold Dunhill, then inhaled deeply, gratefully, in the manner of a man reprieved from a bad dream.

For a brief moment he stared out the starboard window, trying to fathom where they were. But there was no recognizable break in the seemingly endless jungle that unreeled below them like a banal travelogue, except for an occasional brown river that snaked through the fronded trees, or a tiny cluster of nipa huts that marked a native village.

It had been an uneventful flight, from the time the plane lifted off the pitted runway at Manila until now, as they approached Balikpapan, on Borneo's desolate southeast coast. During the first hour he had sat in the copilot's chair, listening to the wearisome palaver of the overaged pilot, a mustang two-striper, who chainsmoked atrocious cigars. As the plane bumbled over Mindoro island, and then essayed the Sulu Sea crossing, the pilot delivered a continuous monologue on the hazards of flight in the benighted month of December, anno Domini 1941.

This was, he gloomed, one hell of a way to waste the twilight hours of your life, driving a rattletrap R4D along a route patrolled by the frigging Nips. Especially since the Navy's halfass version of the civilian DC-3 airliner would be monkeymeat for a Jap Zero. Assuming they made Borneo, the Ancient Mariner said dolefully, their situation would worsen, if anything, because there wasn't a landing strip big enough for an R4D between Mindoro and Balikpapan.

The pilot relit the stub of his Philippine cigar for the third time. Mostly he had been staring straight ahead, as if talking to the windshield. But now he turned toward his passenger.

"Ain't this a pisspoor way to celebrate Christmas, Commander?"

The commander, an elegantly slim, deeply tanned officer, smoothed his prematurely graying hair with an indolent hand. His Annapolis ring glinted in the dim cockpit light. He regarded the pilot solemnly for a moment, his dark eyes unblinking beneath his shaggy upswept brows.

"True, Mr. Dawkins. I can think of numerous better ways."

He unsnapped his safety belt and stood up. Despite his rumpled khakis, Commander Prince managed to project an aura of scrupulous neatness. The pilot watched him step lithely through the cockpit hatch and disappear into the cabin darkness, like a genteel wraith. As a mustang, an up-from-the-ranks nonentity, it always graveled Dawkins to be confronted by these quintessen-

17

tial Academy types, who could sweat so daintily they never stank, and whose pants looked impeccably pressed, even when hanging around their goddamn patrician knees as they sat on the can.

Commander Prince was, in his humble estimation, one of the best (or worst) examples of this arrogant breed. As a staff pilot for the Commander-in-Chief, Asiatic Fleet, Dawkins had plenty of standing time for assessing what he derisively termed the Chairborne Commandos. These were the captains, commanders and lieutenant commanders who spent their days and nights trying to evolve ways of turning back the Japs with somebody else's blood and guts. It gave him a feeling of immense satisfaction now to know that Prince was no longer a remote chessplayer, but one of the vulnerable pieces on the Big Board: a cut above a mere pawn, perhaps, yet nevertheless a *thing* to be manipulated by his former associates, with his life dependent on their strategic pencil-pushing.

Suddenly Dawkins thumbed his nose in the direction of the vanished commander. "Screw you, mac," he called softly. It was only a token gesture of defiance. But he felt a lot better. Then he gave his full attention to the lonely business of flying the R4D. Being without a copilot didn't bother him unduly, although it meant five solid hours in the driver's seat, and using a relief tube to keep from wetting his britches.

Besides, there weren't any spare jockeys in Manila, at this eighth inning in the losing ballgame, so what was the sense of complaining. Nobody would listen, anyhow. . . .

A half hour after official sunrise, the plane's interior became bathed with a strange roseate glow, a phenomenon which stirred no aesthetic joy in the soul of Commander Prince, for it portended a period of monsoon rain and wind. He checked his steel wrist chronometer. It was almost six-thirty. They were due to land at Balikpapan in another twenty minutes.

Laboriously, because of an unaccustomed stiffness in his shoulders from sleeping on the hard bucket seats, he bent down to pull on his mahogany-brown jodhpur boots. These were a source of secret pride to Prince, who had ordered them by mail from Abercrombie & Fitch in the summer before the war started. He had kept them hidden in his foot locker at the bachelor officers' quarters, against the time when he could wear them with impunity, away from the mocking gaze of the naval aviators, who maintained that mere surface sailors should stick to their black-shoed last. Dawkins had noticed them, he knew, but that didn't matter, because Dawkins was more a part of the plane's hardware than he was a real person.

When Prince had finished buckling the jodhpurs above his ankles, he straightened and glanced across the aisle. His nostrils twitched slightly as he caught a whiff of stale perspiration from the somnolent Beaver. He speculated whether the delicate subject of deodorants could be tastefully broached and how the Britisher might accept any such suggestion, now that the two of them were slated to share the confined spaces of a tropics-based destroyer. He sighed regretfully. The Beaver was getting deplorably Americanized. He even wore silver maple leaves on his shirt-collar points, instead of proper Royal Navy shoulder boards, to denote his rank.

Besides, the Beaver was his senior by a couple of years, and even nominal seniority made it awkward for Prince to throw his weight around. He could, of course, if it pleased him to do so. For, after all, he *was* taking command of a destroyer division, and the Beaver was simply going along for the ride, until an opportune moment came to offload him on a ship bound for the Allied naval base at Surabaya, 600 miles down the Makassar Strait and across the Java Sea.

There was one ironic crumb of comfort to be derived from the grim thought that the Beaver was running out of home offices to which he might field his complaints. Singapore was well on its way to being transformed into a keystone of Japan's Greater East Asian Co-Prosperity Sphere, by the little men who had come barreling down the Malay Peninsula, despite owlish predictions that nobody could breach that impassable jungle. Manila was plainly doomed. And all that interposed between the enemy and Australia itself was a mythical thing called the Malay Barrier. The United States had assumed defense responsibility for this line after the British confessed in the gloomy spring of 1939 that they couldn't spare a battle fleet for Singapore, once the crunch came.

Prince still had a mind's-eye picture of the Malay Barrier, drawn from his recollections of the original war plan for the Pacific, a bulky document labeled Rainbow 1. It curved southeastward from Siam's Kra Peninsula, past Singapore, along the Dutch East Indies, and finally anchored on Portuguese Timor. It was 2,000 miles long. But with the destruction of the American fleet at Pearl Harbor, on December 7, and the subsequent loss of HMS *Prince of Wales* and *Repulse,* the Malay Barrier was just another figment of the strategists' imagination.

To be sure, there would be a futile attempt to hold this paper line by the few warships available to the polyglot Allied command. A lot of people would get killed in the process. Among them, quite possibly, the six passengers now aboard the Balikpapan-bound R4D.

As Prince listened for a few more minutes to his companion's gargantuan snufflings, he felt a twinge of envy for the Briton's casual ability to cut himself adrift from the world without so much as a finger snap for the perils that lay across the horizon. The Beaver had a contempt for personal danger that bordered on the pathological, Prince thought. He was entitled to wear a DSO after having been creamed in the Mediterranean by a Stuka that dropped a 500-pound bomb down his destroyer's number-two stack, and then taking a swim through an acre of burning oil. In another time the burns he sustained would have been rated a Blighty wound, entitling him to indefinite home leave. But Britain was too hard pressed for manpower by that time to permit such a luxury. So they patched him up and shipped him off to the Orient, considerably east of Suez, once the scar tissue had taken root and that godawful beard had veiled most of the damage.

The Beaver cheerfully admitted his deficiencies as the very model of a modern British officer, or one destined to become an admiral of the King's Navee. Polishing up the handle of the Big Front Door wasn't his forte. His Majesty's officers were considered an elite breed, sometimes tucking their hankies into their coat sleeves, and always impeccable, even under the worst fire, like Horatio Nelson's band of brothers.

"Maybe I'm a throwback," said the Beaver. "Every service has 'em. And the late Sir Francis Drake wasn't what you'd call a Galahad, just to name one example."

Or perhaps it was the bit of Gaelic on his mother's side and possibly somewhere a Cockney bar sinister on the old family escutcheon. Nonetheless, he *was* the Beaver, contentedly unchangeable, irreformable.

Personally, Prince felt no such exaltation at the thought of plunging into a war for which he had presumably been trained all his adult life. The training part, in fact, had been a delightful experience: "a piece of cake," in the flyboys' argot for a soft touch job. Some officers spent their whole careers progressing from one specialty school to another, learning the mysteries of electronics, or air combat intelligence, or the more esoteric trades like aerology and hydrography, without ever having to practice their newfound expertise out where it counted. Prince himself had ridden this pleasant circuit for a number of years, until the previous spring, when he'd had the misfortune to be tagged for Asiatic staff duty. But now the cake-eating was over. And so was the miserable night.

"We're getting ready to put down." Prince plucked irritably at the seat of his trousers, to free the damp khaki from his aching buttocks. "Christ, but it's hot in this lousy bucket!"

The Beaver bared his snaggled teeth in a horrible parody of a grin. "Wait till you've tasted Balikpapan at high noon," he said, "before you decide what heat really is."

Prince returned to the window. Ahead he could make out the barren, smokeless towers of the oil refinery which had been Balikpapan's sole reason for existence, and a minuscule break in the jungle that denoted the airstrip. Dawkins had throttled the R4D down to an appallingly slow speed. It was mushing, rather than actually flying, just above the treetops which clutched at the plane with great green claws. They should be landing, Prince reckoned, in another five minutes.

He got to his feet and lurched down the corrugated aluminum decking to where the four enlisted men still slept, sluglike, in the half gloom. They also had the Beaver's annoying knack of blotting out the world by the simple act of closing their eyes to its troubles. But in their case, Prince supposed, this feckless disregard for life's hazards was attributable more to ignorance than bravado.

Yet making the mental descent from hallowed officer country to the abject poverty of the forecastle proved quite impossible, especially as Prince gazed down at the unconscious profile of Chief Yeoman Elliot Bream.

It suddenly occurred to him that he knew absolutely nothing about Bream, although the fellow had been his confidential clerk for the better part of a year. If Bream enjoyed any life of his own, apart from the humdrum one he had led on the fourth floor of Asiatic Fleet headquarters inside Manila's ancient Walled City, Prince was unaware of it.

The unfathomable Bream was always there, his slightly balding blond head hunched over a sheaf of incoming dispatches, or his long graceful fingers typing out the outgoing messages.

Every hour on the hour he would fetch a mug of Earl Grey's tea for Prince. Bream brewed the tea himself, precisely to the commander's taste, making sure that a half-inch slice of sweet Philippine lime was on the saucer to give the potion a bit of zest. Prince suspected that Bream, like most yeomen in command setups, was an accomplished operator who gloried in being a man of many secrets, all of them gleaned from official communications. Hence Bream would undoubtedly be held in awe by his witless inferiors, who had only brawn to sustain them.

What Prince did not know, could not possibly know, was that Bream considered *everyone* on the staff his inferior, including the commander himself, whom Bream had written off as an ineffectual, posturing horse's ass fifteen minutes after they'd first met.

Prince reached down for the chief's bony shoulder and gave it a gentle tug. Bream rolled over on his back. His pallid blue eyes stared up impassively, as if divorced from the thin lips that slowly curved into a sardonic grin.

"Top o' the morning," he drawled, adding *sir* after a barely perceptible pause. "What's our ETA?"

"Estimated time of arrival is five minutes from now. Maybe less. Get cracking."

"Roger." Jackknifing his gaunt frame into an upright posture, Bream stretched a long arm toward the enlisted man nearest him on the bucket seats. "Pass the word, Marcus," he said conversationally. "We're landing."

As the seaman moved fumblingly along the aisle to rouse the other two enlisted passengers, the plane gave a lurch, lifted, then seemed to hesitate, like a roller coaster poised at the apex of its highest rise before it hurtles down the slope.

Prince sat down abruptly and twisted himself toward the window. The jungle was frighteningly close. For a split second he thought Dawkins had misjudged their height and blundered into a clump of trees. But the pilot hadn't. Instead, striving to make full use of every spare centimeter of runway, he had figured his glide path with a suicidal coolness. The lurch was caused by the unlocking of the R4D's wheels, which were now almost brushing the palm tops that grew almost to the perimeter of the truncated airstrip. Dawkins was compensating for the extra 500 feet of runway which he desperately needed but couldn't have.

"For Christ's sake," Prince yelled futilely, "get her up!"

Only the Beaver answered him. "Steady, old boy. Hold fast."

Prince gripped the steel edge of his seat so tightly that his knuckles showed white as the plane dived for the ground. At the ultimate moment, Dawkins leveled off, and the R4D touched down with a bone-jarring impact. It was still traveling at better than sixty miles an hour when it swept past the nether limits of the runway.

For an excruciating few seconds it slewed through the rain-moistened sand beyond the tarmac. Just before it reached the first row of trees, a tire blew. The plane tilted crazily, ground-looped, then caromed into the palm grove, coming to rest at a forty-five-degree angle, like a broken kite.

The brutal collision threw Prince out of his seat. Slightly dazed, he started crawling down the canted passageway toward the emergency exit. Bream was already there, undogging the bolts that secured the hatch on the upper side of the R4D's fuselage. Somehow they managed to clamber out of the wrecked craft and slide down its crumpled aluminum flank. Behind them scuttled the three enlisted men. A thin plume of smoke had begun to eddy from the port engine, which was imbedded into the earth, harbinger of the fire that would soon follow.

Prince glanced around, conscious for the first time of his painfully aching right knee and the blood that was slowly trickling down his forehead.

"Where's Commander Monk?" he croaked.

Bream shook his head. "Trapped inside, I guess, with Lieutenant Dawkins."

24

From the nether end of the airstrip, where the communications hut was located, Prince caught the faint whine of a siren, and he saw the Dutch firefighting jeep heading their way. It seemed miles distant, crawling like a poisoned garden snail.

He turned back to the plane. Flames were clearly visible under the nacelles of both engines, ugly little red gouts that grew larger as he watched, licking upward and outward like dragon tongues. He didn't know enough about the workings of an aircraft to estimate how quickly the fuel would ignite, but he supposed it would happen in a matter of minutes or less.

"Somebody has got to bring them out of there," he muttered.

"Yeah," said Bream. "Somebody."

Neither the chief nor his three men made a move. They remained motionless, frozen, gazing at the commander as if they were part of a tableau entitled *Military Circumstance,* caught at the precise instant of a key decision. Prince swallowed hard. Somebody indeed had to fetch Dawkins and the Beaver out of the bowels of the doomed R4D. And according to the Navy Book, that somebody was Prince, because the Holy Writ ordained that when an impossible one-man task loomed and no one else stepped forward, you goddamn well did it yourself.

He accorded Bream a last, smoldering stare. The chief said nothing, although the expectant gleam in his pale eyes was unmistakable. Without speaking, Prince limped toward the plane. Behind him he could hear the jeep's siren, louder, yet still too far away to justify any further delay in his self-imposed rescue attempt. Besides, the Dutch wouldn't understand, either, a commander's refusal to plunge into danger, however hopeless that plunge might be.

As he reached the R4D, Prince remembered the auxiliary tanks in the main cabin, filled with 500 gallons of high-octane gasoline. Once the flames touched them, they would explode like so much TNT, leaving nothing but a scorched crater where the plane had been. Involuntarily, his sphincter muscle spasmed,

25

and he clenched his teeth. Prince thought wildly for a moment that he was about to disgrace himself in front of the four men who had stayed at a prudent distance, silently watching his erratic race to the aircraft.

The dun-colored metal felt hot to Prince's hands as he struggled up to the open hatch, favoring his injured leg. Although the heat was caused by the furnace blast of the sun against the plane's naked skin, it heightened his sense of numb terror at what might happen any second inside the cabin.

Prince stopped once, a yard short of his goal, and fought back an impulse to turn tail and run. But he forced himself on. Then, abruptly, the Beaver's mammoth head emerged from the smoke-filled aperture, his face blackened.

"Got him," he called. "Poor devil's pretty well beat up. But he'll live, if we can haul him out of here."

Together they hoisted Dawkins through the hatch, none too gently, and handed him down into the waiting arms of Bream and Marcus, who had finally galvanized themselves into action.

Ten seconds after the two officers leaped clear of the smoldering wreckage, the R4D blew up with a horrendous roar. All that remained for the tardy Dutch firefighters was to hose down the rubble and extinguish a blaze that had started in the adjacent palm trees.

The officer-in-charge of the detail, after seeing Dawkins off to the hospital in an ambulance, finally got around to the walking wounded. He gave Prince a commiserating look.

"Are you all right, *overste?*"

"Approximately." Prince was uncomfortably aware that his voice quavered as he spoke. "If you'll just find me a goddamn head."

"A head, *overste?*"

"Latrine, can, toilet. It's an emergency."

"Ah." The Dutchman brightened. "At once."

He motioned toward a personnel carrier that had just arrived, flying the Dutch Navy's ensign on one front fender, a miniature blue flag embroidered with the legend *Nederland zal Herreutzen* on the other. This, it was explained proudly, signified that Holland would arise again.

Prince and the Beaver took the rear seat. Neither spoke as the trucklike vehicle threaded its way through the barricades of palm boles and barbed wire that lined the airfield, ready for emplacement across the landing strip at quick notice. Razor-sharp bamboo stakes driven into the ground completed the airfield's sketchy invasion preparations, aside from a scattering of sandbagged bunkers containing .30-caliber machine guns.

Prince was grateful for his companion's silence. He had been waiting, with no suitable reply in mind, for the Beaver to ask him why in hell he'd bugged out when the R4D hit, instead of sticking around and lending a hand in the cockpit.

Later, after a brief pit stop at the administration building, the Beaver finally broke the ice. But what he said had nothing to do with the crash. He jabbed a ragged-nailed thumb in the direction of the traffic that roiled past them, composed mainly of bicycles pedaled by white-clad Malays and Dayaks who wore curious little black caps on their cropped heads, like upside-down flower pots.

In a sententious tone he announced: "Welcome to lovely Balikpapan, Commander."

Frankly, Prince doubted very much that this abysmally drab morning could hold joy for anybody, including the devil-may-care Beaver. The skies were clouding up, intensifying the Turkish bathiness of the weather and threatening to rain at any minute. But above all else there was the undeniable fact of their forlorn mission, which they were approaching in such lubberly fashion.

Closer to home, there was the fact that they had lost everything of value in the flaming wreckage: their personal gear, their clothes, and whatever cherished mementoes sailors burden themselves with, on going to sea, in order to lend their ship-board quarters a semblance of dry-land gentility. This was one of the anomalies of nautical life. One professed to glory in its isolation, while accoutering his stateroom (if he were an officer) or his locker (if he were a forecastle hand) with all manner of nostalgic reminders. Treasured photographs. Well-thumbed books. Perhaps an artifact or two which, used faithfully, served as a reminder of the sweeter existence that awaited them, some-day, if they managed to survive.

In Prince's case, the artifacts consisted of a napkin ring bearing the seal of the old battleship *Texas,* in which he had once served in the prewar Atlantic, and a table lighter fashioned from a 50-millimeter shell casing. Both of these were nice, seamanly items, calculated to impress a wardroom mess and give an aura of naval solidarity to their owner. He would miss them for several valid reasons, none sentimental.

But Prince did regret the loss of his clothes: the khaki shirts and trousers made for him by a Filipino tailor outside the naval-base gate at Cavite. Unlike the government-issue stuff, the garments produced to order in that cluttered shop fitted perfectly. Shoulders didn't droop, nor was there that voluminous bulge around the shirt waist which gave even the trimmest wearer an incipient CPO's potbelly. And the narrower pants fell neatly to one's shoetop, instead of halting three inches too soon, or too late. Although Prince would have denied the adage that clothes make the man, he held firmly, if privately, to the belief that a de-cent wardrobe was an essential part of an officer's image.

Despite their irreplaceability, Prince was less concerned about the destruction of the other *lares et penates* that had been packed among his clothing: the enlarged snapshots of Gwyneth and Mari and the studio portrait of MaMa, which he had in-tended to display on the steel desktop in his eight-by-ten cabin.

Staring rather fuzzily from the mildewed leather frame, Gwyneth looked her usual haughty self, ready with some acerbic remark about the boorish naval hierarchy's contrast to the gentlemen for whom she worked in the High Commissioner's office on Dewey Boulevard. Prince guessed he wouldn't miss her as much, really, as he'd miss the *Texas* napkin ring.

As for MaMa's picture, encased in silver, which his messboy had kept brightly polished, Prince felt no pangs whatsoever. Ever since he had come to the Philippines, Prince had been intimidated by the sight of MaMa, whose cold eyes pursued him around his bachelor officer's digs, monitoring his every movement, from the time he crawled out of the sack, washed in the handbasin, shaved, deodorized, powdered and finally donned his khaki tailor-mades. No. MaMa would not be missed a goddamned bit.

Mari was a different story.

She would have made one hell of a conversation piece, using the operative word *piece* advisedly, because she herself had given him the photograph that night they'd spent in her miniature apartment over the Escolta boutique. Just looking at it made him hunger for her tiny breasts and her soft shoulders and her curved brown thighs, which now he could never vicariously share with his brother officers of Destroyer Division 11.

This depiction of Mari, exposed in all her wanton nakedness, artfully sprawled upon the satin-sheeted bed, had left nothing to a lustful male imagination. But now it was gone, irrevocably, and so was Mari.

Prince sighed a minimal sigh, shrugged and addressed his attention to the passing scene.

Ahead of the personnel carrier stretched Balikpapan harbor, a wedge-shaped expanse of brownish water bordered by a sandy swamp, along whose margin grew clumps of casuarina trees, mangroves and the ubiquitous nipa palm. Only five vessels lay at anchor in the roadstead. They were the four-pipers of DesDiv 11 and their venerable mother ship, USS *Gray Eagle*.

A motor whaleboat was nudging against the pilings of the wharf as they drew alongside. The ensign in charge stepped nimbly onto the pontoon landing and hastened up the splintered steps to greet the newcomers and tossed them a crisp salute.

"Commander Prince?"

Prince saluted back. "Why weren't we met at the airfield?"

The ensign stammered, "Golly, sir, they only gave us the word fifteen minutes ago that you'd arrived. That didn't allow enough leeway to get organized. And our skipper was—"

Prince interrupted, "Wasn't our schedule radioed ahead?"

"No, sir. Just the fact that you'd be coming in sometime to-day." The ensign's worried expression deepened. "Communications have been awfully bad since the Japs bombed Manila yesterday."

Prince suddenly noticed that the ensign, for all his seeming briskness, was a bone-tired young man. He had dark crescents under his eyes, and there was a tautness about his thin lips, as if he were making a special effort to keep them from trembling as he spoke. Remembering his own earlier embarrassment, Prince relented slightly.

"Things are tough everywhere, mister."

"Yes, sir."

"What's your name?" asked Prince in a gruff voice that sought to mask his discomfiture.

"Rand, sir. Tom Rand."

"Okay, Rand. Let's climb aboard."

"Where's your gear, sir?"

"We had a little trouble when we landed," the Beaver cut in. "The plane burned. So we're traveling light."

A thin rain had begun to fall before the motor whaler was halfway to the moored ships, warm, sticky and with the apparent consistency of beef consommé. Crouched in the stern, cupping his hands over his eyes to filter out the fine downpour, Prince stared with skeptical loathing at his new command.

Tiny wisps of gray smoke plumed from the after stacks of the four destroyers, indicative of their readiness to get underway with reasonable promptitude should an emergency arise. But aside from this meager sign of preparedness, DesDiv 11 looked appallingly incapable of meeting the Navy's standard dictum: "When in all respects ready for sea, proceed on duty assigned."

Nevertheless, it would soon be *his* responsibility to respond affirmatively to such an order, however unready he might find himself, because the Service brooked no *ifs, ands* or *buts* from a commander when the exact moment came to weigh anchor. And only a man with a career death wish would pretend he wasn't.

This uncompromising rule, more inflexible than ever in wartime, troubled Prince deeper than he would ever have admitted. It was so colossally unfair. When a commander was directed to take his ships into combat, he should be permitted to make sure that any deficiencies in manpower and hardware were corrected before exposing them to enemy gunfire. Otherwise it could be plain suicide.

Looking now at the scrofulous, paint-peeling, hedge-fence profile of USS *Henry P. Davidson,* his divisional flagship, Prince was more than ever haunted by the grave self-doubt that had blossomed from a small seed of worry, sown the afternoon when the admiral first suggested him for this business. Had he been really honest with himself, Prince would have attributed this massive uncertainty to the fact that he was ill-equipped professionally to take over a combat command. He might also have acknowledged the fact that he was a personal coward. No matter. Given competent underlings, an exec or a couple of twenty-year chiefs, one could camouflage the first truth; but the second must be kept concealed beneath a layer of spurious courage, which might stretch transparently thin under the pull of circumstance.

The sight of *Davidson* and her three siblings, *McGraw, Travers* and *Vincent,* was not calculated to ease this doom-feeling. They had been overly long in the fang when Prince was a raw plebe in 1924. Now they were almost a quarter-century old and looking every dreary hour of it.

Davidson typified the breed. She was a rusty, creaky, pseudo-greyhound, named after an evanescent hero of the brief Mexican-American imbroglio of 1914.

Along with her twelve Asiatic Fleet sisters, *Henry P. Davidson* was as American as the Model-T and as aesthetically designed. Unlike a number of this 1917–18 class, which had been refitted for such mundane chores as mine-sweeping, troop-hauling and chasing rumrunners in the Twenties, *Davidson* retained her distinctive four smokestacks. Hence the sobriquet: four-piper.

Davidson herself (despite her masculine name, nobody ever thought of her as a *he*) had led a whore's life since her birth at the Bath, Maine, ironworks. Like a premature or unacknowledged bastard infant, she had been gestated in fewer than the customary nine months. From keel laying until the instant her unfinished hull slid into the ice-cold Kennebec River estuary, barely thirty-nine days had elapsed. She was commissioned less than two months later.

By then the need for haste was long past. For it was the early spring of 1919. During the period of "normalcy" that immediately followed the war, *Davidson* drew a coveted Presidential convoy, escorting the doomed Warren Gamaliel Harding to Alaska in the summer of 1923.

That same year, in September, she survived a disaster that wiped out seven four-pipers. Fourteen destroyers of the battle fleet, making a round-the-clock test run from San Francisco to San Diego, blundered into the Point Arguello nautical grave-yard because of a pea-soup night fog, abnormal currents whipped up by the huge Tokyo earthquake and some woefully bad navigation that put them nine miles off course.

Bruised and shaken, *Davidson* was relegated to the inactive list early in 1924. With several dozen of her sisters she remained nested in the backwaters of San Diego Bay for six long years, until the harassed economy-era Navy recommissioned sixty four-pipers as replacements for sixty others that had become thoroughly worn out.

Certain postwar embellishments increased her original displacement from 1,100 to 1,240 tons and deepened her draft to a shade under fourteen feet. But her "fine"—meaning excessively slim—hull ratio stayed unchanged. *Davidson* was 314 feet long, with a thirty-one-foot beam. This ten-to-one factor made her tricky as a drunken ballet dancer in a high sea, a trifle top-heavy because of her tall funnels, and given to heart-stopping rolls of fifty degrees or more when a chasmal wave trough engulfed her.

Davidson's two geared turbines, fed from a quartet of midships boilers, generated almost 30,000 shaft horsepower, enough to drive her at approximately thirty-five knots when her bottom was clean.

As the whaleboat maneuvered to come alongside, Prince saw that she was barnacled and slime-festooned. Thus, her long legs, which under optimum conditions could carry her 5,000 miles without replenishing her fuel bunkers, had grown distressingly short.

Davidson was suited with the standard array of popguns for her outmoded type: four single-purpose four-inch rifles, one three-inch antiaircraft peashooter, four .30-caliber machine guns. Her four-inch main battery weapons couldn't elevate their muzzles past the forty-five-degree mark, which was reckoned the necessary maximum for surface engagements, a hobbling circumstance that made her less than threatening to an aerial foe. Whenever she stepped past her normal fourteen-knot cruising speed, *Davidson's* low-slung fantail became awash. And this being the ridiculous place where the refitters had implanted the three-inch AA gun, her potential response to an oncoming enemy plane was even less impressive.

33

The British, having gratefully accepted fifty four-pipers in Mr. Roosevelt's celebrated ships-for-bases swap, quickly discovered some of the least charming aspects of this archaic class. As the Beaver told it, when he heard about Prince's new orders in Manila, their inordinate skinniness, plus the close juxtaposition of their twin screws, caused them to behave clumsily in tight turns. What's more, he said, you had to keep the buggers' fuel tanks topped off—or ballasted with sea water—lest they exceeded design specifications for pitch-and-roll and maybe wound up playing submarine, something which every destroyerman mortally feared. Ballasting was essential but damned bothersome, since the infusion of sea water tended to louse up the next batch of oil.

Other little idiosyncrasies of this breed, which Beaver had learned firsthand during a couple of shakedown runs with the exchange fifty, included a deplorable tendency to ship water through the weather-deck hatchway that led to the crew's quarters beneath the bridge superstructure.

Also, the steering engine beneath the fantail was controlled by cables attached to the bridge wheel. These attenuated lines extended through the engine and boiler rooms, the Beaver reported gloomily, and were apt to get snafued beyond mortal man's ability to comprehend or correct.

None of the four ships of DesDiv 11 boasted radar, either for searching out hostile vessels, spotting aircraft or for accurate gunnery beyond the range of the pointer's naked eye.

Davidson carried a 186-man crew, in quarters built to hold nine officers and 144 men. Since at least a third of them were regularly on watch, there was sleeping space for everyone, provided nobody objected to the hot-bunk principle which stateside tourist cabins had lately made so popular with the twenty-four-hour liberty-pass set around the military bases. These accommodations were austere, sternly utilitarian. The officers' staterooms, on the level immediately beneath the main deck, were less than eight feet square apiece and obviously designed by a sardine-can manufacturer. Two officers were allocated to each cubbyhole.

Between these four staterooms and another set of fractionally larger quarters which housed the captain, the engineering officer, the ship's office and the pantry was the wardroom. This bleak expanse of paint-scraped deck, bolted steel tables, chairs and transoms extended for twenty-four feet across the narrowing bow. It was only ten feet wide. But for the nine officers of DesDiv 11's flagship, who were soon to be eleven, this was the focal point of off-duty life. Here a man wrote his most private letters, risked the few dollars left over from his family's allotment in cutthroat poker, or just sat around shooting the breeze about wine, women and the songs played by Tokyo Rose on the short-wave.

As Prince clambered up the steep ladder, still favoring his sprained knee, it struck him that Lieutenant Commander Roger Thornburg, *Davidson's* captain, might also be displeased. Since the departure of the previous divisional commander a week earlier, for a prospective four-stripe job in San Francisco, Thornburg had been acting commander. More than likely he had wanted to keep the job, even if it meant skippering *Davidson* as well as riding herd on the other three destroyers, a tandem responsibility which Prince would have abhorred, even feared. Now Thornburg would have to play second fiddle to a stranger, a despised staff type at that, who would undoubtedly expropriate the more comfortable lower bunk in *his* sacred cabin.

Solemnly, as if in formal deference to the arrival of a new-crowned king, the officer-of-the-deck returned Prince's quarter-deck greeting. Prince had first saluted the Colors, which hung limply in the rain from the fantail staff, before acknowledging the lieutenant (junior grade) at the accommodation ladder brow. Then he limped through the small corridor formed by a quartet of sideboys. They were not a prepossessing lot. Except for their battered white caps, the four dungaree-clad men might have been a work gang on any waterfront in the world. Like Ensign Rand, the jg looked tired. His wet khakis, clinging to his thin frame, accentuated the droop of his narrow shoulders and his concave chest. This traditional coming-aboard exercise usually gave Prince a quick lift of Nelsonian pride. But now that special pride was lacking. The dreary morning, the forlorn ship, the hollow-eyed aspect of the ship's crew, all increased the sense of inadequacy and depression which had gripped him from the instant he first glimpsed the *Henry P. Davidson*.

Prince was surprised, and somewhat annoyed, to find a two-striper on hand to greet him, rather than the destroyer's skipper. He was shaping an acid comment on this egregious discourtesy when the two-striper cut in with an explanation.

"I'm Lieutenant Rodney, the executive officer. Mr. Thornburg has dengue fever. The doc ordered him into *Gray Eagle*'s sick bay last night, when his temperature hit a hundred and four."

"That's a damned shame," Prince said, trying to inject more sympathy into his tone than he actually felt. Dengue was also called bonebreak fever. It hit a man like a dum-dum bullet and stayed with him for a week or more, and even after that he was weak as a field mouse. Prince scowled. The thought of taking a captainless *Davidson* out into the poorly charted waters of Makassar Strait, and probably tangling with the Japs, made genuine concern for Thornburg's plight hard to come by. It was such confounded bad timing.

The exec sensed Prince's displeasure. "You needn't worry, sir. I've had to assume command before when the skipper got sick." He matched scowl with grin. "We survived."

Prince moved toward the superstructure hatch. "I'll visit Mr. Thornburg later, after I've had some chow and toured the premises."

"Yes, sir."

"You want to join me, Beaver?"

"Bloody well right I do." The Briton glanced around the cluttered amidships deck, paying special attention to the cosmolined torpedo tubes, the davited wooden lifeboats, and the naked four-inch rifle that was mounted atop the boxlike galley shack. "If we're going to fight this little bastard, we'd better get acquainted."

"Hell," said Prince, "when you've seen one four-piper, you've seen 'em all. It's just a matter of comparative readiness."

"Balls." The Beaver fired off a monumental snort that might have been a hunger belch. "I've ridden three of the blighters, during shakedowns, after your President was kind enough to lend them to us. Granted. They look alike. But they're different as hand-blown whiskey bottles."

Prince intercepted the exec's look of astonishment at this exchange, and he surmised what Rodney was thinking: It was one hell of a note when a Limey officer professed to know more about a Yank ship than a veritable Yank did.

He snapped, "Maybe that's true in the British fleet, mister, but not here. Our standards don't vary."

"I repeat," said the Beaver, "balls."

Having introduced himself more formally as Lieutenant Michael Rodney, USN (Annapolis class of '35), the exec ushered them through the narrow passageway at the base of the bridge superstructure, down the ladder that gave access to the first deck, and into the low-ceilinged wardroom.

As he followed in Rodney's wake, Prince was acutely conscious of the early-morning sounds and smells of the venerable warship. Over the loudspeaker came the shrill whistle of the boatswain's pipe, summoning the work detail to its housekeeping chores, decreeing a clean sweepdown fore and aft. From portside echoed the squeal of hemp sliding through wet wooden pulleys as another whaleboat was lowered into the harbor for use as a supply craft. A heavy, metallic rumble overhead signified that the number-one battery crew was limbering up their four-inch gun, making sure it revolved smartly, and aiming it emptily at distant palm trees. There was also the tympany of pots and pans being shuffled like colossal dice on the galley stove.

Cooking smells, wafting below from the topside shack, dominated all the other odors which told in olfactory terms the serried twenty-three-year history of USS *Henry P. Davidson*. It was the cook's proud boast that the twenty-gallon soup kettle had never gone cold during the weeks since the destroyer fled the menaced waters of Manila Bay. Day and night, watch on and watch off, he had kept the dried-bean soup flowing. On an all-night vigil, when the crew remained at General Quarters, the average consumption was almost a gallon of the scalding stuff per man, counting spillage in a heavy sea.

Like the galley odors, which consisted also of boiled onions, rancid grease and villainously strong coffee, the other smells were woven into the warp and woof of the old ship. Even paint-scraping couldn't eradicate them. They were *Davidson*'s own bouquet. Prince's sensitive nose was able to identify some of them: hot oil from the deep-down engine spaces, brackish sea water seeping into the bilges, mildewed wood and canvas, stale tobacco, smoke and human sweat. If anything was missing, he concluded, it was the honest, acrid stench of burnt gunpowder, a proper smell for a man-of-war.

Yet these pervasive, familiar aromas demonstrated the basic truth of what he had tried unsuccessfully to tell the Beaver. Four-pipers were all alike, goddamn cast-iron peas in an enormous watery pod.

Then Prince noticed the Yuletide decorations, and he remembered that it was indeed Christmas, despite the war and the faraway place and the total lack of civilized amenities. From somewhere the wardroom crowd had harvested an assortment of baubles and bangles, tinsel improvised out of machine-shop shavings, strung popcorn, branches of an evergreenish tree that wasn't quite an authentic fir. These laced down from the steel crossbeams, requiring anyone who entered the wardroom to duck slightly as he navigated the narrow space. The over-all effect was more melancholy than festive.

Rodney indicated a straight chair at the end of the baize-covered dining table, which was set for eight. With the exception of the ailing skipper, the OOD and the junior engineering watch officer, *Davidson*'s entire commissioned complement was on hand for breakfast with the new divisional commander. It was, Rodney explained, a most unusual gathering. Generally they ate in relays, depending on the watch they stood, or grabbed a catch-as-catch-can bite at the battle stations during GQ, a condition they had sustained almost constantly since the Jap attack on December 8.

Commander Pryor, DesDiv 11's erstwhile bossman, had sat at the tablehead, Rodney added, although by rights this was the captain's proper place.

"Mr. Thornburg only joins us when we're in port, which isn't often. As a rule he eats topside, in his sea cabin."

"That must get rather uncomfortable," Prince said.

"Not for the skipper, sir. He prefers it. He has a tendency toward seasickness."

After Rodney introduced each of the six officers, Prince motioned them to be seated. Steel chairs scraped noisily on the bare metal deck, which had once been covered with inflammable gray linoleum, and they sat down, looking boyishly expectant. The Beaver occupied the place opposite Prince. He picked up a damask napkin, relic of *Davidson*'s peacetime euphoria, and tucked one end beneath his open shirt collar, after carefully parting his fierce beard. A young ensign, sitting next to him, made a giggling sound, but subsided abruptly when Prince shot him a cold glance.

For a moment there was unprayerful silence, while Prince tried to fix the various names in his mind. If he had to be charged with running this odious tin can, as well as commanding the division, he couldn't hope to fake it by addressing them each vaguely as "fella," an all-purpose title used by an elderly battleship captain under whom he had once served. Accurate names were important. They made a man feel wanted, a part of the team, as the Command School handbooks so cogently explained.

Later, of course, he would learn more about them, and their names would begin to fit their idiosyncrasies of dress, speech and manner. Now they were merely an array of eager faces.

Take Lieutenant Rodney. Average height, average weight, average good looks, with a reddish furze on the back of his hands to match his crewcut hair. He appeared soft, though Prince guessed he wasn't, since playing exec on a ship like *Davidson* tended to harden a man in damned short order. Rodney kept his khaki sleeves rolled down and buttoned, doubtless because he burned easily under the pitiless tropical sun. He was in his latter twenties.

At Rodney's right sat Lieutenant Eric Hagen, USN, a man considerably older than the exec. Prince figured him in his upper thirties. This meant he was a mustang, like the ill-fated pilot Dawkins, who had achieved his present status as gunnery officer the hard way, through the deck ratings. Prince had heard the younger men call him "Dad," a positive sign that he was both popular and respected. Born in Denmark, Hagen still spoke with a slight accent, although he had come to the United States as a child. He was almost bald. Remnants of pale blond hair wisped over his large ears and straggled down across his unbuttoned collar. He regarded Prince with bright bottle-green eyes, unblinking, owlishly solemn, quietly curious.

Next came Lieutenant (junior grade) Robert Slattery, USN,

class of '36, the ship's overworked engineering officer. He was ruddy-faced, strangely portly for someone who couldn't have been much over twenty-five and who sweated so copiously while on duty with his boilers and turbines. His nickname, inevitably, was Slats.

Across the table from the exec, at Prince's left, sat Ensign Peter Blue, USNR, who had been introduced as one of *Davidson*'s two V-7 graduates. He'd taken his training at Cornell. Just turned twenty-three, he was the destroyer's first lieutenant, damage control and *de facto* supply officer, and (he announced bitterly) mess treasurer as well. "If there's any lousy job to be done that no one else wants, I'm Mr. Rodney's dog'sbody." For self-evident reasons, Peter Blue was known as Blue Peter, after the signal hoist that chivvied the crew back aboard when a Navy vessel was due to sail.

Ensign Tom Rand followed. He was twenty-two, Annapolis '41, only six months removed from midshipman. The nervousness which Prince had detected in Rand seemed to have eased, although the kid was still tense, vibrating like an idling motorcar with a badly tuned engine as he waited for the Negro mess attendant to pass around the platter of fresh fruit. As communications officer, perhaps Rand had decoded too much information, most of it uncompromisingly grim, in his monitoring of the Asiatic fleet's short-wave circuits, so that the constant drumfire of all this dreary intelligence had unsettled him. Whatever, Prince decided that Rand had strung himself too tight. He would bear watching and some competent backstopping from Chief Yeoman Elliot Bream.

Finally there was Ensign William Savage, USNR, a fresh-caught product of the University of Maine. Tall, burly, unflappable, he was the antithesis of young Rand, for all his reservehood. He had thick, sandy hair which he kept plastered tightly over an overlarge skull and a New Englandish manner of speaking that reminded Prince of Gary Cooper's monosyllabic drawl.

Savage meant it that way. His *yups* and *nopes,* for some odd reason, proved irresistible to women. He was also twenty-two. As assistant gunnery officer he was responsible for the functioning of *Davidson*'s outdated torpedoes, if, as and whenever they finally closed the enemy in a surface engagement.

Under the combined stare of the half-dozen officers, Prince felt like a ship trapped in a bracketing broadside after her *T* had been crossed. They looked so goddamned anticipatory, so blasted dewy-eyed, despite their manifest weariness, waiting for the Word they knew Prince must be carrying from Fleet head-quarters. And the Beaver wasn't helping things much. His expression contained its habitual mix of irony, assuredness and skepticism, as if he had just assayed the world's content and found it jolly amusing, albeit more dross than pure metal.

Prince ladled an assortment of sliced papaya, mango, red banana and pineapple onto his plate before he spoke. Then he surprised them by posing a broad question of his own rather than issuing the profound statement for which they were so patently ready.

"How's it been since Manila?"

Lieutenant Rodney's ginger eyebrows arched a millimeter upward. "You mean, sir, what have we been doing?"

"More or less."

"Mainly chasing our own tail. We've been down here damned near a month, ever since Admiral Hart got the idea things might start cooking sooner than some other people thought. But beyond an occasional plane, we haven't seen hide or hair of the Nips. Not so much as a patrol boat. Our job is guarding the northern sector of Makassar Strait. DesDiv Ten screens the lower half. They're based at Sumbawa. You know, the island that sits right in the middle of the Lesser Sundas, about five hundred miles south—"

"I know all about that," Prince interrupted. "What about morale? Readiness? Shipboard procedure?"

Rodney's freckled cheeks turned a shade pinker. "We're in pretty fair shape, sir."

" 'Pretty fair'?" Prince mimicked, his voice lifting. "That's not half good enough."

"Until we came back to Balikpapan yesterday," said the exec, "we'd spent a week on station, steaming slow to conserve fuel. It's been that way since December eighth. Four hours on, four off tend to wear down the crew after a while. Maybe we're a little punchy."

"The whole fleet's punchy," said Prince. "What about your gunnery?"

Rodney surrendered the defense to Lieutenant Hagen, who said in a tone which only a crazy Dane mustang would have dared use in the presence of such chill majesty: "God knows, Commander. I don't. There's been nothing to shoot at."

"Don't you practice?"

"Negative."

"And why not, may I ask?"

"Flat orders to save ammo. When it's gone, it's gone. *Kaput*. Unless they send us into Surabaya for replenishment, which isn't likely, we've got just enough in our lockers for one good shoot-out."

Prince demanded incredulously, "Doesn't *Gray Eagle* carry spares?"

"That's one dispatch you must've missed, sir," Hagen drawled. "*Gray Eagle* was lucky to escape from Cavite with her feathers intact. All she carried away with her were the stores already aboard, and that didn't include any ammo."

Prince decided to ignore the gunnery officer's thinly veiled insubordination. He would deal with the fellow later, in his own fashion, under less public auspices.

The Blue Peter cleared his throat timidly. "In case you're wondering why all four cans returned to Balikpapan at the same time, sir, I can tell you—"

"Please do," said Prince. "I *was* wondering."

"It's because our bunkers ran dry simultaneously, and the nearest tanker is at Sumbawa, with DesDiv Ten. That's why we're sucking oil from the titties of those crumby harbor scows."

"Why didn't Commander Pryor split the division into pairs so he'd always have two ships on station?"

Rodney replied, "Commander Pryor was a bearcat for keeping the division at full strength in case we ran into trouble. He figured we'd be weak enough as it was, considering our lack of real firepower, without raising the odds against us by dividing our forces. So he preferred the once-a-week risk of going off station."

"Who's watchdogging the Strait now?"

"Couple of subs, *Shark* and *Seadragon*. They're based here, too, although we never see 'em. When we're in, they're out, and vice versa."

"How long will it take you to refuel?"

"Practically the whole day. It's a damned tedious process. We should top off around seventeen hundred hours, give or take a few minutes."

"And when d'you propose to resume patrol?"

Rodney gave Prince a startled look. "Ordinarily we'd leave at first light tomorrow. Without radar, we're not much for night scouting. But now that you're aboard, Commander, I guess it's your decision."

"Thanks," said Prince. "I'll remember that."

Hagen's gravelly voice interposed. "You asked about gunnery practice. *Shark* and *Seadragon* have had several bites at the Japs. They should've gotten direct hits. But the mucking torpedoes broached, curved, sank, aborted—and did everything else except what they were supposed to do, which is sink the enemy."

"What's wrong with the goddamned fish?" Prince demanded.

"I wish to Christ I knew. We use the same kind. But before the crap hit the fan, all we were allowed was dummy runs. You

44

don't learn anything valuable from those. It's like screwing with your pants on."

Prince gave up his interrogation. After a brief pause, Ensign Rand found courage to say, "Last night I intercepted a news broadcast from 'Frisco."

"*San* Francisco, son, not 'Frisco," admonished Rodney. "That's my town."

"Yes, sir. Anyhow, it was FDR giving his Christmas Eve talk. He warned everybody they'd better get braced for a long war. And he sort of implied we'd have to take care of Europe first before really pouring on the coal in the Pacific."

"This war," opined Rodney, "could last a year. Maybe longer."

From the far end of the table came the Beaver's pre-emptive snort. Six heads swiveled in his direction. He remarked dryly, almost pityingly, "Lads, you forget that this war's already more than two bloody years along, with no end in sight. We've merely started a new phase. You've got a whole army to train, to say nothing of a navy to build." He checked himself. "You chaps took a frightful drubbing at Pearl, you know. Perhaps the operative word is *rebuild*."

"How long do you reckon it'll go on?" Rodney asked in a chastened voice.

"Twice what it's taken so far," said the Briton. "Four more everlasting years."

"But that would be nineteen forty-five!"

"Precisely."

Nobody sought to challenge the Beaver. He was too overwhelmingly positive; his credentials were too solid. Prince fell to eating his granular eggs and fatty bacon. He had intended to close the proceedings with a nice little set speech, which would help bolster their spirits and at the same time stamp himself as an officer of sterling character and discernment. But he was thrown off stride by their slavish acceptance of the Beaver's

45

harsh prophecy and the way they seemed to hang on his words, as if the bearded bastard was somehow privy to all the wisdom of Solomon.

Prince finished the rest of his Spartan meal in hurt silence. Then he pushed back his empty plate and stood up.

"Have the whaleboat brought alongside," he instructed Rodney. "I'm going over to *Gray Eagle* to see Mr. Thornburg and get some clothes. Coming along, Beaver?"

"Right-ho."

The exec said, "Don't you want to inspect the ship first, sir?"

"That can wait." Prince rubbed his aching knee. He turned to Ensign Rand. "Send a signal to *McGraw, Travers* and *Vincent*. I want their COs aboard *Davidson* at thirteen hundred sharp for an operations conference."

"Yes, sir." The communications officer hesitated. "There's a message from the Dutch liaison officer, Lieutenant Commander van Dekker. He needs to see you as soon as possible."

"Trouble?"

"I don't know, sir. But it generally is."

PART I

2

"All the World's a Stage"

THAT SUMMER in Manila had been easygoing, pleasant, almost carefree for those who didn't know or who didn't much worry about what was happening in places like Tokyo and Washington, D.C. Knowing the score, appreciating the nuances of the Big Picture, was a privilege vouchsafed to a minimal number of high-ranked personages, both military and civilian, who seemed to be acting under instructions not to alarm the non-cognoscenti among the 12,000 American troops, the officers and men who flew the 35 bombers and 72 fighters of the inadequate Far Eastern Air Force, and those who crewed the three old cruisers, 13 World War I destroyers, 27 submarines, six torpedo boats and 28 patrol seaplanes of Admiral Tommy Hart's fleet. Plus, to be sure, the lone Marine regiment whose hard-bitten officers never expected to be phased into the Big Picture anyhow, since their job was fighting at the drop of General Douglas MacArthur's gold-crusted cap, and to hell with the grand strategy.

By and large, as personal aide to the doughty bantam cock of an admiral, Commander Prince himself had a fair notion of what was cooking and why. The Old Man, who rightly fancied himself a competent student of war, had it pretty well figured out. On an off night, when things quieted down temporarily in the fleet's GHQ in the barrackslike Marsman Building, which crouched within the Walled City, he was apt to expound on the potentially disastrous situation that confronted all of them.

Washington had left the choice up to him, back in the fall of 1940, whether to haul his patchwork Asiatic Fleet out of Shanghai and base it in Manila, or to take the chance that the Japanese wouldn't pose an international threat to the big Chinese seaport. In the face of a few critics who cried "retreat," Tommy Hart wisely chose the former course. This would, he reasoned, make for better naval coordination with MacArthur and their British-Dutch allies.

Besides, the admiral was damned well convinced the Nips wouldn't delay much longer. Being of such a mind, he was appalled by the relaxed attitude of both the American diplomats and the Philippines authorities, who seemed to feel (like Scarlett O'Hara) that the danger would go away if they just stopped thinking about it.

Then came July.

The Japs swarmed into Indochina, the French quit, and that finally got the Pollyannas off their lazy duffs, as Tommy Hart told it privately. This abrupt enemy move meant that the Philippines were three-quarters hemmed in: on the west by the surrendered French colonies and an embattled China; on the north by the main Japanese islands; and on the east by the jealously guarded, mysterious Marshalls and Carolines, where the Nips were known to have concentrated sizable forces.

Although Commander Prince had access to many classified documents in the course of his daily duties, he had never been permitted to scan that formidable compilation of orders, assumptions and uncertainties known as Rainbow 5. This was the latest war plan drafted by the Army and Navy after a three-month Allied conference in Washington. It condemned, perforce, the skeleton legions under MacArthur and Hart to operate in a purely defensive manner, in concert with the even more skeletal forces of the British and the Dutch.

Once the Philippines fell (Rainbow 5 appeared to regard that bleak outcome as inevitable), Tommy Hart would flee south with his naval remnants, where they would then come under British command for the protection of the Malay Barrier.

Belatedly, though, the Washington wizards came to the conclusion that the Philippines might indeed be brought up to combat readiness. They were encouraged in this new optimism by MacArthur, who said 200,000 men would do very nicely for the insular defenses, provided they were available by April 1942, when *his* wizards prophesied the Japs would make their next leap forward.

So it was agreed. The ponderous wheels began to turn, with agonizing slowness, and the manpower-airpower trickle started.

Prince happened to be in the Old Man's office, which overlooked the cluttered inner harbor and the port facilities, when Hart received advice from his chief of staff that the earlier defeatist strategy had been shelved in favor of a maximum defense effort.

The chief was almost apologetic as he relayed his message. "This decision," he said, "was reached by the Army General Staff two mortal weeks ago. But we just learned about it today."

Hart glanced at his desk calendar. It showed October 27.

"How did we get the Word, Captain?"

A stranger might have interpreted the admiral's quiet tone as one of normal curiosity. But it wasn't. Hart was less than enchanted by the realization that the Army was treating him like a bench warmer in the championship game, useful enough to have around in case the varsity collapsed, yet hardly to be entrusted with a complete catalogue of the plays.

"Totally by accident," the chief said, with a deprecatory shrug, "and a bit of intramural espionage."

"I'm glad our intelligence is functioning." Hart put aside his pique to concentrate on the main issue at hand. "Very well. So Doug's going to get more toy soldiers. Maybe. And a lot more planes. Also maybe. But one thing is dead certain. *We're* not going to get another blessed scrap of hardware, except for what we can steal from the Pearl Harbor convoys."

"Right, sir. There's nothing in the cards. Everything has been earmarked for the Atlantic."

"So we'll make do with what's on tap." The admiral turned to Prince. "Draft a dispatch for the Navy Department. Tell the Secretary and Betty Stark in CNO we want to keep the fleet intact in Manila Bay, in view of the Army's planned build-up, rather than running part of it south. Tell them also that we haven't gotten past first base in our joint planning with the British and the Dutch, so that combined operations could be a bloody shambles. We can do a better job right here, where we happen to have a moral commitment to hold the line."

"Yes, sir." Prince gathered up his hastily scribbled notes and headed for the door.

"Mark that message 'urgent,' " Hart called.

"Yes, sir."

It was countersigned by the admiral, encoded by Yeoman (first class) Elliot Bream and sent within thirty minutes. But the Navy Department, in its august wisdom, waited three long weeks before bothering to reply.

At 1800 hours, as the nearby cathedral's iron bells began chiming six, the admiral closed up shop. Things were quiet, operations reported, with zero readings from the aerial and submarine reconnaissance units. So it looked like a salubrious evening for a few rubbers of bridge with the chief of staff and a couple of amiable generals, over a bourbon or two in the Flag quarters at the Manila Hotel. Just possibly the generals, warmed by the whiskey, might do some talking.

"Will you need me, sir?" Prince asked.

"Negative. But behave yourself, Commander, and keep a clear head for tomorrow."

"Tomorrow, sir?"

The admiral's hooded gray eyes were noncommittal. "In our trade, almost anything can happen, and usually does." He smiled frostily. "I might even want you to fill a foursome in golf. If you do go out, let the duty officer know where you are."

"Yes, sir."

Prince went back to his office and got his cap. He studied himself briefly in the mirror that was affixed to the small coat-closet door. With his right index finger he preened both bushy eyebrows, combing them upward, and then scowled at his reflection, hardening his glance in conscious mimicry of the Old Man's fierce look when angered. Barbers always wanted to trim his eyebrows. But Prince wouldn't let them. They were his sole unkempt feature, albeit a studied one, and he knew it impressed strangers meeting him for the first time.

Regretfully, he had been forced to shave off his stateside mustache, a thing of hirsute splendor, when he joined the Asiatic Fleet that previous July. The admiral, who considered mustaches inappropriate for a modern American naval officer, announced dourly that full beards might be acceptable, provided the wearers grew them on their own time and didn't appear in the Flag's presence until they were matured, like an oak tree transplanted secretly at night. Nobody took him up on his grudging offer. Nobody, that is, until the Beaver happened along. But this was much later, when the admiral couldn't have cared less about beards, full-grown like Rip van Winkle's, or merely sprouting, at that critical stage of the ball game.

Prince gave the visor of his cap a slight tug. Satisfied that it was tilted at a proper jaunty angle and that his high-collared white uniform jacket showed no telltale spoor of carbon paper, green tea or red grease pencil, he departed.

On his way to the second-floor elevator, Prince passed the desk where Yeoman Bream was still engaged with a sheaf of dispatch flimsies, sorting them and placing each on its appropriate spindle for easy reading by the various staff officers who had the duty that night.

Bream looked up. "Going out on the town, Commander?"

As always, in addressing Prince, the yeoman's voice was languid, a decibel shy of quiet insolence, and his pale-blue eyes gave no hint of what lay on his mind. Prince detested Bream. But he had inherited him from his predecessor, who was loud in the fellow's praises as a paragon of a naval clerk, quick-witted, accurate and resourceful. Bream was indeed all of that. But he was also a crafty buzzard who knew a hell of a lot more than was good for him and probably wouldn't be above turning such illicit knowledge to his own advantage.

In spite of himself, Prince felt a certain reluctant admiration for Bream, partly because of the man's reputed social background and partly because of his indubitable style, which came from good breeding and the right schools. Bream had a graceful manner of speaking, of gesturing, which Prince envied. Even the ridiculous swabbie costume that enveloped the tall, lanky yeoman like an ill-fitting glove could not wholly conceal his inbred aristocracy.

Bream was twenty-seven. He seemed older, older perhaps than Prince, who was thirty-five. Ten years earlier he had run away from an upper-crust New England prep school, thumbing his hawkish nose defiantly in the direction of his family's big mansion on the Chicago Gold Coast, and joined the Navy. Service life suited him perfectly. Bream had twice risen to chief and twice been broken back to yeoman first class, after having too blatantly breached that invisible line which separates ingenuous frankness from rank insubordination. But he had learned his lesson. He didn't intend to make the same mistake again.

Instead, Bream displayed his independence in subtler, less

abrasive ways. He always had a taxicab awaiting him at the front door of the Marsman Building, while the others stood in line for the malodorous downtown bus; and inevitably he would show up at the watering holes where officers congregated at night, with a statuesque *mestiza* clinging to his arm and plenty of money for champagne. It was rumored that Bream lived in a thatch-roofed bungalow on the banks of the Pasig River, upstream from President Quezon's stately Malacañan Palace, a luxury made possible by the fact that his father had conveniently died a year ago, leaving him a sweet bundle.

Now Bream said, "The staff duty car has a flat tire, sir, and won't be available for an hour or so. Would you like to borrow my cab?"

"No, thanks, Bream. I can't take your wheels." Prince emulated the admiral's frigid smile. "Use 'em in good health."

The yeoman stifled a yawn with his elegant left hand. "Hell, Commander, health is no problem. I only deal in triple-A prime government-inspected meat. And there's always sulfa."

"You're a very prudent man, Bream."

"Sometimes, sir. Where it really counts."

Feeling oddly nettled, as if he had lost a fast rally in the crucial game of a tennis match, Prince headed once more for the exit and pushed his way into the jam-packed elevator. His disposition wasn't improved by the expectable lack of taxis at the curb, save for Bream's private coach, which was parked discreetly near the corner, with its flag down.

Before he reached the Santa Lucia Gate, leading from the Walled City to the broad reaches of Dewey Boulevard, the perspiration was already trickling down his spine. It had wilted his starched jacket and threatened another onslaught of prickly-heat rash. The beauty of Manila at this hushed moment of opalescent twilight failed to inspire him. Through a sweaty haze Prince glared at the crowded harbor, which had assumed an evilly beer-colored cast, bubbling as if someone had mulled its shallow depths with a red-hot poker. Everything he saw and smelled and heard added to the discomfort that boiled up inside: the Chinese fruit stalls reeking of burnt kerosene from the lamps which fitfully illumined their dank interiors; the universal whitewash that caused a thousand stuccoed façades to hurl back the hot rays of the setting sun; the dog-eat-dog homeward-bound traffic, a melange of ancient trucks and taxis and official limousines which spewed their gassy garbage into the humid atmosphere; and the Mayan hulk of the hotel itself, looking like a giant loaf of crisped brown bread, as he passed under the ornate iron archway.

A sign on the parched lawn proclaimed, *Bawal Dumaan;* another read, *Bawal ang Pumasok.* Tagalog for *No Trespassing.* And *Do Not Enter.* Prince wondered whether the Japanese invaders, if they were finally successful in breaching MacArthur's vaunted "inland sea" defenses, would obey these quaint admonitions. Then he put the vagrant notion out of his mind. It was a stupid conceit, the sort of brittle whimsy he might expect from a blasé High Commission secretarial type like Gwyneth Dean, whom he would be seeing soon enough anyhow and jousting with over a pitcher of martinis in her extravagant Edwardian apartment near Luneta Park, where the nannies still wheeled their infant charges in their Edwardian prams.

But first he would have to shower, shave and climb into a fresh set of whites.

When he was three months old, MaMa arranged to have him baptized in the very Anglican, determinedly high-church chapel of St. Swithin's, whose slate spire and white columns provided a landmark for sailors navigating the broad reaches of the lower Potomac. St. Swithin's was the spiritual and social center of Province Beach, where MaMa managed her effete boarding house, with PaPa's desultory help.

The pastor, an expatriate Londoner with a formidable accent, sprinkled a few drops of holy water across the infant's brow, thus insuring that the regenerated tyke would mature into a man of stalwart character. PaPa held the mewling baby, while MaMa stood proudly by with two of her most valued roomers, a pair of male and female schoolteachers, serving as *de facto* godparents.

He was christened Custis Hensley Morgan Prince, after an array of ancestors, all maternal.

PaPa shuffled off his mortal coil (in MaMa's words) shortly before Prince's eighth birthday. He was worn out from fifty-three years of being constantly onstage, including nine when he actually trod the boards (in PaPa's idiom) as a supporting actor with a Shakespearean troupe that played mainly in tank-town high-school auditoriums.

During his eight brief years with the boy, he coolly took over the task of instilling what he termed "the elements of gentlemanly conduct" into the preschool Prince, once his son grew big enough to straddle a horse, grip a tennis racket and handle a tiller.

Another facet of Prince's emergent character, to which PaPa paid earnest attention, was his inherited gift for theatrics: an ability to play for an audience of one, himself alone, if nobody else were around to watch. Prince's talent was less histrionic than PaPa's, carefully toned down, until a later generation might have termed it Method acting. Like PaPa, Prince consistently played himself, to the hilt.

After PaPa died, Prince grieved briefly, then came to the conclusion that he didn't miss him very much, and so stopped grieving. It was more as if PaPa had exited permanently, stage left, having turned over the part to his understudy-son.

It pleased him to refer to MaMa's boarding house, when he was away from Province Beach, as an ancestral estate in tidewater Virginia. That was arrant hyperbole, for Province Beach wasn't tidewater by any stretch of the imagination, but a raunchy little upstate sandspit, a long way from the *real* tidewaters of the historic rivers, like the York and the Rappahannock and the James. Province Beach was a lot nearer to Annapolis, for example, just a short boat ride down the Potomac, around the Maryland delta, and then up the Chesapeake.

Upon his graduation from Province Beach High, where he had taken a profound interest in the less disciplined subjects, like English lit and English composition, Prince was accepted by the Naval Academy.

This was in the autumn of 1923.

Calvin Coolidge had become the thirtieth President of the United States, owing to the untimely death of handsome Warren Gamaliel Harding, sworn into office by candlelight in his father's Vermont village home. The world was safe for democracy.

That same year Silent Cal proposed to spend a paltry quarter billion dollars on the military—all species thereof—although Britain and France were budgeting almost twice that amount apiece.

Under such auspices a naval career might have struck Prince as something less than promising, had he been concerned with the finer points of history or taken the trouble to discuss his service future with the occasional officers who visited Province Beach during the summer doldrums. But he did neither. Moreover, life in the Navy was certain to be placid, safe and free of sudden alarums and excursions.

From his earliest days at Annapolis, Prince's somewhat calculated air, embodying hauteur, disdain and a certain detachment from the other midshipmen's affairs, had the effect of keeping him out of the Academy mainstream. His baffled confreres invented no nickname for him, although a few hackneyed wiseacres tried to make something out of his middle initials, H.M., and thus label him "Your Majesty." That failed. Prince was Prince. Period.

In his entire quadrennium, Prince never gained real popularity, nor did he seek it. He was even a little feared as being too clever, too biting with words, too introspectively organized. Again he avoided bone-crunching athletics and went after the managerial jobs, which involved behind-the-scenes power instead of instant glamour.

On his passage up the slow, arduous promotional ladder, from ensign to jg in June 1927, and to lieutenant four years later, Prince took on the requisite number of menial assignments. After each, his superiors stamped his fitness report as "most suited" for higher rank, when such a vacancy should occur, if ever. He was second assistant gunnery officer on the old battleship *Texas,* sub-operations officer for the Eleventh Naval District at San Diego, exec of a four-piper destroyer based in Norfolk, instructor in English at the Academy.

Prince made lieutenant commander in 1937.

By that time, most of his peers were comfortably, if not always happily, married to the girls they had wooed during their junior-officer years. But not Prince. Unsurprisingly, MaMa never urged marriage for her son, chiefly in her own self-interest, but also because she didn't think the girls in prospect measured up to his Princely standards, as one of the Navy's bright young men.

At a relatively early period in his career Prince was tabbed as good staff officer material by the personnel analysts who from time to time prowled through a man's files to see whether he was a square peg jammed into a round hole and if so, whether his usefulness to the Navy couldn't be improved by beveling off a few rough edges. Prince impressed them with his complete lack of such rough edges, a factor of some importance in adapting to staff duties, which entailed a certain amount of native diplomacy as well as professional savvy.

Some ambitious young officers might have been distressed that the Bureau of Navigation hadn't seen fit to give them seagoing commands, however modest, by the time they had reached the quasi-seniority of two and a half stripes. But Prince was delighted when BuNav chose him, instead, for the Naval War College at Newport, Rhode Island. That year Prince was the youngest lieutenant commander among the class taking the formidable ten-month obstacle course devised almost a half century earlier by Captain Alfred Thayer Mahan, the eminent authority on sea power.

The European war had degenerated into its quiescent, or phony, stage when Prince finished his studies at Newport. That fact may have tempered the thinking of his War College mentors, who still inclined toward doctrinaire Mahanism. While France's vaunted Maginot Line held the Nazis at bay, they figured, Great Britain's dominant sea power would soon strangle an almost landlocked Germany. There would be no need for the United States to dirty its hands with what was essentially a European concern. We could retain the bulk of our fleet in the Pacific, safely moored within the impregnable shelter of Pearl Harbor between exercises, with no fear of sudden attacks, as long as we kept a close watch on the Japanese.

During his War College stint Prince came to know the handful of British officers who had been sent to Newport for indoctrination into American methods, against the improbable day when the Yanks might be fighting alongside His Majesty's Navy. For all their confident talk, they were doom-filled types, blooded veterans at a too early age, and most of them had seen ships shot out from under them.

Certificated as a War College graduate in the spring of 1941, Prince was immediately ordered to the staff of the commander-in-chief, U.S. Asiatic Fleet. The Philippines assignment suited him perfectly. It gave him a ringside opportunity to observe how his seniors, especially the sagacious Old Man, handled their weighty responsibilities. Like the British, although in a quite different way, the upper echelon of Tommy Hart's close-knit staff had class. They were a rugged crew, dedicated to a superhuman task; and all of them were very much in awe of their peppery sixty-four-year-old boss, who had been around the Navy longer than Neptune himself.

Prince's equerry duties were of such a nature that he was not required to accept any direct responsibility other than making sure the Flag dispatches and letters were kept shipshape, the Old Man's black Buick sedan and teakwood barge instantly available, and his off-duty engagement calendar unsnafued.

It was a position of singular prestige and social importance, honored by custom, beloved of naval hostesses, and with it went more than a modicum of reflected glory. This mirrored glow, the smart tropical worsted uniform he had tailored for him in Cavite, and his nearness to the throne, all helped to diminish the gnawings of self-doubt that occasionally afflicted him whenever he paused to realize that he mightn't always be so nicely sheltered from the gathering storms.

For public purposes, and as protective coloration in this social jungle, Prince kept Gwyneth Dean on the string. Gwyneth was the acknowledged queen bee in the High Commissioner's paperworking hive, a coolly remote, supercilious, enameled beauty in her late twenties who understood Prince far better than he suspected. Moreover, her cultivated ego was a Mexican stand-off match for his own, in hauteur, vanity and the serene satisfaction of being Gwyneth Dean.

His favorite therapy was to slip away, after a long evening with Gwyneth, for a late-night expedition, quite alone and out of uniform. Generally he would visit one of the vast subterranean dance halls that abounded in the area around the Escolta. Most of them were so-called "clubs," which granted instant membership privileges for a few pesos, plus the equally instant availability of their painted hostesses. His favorite was the Yum-Yum. This was not the kind of establishment he would ordinarily have entered, since it catered mainly to enlistees and merchant seamen and hence was considered *déclassé* for commissioned officers. But Prince, incognito, never reckoned he'd bump into any of his peers in the small hours of the morning in such an unlikely place. He would fog down a fast beer or two, ogle the scantily clad bar girls and sometimes select one of the more prepossessing of these dainty whores. They each had access to a nearby flophouse, it seemed, where you could romp away the rest of the night, if you wished, for a dozen or so pesos above the "membership" rate. They were very experienced, very sportive and peculiarly enticing to a libidinous American male because of their smallness.

Because it faced the blind wall of a narrow courtyard, rather than the harbor or the hotel gardens, Prince's room never caught the direct rays of the sun. It was always gloomy. And now, at seven o'clock, although the tropical sunset still shed a painful brightness over the rest of the city, he had to turn on the overhead light.

Prince rummaged through the tangle of clothes that hung haphazardly in his closet to find a fresh pair of white duck trousers and a *barong tagalog* shirt. Accepted as evening wear for pub-hopping males, this Filipino blouse took the place of a restrictive coat and tie. Prince chose a pale-blue, short-sleeved model, open at the neck and daintily pocked with embroidered eyelets. He fancied this costume, which was worn outside the trousers. It made him feel rather like a beachcomber, slightly raffish and quite removed from service formality.

Before leaving, he splashed three fingers of Haig & Haig pinch bottle into a thick-glassed tumbler and downed it in a single gulp. At long last he was ready for Gwyneth.

The quick twilight had surrendered to typical Manila autumn darkness, a deep lavender canopy pierced by huge incandescent stars, and the heat was no longer insufferable when he reached the verandah. Prince savored the air appreciatively. When night fell, the city's abominable odors also departed, borne away upon the faint monsoon breeze. In their wake lay the sweet scent of flowering acacia and magnolias.

He crossed Dewey Boulevard and struck out through the tree-shaded Luneta toward Taft Avenue, inevitably pondering, as he strolled along the graveled pathways, the bygone and triumphal era these streets commemorated. That would have been a glorious time in which to live, Prince mused enviously, when an emergent United States rode high and couldn't lose for winning. Dewey had riddled the Spanish fleet in the shallow waters off Cavite, where the dons chose to make their futile stand so that they could paddle ashore after it was all over. The Navy was king. There were no more wars to fight, no more potenial foes to challenge.

Regrettably, it wasn't that way now, with enemies springing up on every side. No. Make that a single enemy in the Pacific. The Japanese were plural only in their menacing numbers, which outstripped anything the Americans, British or Dutch could muster, and in their obvious superiority in bases from which they might strike from a half dozen directions.

Prince slowly ascended the creaking stairs that led to Gwyneth Dean's apartment.

Phonograph music, played much too loudly, bombarded the heavy oak door. Gwyneth was taking her shower, he guessed, and had turned up the volume so that she could hear the cacophonous sounds in the bathroom. She hated silence. The portable Victrola was always yammering, day and night, whenever Gwyneth was around. She got all the latest popular records from the States. Sometimes they came by slow freighter; but more often they were brought to her by High Commission staffers returning from home leave who figured it paid to keep Gwyneth happy. This summer the hit tunes were "Blues in the Night," "Martha," "The Breeze and I" and a thing called "The Hut-Sut Song."

Gwyneth's overworked phonograph was playing that pandemoniac ditty now. Standing alone in the empty hallway, Prince grimaced and then raised his shoulders in a dramatic shudder before he pressed the buzzer.

Hut-Sut Rawlson on the rillerah
And a brawla, brawla soo-it—

After five minutes the door swung open. Gwyneth stood there, coolly elegant in her purple terrycloth robe, despite moist face and damp ringlets of dark hair. Smiling, she took him by the hand and led him into the high-ceilinged parlor, switching off the phonograph in mid-passage as she went. The room was filled with souvenirs of her service in diplomatic stations around the world: filigreed brass tables from India, superb porcelain birds from Germany, a llama rug from Peru, a camel's saddle from Egypt, a *shoji* screen from Japan. All of them were gifts. Gwyneth saved her money. She bought nothing for herself except the minimum in groceries and the expensive clothes which graced her handsome body.

Prince noted with pleasure that she had laid out the cocktail-hour gear on one of the Indian chow tables. A silver shaker glistening with icy sweat, two long-stemmed crystal glasses, a virgin bottle of Bombay gin and a flagon of Noilly Prat vermouth testified to Gwyneth's appreciation of the important little items that separated civilized man from the unthinking beasts. The Bombay gin was typical. It cost more than the Gordon's, which most of the resident Americans drank. And it permitted Gwyneth to explain, each time she produced the bottle, that you could always gauge your sobriety by watching the portrait of Queen Victoria on the label. When the old bag's prunish face started looking like a Wampas baby starlet, then you jolly well knew you'd had enough.

"Just as," Gwyneth told Prince with a caustic, meaningful glance, "a sailor should know he's been out here too damned long when the native damsels begin turning blonde, like Betty Grable."

Gwyneth herself never reached the point of alcoholic no return. Her lovely legs were hollow. She took her martinis eight

64

to one and could absorb a half dozen of them without crossing an eye or slurring a syllable. After cocktails Gwyneth liked a good French wine with dinner and later a decent cognac. There was, Prince saw, a bottle of Châteauneuf-du-Pape basking in a pewter ice bucket alongside the card table that Gwyneth had set for dinner. He winced. Despite the Bombay gin, Gwyneth would never accept all of the niceties, such as never, but never, chill burgundy. Or perhaps she didn't want to. Gwyneth preferred things cold, and that was how she generally got them.

"Build me a martini," she ordered. "Veddy crisp. While I crawl into something less comfortable . . . darling."

The *darling* emerged the way Tallulah Bankhead might have said it, all drawling and throaty. Gwyneth loaded a fresh stack of records on the phonograph before she left for the bedroom. When the music started, Prince was relieved to hear the opening piano strains of Freddy Martin's version of the Tchaikovsky B-flat minor concerto, which was so much the rage that autumn. He had been afraid of more "Hut-Sut" or possibly Helen O'Connell belting out "Six Lessons from Madam LaZonga," since that had seemed to be Gwyneth's mood, so the bowdlerized Tchaikovsky came as a welcome surprise. It meant that Gwyneth was thawing.

Prince poured a generous portion of straight Bombay over ice and dropped a lime twist into the glass to disguise the raw nakedness of his drink. Then he lowered himself into one of the overstuffed chairs that made the apartment seem even smaller than it was and propped his illicit jodhpur boots against the edge of the chow table. He knew Gwyneth would take at least twenty minutes to lily-gild the perfection of her face, repair her damp coiffure and make damned sure that whatever gown she selected was impeccably adjusted before mincing onstage to receive the cheers of her audience of one. In eighteen minutes he would mix *her* martini.

The thought of such careful timing for this inconsequential

act amused him. Gwyneth was one of those women who constantly demanded to know the exact hour and minute of the day, even though she never kept wound the infinitesimal diamond watch that sparkled on her wrist.

"Women," he once told her firmly, "don't have to know what time it is."

"They don't?"

"Christ, no. Only things like how long it takes a person to travel from Point A to Point B, or the interval between rare and medium in a filet mignon." He blew a smoke ring. "Mine, incidentally, should be on the rare side."

"Bullsweat, Prince!"

"There's more?"

"Lots. Such as how long a gentleman will wait for a lady before he blows his stack, or how long that selfsame gentleman will keep on being a gentleman when he finally gets that lady alone . . . in her apartment on a moonshiny night."

Freddy Martin had relinquished the turntable to Glenn Miller's disciplined swing, which was followed by Tommy Dorsey's trombone and a couple of other geniuses whom Prince didn't recognize, before Gwyneth made her entrance, precisely on schedule. She was wearing a brocaded Hong Kong silk *cheongsan,* cream-colored and slit to her thigh, which lovingly reproduced every curve of her splendid frame. In spite of his determination not to be impressed, Prince pursed his lips in a soundless whistle as he handed her the martini glass.

Gwyneth elevated the corners of her eyes with both forefingers and gave him an inscrutable Oriental stare.

"You likee?" she purred.

"Adequate," he said, recovering. "Just adequate."

"Go to hell, Commander." Gwyneth tasted the cocktail. "Also just adequate," she said mockingly. "A bit too heavy on the Noilly Prat."

"You should try my recipe," said Prince.

66

"What's that?"

"Straight gin."

Gwyneth wrinkled her patrician nose. "Ugh."

"Straight's the only way."

"Double ugh." Putting down her drink, she went to the table and began lighting the candles that stood in crystal holders between the sterling place settings. While her back was still turned, Gwyneth said in a deceptively innocuous tone, "Is there anything else you take straight, Prince?"

"Just what in hell does that mean?"

"Federal census information. Trying to find out how a government-issue operator operates."

"Muchas gracias," he growled. "You're so damned charming. Especially when you twist the knife."

"That's part of our irresistible appeal for each other, darling. We don't keep secrets."

"Whole bloody truth and nothing but the truth?"

"Hardly that, dear heart. Candor, perhaps, but not always the truth."

Prince tired of the brittle game. "D'you want me to burn the steaks? Or is it your turn?"

"You relax from your grueling day at the factory, poor baby, and let Mama do the nasty housework." Gwyneth swept into the Pullman kitchen that formed one end of the parlor and opened the refrigerator. "Just see to it that my martini cup overfloweth."

"Affirmative."

While Gwyneth made domestic noises with pans and chinaware in the galley, Prince leafed through a week-old copy of *Time* magazine. It didn't make for cheerful browsing. *Item:* The Nazis were only one hundred miles from Moscow, ready to macerate the last major army that confronted them in Europe. *Item:* FDR was fracturing the Neutrality Act ten ways to Sunday by arming U.S. merchant vessels. *Item:* USS *Kearney* got herself torpedoed during a tangle with a German U-boat wolf pack off

67

Iceland. Eleven crewmen were listed as "missing," though probably trapped in the year-old destroyer's flooded compartments.

Prince was deep into his fourth drink and Gwyneth her double catch-up third before dinner was pronounced ready.

"Uncork the vino," Gwyneth said, "and dim the overhead lights, darling."

He saluted the kitchen, quarter-deck fashion, and stood up, grinning. Some things were also comfortably immutable in Manila. Gwyneth's calculated arrangements for a *dîner à deux,* with all the details worked out like a well-structured scenario, including lights, camera and a certain amount of permissive action, depending on how the star felt at the moment.

But the dialogue was eminently predictable.

Gwyneth opened the scene by remarking with a disarming smile, "You look a trifle world-weary tonight, *mon cher.* Or is it hag-ridden?"

"I guess I'm suffering," Prince said finally, "from some rare strain of *Zeitgeist.*"

Gwyneth shrugged a delectable shoulder. "There's no such thing as a rare strain of *Zeitgeist,* sweetheart. It's a common ailment. We all feel it nowadays, because of Europe."

"So what?"

"So it's not like you, *bébé,* admitting that you share the malaise of us commonfolk." Gwyneth paused, then added maliciously, knowing the paltriness of his staff duties, "Job getting you down?"

"Sure. I'm a walking bundle of ganglia. Hand shakes constantly. I'm so nervous I can hardly hold it steady enough to light the Old Man's cigarettes."

"Bullsweat. You wouldn't change jobs for all the tea in China. Where else can you be so safe, sane and sinecured."

"It's something to do," Prince said unwarily, "while I wait for a seagoing command."

Gwyneth's knife thrust cut through his pretense. "You're a fourteen-karat liar, *mon commandant.*"

"A certain amount of lying is good for the soul," said Prince in a manful attempt to recoup lost points. "Teaches it proper humility. You should know that, *mon enfant.*"

"I do, darling, indeed I do." Gwyneth reached across the table and expertly snuffed out the candles with a thumb and forefinger. "Now let's forget this silliness and go watch the ever-lovin' moon. We'll have our cognac on the balcony. Fetch the bottle and the glasses."

When he joined her on the narrow balcony, which looked out upon the municipal golf links and the Muelle San Francisco, where the shipping piers extended their long fingers into the harbor, Gwyneth had drawn two wicker chairs close together and was reclining in one of them with her gold-sandaled feet braced high against the iron rail. The restful posture brought the clinging *cheong-san* up even higher and exposed the whole of her left thigh to his appreciative gaze. As he had suspected, Gwyneth wore absolutely nothing under the revealing gown. Prince knew that she had planned this deliberately, as she planned everything, to provoke just such a Pavlovian response. It also signaled her availability for the night.

Gwyneth did not dispense her favors lavishly, but when she offered them they were tendered with a minimum of coy nonsense. She set a sound market value on her physical wares—not in money (that would have whoreified her, Prince thought ironically) but in equally negotiable terms. Distributed wisely, her vaunted charms guaranteed Gwyneth an enviable position in socio-diplomatic circles and placed her on a first-name basis with a surprising array of Very Important People.

Prince slipped into the chair beside her and hoisted his jodhpurs onto the railing. Gwyneth thrust her leg against his. He drew his right hand across the inside of her bare thigh and squeezed it gently. It was very warm and very soft, a phenomenon that never ceased to astonish him, considering Gwyneth's normal aura of encapsulated coolness.

For a while they sipped their cognac, not speaking, watching the moon course through the faint mist that lay over the glimmering waters of the bay. In the middle distance a passenger vessel, one of the big President liners, was creeping into port with all her lights ablaze. Prince wondered idly what sort of people still traveled for pleasure, now that half the world's harbors were closed to everything except convoys laden with war goods. True enough, the Pacific was still open, after a fashion, although even its peaceful days seemed numbered.

Gwyneth laid her coiffed head against his shoulder, sighing luxuriously, and made no effort to dislodge his questing palm.

After a moment he removed his hand reluctantly. "First I've got to make an urgent telephone call," he said.

He went inside and dialed Fleet headquarters. The duty officer said there were two messages for Commander Prince, one directing him to join the admiral on the golf course at 0800 sharp, the other belaying that order and advising him instead to report at 0730 for a joint powwow with General MacArthur's staff.

"Something extra special?" asked Prince.

The duty officer yawned. It was Pokey Benson, who yawned frequently and with good reason. He was somewhere down the indeterminate line in Fleet logistics, with not a hell of a lot to be logistical about.

"Sounds like a hot one," Pokey said. "But you never can tell with MacArthur. Maybe he just wants to lead us in prayer."

"It's awfully goddamned early for sermons."

"Amen, brother."

When Prince came back to the balcony, Gwyneth was asleep, or pretending to slumber. So he picked her up in his arms and carried her with some difficulty into the bedroom. Gwyneth was heavier than he would have imagined. She didn't stir when he peeled off her *cheong-san*. But after he had undressed and carefully draped his clothes over a chair, then stood frankly appraising her uninhibited nakedness, she fluttered her eyes.

3

"Too Late for the Panic Button"

THE FIRST IMPRESSION a stranger received, upon entering the inner sanctum of the commanding general, U.S. Armed Forces of the Far East, was one of twilight gloom, despite the tropical sun's determined assault against its latticed window shades. The general preferred it that way, subdued, quiet, even restful, for the purposes of better cerebration, as he explained to his frequent visitors from the power and publishing centers of the United States. His headquarters occupied one of the proudest structures within the 400-year-old Walled City, Fort Santiago, whose original masonry was emplaced by Miguel Lopez de Legazpi, conqueror of the Philippines and founder of Manila.

Four centuries of history had culminated in the stately arrival of General Douglas MacArthur to take over the undernourished command called USAFFE by an abbreviation-happy officialdom.

Now almost sixty-one, ramrod straight in his imperial dignity, MacArthur had come a long way to this post, some of it ruggedly uphill, some down. His father had been military governor of the islands; and he himself had served his initial duty here in charge of the Philippines Department thirteen years earlier, before he'd reached the Army's pinnacle as chief of staff. In July, four years retired, he was recalled to active duty and given the USAFFE chore. During his retirement MacArthur served the people he loved so well as architect of their defenses.

It angered him more than he would admit that the War Department had accorded him only the three stars of a lieutenant general, one less than the fulgent four which he wore upon leaving the service. Moreover, this oversight (to use MacArthur's kindest phrase for the Army's niggling action) put him at a temporary disadvantage, rankwise, with his naval counterpart, Admiral Thomas H. Hart, whose four-starred blue flag waved over the Marsman Building, just down the cobbled street from Fort Santiago.

On the massive mahogany desk behind which he now sat, puffing away at his long-stemmed corncob pipe, lay the elaborate gold filigreed cap he had sported on that presumably sunset-years assignment as a Filipino field marshal.

A gigantic map of the southwest Pacific area, known for communications purposes as SouWesPac, hung against the opposite wall.

Admiral Hart perched at MacArthur's right, awaiting the G-2 (intelligence) officer's report. The Old Man's dour little face was also devoid of any obvious feelings. Military-naval operations that hinged upon the Philippines fulcrum were a joint affair, with MacArthur and Hart playing equal roles. This pertained as well in the much larger, more prestigious Hawaiian zone, where General Walter C. Short and Admiral Husband E. Kimmel pursued their separate but supposedly integrated courses.

Pointer in hand, the G-2 bird-colonel took his stance in front of the chart and began elucidating the plusses and minuses inherent in the task of defending the Philippines archipelago at 0745 on October 28, 1941.

"Why," the G-2 staffer asked rhetorically, with a respectful glance toward his pipe-smoking general, who had written the prologue, "are we concerned about a Japanese thrust toward the Philippines? And why would they want to invade these islands, if indeed they do entertain such a purpose?"

He answered his own question: Whoever controls the Philippines sits athwart the sea lanes leading from the United States to the southwest Pacific, where Australia formed the terminus of the vulnerable 7,000-mile line. That was axiomatic.

Industrially, the islands along this route weren't worth a tinker's dam, and they contained few raw materials of the sort needed by the Japanese. Manchuria and China furnished the Nips with a certain amount of their basic requirements. Korea provided security. But to fuel their war machine, they desperately craved much more. Thus, said the G-2 man in his kindergarten tone, their real aim was Malaya, the Netherlands East Indies, Burma and Siam, where oil, rubber, cotton and rice were available in limitless quantities.

"Right there for the taking, you might say," the G-2 man said with a gentle smile. "So our mission is to interdict the Japanese by placing our combined forces between them and their latest territorial aspirations for expanding the Greater East Asia Co-Prosperity Sphere."

Prince saw the admiral's lips tighten at this egregious oversimplification. Having belatedly learned that the Washington geniuses were now convinced of the Philippines' defensibility, Tommy Hart was blessed if he'd swing his own strategic compass around a full 180 degrees, from a workable hit-and-run concept to one based upon an inflexible stand-and-fight plan.

The G-2 fellow continued, unaware that he had almost lost part of his audience.

"History demonstrates," he said brightly, "that overseas expeditionary operations can be disastrous, as witness Gallipoli in nineteen fifteen, and last year's abortive British landings at Narvik. Moreover," he plunged on, with the triumphant air of a

73

mathematician who had solved a difficult equation, "one should consider the present quandary faced by Adolf Hitler as he tries to figure out how to bridge a mere twenty-five nautical miles between Calais and Dover, across the English Channel."

The Japanese must also realize (he said) their immense vulnerability to Admiral Hart's fast ships at the outset of any such risky enterprise and to the many others which would be dispatched from Pearl Harbor the instant they embarked on such an amphibious operation.

Prince intercepted the smoldering glance that flickered between the Old Man and his chief of staff, and he thought he observed the admiral's narrow shoulders lift in a barely perceptible shrug. But he couldn't be sure.

He wrenched his attention back to the G-2 lecturer and listened to the all too familiar litany of comparative Allied and Japanese naval strength in the Pacific, along with G-2's best estimate of where all this hardware was floating at the moment. Battleships, 10 each and pretty well confined to home ports; aircraft carriers, 4 U.S.-British, 10 Japanese, scattered from hell to breakfast; heavy cruisers, 17 versus 18, most of them escorting the aforesaid dispersed carriers; light cruisers, 27-17, ditto; destroyers, 93-111, ditto; submarines, 70-64, playing hide-and-seek with their respective adversary's surface iron.

So it continued.

There was satisfaction to be gleaned from the marked successes of lend-lease U.S. Flying Fortress bombers over Germany and from the expectation that a batch of these formidable aircraft would soon arrive in the Philippines. While the troop build-up proceeded (said the G-2 man, resuming his tutorial role) we would aerially blockade the South China Sea, operating around the clock, if necessary, from Clark Field. General MacArthur's great expectations included 75,000 American soldiers for his insular armies, 250 modern bombers and 250 pursuit planes to take care of any Jap Zeros that might show up.

Even though we are presently outnumbered (said the G-2 staffer), it should be borne in mind that ship for ship, plane for plane, man for man, our forces outclass those of the enemy.

"Training and *esprit de corps,* gentlemen, count for a vast amount in this business."

Admiral Hart greeted this announcement with another audible snort. "I'll accept your equation, Colonel, but only if you'll append a slight codicil. Not even training and *esprit* can overcome impossible odds, as the Light Brigade amply proved. If we get those reinforcements in the quantity you have suggested, very well and good. If we don't—" this time the Old Man's shrug was unmistakable—"then we're right back to Rainbow Five."

He didn't have to amplify that bald statement. Under the five-months-old war plan, the Navy would bolster MacArthur's efforts to hold the Philippines as long as dry-land defense was possible. But when, as and if it appeared certain that the jig was up, any surviving U.S. naval units would hightail it to Dutch or British bases and assume their positions along the Malay Barrier.

Nothing in MacArthur's existing arsenal of manpower and hardware gave the Asiatic Fleet commander much reason to believe that Rainbow 5 wouldn't ultimately prevail as written. Of some 130,000 men now in uniform, almost 100,000 were Filipinos, most of them formed into an amorphous Citizens' National Army, whose sketchy training ran largely to field drills and whose weapons consisted mainly of ancient Enfield rifles which they hesitated to shoot for fear of barrel explosions. Far from the 250 Flying Fortresses that might eventually reach Clark Field and its vulnerable satellite bases, MacArthur now had a mere thirty-five, plus 107 P-40 fighter planes and God only knew what else of a similarly depressing nature.

The British, for their part, were immersed in the defense of Singapore. To be sure, the battleship *Prince of Wales* and the battle cruiser *Repulse* were due soon. But they would have to operate against the Japs virtually without air support.

As for Hart's own wretched, misnamed fleet, it was woefully shy of ammunition and back-up auxiliary bottoms to keep its three old cruisers and thirteen even older destroyers running, once the outbreak of hostilities drove them to the high seas.

On that joyous note the conference adjourned.

Slowly at first, as when a destroyer is flagged into action, and with the destroyer's accelerating momentum, the tempo of events throughout the Pacific theater began to quicken. Early in November came a report of a Japanese submarine off Oahu. This enemy boat, according to the dispatches from Pearl Harbor, kept a constant 2,000-yard margin between her paper-thin skin and the coastal batteries' maximum range. So everybody got a chuckle out of the ludicrous situation, imagining the Nip sitting out there like a waterlogged duck, and the matter passed. But the loudest horse laugh, unheard at Pearl, was that of the Jap skipper, whose assignment was tabulating the sorties from the bottlenecked lagoon anchorage, counting the battleships and aircraft carriers and then sending the Word back to Yokosuka.

For at this juncture neither American fleet, Kimmel's Pacific nor Hart's Asiatic, had received shoot-to-kill orders. All they could do was watch, wait and try to guess what mischief their putative enemy was conjuring up in his wily brain.

They shadowed the Japs as best they could, with their inadequately ranged planes and with their own subs, and every once in a while they sent their surface forces out to maneuver in battle array and to shoot at towed targets. The Pacific Fleet ships held the advantage in that department because they possessed ample supplies of ammunition. But the Asiatic Fleet, at the far end of the line, had to husband its slender resources against a crisis when the objective might be something more lethal than a canvas bull's-eye mounted on a sled, or a cloth sleeve fluttering at the end of an aerial cable.

The various commands in Manila had started ferrying military and civilian dependents back to the States. This was the most doleful business of all, symbolic of the quiet confusion that prevailed in the late autumn of 1941, along the entire periphery, wherever the Americans, British and Dutch faced the enigmatic Japs.

Unattached females, of course, were permitted to stay in the Philippines at their own risk. Thus Gwyneth Dean continued her queen-bee reign at the High Commission, more glamorous than ever now that she was sharing all sorts of delicious dangers with the Army colonels and the Navy captains and the deputy commissioners, to say nothing of the subalterns and j.o.'s and the minor luminaries of Mr. Sayre's elegant satrapy. Gwyneth's regal status was enhanced by the fact that American females, always in short supply, had now become an almost priceless commodity.

Prince soon discovered that his own dates with Gwyneth were severely rationed. This did not fret him unduly, however, because of his firm resolve to lay aside childish things, devoting more attention to his staff duties and less to the temptations of the Civil Service flesh.

His newfound diligence was rewarded by a very rare invitation to play golf with the Old Man. After the admiral's personal call, which had awakened him at the ungodly hour of six o'clock of a Sabbath morning, he was assailed by a paradoxical mixture of relief and apprehension. These imperious golfing bids often had a diabolical way of turning into a catastrophe for the Old Man's guests, especially when, as in this instance, the summons came on the spur of the moment. The chief of staff was the only person who seemed immune to such treatment.

Others, with less standing, were known to have been given the Deep Six between putts on the eleventh green.

Prince was not reassured, either, by the prospect of a ride to the Manila Golf Club in the four-star Buick, sharing the back seat with the Old Man and nodding respectfully at his acidulous remarks on the world and what's wrong with it. The admiral had indicated he wished to play as a twosome. That in itself was an ominous portent.

They reached the course while the dew was still glistening on the fairways. Because of his stratospheric rank, the admiral was waved through the meager knot of early-morning golfers and given an immediate starting time.

"Let's shove off," said the Old Man, "so we can play nine holes before the sun gets too blamed hot for comfort."

"Yes, sir," Prince said.

They picked up a pair of caddies, small brown youths who looked no bigger than their golfbags, and strolled to the first tee. Prince stepped aside to let his august opponent drive first, but the Old Man insisted on flipping a coin for honors. Prince was secretly gratified when the admiral won the toss.

The Old Man took two brisk practice swings, and no more, before he lofted his ball straight down the fairway. Not much distance, Prince saw, but true. He envied the admiral's resolute accuracy. His own drive traveled a good hundred yards farther, then hooked sharply and rabbited into the rough.

"Tough luck," the Old Man said curtly. "Want to try another?"

"Negative, sir. I'll play it."

"Good."

They started walking down the undulant hill, and soon the one-story clubhouse was lost to view below the rise. Except for themselves, the course appeared to be deserted. As far ahead as Prince could discern through the morning heat haze there wasn't a living soul. Even the greenskeepers had fled, leaving their automatic sprinklers on full blast. Having achieved such utter solitude, in an atmosphere conducive to serious dialogue, Prince supposed the admiral would now reveal whatever it was that concerned him enough to arrange this *tête-à-tête*.

But the Old Man waited until they had reached the fifth tee, a country mile from the clubhouse, before he unlocked the mystery. By that time both of them were wringing wet, and Prince was four strokes down, thanks to his adversary's accurate, dogged, annoyingly consistent game, and to his own mounting exasperation which betrayed itself in muffed approach shots and triple putts. Prince had no intention of winning. But neither did he wish to look like a raw-assed duffer in front of this man who prized professional skill above all else.

"Let's drop anchor here for a few minutes," the admiral said, indicating a magnolia-shaded bench beside a drinking fountain. "Smoke?" He proferred a crumpled pack of cigarettes.

"Thank you, sir." Prince took one gratefully. "It's hotter than a tin can's boiler room."

The old Man grunted but made no other response. Then he announced without preamble: "Tomorrow I'm ordering four destroyers—DesDiv Eleven—into Balikpapan, with their tender *Gray Eagle*," said the admiral. "DesDiv Ten will go with *Marblehead* to Tarakan, also in Borneo but a bit farther north, so we can bird-dog both Makassar Strait and the Celebes Sea. Eight tin cans and a light cruiser isn't much for the job. But that's what Washington wants—to clear our hardware out of this area in case the Japs strike." He drew deeply on his sputtering cigarette. "We'll also send *Houston* down to Iloilo, on the southern tip of Panay, where she'll be available to Admiral Glassford when he takes over Task Force Five. He rates a heavy cruiser."

Prince nodded to indicate his comprehension of these fleet movements. But he was still puzzled. The Old Man wasn't given to discussing tactics with his juniors, particularly in advance of their execution, unless he had a definite purpose in mind.

"If Manila proves untenable," said the admiral, "I'll move my headquarters to Surabaya."

Prince nodded again, although a chill feeling of doubt was beginning to assail him as the Old Man pressed obliquely toward whatever goal he was aiming at, using short conversational strokes, the way he played golf.

Then, as if chipping onto the green, within inches of the pin, he said abruptly, "There's going to be a new billet for you in this exercise, Prince."

"Sir?"

"Your record is excellent—on paper."

"Sir?" repeated Prince, aware that he sounded appallingly stupid.

"Command and staff school," the Old Man barked. "Damned fine grades."

"Thank you, sir."

"Only one lack, and it's hampered you for a long while. 'Command and staff' tells the story. You've had all you need of 'staff.' Now you're going to pick up the 'command' part."

"I don't think I quite follow you, sir."

"If you expect to advance in this business, you've got to put some solid command experience under your belt. Seagoing stuff, not shore-based."

"Yes, sir."

In a ruminative tone, the Old Man went on: "DesDiv Eleven might be just your dish of tea. It's heading into a situation that could very well take imagination, resourcefulness, plus a certain amount of—" he groped for the right word—"gall."

This was hardly the characterization which Prince would have applied to himself. He wondered whether he had succeeded so well in his role of faithful servitor that the Old Man had been gulled by the act, like any ordinary mortal.

But all he said was "Yes, sir," in a voice that was as devoid of expression as he could manage.

"You also know exactly where the Asiatic Fleet stands in relation to the whole fouled-up picture," said the admiral. "We're strictly a holding operation—like what's-his-name at the bridge."

"Horatio," supplied Prince, numbly.

"Correct. So we take what we've got, and we run with it. Nobody reporting out here fresh from the States could even begin to understand this mess the way we plank-owners understand it. And by the time they might get around to learning, it would be too late."

"Yes, sir."

"Warren Pryor commands DesDiv Eleven for the moment," said the admiral. "He'll take his division into Balikpapan and get it properly established. But Pryor is about due for Stateside duty, and I don't think we can hang onto him much longer. So that's where you come in."

"Yes, sir," Prince said. He was sounding like a broken record.

"I've given this matter a lot of thought, Prince. You don't have that instinct for mayhem which drives some of the other three-stripers who might qualify. But maybe it's just as well you don't. We haven't enough ships to risk unnecessarily, so a moderate sense of self-preservation could be a good thing, under the circumstances."

Prince nodded glumly. He had a sudden guilty feeling, almost visceral, as if he were letting the Old Man down even before he undertook the assignment. Worse yet, he knew the "self-preservation" to which the admiral had alluded wasn't really that at all, but sheer cowardice.

By the last of November, scarcely a week after Prince played his losing match with the admiral, there could be little doubt that the Pacific and peace were no longer synonymous. From the Chief of Naval Operations, Harold R. (Betty) Stark, came a dispatch that was flatly labeled "a war warning." His message to Kimmel at Pearl and Hart in Manila declared:

"Negotiations with Japan looking toward stabilization of conditions in the Pacific have ceased. An aggressive move by Japan is expected within the next few days. The number and equipment of Japanese troops and the organization of naval task forces indicates an amphibious expedition against either the Philippines, Thai or Kra peninsulas, or possibly Borneo."

Whereupon CNO, in all his distant wisdom, instructed his far-flung lieutenants to "execute appropriate defensive deployment" preparatory to activating the Navy's share of Rainbow 5.

The Old Man read this extraordinary dispatch aloud, for the benefit of the chief of staff and Prince, with tightening jaw and darkening countenance.

"I wish to high heaven," he exploded "they'd make up their minds back there. Three weeks ago Betty Stark was giving as his personal opinion the belief that the Japs weren't about to 'sail into us,' whatever in hell *that* meant. Now this! We've got to find some way, damn it, to inform those people that theory stops at the water's edge."

Since receiving the unpleasant notice that he would soon be given command of DesDiv 11, Prince had virtually memorized the details of Rainbow 5. It wasn't nice literature for a tethered sheep, postulating as it did a rear-guard operation by the Asiatic forces while the main body of the Pacific Fleet stormed the Japanese bases in the Marshalls and the Carolines. This optimistic endeavor included capturing the giant stronghold of Truk, which was reputed to be even larger than Pearl Harbor itself and incalculably more mysterious, since the United States had no convenient consul there to spy on the Mikado's ship movements.

Rainbow 5 concluded that the Pacific Fleet, maybe six to nine months later, depending on its expeditionary successes, would steam west to lift the siege of the Philippines.

The hour was long gone for pushing the panic button. Everything possible had been done. The last residual forces were moving out of China, first the Marines and then the gunboats, in a race against time. Minefields were laid in Manila and Subic bays. All, or what passed for all that late autumn, was in readiness.

And, finally, the Asiatic Fleet and MacArthur's USAFFE agreed on a combined air reconnaissance, using the Army's Flying Fortresses to scout the northern sectors as far as Formosa and the Navy's lumbering twin-engined Catalinas to probe along the Indochinese coast. To date, after three days of unremitting, exhausting missions, they had sighted nothing worth mentioning locally, much less relaying to Washington, D.C.

Yet, unbeknownst to the worried staffs at Pearl and Manila, the enemy was indeed on the prowl. At Tankan Bay in the fog-shrouded Kuriles, which stretched between the nether Japanese island of Hokkaido and Russia's Kamchatka peninsula, the combined fleet was assembling. Even farther north, starting its great sweep toward the unsuspecting Americans at Pearl Harbor, was Vice Admiral Chuichi Nagumo's lethal striking force: six aircraft carriers, plus a mighty array of battleships, cruisers and destroyers.

4

"The Man's in a Hurry"

COMMANDER ALGERNON MONK, R.N., reached Manila on December 3. He arrived aboard one of those preposterous Royal Air Force flying boats that seemed more albatross than airplane and which had taken thirty-six mortal hours to traverse the 1,500 miles from Singapore. But this included a bibulous stopover at Brunei, in Sarawak, where a *soi-disant* white rajah ruled that aboriginal portion of northwest Borneo. The drinks had flowed freely, partly because the rajah hadn't found a decent opportunity for a social bash in a good many weeks and partly because Sarawak itself was admittedly in the direct path of any southward Japanese push. So even this transient sight of the RAF was reassuring. Britain was still there. A trifle remote, perhaps, but somewhere in the vicinity.

As soon as the Asiatic Fleet barge pulled alongside the high-winged craft, whose accommodation hatch was flung open the instant it mushed to a halt, Commander Monk leaped out. He was rumpled, redolent of stale sweat and exceedingly hung over. But his grip, when he clasped Prince's tentatively outthrust hand, was like the embrace of a Kodiak bear.

By the time they reached the Manila Hotel, he was the Beaver, and Prince had become resigned to the thought of having him briefly occupy the spare twin bed in his air-shaft room.

Admiral Tom Phillips, said the Beaver, would pop in on Friday, the fifth, for a brief *tête-à-tête* with Admiral Hart, General MacArthur and whomever else it seemed logical to invite. There was no need for ceremony or a vast amount of elaborate preparations, because little Tom was a chap who didn't stand much on ritual, despite his haughty Royal Navy upbringing. They'd simply exchange a few ideas, help each other tighten the old belt a couple of notches, and then go about their business of readying a proper welcome for the bloody Nips.

"Of course," said the Beaver, "I'll be staying on with you fellows."

"Of course," Prince said, none too graciously, as his unwanted guest flung himself, wet boots and all, upon the protesting bed. "But we'll have to find you a decent place to live."

"This is top hole," said the Beaver. "I rather like it." He appraised the minuscule chamber with a swift eye. "Room to swing a cat. A very small cat, less than nine tails, but adequate." He grinned like a honey-sated bear. "After convoy duty in the Mediterranean, old man, this resembles Claridge's."

Prince gave a hopeless shrug. "Hell, why not? Make yourself at home. I'll be shoving off fairly soon, anyhow."

"So?"

"They've got me ticketed for a busted-ass tin-can division that's been sent to Balikpapan."

"Lovely spot. Lively duty."

"You know Balikpapan?"

"Well enough to recognize it's where evil Singaporeans go when they die. Sort of Purgatory with palm trees." The Beaver stretched luxuriously. "As for destroyer duty, me lad, that ices the cake."

"You've had it?"

"I," said the bearded traveler, "have indeed had it. As you Yanks phrase it so cogently, in spades."

Prince consulted his watch. "It's five past five. The admiral told me to give you a night to relax before fetching you around to Fleet headquarters. What's your pleasure?"

"Screwing," the Beaver said, grinning lewdly. "But I'll settle for whatever comes naturally in this Pearl of the Orient."

"Maybe we can arrange something," Prince said, "after we wash up."

"Splendid."

"You're still company. The head's all yours."

"Thanks."

The Beaver heaved himself off the bed and picked up his canvas flight bag. From it he extracted a clean but horribly wrinkled white uniform, above whose breast pocket was sewn a single red and blue ribbon. Prince recognized the decoration as the Distinguished Service Order, an honor not given lightly by a nation used to gallantry in action. He was impressed.

After ten minutes in the bathroom, during which he took a shower and noisily used the W.C. without bothering to shut the door, the Beaver burst forth looking like the contents of a laundry bag. But at least, Prince noted, he smelled a lot better.

"I borrowed your cologne," the Beaver said. "It's rather elegant. Better than bay rum."

"What's mine," Prince observed ironically, "is yours, *effendi*." He reached for the telephone. "I'll order up a staff car, and then we'll imbibe a little nourishment at the hotel pub before hoisting anchor. Okay?"

"Okay."

It was five-thirty by the time they went downstairs. As always at that hour, the main saloon was already crowded, mostly with uniformed Americans who seemed bent on preserving the island's entire limited alcoholic supply from threat of enemy capture. All the tables, even the bar stools, were taken. So Prince and the Beaver had to be content with an SRO niche near the jangling cash register.

The Beaver asked for Scotch and water with plenty of ice. When Prince questioned him, he explained that the only reason the British made such a godawful fuss about taking their whiskey warm was because they lacked refrigeration facilities. It was pure defensive pretense. Taste didn't enter into the silly custom.

Prince deliberately ordered his without ice.

"From the way you talk about Balikpapan," he growled, "I'd better start getting used to drinking the stuff this way."

"Hell, man, you'll be uncommon lucky to get any Scotch at all in that bloody wilderness," the Beaver said. "Holland gin is more like it. And that's a ruddy vile potion, iced or not."

Over their whiskies, as they leaned companionably against the polished mahogany bar, they chatted about the European conflict, which the Beaver had seen and felt, but about which Prince could only surmise, from official action reports and what he had learned from the tired young Britons at the War College. The Beaver reluctantly disclosed how he had won the DSO and grown his monstrous beard, to hide the damage done his face after he'd been dive-bombed off Malta. But he had saved his ship and earned the medal. With a wry grimace, he opined that he mightn't have survived at all had he been standing on the bridge of a Lend-Lease four-stacker instead of a reasonably modern Royal Navy destroyer.

Four-pipers, drawled the Beaver, were originally designed for a more innocent kind of combat, before precision bombing was invented or even dreamed of. Nothing, really, could be done to improve the ugly breed at this late date. They were too slow, too unmanageable under certain emergency conditions and their armament was never meant for dueling with fast-flying aircraft.

"But you fellows were glad enough to get 'em, weren't you?"

Prince demanded, suddenly stung by the Beaver's left-handed criticism.

"Beggars," said the Beaver, "jolly well can't be choosers."

Prince glanced around. The cavernous room was smoky, like a volcano on the verge of erupting, and its atmosphere seemed almost as volatile. The laughter was too hectic, the voices too loud for normal creature comfort.

The Beaver was rambling on again above the conversational hubbub in the bar and the constant metallic clangor of the cash register. What he said was meant for Prince's ears, but others around them soon became interested listeners.

"You have my sincerest sympathies, old cock, you and your Asiatic squadron."

Prince continued to be annoyed at the Beaver's pejorative references to the American forces, regardless of the truth in what he was saying. "It's officially designated a fleet," he snapped.

"Balls. Squadron. And that's being ruddy kind to the little bugger."

"What about your own so-called British 'Eastern Fleet,' mister, now that it's finally arrived in Singapore?"

The Beaver fired off an ursine belch. "Charity really does begin at home, you know. It has my sympathies, too." He belched again. "We were supposed to have brought an aircraft carrier with us, the *Indomitable*, but the silly wench managed to hang herself up on a reef near Jamaica, so we had to go it alone."

Prince shot him a warning look. "You're talking pretty goddamned freely, aren't you?"

The Beaver retorted with an explosive obscenity. "There are enough spies in Singapore to fill a regiment. Tom Phillips' combat strength isn't a mystery to anyone, much less the Nips who shadowed us the whole way." He pounded upon the bar for another drink. "Make it a double," he told the white-clad bartender. "I need it. And a double for my stouthearted young friend here."

Prince had to laugh. "You sound like the Ancient Mariner. In spite of the shrubbery, you can't be all that senior to me. I'm thirty-five. How the hell old are you?"

"By the Gregorian calendar," said the Beaver, "I'm still on the sunny side of thirty-eight. But on top of that you've got to add my sea duty since 'thirty-nine, which equals another century or so." He gulped at his whiskey. "Losing our arses at Narvik, at Dunkirk, at Crete, on the bloody Atlantic and Mediterranean convoy runs . . ." For a moment the Beaver was silent, brooding, his pitted face unwontedly solemn. Then: "Small wonder Tom Phillips has a favorite epilogue for bidding his staff good night. 'God rest ye, merry gentlemen,' it goes, 'for this day we're that much nearer the yawning chasm of the tomb.' "

"Sounds pretty goddamned doom-filled."

"It is, it is. And now we've extended the chasm to Singapore. Christ! The blasted fortress guns are frozen seaward, if you can imagine such utter stupidity. Yet an attack, when it comes, will hit us from up the Malayan peninsula." The Beaver polished off his double whiskey. "I tell you, mate, we're still living in Sir Stamford Raffles' time."

Prince sought to end the lugubrious dialogue. Peering through the tobacco miasma, he made out several of the better known, or more notorious, camp followers of Manila, whom he described in lurid detail for the Beaver's edification. It amused him to include Gwyneth Dean among this roster of hard-drinking, chain-smoking *houris*. He had glimpsed her at a center table, surrounded by a quartet of Army brass, the junior of whom was a grizzled bird colonel.

The Beaver was moved to almost lyrical comment by the sight of Gwyneth's generous décolletage and the shape of her bare thigh along the split of her inevitable *cheong-san*.

"Your Miss Dean," he said, "has the dulcet look of a predatory swan."

Prince sighed. "You're guilty of contradictions in terms, my friend. First, she's not 'my' Miss Dean, because I've obviously been outranked. Second, swans aren't predatory—even if Miss Dean damned well is."

The Beaver fondled his ferocious mustache and gave his pirate's beard a tweak. "I think I shall present my diplomatic credentials to the charming lady."

"She'll cut you cold," warned Prince.

But the Beaver was already plowing through the clot of predinner celebrants, forcing his way like a plunging fullback, straight toward Gwyneth Dean's table. Prince saw him stop, bend down, speak a few words and then take her slim hand in his. Amazingly, the Beaver lifted her fingers to his coarse lips and kissed their tips with consummate gallantry. They chatted together briefly, and it became apparent that Gwyneth was urging him to join her brass-bound claque. But the Beaver demurred graciously. Instead, he looked at his watch, baring huge teeth in a Teddy Rooseveltian grin, and said something that made Gwyneth smile. Whatever it was, the remark elicited a much less appreciative response from her guard of honor. The Army was not amused. It scowled nastily. Undaunted, the Beaver completed his mission and returned serenely to the bar.

"What in God's name did you say to Madame Pompadour?" Prince asked.

The Beaver simulated a colossal yawn. "It seems we English have a certain charisma, you know, whose source eludes even ourselves. But it does have a marked effect on the ladies. American ladies, that is. I merely informed *our* Miss Dean that I was the new British liaison chap with the Asiatic Fleet—*Fleet*, mind you, laddie—and that her beauty had impelled me to forgo my typical Anglo-Saxon reserve. Actually, old man, it was frightfully easy. Quite simple. She is bored with the American military. Even with the Navy and Marine Corps. She craves something more, shall we say, continental. Possibly she imagines that I can supply it."

Prince stared in disbelief at the Beaver's scarred face, at his unkempt beard and shock of ginger hair. "I'll be forever goddamned," he muttered, almost reverently.

The Beaver took no offense at Prince's patently low assessment of his masculine attraction.

"Miss Dean will join us," he said complacently, "as soon as she can dispose of the United States Army. I suggested that seven o'clock would be an appropriate hour. She agreed."

From the outset, it was a weird sort of evening, for Prince was determined to show Gwyneth something of the Manila she'd missed on her regular beat of grand hotels, fancy clubs, posh bars and her perfumed seraglio on Taft Avenue.

He selected a place on the Pasig River, beyond the Malacañan Palace, where the Commonwealth's indomitable, ailing President lived. Here you could listen to authentic *folklorica* music and watch the Tagalog dancing, while drinking rum potions and dining leisurely on exotic native dishes.

The main attraction, Prince explained, was an improbably wild dance called the *tinikling*. During it, the performers leaped nimbly between the interstices of huge clashing bamboo poles, wielded by a quartet of muscular Filipinos who squatted on the floor. One false step could mean a broken ankle, or worse.

A minnow-slim girl, hardly five feet tall, yet a splendidly proportioned figurine with shapely legs set off by her embroidered skirtlet, was the darling of the audience. Her elfin toes flickered like hummingbirds' wings, the bamboo staves thundered, and each time she appeared to have eluded their terrible grasp with less margin to spare.

After it ended, the leader guided his miniature star across the candlelit verandah to the table where Gwyneth, Prince and the Beaver were sitting.

"This," he said, "is the incomparable Mari, the finest dancer in the Philippines. We saw that you lacked a second lady, and it occurred to us that you might wish to have her join you."

Prince and the Briton had risen deferentially as Mari approached. Both sprang to assist her into the vacant chair.

"Charmed," said Prince.

Gwyneth stared glacially at the girl opposite her. Mari's breathing was curiously normal for someone who had just survived the rigors of the *tinikling*.

"You do have some rather extraordinary talents, my dear, and not all of them entirely hidden," Gwyneth purred.

The Beaver took over. "By all that's holy, this child's a ruddy wizard." He motioned to a waiter. "Break out another tot of rum. After this example of courage under fire, we've got to splice the main brace—with double Demeraras!"

Shortly after midnight they went back to La Luna for the car. Prince dropped the Beaver off at Gwyneth Dean's place, by unspoken mutual agreement, and then retraced their route downtown, to the Escolta, near which Mari had her own one-room apartment over a dress shop.

Prince looked around. "Elegant quarters, *señorita*."

"It is not much," she said. "But it suffices."

Mari made no move to switch on the lights. Instead, after closing the hallway door, she stood immobile in the center of the room, gazing at him expectantly, as if awaiting something that was both inevitable and much to be desired.

The moon shone obliquely through the dainty *piña* lace curtains, transforming the room into a chamber of almost medieval mystery. The high-postered bed in the far corner, with its mosquito netting, could have been a queen's canopied couch; and the window itself was the casement from which the captive princess had brooded out across the darkened moor.

But Mari was no captive. She was doing exactly what she wished to do.

Docilely, she allowed Prince to undress her, pirouetted once so that he could view her exquisite body, and then slipped into the bed. She reclined there, solemnly watching him disrobe, intrigued by the meticulous way in which he arranged his clothes over the straight-backed chair, so they would betray no telltale wrinkles next morning.

He joined her in the narrow bed, where they lay quietly for a moment before he asked wonderingly, "Why me, child?"

Her answer was simple. "As I danced, I observed you, and you seemed so lonely, even with your two friends. Sometimes I am lonely too. Very."

"How could you have been watching me," Prince marveled, "while those bamboo sticks were slamming at you like goddamn cannonfire?"

"The *tinikling* is a matter of instinct. If you must watch your feet, then you are lost."

"Do you always feel this humanitarian about castaway males?"

"Not often," said Mari with quaint dignity. "It is not what you are thinking. I am not a prostitute."

"I wasn't thinking that at all," he protested.

She gave Prince a cryptic smile as he drew her against his lean body, gently kissing her earlobes, nuzzling at her soft cheeks.

"You taste delicious," he whispered, transferring his lips to her dark-aureoled right breast. "Much sweeter than a mango."

Mari giggled. "You are tickling me."

He moved his hand slowly downward, across her smooth belly, until it touched her velvety pubic fleece. "Does that tickle?"

"Not really . . ."

"Or this?" he teased, probing. "Or that?"

Mari responded with a gentle laugh, deep in her throat, but did not talk again until their love play ended. She was a very satisfactory partner. She had few inhibitions.

After a short while Prince raised himself on an elbow, reached out through the netting for his silver cigarette case, which he had deposited on the bedside table. He lit one for each of them. They relaxed against the thick bolster that served as a double pillow, tranquilly smoking, listening to the gabble of night birds in the courtyard palms.

Mari was the first to speak. "You asked me 'why' when we first came to this room. Now I shall repeat that same question. Why do you like me, Prince, if indeed you do?"

Before replying, he stubbed out his cigarette in the ashtray balanced on his naked chest and pondered the issue thoughtfully. At length he answered in a somewhat ironic tone, "Maybe it's because you say 'like' instead of 'love' when you put such a foolish question."

"Foolish?"

"Certainly. We enjoyed each other, didn't we? No commitments asked or given. Wasn't that enough?"

"I guess so." Mari leaned over to extinguish her own cigarette and peered up at him through half-closed lashes. "But sometimes I truly wonder what is in a man's heart at such a moment."

"Perhaps I don't have a heart," he countered. "Didn't that possibility occur to you?"

She smiled enigmatically, as she had earlier. "No, *querido,* it never did."

"In which case, the defense rests, body and soul."

When Mari went down the hall to the bathroom, clad only in a sarong-wrapped towel, he got dressed. On her return he said it was past time for him to go. Almost two A.M., and he had the duty in the morning. One more late arrival at GHQ would spell "So Long, Prince!" in flaming letters you could see from here to Cavite.

But before he departed, Mari went to her bureau, found a small envelope and wrote his name on it with a purple pen.

"This," she said, "may help you remember me. But do not open it here. Wait until you have gone."

He slipped the envelope into a pocket of his khaki shirt.

"Thank you," he said, "for everything."

"Shall I see you again, Prince?"

"Hell, yes!"

But he was wrong. Abysmally wrong. This would be their only encounter, although what she had given him as a keepsake did, indeed, cause him to remember her often. Prince sat in his staff car, with the dome lights on, and inspected the contents of the envelope. It was a photograph of Mari, entirely nude, stretched across the very bed upon which they had made such abandoned love.

He put the envelope and picture back in his pocket. Then he sparked the Chevy into life after several tries and drove slowly to the Manila Hotel.

The Beaver stormed into their room around six A.M., reeking of Chanel Number 5 and Courvoisier cognac, to catch a roaring forty winks before he had to pay his respects to the Old Man. Prince came awake only long enough to ask him sleepily how he'd made out.

"How d'you Yanks phrase it?" The Beaver sighed contentedly. "Four-bloody-oh."

Like a disdainful conscience, Chief Yeoman Elliot Bream brought the sheaf of operational dispatches, Asiatic Fleet letters, directives and intelligence data, sitreps (situational reports) and an avalanche of minatory advices from Washington, which Prince had asked him to accumulate for Commander Monk's appraisal. It was only eight-thirty A.M., but the staff bullpen was steaming like a Turkish bath. Bream had been laboring over these bulky archives for more than two hours. He was bored stiff with his monotonous task, although in the process of putting together this sum total of everything the Fleet knew (or presumably ought to know) about the rapidly worsening conditions in the Pacific he had acquired a considerable education for himself, which would stand him in good stead when next he held court at the Non-Commissioned Officers' Club. Bream was, after all, a very junior NCO. He needed a bit of extra clout. This would give it to him, raising him from the usual chief's scuttle-butt status as a purveyor of mere rumor to that of a man who dispensed the True Word.

Bream had been promoted only two days earlier, from first class yeoman to chief, on Prince's recommendation. He wore his new honor lightly, accepting it as his overdelayed due, and whatever gratitude he might have felt was occasioned mainly by the fact that now he could lay aside his bell-bottomed swabbie's costume for the more modish uniform of a chief. Besides, the hard-drinking NCO club was much to be preferred over the en-listed men's club, where San Miguel beer was the drab alcoholic staple.

The Beaver was visibly impressed by Bream's diligence. After the neatly collated file folders had been spread out on the desk assigned him near the Flag Lieutenant's, he said admiringly, "A good yeoman, like a good woman, is damned hard to find, old cock."

Prince glowered at Bream's retreating back, noting the el-egantly tailored cut of his tropical worsted jacket, which the fledgling chief insisted on wearing despite the sodden heat. Bream *was* useful. Probably indispensable. But Prince hated to be reminded of it so all-fired early in the morning, especially by a practical stranger who had observed—and doubtless measured —his tenuous master-servant relationship with the crafty bastard for less than twenty minutes.

"Thanks for the advice," Prince snarled. "I'll give the proposi-tion some thought."

"Do that," the Beaver replied imperturbably. "Believe me, you won't regret it."

Then the Briton stripped off his coat, necktie and shirt, ob-livious to Prince's look of fastidious censure, and began wading through the small mountain of documents. Whistling tunelessly between splayed teeth as he riffled the pages, the Beaver read with remarkable speed for a man who appeared to be so phlegmatic. By ten o'clock, the appointed hour for his meeting with the admiral, he had digested the whole lot.

At that exact moment the intercom on Prince's desk buzzed, and the Old Man ordered them into his office. The Beaver cursed mildly as he struggled back into his wrinkled uniform.

It wasn't a very protracted session. The Old Man wanted to know whether proper arrangements were completed for Admiral Tom Phillips' visit. The Beaver, who hadn't lifted a finger to make any, beyond ascertaining the readiness of hotel space for Admiral Phillips and his top staffers, allowed that everything was top-hole. The Old Man harrumphed and said this was fine. General MacArthur, his air chief, Lew Brereton, and High Commissioner Sayre would all go down to the Muelle Tacoma with him next morning to greet the British admiral's plane when it taxied into the inner basin.

"What's the ETA?" asked the Old Man.

"Estimated arrival time is seven A.M.," the Beaver said promptly.

"Reckon you two young studs can make it?"

"Tonight," said the Beaver, conscious of his bloodshot eyes and aware of what the admiral was thinking, "we'll comport ourselves like monks."

The Old Man accorded him a frosty smile. "That *is* your surname, isn't it, Commander?"

"On rare occasions, sir."

"Good."

So the audience ended. Prince and the Beaver departed. When the door was safely shut, the Briton said, "Your boss is a refreshingly trustful soul. Rather like my own little chap."

"Maybe he is," said Prince. "But don't let first impressions fool you, and don't ever let him down. He won't tolerate screwups."

Clambering laboriously past the legs of his three subordinates, who were seated beneath the ropework canopy of the Flag Barge, Admiral Tom Phillips was the first to reach the brow of the pier and accept the salutes of the assembled American brass.

He was a diminutive man, almost runty in stature, who stood barely five feet four in his trim black shoes. He was a full inch shorter than Napoleon, and his nickname was "Tom Thumb" to those of sufficient rank or intimacy to risk the appellation. Still in his early fifties, a youngish age for a flag officer, he was ticketed to go far in the Royal Navy, should he survive the Herculean task that had been given him, intervening his paltry Eastern Fleet between the rampant Japanese and the menaced stronghold of Singapore. There was a distinct whiff of salt about Tom Thumb as he swaggered like a miniature bantam cock across the splintery wharf to shake the outstretched hands of Admiral Hart, Generals MacArthur and Brereton and their sundry attendant aides. The Old Man had even ordered up a six-piece band from the Cavite Naval Yard, which played "Rule, Britannia" as Phillips stepped ashore. It was an emotional moment, to Prince, enough to make a quasi-hero of any man who took part in the ceremony that crisp December morning.

Since the British commander had already breakfasted aboard his RAF seaplane, they proceeded immediately to the Marsman Building, adjacent to the waterfront, where the U.S. Asiatic Fleet was headquartered. In consideration of Phillips' urgent responsibilities back at Singapore, only three days had been allocated to the meeting, long overdue as it was.

For openers, he recalled that Sir John Fisher, the Empire architect of World War I sea power which preserved Pax Britannica, had a cherished saying: "The Royal Navy always travels first class."

Phillips amended the ancient quotation with just a trace of a smile: "In this instance, gentlemen, 'first class' consists of one dreadnaught, one battle cruiser, seven destroyers—and no visible means of air support beyond a handful of rather antiquated RAF fighters that have several dozen other tactical fish to fry, besides covering my fleet units."

There were additional opinions of a classical nature worth mentioning in this context, said Phillips. Sir John also believed in Nelson's dictum: "Think in oceans, sink at sight." Again, excellent, provided you had the wherewithal for such impetuosity. And Winnie Churchill, a certified theorist, held that the Allied naval forces in the Far East should "exercise that kind of vague menace which capital ships of the highest quality, whose whereabouts are unknown, can impose upon all hostile naval calculations . . . going to sea and vanishing among the innumerable islands."

Hart interrupted in a testy voice: "Maybe the Japs will be impressed. I sure as hell am not. We've been stamping 'whereabouts unknown' on their movements for the past week like so many postal clerks. There's been a convoy in Camranh Bay, Vietnam, another in the Hainan-Formosa area, and a third one God-only-knows-where. But our reconnaissance hasn't produced much of a clue as to their intentions."

"I know," soothed Phillips. "It's damned vexing."

"Vexing is a pretty mild word, Admiral. It's a potential disaster." The Old Man looked at the wall chart, on which a greased-penciled series of lines seemed to begin nowhere and end nowhere. "We've got two patrol craft on station, armed with popguns, crewed by Filipinos under U.S. naval ratings. Their orders, straight from OpNav in Washington, are 'to observe and report by radio any Japanese movements in the west China Sea and the Gulf of Siam.'" He laughed harshly. "Those ships—if you can call 'em ships—are all we have operating beyond the extreme limits of our aerial searches."

Phillips demurred politely. "My flying boats are also operating in the sector south of the Cochin-China peninsula, off Cape Ca Mau."

"What've they reported?"

"Nothing as yet. The whole area remains blanketed with cloud cover."

General Brereton intervened smoothly. "Something should develop any time now, considering the number of planes we've laid on."

"Let's hope so," said the Old Man. "But the basic issue remains—are they merely bound for supplementary landings along the Siamese coast, or do they intend to try a Malayan beachhead?"

On over-all strategy, it became readily apparent, Hart and his august visitor stood in essential agreement. Singapore was vulnerable, deplorably so, whereas Manila was a more secure base from which to launch a counterattack against the enemy when the shooting war broke out. The British were virtually prisoners in their vaunted stronghold, pinned down without adequate air cover for any major moves toward the east.

Thus, reluctantly, the American admiral said he would pare off four of his overaged destroyers to bolster Phillips' forces in the threatened Malayan area, if the Briton would fetch three of *his* destroyers down from Hong Kong, which was a sitting-duck harbor anyhow if the Japs struck.

The Old Man addressed his chief of staff: "We'll tap DesDiv Eleven for this assignment. Use plain language in your dispatch sending 'em from Balikpapan to Batavia, on the pretext of rest-and-recreation. Let's make sure the Nips figure it's just a simple R-and-R exercise. But actually, they'll swing past Java and make for Singapore." He turned to Prince, who had been listening to this high-level discourse with rapt attention. "You may have to leave a bit earlier than planned, Commander."

Prince nodded unhappily. "Yes, sir."

"I think," said Phillips, "that it would be worthwhile to send my force up Malaya's east coast on a show-the-flag mission, as a deterrent in case the enemy really has some notion of invading."

"Churchill's theory again, Admiral?" asked the Old Man.

"No," Phillips growled. "Mine. We'd be ready for a fight."

He ticked off his available ships: *Prince of Wales, Repulse,* plus the destroyers *Electra, Express, Tenedos, Vampire.* Three others were under repair, and the Hong Kong contingent wouldn't make it in time. Formidable names, thought Prince, colorfully heroic, and far superior to the mundane christenings which the U.S. Navy culled from its dusty archives. What were the names of DesDiv 11's miserable four-piper quartet? *Henry P. Davidson,* for sweet Christ's sake! *McGraw, Travers* and *Vincent.* Yet appropriate enough, he supposed, for the Smithsonian relics whose rusty fantails they adorned.

At five P.M. the session was adjourned until next morning, Saturday the sixth of December, to allow the big brass a chance to huddle privately over cocktails and steaks in General MacArthur's penthouse suite at the hotel. Not a great deal had been accomplished. But they had become better acquainted, as a Nelsonian band-of-brothers taxed with a monstrous job, and there was tacit agreement that an enemy strike against one was an attack against all.

This assumption wasn't especially new, of course, for it was inherent in the latest dispatches, however purposefully vague, from the Navy Department and London's Whitehall. Moreover, as Tom Phillips reminded his American peers, he had attended a conference in London almost four years earlier at which it was privately agreed that the U.S. fleet would rush to the aid of the Royal Navy's Singapore-based battle force in the event of a southward push by the Japanese into the sacred waters of the British raj. Only trouble was, gloomed Phillips, the Yanks would have to steam west from Pearl Harbor, where they had elected to keep the bulk of *their* combatant units, a journey of some 6,000 miles as the crow flies.

Admiral Hart shrugged. "Hell, Tom, if some people had

gotten their way, the Pacific Fleet would still be anchored in mainland ports."

Like blindfolded chess players confronting an opponent with 20/20 eyesight, and further handicapped by having their queens sequestered before the game, the admirals and the generals reconvened early next day. Charts and files were brought out again. Strong black coffee was served in four-starred mugs from the Old Man's private mess. By midmorning the humid atmosphere of the big room was reeking with tobacco smoke as the conferees, in owlish ritualistic fashion, puffed away at their cigars, pipes and cigarettes.

The business at hand dealt with the Japanese intentions and the proper Allied response to the presently inscrutable foe— once his intentions came into focus.

But that was the rub. Nothing had occurred overnight to clarify the situation. The Nip convoys continued to be an X-quantity, both in size and location, and the whereabouts of the Japs' major fighting units remained even more of a mystery despite the best efforts of short-wave listening posts from Cavite, P.I., to Bremerton, Washington. Long ago American intelligence Merlins had cracked the Japanese codes. Under a complicated system called MAGIC, they overheard, translated and sought to evaluate the potential enemy's topmost secret radio traffic. It was a tricky process, one which could lead a man, or a whole fleet, woefully astray if the decoded messages were misunderstood.

"Our latest information," said Admiral Hart, "has them laying plans to inveigle the British into invading Thailand—so they can rush in as rescuers of a threatened nation."

Tom Phillips unleashed a salty epithet. Such a prognosis, he asserted, was about as plausible as something plucked out of the tea leaves in the bottom of a china cup.

The Old Man agreed. But it *was* the most recent intelligence data from MAGIC, aside from the not unexpected news that the Emperor's diplomats were busily destroying their coding equipment and cremating their files.

"We don't," he admitted, "have the foggiest notion where the goddamned Jap carriers are."

"Perhaps it's just as well," said Phillips, "since we've got nothing to counter the blighters with."

"Our submarines are still operative."

"How many d'you have?"

"Twenty-seven."

Phillips cocked a speculative eye at the bulkhead chart. "It's a bloody big ocean."

The Old Man acknowledged his fellow admiral's skepticism with a courtly gesture. "You're right, of course. And what I didn't mention was the fact that eight of the twenty-seven are undergoing overhaul at Subic Bay. The rest are scattered from hell to breakfast, trying to keep tabs on the Nips' movements, but with damned little results."

As a sort of final accounting, Hart reported that everything the Asiatic Fleet possessed, beyond those laid-up subs, was at full combat readiness. Live ammunition had been loaded on hoists and racks; torpedoes were armed with warheads; the insular bays were mined; his three cruisers and thirteen destroyers were strategically deployed from the Philippines to Borneo.

"Not much"—the Old Man shrugged—"but there you have it."

Then the Army's air staff added their sitrep to the Navy's. It was equally depressing. Thirty-five Flying Fortresses, maybe two dozen of them on the immediate line in airworthy condition; only ninety of the 107 P-40 fighters available for instant service. The other 140-odd aircraft nominally counted among the USAFFE arsenal were too obsolete to be considered for any practical warlike purpose.

"Of course," said one of the air staffers, "even one B-seventeen is a pretty formidable weapon against a surface ship."

"Bombing from twenty thousand feet?" asked the Old Man.
"Our bombsights have been vastly improved, sir."

The Old Man let the debatable subject drop. Nobody mentioned ground forces, although General MacArthur's immense training problems were well enough known. Like doctors debating how best to prevent an epidemic without adequate serums, they were desperately seeking some means of interdicting an enemy invasion before it began.

At three P.M., less than an hour after they returned from a leisurely lunch at the hotel, Chief Yeoman Bream slipped into the conference hall with a message that had just been received from a RAF flying boat, via Singapore, Reconnoitering at high altitude, this search plane had sighted two massive convoys standing northwest from the lower tip of Indochina. Through intermittent cloudbanks the RAF spotter had counted one formation of thirty-three merchant-type ships, accompanied by a battleship, five cruisers and seven destroyers. Another convoy, twenty miles away, comprised twenty-one merchant ships, a pair of cruisers and seven destroyers.

The Old Man read the dispatch aloud, then said, "Your two big boys and those four operable little fellows don't look as good as they did a few hours ago, Admiral."

Phillips responded with a tight smile. "To paraphrase your own estimate," he said, "they're not much, but they're all we've got. Or I can quote Mr. Shakespeare—'An ill-favored thing, sir, but mine own.' "

One of the younger Army air officers made bold to offer his personal opinion: "At least, gentlemen, they're not heading toward British territory."

"Not now," said Phillips. "But I'd suggest we don't rule out the possibility. Let's wait awhile and see what those RAF chaps turn up."

Shortly before six P.M. the blow fell. Bream returned to the smoke-laden room with a second message from the reconnaissance plane. His thin, pallid face was extraordinarily grave.

"Take it to Admiral Phillips," Hart said. "It's his baby."

"Yes, sir."

The British fleet commander accepted the flimsy bit of paper and seemed to weigh its contents physically before he opened the folded sheet. He scanned it hastily. Then, as had the Old Man earlier, he read the dispatch aloud: " 'Enemy convoys changed course at seventeen-oh-five to a heading of two hundred and forty degrees. Presently located at eight degrees north latitude, one hundred and four degrees east longitude.' "

Phillips stepped to the chart and laid a wooden ruler along the course given by the faraway aircraft. This was an instinctive yet unnecessary gesture, for his trained nautical mind had already told him precisely where the enemy armada lay and where it was going. If it continued along course 240, roughly southwest, it would intersect Malaya's unprotected coast in the vicinity of Khota Baru, the largest seaport north of Singapore. Phillips had no doubt in the world that this was what the Japanese intended. It was totally logical, obvious and inevitable.

The Old Man regarded him compassionately. "When did you say you were flying back, Admiral?"

"I'd planned to leave tomorrow morning."

"If you want to be there when the war starts," said Hart, "you'd better take off right now."

When it is eleven P.M. in Manila the clocks of Honolulu are striking four A.M., and since the international date line intervenes in mid-Pacific, Hawaiian citizens are enjoying their best pre-dawn Sabbath slumber, while Philippine residents are apt still to be celebrating whatever there is to celebrate on a Sunday night.

Thus it was on the evening of December 7, less than a day after Admiral Tom Phillips had sped back to threatened Singapore, that the officers of a newly fledged Army air bombardment

105

group elected to stage a formal dinner party for the USAFFE's top air command. Music and dancing and splendid food were requisitioned; and the staff of the Manila Hotel outdid itself to make the event one that would endure in the city's social annals. It might well be, they also knew, the last of the great *soirées*. The Americans, who were here to protect them, deserved the best.

Of course, the jubilant host group wasn't in much of a position to defend the islands as yet, being a paper force of 1,200 men without planes. But their Flying Fortresses, thirty of them, were even now en route from California. These giant bombers were scheduled to make a fueling stop at Hickam Field, on Oahu, in a couple of hours, and then proceed on to Clark Field, a few dozen miles north of Manila.

As an Asiatic Fleet staffer, Prince was invited to attend, bringing along a lady of his choice. Ordinarily he would have asked Gwyneth Dean. But he had delayed so long, pondering whether it was worth the effort, that the Beaver had beaten him to the punch. All of the service wives and many of the female civil servants were long gone, and he had only a limited acquaintance among the more eligible Manila families. So Prince went solo.

Unruffled, he wandered around the great verandah, ironically amused by the fact that its principal illumination came from the glow of brightly hued Japanese paper lanterns. He was in a strangely euphoric mood, amused also at the thought of a party given by a band of wingless Army aviators, as he paused occasionally to chat with his dress-uniformed peers and their elegant consorts. After a mammoth buffet, the dancing began.

Around midnight, Prince found a convenient vantage in the shadows of a potted palm to observe the Beaver foxtrotting with Gwyneth Dean, and to check his emotional pulse to discern whether the sight of their cavortings made him jealous. He decided that it didn't. A few yards past him, beyond the shrubbery, the Old Man's chief of staff was talking with the air group colonel. Prince unabashedly listened as the chief said, "It's only a matter of days, maybe hours, before the balloon goes up."

"Hell," the colonel retorted, "the shooting could start any minute. I've got all my people on combat alert."

"That's fine," said the chief. "So have we. Two tin cans patrolling off Corregidor, a pair of minesweeps combing the harbor, twenty-three Catalina flying boats operating out of Olongapo. End of message."

"We'll soon have our extra B-seventeens," the colonel said in a more confident tone, "and there's a convoy due here right after the first of the year with fifty-two dive bombers, a couple of artillery regiments, plus all the hardware they need."

"I thought you said it could happen any minute," the chief reminded him.

"I did." The colonel smiled ruefully. "But I still live in hope."

At one A.M., leaving the Beaver to Gwyneth's tender mercies, or vice versa, Prince caught an elevator down to his fourth-floor room. For a change, he dropped off to sleep immediately, as if he'd been swallowed up by an avalanche. What seemed like scant minutes later he was awakened by the insistent ringing of the telephone. Prince picked up the receiver without switching on the light. His luminous bedstand alarm clock showed five minutes after three A.M.

A very young, very shaken junior watch officer at Fleet GHQ was on the line. For a moment he stuttered, until Prince advised him to calm down. In a more controlled voice, as if delivering a rehearsed speech, the j.o. then said, "Sir, we've intercepted a message out of Hawaii, originated by the Naval Air Station at Ford Island, which advises as follows: 'Air raid Pearl Harbor. This is no drill.' The dispatch was marked at seven fifty-eight A.M., Oahu time."

Prince calculated rapidly. "That's less than a half hour ago."

"Yes, sir. The senior duty officer thinks you'd better get the Old Man—I mean, the admiral—up right away."

Prince's mind was clearing rapidly. "Tell him we'll be right over. Has the chief of staff been informed?"

"He's next on the list."

"Okay. Send the Flag sedan around to the front door, *muy pronto.*"

Prince slammed down the receiver, lit the lamp and squinted across the narrow space between his bed and the Beaver's. For a change the Britisher was where he belonged, instead of with Gwyneth Dean, snoring like a bearded grampus. On his way to the bathroom Prince pummeled him savagely.

"Wake up, mister!"

The Beaver came alive in remarkably short order. He sat up in a welter of scrambled bedclothes, zestfully awake and already leaning over for a cigarette, before Prince had reached the door.

"What's the drill, matey?"

"Pearl Harbor's been attacked."

"No!" Rather than disbelief in the Beaver's tone, it was more that of a man commenting upon the ugly splendor of the inevitable. "The bloody sons-of-bitches!"

"That's the Word from Hawaii. We've picked up a plain-language message beamed to anybody listening."

As the Beaver began struggling into his unpolished shoes, Prince noted with detached curiosity that he slept with his socks on. Then Prince went into the W.C. and urinated without shutting the door. This elemental act made him think again of the uninhibited Englishman. But now was no time for the social niceties. The sudden onslaught of war, he had discovered, exerted a drastic effect on a man's kidneys.

Prince took less than four minutes to slosh water over his face and get dressed. "Meet you at the entrance," he shouted, leaving.

"Tally-ho," acknowledged the Beaver.

The Old Man was already up and pulling on his starched khakis when Prince knocked on his door. He had been roused by a follow-up call from the chief of staff, who reported receipt of a second confirmation message telling of the attack, this one signed by Admiral Husband E. Kimmel himself, the Pacific Fleet commander.

While the Old Man was still meticulously knotting his black tie, he ordered, "Take down a message."

"Yes, sir."

Prince found a hotel memo pad and pencil, as the admiral began dictating in an unimpassioned voice: " 'Japan has begun hostilities. Govern yourselves accordingly.' Tell communications to move this in the clear to all our operating units, with info copies to MacArthur's people at the fort."

"Yes, sir."

Prince dialed the emergency GHQ number that put him straight through, without bothering the switchboard. The Old Man had guts, he thought. Anybody else might have waited to find out if it really *was* the Japs, or a chance German raider, or maybe the goddamned Hottentots who had attacked Pearl. But not the Old Man.

The Beaver was waiting for them at the front steps, where the four-starred Buick, engine running, was parked. He crawled into the seat beside the driver and kept discreetly silent until the admiral could speak his piece. It wasn't long in coming.

"Well, we've finally joined your private war, Commander."

"Yes, sir," said the Beaver. "It's a distinct pleasure to have you aboard with us."

The rest of the night, and well into the dawn-breaking hours, GHQ was a crazy kaleidoscope of dire information received and curt commands given; of grim-demeanored Fleet department heads coming and going to set in motion the plans upon which they had labored for so many weeks; of impromptu joint conferences with their taut-faced opposite numbers in USAFFE; of charts drawn and redrawn to match the fragmentary data that kept pouring in from short-wave centers at Cavite, Olongapo, the Army's Nielson Field in the Manila suburbs, and from Pearl itself.

It was learned that the Army air force boss wanted to clobber Formosa at first light with his Flying Fortresses, to minimize the enemy's air potential, but had been held back on the debatable thesis that the United States shouldn't make the "first overt act" in the southwest Pacific. At this, the Old Man unzipped his carefully nurtured store of profanity and demanded of nobody in particular whether the Pearl Harbor attack couldn't be construed as a sufficiently "overt act" to draw the rest of the triple-bloody-blasted U.S. forces into action. No reply was expected. None was offered.

But the Japs themselves provided one at five-thirty A.M., Manila time, by unleashing a flight of bombers and fighters— Bettys and Zeros from a carrier lurking off Palau—against an old seaplane tender anchored in Davao Gulf, on the southeastern tip of Mindanao. Little actual damage was done to the ship, but a brace of irreplaceable search Catalinas were lost in the brief melée.

Yet the American high command continued to delay. MacArthur, the Old Man had to admit, *did* have a tough decision to make. Beset by the Filipino leaders, who still hoped against hope that the Japanese wouldn't launch an all-out assault against their quasi-independent country, MacArthur waited with growing doubts and soaring impatience.

Finally, at ten-fifteen A.M., Washington dispatched its overdue official command: "Execute unrestricted air and submarine warfare against Japan."

The Beaver studied the message over Prince's shoulder. "It loses something in translation," he commented mordantly, "seven hours after the other side started shooting at our sitting ducks."

Providentially, the weather was reported socked in over Formosa, giving the Philippine defenders some reason for optimism that further raids might be delayed. But they weren't. As if the Japs couldn't care less whether their hardware returned to the take-off fields or not, planes emblazoned with Nippon's blood-red meatball on their fuselages swarmed over the summer capital at Baguio at midmorning, hitting military concentrations, and then sped on to plaster an air base in central Luzon.

American fighters and bombers from Clark Field, which had been in the skies for several hours, returned around noon without finding any targets. While the All Clear sounded, their pilots sat down for a hasty lunch, leaving only two of their planes in the air as a protective umbrella over the sprawling complex.

Suddenly, out of nowhere, the Japs appeared, spewing bombs and strafing at near ground level. Damage: a dozen B-17s, thirty P-40s destroyed and Christ only knew how many others damaged beyond immediate repair. So there went a third of the Army's fighters, half its bombers—with nothing more expectable from Pearl, where everything that could fly was being high-jacked en route from the mainland, including the Fortresses originally slated for the Philippines.

For the moment Manila itself was spared by the heavy overcast. Its population that Monday pursued their normal business rounds. In the nearby *barrios* and villages the people were celebrating the Feast of the Immaculate Conception. Those few who bothered to listen to the civilian radio heard about the war, but many of them didn't believe it and were inclined to scoff at such nonsensical rumors, because it could neither be seen nor heard from their peaceful abodes. Even a few Americans were skeptical, remembering Orson Welles's notorious Martian-invasion scare of three years earlier.

A strange lull descended over the doomed islands for another forty-eight hours.

The Japanese resumed the attack on Wednesday noon. This

time they bore-sighted in on the Navy base at Cavite, less than fifteen miles across the crescent arm of the bay from Manila itself. For three hours, with maddening, unimpeded ease, sixty bombers and at least 100 Zeros cut lazy patterns in the clear blue sky. The relatively few U.S. planes that rose to meet them had been quickly dispersed, so the Nips were able to unload their explosive wares over the hapless, helpless base with insolent accuracy.

Disregarding his staff's anguished pleadings, the Old Man climbed up to the roof of the Marsman Building to watch the carnage and grind his teeth in impotent fury. Beside him stood his chief of staff, Prince, the Beaver, and a handful of awestruck lesser officers. Great gouts of dark smoke poured up from Cavite as the enemy, apparently without squandering a bomb, laid waste the entire installation—everything, it seemed from where the staff watched, including a good part of civilian Cavite itself.

In *sotto voce,* the Beaver said to Prince, "This is a bit like when the Nazis blitzed London—yet without the inhibiting aspects of the RAF."

Prince nodded dumbly but said nothing. He was, he had to admit privately, too goddamned scared for any response to what sounded like airy persiflage from this idiot Britisher.

A message cranked out by the stricken base's auxiliary radio confirmed the worst. One of the Fleet's precious submarines had been blasted. And 230 torpedoes, already in short supply, blew up when the arsenal absorbed a direct hit.

That same day the Old Man decided to send the vulnerable remnants of his naval air arm to join Admiral Glassford's combatant units at Iliolo, in Panay, and to deploy his last Philippines-based surface ships south. There wasn't much to deploy: a pair of four-pipe destroyers, three gunboats, two submarine tenders, two minesweeps. That was it. Only the subs themselves stayed behind, diving by day and skulking by night, to wage a futile rear-guard action against the rampant Japanese and, when possible, to report on the enemy's increasingly mysterious movements.

Next morning the disaster toll was multiplied when a terse dispatch arrived from Singapore reporting that HMS *Prince of Wales* and *Repulse* had been sunk with an appalling loss of life. Admiral Tom Phillips, who had gallantly thrown his squadron against the foe despite a total lack of air cover, had gone down with his flagship.

As an informational addressee on the message from British Eastern Fleet headquarters, the Beaver was among the first to receive the terrible news. He read it, then looked bleakly at Prince, who had delivered it to him. When the Beaver spoke, after swallowing audibly, his voice sounded choked, and Prince could have sworn that tears were glistening in his bloodshot eyes.

"God damn the bastards to hell!" The Beaver's curse was delivered earnestly, with intense feeling, not at all like his customary offhand profanity. "There but for the grace of an incomprehensible Providence go I."

"I'm sorry," said Prince numbly. "Your boss was a great guy."

"That he was." The Beaver pretended he'd gotten something in his eyes, wiped them with a soiled handkerchief and blew his vast potato of a nose vigorously. Then he asked, "How soon did you say you were leaving for your new command?"

Prince shrugged. "I didn't. Whenever the Old Man gives the word. Damned soon, I guess. Why?"

"Because I'm coming with you, mister." The Beaver thrust the balled-up handkerchief into his hip pocket. "With *Wales* and *Repulse* gone, there's not much left for a liaison officer to liase around here. One day you'll probably make it to Surabaya, where you can drop me off. Meanwhile," he added in a tone that was oddly placative for the Beaver, "perhaps I can lend a useful hand. I *do* know something about your bloody four-pipers. Remember?"

"Okay," Prince said doubtfully. "If it's all right with the Old Man, then I guess it's copecetic by me."

For the next fortnight there were alarums and excursions, some false, but enough of them sufficiently valid to remind the Manilans that war had indeed come. It was abundantly clear to the beleaguered staffs of the Army and Navy—who saw their material resources dwindle from inadequate to virtually nothing, as the enemy's pressure mounted against exposed sectors along the Luzon coast, first feinting, then probing, then getting poised to leap—that invasion was only a matter of days.

The main Nip amphibious expedition was still loading somewhere in Asia and wouldn't set sail for another ten days or so, on a schedule timed to coincide with the islands' Christmas celebration.

"Makes sense," argued the Old Man. "Damned ugly, logical sense."

Back in Washington, D.C., a new team came in for the Navy: Ernest (Jesus) King replaced Harold (Betty) Stark; Chester Nimitz took over from the tragic, beaten Kimmel. Even Prince, who had some knowledge of Admiral King's tough sundowning methods, dared hope that the islands might finally rate a better priority in their fight for survival.

But the Old Man dashed cold water on *that* fatuous assumption. "Forget it, Commander, and start packing your ditty bag. I've a nice little Christmas present for you."

"Sir?"

"That's the day you'll leave for Balikpapan." The Old Man permitted himself a frosty smile. "As things shape up, you may be better off than staying here. We'll hang on a while longer, then move along to Surabaya by sub, to set up shop there, with the Dutch and the British."

"Yes, sir," Prince said without much conviction. Then he remembered his halfhearted pledge to the Beaver. "Commander

Monk has asked whether he can accompany me when I take over DesDiv Eleven. I told him it was pretty much up to you, sir."

"I think it's a damned salubrious idea," said the Old Man promptly. "Good experience for a liaison fellow. Should've thought of it myself."

Eighty Japanese transports were spotted by a U.S. submarine in an area forty miles north of Lingayen Gulf late on the afternoon of Saturday, December 20. In addition to fourteen that had already been reported assembling off Davao, this represented the closing of the pincers on the two main islands. Moreover, it was learned that the Nips were solidifying their beachhead in northeastern Borneo, 400 miles across that huge land mass from Balikpapan, where DesDiv 11 was precariously stationed.

At this juncture, like a man vainly shaking the handle of a slot machine that had ingested his last quarter, General MacArthur radioed Pearl Harbor to determine—once and for all—whether any aircraft carriers were available for support against these imminent landings.

They weren't.

Nothing was available for the Philippines—neither ships, planes nor manpower.

So the end began. USAFFE's last four Flying Fortresses were ordered to northern Australia. As they departed, they unloaded their bombs on an enemy convoy, a lesser and hitherto unreported flotilla, that was steaming toward Mindoro. Two untrained Filipino divisions were routed, badly mangled, by the initial Japanese who stormed ashore at Lingayen. But the other defenders held tough, falling back slowly before the foe's meatgrinder advance.

It was then, too, that MacArthur decided to abandon any attempt to maintain the coastline. While the bulk of his troops retreated to Bataan peninsula, the rest were told to make a last-ditch stand on the outskirts of Manila itself. They did. Their gallant effort gained precious time, enough to allow establishment of the Army's GHQ inside the rocky fortress of Corregidor, along with President Quezon's civilian government and a selected few of High Commissioner Sayre's staff.

Gwyneth Dean was among those chosen. She telephoned Prince shortly before she left, on the twenty-third, to tell him goodbye and, in a subdued tone, to wish him well in the dark days ahead.

"Maybe we'll see each other after this blows over," he said, "back in the States."

"Maybe," said Gwyneth. "Let's try to keep in touch—one way or another."

"You sound scared," he said.

"Your ears don't deceive you, Prince. For once in her life, little old hard-shelled Gwyneth Dean is goddamned well scared."

Early in the forenoon of the twenty-fourth, a crystal-clear, magnificent, cloudless morning, Admiral Hart convened his entire staff for a final briefing. The jig was definitely up, he said. They were going to shift their headquarters as scheduled, to Surabaya, the Dutch naval base in eastern Java, leaving the district commandant in charge of whatever odds and ends remained. Mainly, this rear guard would blow up the fuel dumps and anything else of value to the enemy.

This move, said the Old Man, would take place within the next few days, as soon as they could assemble the two submarines that would serve as their transports.

He swiveled his chair around to confront Prince. "As for you, son, you'll leave a trifle earlier than I'd originally intended. There's one C-forty-seven still operable at Nielson Field. If the Nips haven't gotten it before then, you'll take off after dark, to avoid detection en route south."

"Yes, sir." It seemed to Prince, suddenly, that he'd been replying "Yes, sir," all his life to orders that either didn't make any sense or were too preposterous even to consider. "We'll be ready." It occurred to him, also, that now he wouldn't be seeing Mari—or Gwyneth—for a personal farewell.

Three times during their conference waves of Japanese planes thundered over Manila, in the first major assault on the impotent city, bombing with complete impunity. As each echelon came, the Old Man would stride to the opened window and glower out at the whirling, dipping, diving aircraft. Prince forced himself to stand beside the Old Man, uncomfortably aware of the clammy fear that gnawed (as always) at his own guts, yet ashamed not to remain there, Faithful Achates to the bitter end, while the admiral insisted on exposing himself to the enemy. An air-raid shelter had been provided for the staff in the bowels of the Marsman Building. Prince wished the Old Man would dispense with his stubborn heroics and adjourn the meeting to the basement.

Once a bomb struck the GHQ, shaking plaster off the ceiling and shattering glass. But the Old Man stood fast, issuing orders a mile a minute, winding up the scattered Fleet's logistical affairs and behaving in general like a dying millionaire making out his last will and testament.

It was a scene out of the *Inferno*. Along the Muelle San Francisco, where the great liners and cargo vessels had anchored in happier days, everything was ablaze, and greasy smoke fouled the erstwhile clear sky. Inshore from the wharves, Prince could see bomb craters blossoming at strangely regular intervals in the roads that surrounded the Walled City: Bonifacio Drive and Burgos Avenue and Aduana Street. A near miss had catapulted a loaded tram across the railroad tracks, sending it caroming against a warehouse, with its wounded passengers screaming out in mortal terror.

Farther uptown, away from the windows that overlooked the

117

waterfront, Prince could hear the *crump-crump-crump* of more bombs as the Japs made their third and, as it turned out, final assault on the prostrate city. The Pasig River, the slow-moving stream that bisected Manila, had become dark as flowing blood under the ugly smoke pall.

At last the bombers left. An ominous calm descended upon the stricken metropolis.

While the staff wolfed down a hasty dinner of sandwiches and coffee, before finishing their melancholy task of dismantling the command, Prince assembled his small expedition. He instructed Chief Yeoman Bream to round up a personnel carrier, which could handle the pitted streets better than a sedan, locate a driver and find two other men to help handle the gear.

"They won't be coming back," Prince said. "So pick men who'll be useful when we get to Balikpapan."

"I know just the guys," said Bream. "Peter Marcus. Remember? He drove us to Cavite—and conned that damned boat back to Manila. Pete's bucking for quartermaster. He's always wanted to steer a real, live destroyer. He'll be our lead man."

"Fine." Prince had been sitting for the first time in hours. Now he rose stiffly to his feet. "Commander Monk and I will go over to the hotel to pack our stuff. Pick us up there in thirty minutes."

"Aye, aye, sir." Bream tossed him an illegal hatless salute. "On the button."

They pulled onto the tarmac at Nielson Field shortly after eight P.M., after a mad drive through rubbled streets. Propellers idling, twin engines spitting blue flame into the night, the dun-colored C-47 was waiting for them, ready to roll. A middle-aged Navy pilot, with the much chewed butt of a Philippine stogie clamped in his mouth, stood at the foot of the spindly aluminum ladder.

"I'm Lieutenant Dawkins," he said churlishly, "your pilot,

co-pilot and stewardess. Hope you'll enjoy your trip." He cast an uneasy eye at the dark overcast. "Now let's bug out before the frigging Japs come back."

"Toss the gear aboard, Bream," Prince ordered. "The man's in a hurry."

"Affirmative, sir. So are we, if I might say so."

"You might," snapped Prince. "We are."

Like survivors loading rations into a lifeboat suspended from the davits of a doomed ship, Bream and his three companions manhandled the baggage into the almost empty plane. As soon as it was safely stowed and secured with ropes, Lieutenant Dawkins revved the engines, and the officers sprinted up the ladder. The C-47 started waddling down the runway before the Beaver, who was last aboard, could get the cabin door closed.

Dawkins barreled the plane up fast and straight without bothering to make the usual climbing turn. Prince looked back only once. Manila was already lost to view, even the red glow from its funeral pyre hidden in the murk.

PART II

5

"We Can Hang On Until Things Work Out"

THE CAPTAINS AND THE KINGS, for such they could justly be called with a definite degree of nautical logic, considering the absolute sway they held over their encapsulated domains, began coming aboard *Davidson* at 1300 hours. By 1330 the three destroyer commanders were assembled with their execs in the cramped little wardroom. Most of *Davidson*'s off-duty officers attended the session, too, at Prince's invitation. Sipping their jet-black coffee meditatively, they were clustered in the rear of the barren steel chamber, auditing carefully.

Like the skippers of *McGraw, Travers* and *Vincent,* they hoped that they would finally get word on the Word, from the horse's mouth, as it were, after weeks of what seemed like aimless maneuvers around an increasingly puzzling reconnaissance station.

The senior among the three captains, Lieutenant Commander Perry Koch, was first to arrive in his whaleboat, on whose bow, in discreetly small numerals, was *McGraw*'s designation: DD

208. This meant that USS *Howell J. McGraw,* the four-piper's full commissioned name, was 208th on the list of American destroyers built before or after World War I which were either in action now or had been scrapped after the earlier conflict.

Commander Koch was three years younger and three Academy classes behind Prince. But this afternoon, in the shrouded light of the stifling wardroom, he looked older than his division chief. He was a chunky man, perhaps five feet eight, balding, saturninely jovial while expressing the frequent total pessimism he felt for DesDiv 11's plight, which was often. Prince, who had known him slightly at Annapolis when Koch was a lowly plebe, suspected that he was Jewish, and therefore, owing to the unspoken yet omnipresent discrimination that prevailed in the Navy, neither ticketed for higher command nor altogether to be trusted in his present assignment. To use the phrase often applied to the fellow, he was too goddamned Koch-sure of himself, too volubly arrogant in his superior knowledge about the world and its myriad of troubles, of which he alone seemed to possess the key for a sensible solution.

Nevertheless, Prince knew Koch was reputed to be a sound skipper, running a good if somewhat loose ship, with a crew that made no secret of its immense liking for their captain. Koch kept them informed of what was going on. For some reason very few American COs had either the ability or the willingness to take their enlisted complement into their confidence, to tell them what *might* happen around the bend of the next palm-studded atoll, on the basis of their orders from on high. Those who occasionally did, found that their crews responded with surprising new bursts of vigor, like surgical patients finally permitted to comprehend the seriousness of their condition, yet who, given a 50-50 chance of survival, develop a sudden will to live.

The other two DesDiv 11 captains were Lieutenant Commanders Samuel Pierce and Horton Naylor. Each was thirty-one, a year younger than Koch, but of the same Crabtown class of 1930. Pierce, who had USS *Melville Travers,* was tall, spare, angular. Unlike Koch, he was almost unbearably taciturn. His four-piper was sometimes dubbed the *Terrible Travers,* or the Slaveship, because of Pierce's insistence that all hands must toe the line, obey orders instanter and behave in principle as if they were on a stylish shakedown cruise off Mare Island, California, rather than suddenly caught up in a war, with Mare Island and all its wondrous facilities a quarter of the way around the globe from them. Prince admired Pierce as a sort of junior-grade Ernie (Jesus) King, who would one day make a fine sundowning admiral.

Horton Naylor was called "Broad Tail" by his more irreverent associates, in the tenuous fashion of Academy sobriquets, who split his given name into two parts, coming up with "whore" and "ton." Ergo: "Broad Tail." Naylor didn't give a tinker's dam. He wore his dubious honors as a four-piper captain lightly, tied a length of Manila hemp around his copious middle in lieu of a regulation webbed belt and treated the 184-man crew of USS *Manfred H. Vincent* as virtual equals, at least in the realm of humankind, once they hoisted anchor and got safely out to sea. Yet they responded to his demands with an immediacy that the taut-ship Pierce secretly envied, even when he was solemnly admonishing Naylor, over a beer at the small waterfront café which had become DesDiv 11's *de facto* officers' club, about the dangers of fraternizing with the hired help.

As he scanned his three destroyer skippers, Prince strove to maintain the sober demeanor he knew they expected of him: a slight frown, an aloof look that might betoken the omniscience they obviously hoped he'd inherited from Fleet headquarters, a quiet assurance which he was far from feeling, despite his best efforts to conceal this lack of confidence in himself or the impossible job the Old Man had so cavalierly thrust upon him. Prince made a mental note to suggest that Broad Tail forgo

125

the rope belt for something more regulation. It was bad form, damned bad precedent.

Prince was wearing the new khakis he had procured from *Gray Eagle*'s stores. Conscious that they didn't fit very well, having been designed for the standard Navy man (if such a creature existed) and thus were too large both in the waist and shoulders, he took a measure of compensatory pride in the fact that the silver maple leaves on his collar set him apart from the rest, the mere lieutenant commanders, who wore the gold leaves of lesser rank. Moreover, he had visited Thornburg, and the medics said *Davidson*'s skipper was progressing well. He should be able to resume his command functions in a few days. This was an immense relief. The more Prince had pondered it, the notion of captaining the destroyer, while at the same time directing divisional battle tactics, had grown more formidable by the moment.

During his stay on *Gray Eagle* Prince had also instructed that Lieutenant Dawkins be transferred from the shoreside Dutch hospital to the tender's sick bay.

"Dawkins is an ornery cuss," he said. "*Very* ornery. But a damned good flyboy, which is a scarce commodity right now. We don't want to lose him if we can help it. If you can patch him up, we'll get him to Surabaya one of these days—along with Commander Monk here."

Unlike the slovenly Naylor, the Dutch liaison officer who had insisted on attending their meeting, Lieutenant Commander Pieter van Dekker, was clad in immaculate starched whites, including the detestable chin-high collar. Van Dekker was an improbable-looking squarehead, brawny rather than soft, tanned rather than pink-faced, with surprisingly dark eyes.

"*Mag ik mij even voorstellen*?" he had asked, shaking hands gravely with Prince at *Davidson*'s quarter-deck.

Prince's rudimentary knowledge of Dutch told him that his unwanted guest wished to introduce himself.

"That shouldn't be necessary," he said. "You've got to be van Dekker. Welcome aboard."

The Dutchman grinned, revealing for the first time what apparently was his only physical flaw: a complete mouthful of gold teeth.

"Dank U."

"You do speak some English, don't you?"

"Ik ken een beetje—a little," van Dekker conceded diffidently.

"Then maybe we'd better give it a whirl," Prince said, "unless we resort to sign language. My Dutch is practically nonexistent."

Haltingly, van Dekker said he had two messages to deliver. One concerned a matter of some social importance: His Excellency, the Dutch Resident of Balikpapan, most earnestly desired that Commander Prince, his British associate and the captains of DesDiv 11 attend a Christmas reception in their honor at the Residency that evening. There would be ample schnapps, a buffet, and doubtless (van Dekker flashed his improbable gold teeth in a suggestive grin) some young ladies who would appreciate dancing with the handsome Americans.

"Tell His Excellency," said Prince, "that we'll certainly try to make it, as they say in the South, the Good Lord willing and if the creeks don't rise. Hell, I'd forgotten all about this being Christmas."

Van Dekker grinned again. "You mean I should inform him that you will come."

"That's approximately it."

The other matter, the liaison officer went on, was van Dekker's desire to go along on DesDiv 11's next mission for indoctrination purposes. He hadn't been to sea for months, he said, and was becoming rusty. At least, that was the gist of what Prince gleaned from the Dutchman's painful efforts to convey his meaning in badly fractured English.

Reluctantly, Prince agreed. "I've already got one supercargo," he said, glowering at the Beaver, "so we might as well have another. You can join Koch in *McGraw*. He's a brilliant s.o.b. who probably speaks fluent Amsterdam Dutch."

Now that they were all gathered in the wardroom, Prince glanced pointedly at his watch. "It's almost thirteen thirty-five," he growled. "This session was called for one o'clock sharp. We'll have to do a damned sight better, timewise, if we're going to turn DesDiv Eleven into the kind of outfit I've got in mind."

Precisely what it was Prince envisioned for his destroyer quartet he couldn't have described at that moment. As was the case with his earlier dilemma, when he'd breakfasted with *Davidson*'s officers, he would have liked to speak out dramatically, yet with assurance, about their task and how he aimed to accomplish it. But that was patently absurd even to consider at this particular instant. Their job was a simple, impossible one: halt the Japs. Later, at the Resident's party, he might get away with such pomposity, for there his role would be that of the gallant young American naval officer leading a rescue mission of immediate concern to the good people of Balikpapan. Of course, he would have to speak his piece out of the saturnine Beaver's listening range, for he could already imagine the bearded bastard giving him the upthrust middle finger, that immemorial go-screw-yourself gesture. When you came right down to it, the Beaver *was* the epitome of that mocking ego which had pursued him all his life, to such little purpose, thumbing its nose and telling him the bitter truth about his carefully hidden inadequacies.

So Prince elected to let the more experienced skippers do the talking.

It was a somewhat higher leveled version of what he had heard from his flagship subordinates that morning, minus the geographic elements.

The usually closemouthed Pierce opened up with something he termed the "Pryor Principle," derived from the rules laid down by DesDiv 11's previous commander. Pryor had enjoined them, jointly, separately and repeatedly, "Never tangle assholes with the Nips if they've got you too badly outnumbered—but hit 'em in the balls if they don't. Fast and hard. Don't be polite."

"Cogent advice," Prince said approvingly. "Solid."

The departed Pryor sounded more prudent than he had imagined, content not to stick his neck out too far, nor to play John Paul Jones with DesDiv 11. Prince's kind of man, in fact.

Pierce added, "Thus far, sir, we haven't had to test the alternatives."

Horton allowed they had enough torpedoes on board for one Seventh Cavalry type charge, especially if it were a night engagement. After that they'd have to throw potatoes at the Japs.

Dryly, Koch interjected: "You've forgotten, Broad Tail, that we're out of the real thing. Dehydrated spuds have a tendency to scatter, like buckshot, so they don't have much impact power."

"Let's get back to business, gentlemen," said Prince, although nobody had laughed at Koch's remark, or even grinned, because it was too goddamned true.

As their acknowledged dean, Koch thereupon recited the division's quiescent history since leaving Manila. They had been orphans of the storm, although the storm itself was comfortably removed for the moment. First they'd played a useless game of hide-and-seek off Tarakan, north of Balikpapan, along the lower reaches of the Celebes Sea where it began to narrow into Makassar Strait, in the expectation that the enemy would immediately strike south from his initial Philippine beachhead at Davao. They chased what seemed mostly to be imaginary Nip submarines and wasted an inordinate amount of ashcan depth charges in the process. It might be noted in passing, said Koch, that our own subs hadn't reported sinking as much as a sampan in this area during December, because of faulty torpedoes.

He aimed his forefinger disgustedly at the chart which Chief

Yeoman Bream had affixed to the bulkhead behind the baize-covered table.

"Since Balikpapan *has* to be their target eventually, we've concentrated our patrolling off that little tit of land called Randjung Mangkahilat, where the strait's only eighty miles wide. *Only!* Christ, Commander, after dark, with four destroyers and no radar, it's like hunting for the world's smallest needle in the biggest haystack in Iowa."

If the man was actually Jewish, thought Prince, why did he bother to invoke Christ in their problem? It sounded rather futile.

Koch went on: "At last accounts the British have abandoned Sarawak to the Japs, who are constructing airfields capable of handling medium-sized bombers. Bettys. And they're getting set to move into Tarakan, which is only three hundred-odd miles upstream from here."

"What you're implying," Prince said, "is that day by day in every way we're growing up to be fatter sitting ducks."

"That's about the size of it, sir."

And for this, Prince told himself morosely, my MaMa wrapped me warm. Aloud he said: "So let's face the realities. We've got four tin cans here, plus a damned near empty supply ship. Admiral Glassford has one heavy cruiser, *Houston,* and a pair of lights. Down south, there's DesDiv Ten, also with four lousy tin cans, plus *Marblehead.*" This light cruiser, he reminded them, was almost as old as the Asiatic Fleet destroyers —and a clumsy four-piper to boot.

The Dutchman, van Dekker, intervened. "Vice Admiral Helfrich has three light cruisers of the Royal Netherlands Navy, Commander, all of them excellent ships, and seven destroyers." A tinge of patriotic pride rang in his voice. "Also twelve submarines. We Dutch are well prepared for action."

"Great," said Prince. "I'd forgotten about that. Thanks for reminding me. We've had twenty-six subs on station since the

Japs started this ruckus, too, for all the flogging good it's done us."

The Beaver offered: "We mustn't neglect to mention His Britannic Majesty's contribution to this gaggle of ancient geese, old boy. We can match your heavy cruiser and two lights with a trio of our own, along with three nicely trained destroyers."

"And what have the Nips got?" asked Prince. "If my memory serves me right—and it does—they've thrown the book at us. Several, in fact, from three directions." He ticked the Japanese forces off on his fingers as he spoke. "Battleships, two. Heavy cruisers, five. Light cruisers, five. Destroyers, fifty-eight. Aircraft carriers, seven. And God knows how many subs, including those I-boats that can carry planes in their deck hangars."

"Which, of course, represents a fair share of the Nippers' entire fleet," said Pierce, breaking in for the first time.

"Naturally. But what else have they got to do at this point?" Prince demanded. "After Pearl Harbor, we're in no shape to invade the Japs' home islands. So they're wide open to do anything they goddamn well choose."

For a few moments a strained silence prevailed in the wardroom, while DesDiv 11's skippers digested the Word, finding it more unpalatable than they'd imagined. To Prince, they wore the look of condemned men who had occupied Death Row so long that they didn't really care whether they were gassed, hanged or electrocuted, yet who had somehow made peace with themselves. But self-preservation is an elemental thing, not to be taken lightly. If there were a decent way out, a gentlemanly way, they would probably take it, hoping to live to fight another day.

"So," said Prince, "our orders remain the same. 'Search and destroy.' "

To the Beaver, inspecting the head, thorax and abdomen of a four-piper was very much old hat, as he so often reminded

Prince, since he had served in a Lend-Lease destroyer given to Great Britain by FDR in exchange for use of certain Caribbean bases. Yet it was a refresher course for Prince himself, who hadn't been aboard one of these outmoded crates since he had played exec on such a tin can for six months during the peacetime Thirties.

An officer whom he had not yet met, Ensign Carl Virtue, was standing watch in the forward engine room that occupied most of *Davidson*'s thin-skinned mid-section, just below the torpedo mounts. He was quite unlike the senior rubicund, perennially sweating engineer, Lieutenant (jg) Slattery, who claimed the ability to keep the flagship mobile, somehow, through an occult mixture of tobacco juice, chewing gum and baling wire, the exact components of which Slats never divulged, even to his twenty-one-year-old assistant. Barely seven months out of the Academy, he was *Davidson*'s baby, having graduated a year earlier than most midshipmen. Small, almost birdlike, Virtue was constantly being told by his seniors that he was his "own reward," a heavy-handed Navyesque pun deriving from his name; and he struck back by playing a harmonica, not well but loudly, when he came topside briefly for a breath of fresh air. Virtue was a dusk-eyed Southerner, from Greensboro, North Carolina, a fact that Prince had noted with pleasure. It might mean that the engineering j.o. was a gentleman by birth rather than by mere Act of Congress. He was a bachelor, unsurprisingly, considering his precipitate entry into foreign service. His ribald peers declared that Virtue would unquestionably lose his virtuousness by shacking up with a jungle wench during one of their layovers at Balikpapan, provided he could find a proper midget. Hottentot country, they added unkindly, might have been a better duty location for a five-foot-six ensign.

There was steam in one boiler, as a precaution against a sudden order to haul anchor and make a seaward dash. Prince found Virtue studying the pressure gauges dubiously, like the pilot of an aircraft that wasn't functioning properly at a 10,000-foot altitude when a 12,000-foot mountain range was dead ahead.

"How's she holding up?" Prince asked.

"Moderately, sir," said Virtue, "The pressure wavers, though, because these damned kettles haven't been cleaned in months."

"Well, keep 'em boiling."

Virtue gave Prince a tired smile and brushed away a strand of lank black hair. "That's really Slat's job, sir. I'm just his apprentice sorcerer."

They turned to leave. Even now, lying idle, *Davidson*'s bowels were hot, and the handrails of the ladders leading up to the metal catwalk were uncomfortable to grasp. When the four-piper was moving fast through open seas, generating her full 30,000-shaft horsepower (or whatever portion thereof she could manage, after having been too long away from decent overhaul), the engine room would become a small preview of Hades, Prince knew, and you'd need asbestos gloves to touch these rails and manipulate the levers that governed her speed upon orders from the faraway bridge. But the throttles were only part of the forty-odd instruments which Virtue, Slattery and their chief machinist's mate had to tend. They represented the end result of everything that went on in the series of keel-to-deck chambers which housed two geared turbines, four boilers and Diesel tanks, all of which comprised well over a third of the ship's 315-foot interior. Now that she was berthed, her forced air blowers were idling, thus adding to the almost unbearable heat.

Prince winced, involuntarily, as they stepped through the double air-locked hatches between the boilers and the engine spaces, remembering the purpose of these complex doors: to prevent a flareback from released cold air above from incinerating those trapped below.

Together with the Beaver, he made a quick passage through the after crew's quarters, which were unpleasantly low-beamed to make more room for the powder magazines, provisions and stores that occupied the area beneath, a few feet above *Davidson*'s brittle keel. They emerged from the emergency steering compartment in the fantail, walked the length of the narrow, cluttered deck and finished their tour at the forward crew's quarters. These were slightly more commodious, although still located over fuel tanks, magazines and the sound room, wherein was contained the ship's rather elementary submarine detection equipment.

At length, happy to be free of the constricted, malodorous depths of his new command, Prince led the Beaver aloft to the radio room and charthouse, under the twenty-four-foot-wide bridge. Ensign Tom Rand was waiting for a communications rating to translate the gibberish that crackled from the short wave so that he could reduce it to English, using the coding board whose key was changed regularly on instructions from Fleet headquarters. Neither *Davidson* nor her three sisters had electric crypto machines (ECMs), so it all had to be done laboriously and by hand, running four-lettered code strips through the board and comparing them with the appropriate code-breaker for the day.

"Anything important expected?" Prince asked.

"Negative, sir." The dark circles under Rand's eyes seemed more than ever like splashes of charcoal, and his hand visibly quavered as he reached for the completed dispatch. "Probably just more of the same. Japs reported along the Sulu Archipelago or at Bunju or in God knows whatever pissant place you can hardly find on a chart."

"See that Chief Bream gets my copy of *all* messages," Prince said, "as soon as you've decoded them."

"Yes, sir." Rand's voice was as tired as the rest of him, but he couldn't refrain from letting a faintly hurt note creep into it. "The skipper always gets the original—before the ink dries on the paper."

"Good."

The only officer Prince hadn't met formally during breakfast was Lieutenant (jg) Stanley Krebs, who had been officer-of-the-deck when he had come aboard earlier. Krebs was the navigator. He was an elderly twenty-five, thin and gaunt in the trademark manner of most of *Davidson*'s officers, with brown hair plastered over a knobby skull and disconcertingly gray eyes that seemed to imply an occult knowledge on the part of their owner which others didn't share. Krebs had joined the ship in late autumn. Thus far he had found destroyer duty both frustrating and futile, as well as damned messy, being a man with a passion for neatness. His summons to the Asiatic Fleet came at a time when he was enjoying the best duty of his four years as an officer: shore-side, in his San Francisco birthplace, where he and his family, a pretty young wife and son, lived in an apartment overlooking the magnificent bay. Krebs was a born navigator. He had learned to sail as a kid in the safe waters of the bay. Then, when he became a trifle older and more venturesome, he took his sloop out around the Farallones, where the sea got downright dangerous, especially when an unexpected fog rolled in. His enlisted assistants proudly declaimed that Lieutenant Krebs could god-damn near *smell* where they were, even when you couldn't see the ship's prow in murky weather.

At this moment Krebs was bent over a chart, stepping off a variety of potential courses with a divider, drawing thin red lines between points marked Able, Baker, Charlie, Dog and so on down the Navy's phonetic alphabet.

"You look industrious," said Prince. "Practicing?"

Krebs swung around to greet the new division commander, to whom he gave a full salvo from his remarkable eyes. "Sort of, sir. Since we don't know where we're headed—or why—I figured I might as well work out a few possibilities."

"Sounds like a healthy idea," Prince said approvingly. "Keep it up. Might save us a lot of trouble later on."

Krebs accepted the compliment with a mute nod and delved back into his charts.

The inspection tour wound up on the bridge. Here Prince tested the captain's leather-padded swivel chair for size, found it to his liking, checked briefly the red and green levers that activated the depth charges, the torpedo directors, the radio-telephone which permitted talk between ships (TBS), the compass-carded binnacle and the engine order telegraph. They all pleased him. They were neat and the brass was well polished, despite *Davidson*'s otherwise rundown appearance. He praised Rodney, the exec, for the general excellence of this vital sector of the ship.

"Up here," said Rodney, "it's a piece of cake compared to those poor bastards down there who have to keep this bucket running."

"But it's up here," Prince reminded him, "that we make the decisions that could make their work purely academic."

Rodney waggled his crewcut head in understanding. Since Thornburg's illness the entire responsibility for *Davidson*'s performance had rested upon his plump shoulders. He was glad now that he could resume his less exacting executive-officer chores and leave the immediate command duties to this suave three-striper, who radiated such a positive aura.

There was a photograph on Rodney's desk, in the cubbyhole stateroom which he shared with Tom Rand, a grouping that showed his wife and two butterball youngsters, a boy and girl, who had gone back to Coronado when dependents were ordered home. A third child was due in a couple of months. Rodney's dominant aim was to return to Coronado—a place where old admirals usually went to die—and start living again. That was why he was the most taken aback of all the officers who had listened to the Beaver's pessimistic overview of the war's duration at breakfast. If this outspoken Britisher was right, the latest of the Rodneys would be damned near four before he ever saw him (or her), assuming he didn't get leave, meanwhile. Knowing the Navy's reluctance in such matters, Rodney wasn't very hopeful about the passing of such a delightful miracle.

Even as the captains of DesDiv 11 began arriving at the wharf in their whaleboats, the Resident's party seemed foredoomed as a dismal affair. There was a hint of rain in the muggy sky, a villainous corona around the moon, and the walk up the graveled pathway to the Residency muddied the officers' white shoes. Prince had ordained starched semi-dress uniforms for the Dutch leader's gala, over the Beaver's anguished protests that the divisional skippers would think it too goddamned pretentious to get all togged up in the middle of a shooting war. But Prince was adamant.

"Since we've got to go through this frigging ordeal," he said, "let's do it right and show the squareheads that Americans have class."

"But I'm British," the Beaver complained, "with more than a touch of Gaelic."

"So blame your parents."

"Where'll we get our whites?"

"Find somebody aboard *Davidson* who's your size and borrow 'em. I've tapped young Rand. Rodney looks about right for you, laddie-buck, with the properly established embonpoint."

"Shall we wear dress swords, too?" the Beaver demanded scornfully.

"Negative," said Prince. "I'd thought about that but decided it might be a little *too* much."

"Okay." The Beaver grinned. "Anyhow, a chap can always comfort himself with the knowledge that social intercourse is almost as good as the real thing—and might even lead to it."

"Why don't you inscribe that in the log?" Prince suggested. "It's a goddamned sound philosophy."

"I'll do that, old cock."

On his youngster cruise in the ancient battleship *Texas* in 1927, Prince had visited Rotterdam, and now he nostalgically recalled the Dutch as an amiable, hospitable lot. Even if they might be considered a trifle stodgy, by Yankee standards, they were generous with their gin-and-bitters, a rather viscous potion, as he remembered it, and boldly willing to match drink for drink all night, if the Americans wished to accept the challenge. Prince had. Another memory stirred him, more uncomfortably, that of the worst hangover he'd ever experienced in all his twenty-one years.

But the two dozen or so Balikpapan burghers gathered at the Residency didn't seem to fit his recollections of those earlier days. They were a harried lot. When they infrequently smiled, it was more a fleeting grimace than an expression of pleasure. Which, Prince supposed, was only natural, under the dire conditions that confronted the Borneo Dutch at this exquisite point in history.

They clustered around Prince and the Beaver, who were the senior honored guests, florid-faced and perspiring in the dank heat which the Residency's slowly turning fans did little to dispel. The windows of the huge wooden edifice were flung wide, but shrouded with blackout curtains, which occasionally stirred in the faint breeze from the fans, allowing illegal glimmers of light to stray into the outside night. Unlike the last party he had attended in Manila with the wingless flyboys, this one had no spontaneous we-who-are-about-to-die gaiety about it. There was a determined, grim hospitality. But that was all.

The Resident and his friends doggedly sipped their Bols gins, attempted small talk in approximate English, but made no effort for the moment to broach Topic A: the status of the war and what Prince's destroyer division proposed to do about it so far as Balikpapan was concerned. Their painful avoidance of any attempt to get at this subject, Prince supposed, was caused by some innate awareness that it might be a breach of etiquette to embark upon such a crass discussion about their (and possibly DesDiv 11's survival) unless an appropriate moment arose or some hardy soul seized the bull by the horns and blurted out his forebodings. Instead, they made a masterful effort to make Prince and his fellow officers feel at ease. But it wasn't a very successful exercise.

By the time the preprandial cocktailing had finished, Prince found himself slightly queasy from having consumed too many cloying gins. A fresh cuplet would miraculously appear at the exact instant when he had finished what he figured was surely his ultimate portion, on a silver platter carried by a native house-boy, whose feckless grin was the only authentic evidence of joviality in the room.

The Resident, a tall, worn-looking man of about sixty with a grizzled Moslem beard, a relic of his previous service in Turkey, had started a series of toasts just before they paraded to the long damask-draped table spread in buffet fashion with a vast *rijst-tafel,* which was a sort of Dutch smorgasbord. Prince's nostrils twitched at the violent aroma of curry that eddied from the various dishes, and his stomach involuntarily recoiled at the odor. He despised curry, despite the fact that American naval wives in the Far East took inordinate pride in their ability to outdo the indigenes at their own gastronomic game with this miserable spice, which originally had been designed to conceal the stench of rotting meats in iceless tropical countries.

"To the President of the United States," intoned His Excellency.

All those present echoed him and drained their glasses. More Bols arrived. Prince dutifully responded: "To Queen Juliana of the Netherlands."

Still more Bols.

The Resident hoisted one to His Majesty, George VI of Great Britain.

Another lot of Bols from the cheerfully grinning houseboy.

139

Prince searched his mental archives for the famous toast offered by Stephen Decatur at Norfolk, Virginia, in 1816, when he was still a national hero for his exploits against the Tripolitan pirates in 1804 and later against the British in the war of 1812.

" 'Our countries,' " said Prince, generously multiplying Decatur's single *country* to include his hosts. " 'in their intercourse with foreign nations may they always be in the right; but our countries, right or wrong.' "

"Bravo," said His Excellency, and for the first time his grimly fixed smile was an iota more relaxed.

Prince then explained the origin of the toast and who Decatur was. At twenty-four, he said, the brash young lieutenant commanded a twelve-gun schooner called USS *Enterprise*. When Captain William Brainbridge's frigate *Philadelphia* got hung up on a reef during hot pursuit of a pirate ship into Tripoli harbor in the waning autumn of 1803, there was no choice but to destroy the trapped vessel because her thirty-six guns added immeasurably to the Tripolitans' shoreside batteries in their threat to the blockading Yankees. Decatur drew the assignment. He took his small ship into the menacing bay on the night of February 16, 1804, pulled alongside the trapped *Philadelphia*, set her ablaze and escaped without the loss of a single man. Lord Nelson, something of a naval hero himself, termed Decatur's feat "the most bold and daring act of the age."

The Resident was properly impressed. "Thus, Commander, one does not always have to worry about being outnumbered."

"No," said Prince, "one doesn't. But the Americans had a damned sight more potential in the Mediterranean a century ago than we have out here now."

"Don't you still have an *Enterprise* operative in your fleet today?" the Resident asked.

"Yes. She's an aircraft carrier, the flagship of Admiral William F. Halsey, who's got the reputation of being a Decatur-type himself, although he hasn't had much of a chance to prove it as yet."

"Where is this *Enterprise,* Commander?"

"Working out of Pearl Harbor," said Prince, "and not likely to come within a country mile of here. She's scheduled for hit-run operations against the Japs, I imagine, rather than any close-in support for our Asiatic forces."

The Resident shrugged. "That is what I thought. It makes logical sense." His taut smile faded. "Now let us eat, and we can discuss these serious matters later."

After walking past what seemed to Prince an interminable array of casseroled meats, rice, cheeses and other items he couldn't identify, filling their plates and heaping shredded cocoanut, bacon bits, chutney and raisins atop the whole mess, they went to various tables. Prince and the Beaver, through seniority, sat with the Resident, his wife, and a pair of unattached young women. Both girls were blond, cast in the standard Dutch mode; but the one designated for Prince was the prettier of the two. He thought back, briefly, to his stay in Rotterdam. There had been ample time for amatory dalliance, then, during the three days the *Texas* lay at her berth. But now there was none, although the women's provocatively exposed bosoms, thrusting like cream-filled pastries above their threadbare formal gowns, were as provocative as ever, almost fifteen years later, in Prince's incipient middle manhood.

His partner was called Zaskie, or ZaZu, or something equally outlandish, and she earnestly played the role assigned her, making the gallant American naval officer feel welcome, warmly wanted and perhaps destined for something more romantic than a casual sit-down *rijsttafel* at a more appropriate time. She was not, as Prince had feared, the nervous, giggly type. In fact, Saskia (as he finally determined to be her true name) was calm as the waters of the Zuyder Zee, but not, he guessed, as shallow.

Saskia explained that she was Lieutenant Commander van Dekker's cousin, the daughter of a Residency staffer, and thus had not been required to go back to Holland when the war threatened. Besides, now that Holland was under Nazi occupancy, with the Japanese moving ever southward, few places remained where one could flee.

"*Nederland,*" she said in a firm, girlish voice, "*zal Herreuzen.*"

"You'll rise again," Prince agreed solemnly.

It was the Resident's wife, a determined-looking, curiously frail woman for a Dutchmeister's *vrouw,* who finally induced Prince to speak about what they were all yearning to know: how he viewed their prospects from his lofty combat vantage.

Wasn't it probable, she asked, that the enemy would be so busy assimilating his conquests in northwestern Borneo that he would sit awhile, digesting his spoils, before proceeding south? Was Balikpapan really worth a major battle for them now?

The Resident wanted to know how capable were the *overste*'s four destroyers of turning back a Japanese drive down Makassar Strait.

Prince was torn between the impulse to tell these importunate people the sour truth and his momentary pride in commanding the only American naval units within 400 miles of this godforsaken hole. The latter won out.

"I'd estimate we can hang on until things improve—or we get reinforcements."

His Excellency seemed pleased. Balikpapan itself, he said, was also prepared for the worst, with an "auxiliary town" for 30,000 inhabitants five miles inland. They had 1,500 troops, pillboxes, tanks and some seaward-aimed cannon. Upon receipt of a message from Bandung, the capital of Java, they would blow up the sixty-mile pipeline that led from the mountainside tank farms to the coastal refineries.

As yet, Balikpapan had undergone no air raids. It was Lieutenant van Dekker's judgment that the enemy wouldn't make any aerial visitations for at least another ten days. Meanwhile, they had established an impromptu "early warning" system, using reliable native stations deep in the jungle. Drums would be beaten, and their message relayed, when airplane engines were heard.

"So you'll get maybe a half hour's advance notice," said Prince.

"Possibly," van Dekker conceded.

The Resident signaled an end to this dismal discourse on Balikpapan's lacks. Four natives, bearing odd-looking instruments, had now entered the humid room. They took up their places in a far corner, tuned up halfheartedly and launched into what could have been a waltz.

"Let us *dansen*," said His Excellency.

Saskia danced not at all as Prince had expected she would. From her demureness at table and her resolute abstention from the conversation that must have concerned her as much as the others, he had anticipated an equally modest, restrained dance partner, holding him at arm's length, as if determined to assuage her guest's loneliness by her mere propinquity. His initial hopes for a more specific appreciation of his manly presence had faded long before the Resident pronounced that dinner was over, when Saskia herself had become just another pale pink face in the chattering crowd, although she was perforce sitting very near to him at the small table for six.

But now, suddenly, she was a different creature. She seemed to want Prince to hold her pliant body tightly as they strove to match their disparate dancing styles to the impossible music of the native quartet.

"It is too warm in here," she said. "I should enjoy some night air." Saskia smiled up at him. "There is also a moon, which may allow us to see your brave ships, *kapitan*, as they ride at anchor."

They walked down a footpath leading to a glass-enclosed gazebo on the headland that overlooked the harbor. A distinct corona encircled the moon, indicative to Prince of a change in the weather, doubtless for the worse; and he thought he could detect a fog line off to the east, where Makassar Strait stretched almost two hundred dark miles toward the Celebes. Saskia slipped her left hand into his. It was astonishingly small. The narrowness of the pathway caused them to walk very close together, and Prince could feel the swell of her round thigh against his leg, invitingly warm through the thin batik gown which (he wryly imagined) had been manufactured by semi-slave labor in some Batavian sweatshop factory.

Low on the horizon he could also see the Southern Cross, where Orion's Belt had hung during some stupid astronomics lecture to Gwyneth Dean. Chalk up a second irony, he thought, remembering how he'd sworn he never wanted to see this gorgeous constellation. Yet here he was. Another time, another girl; another set of inexorably revolving stars. Also slightly drunk from all the Bols and the champagne and the saccharine after-dinner liqueurs, before the dancing began.

Apropos of nothing whatsoever, Saskia said abruptly, "It gets lonesome out here for everyone."

"Do you read minds?" Prince asked.

"No, just faces."

"But you're too young to feel lonesome," he said.

Saskia smiled forlornly. "I am *vijf en twintig*—twenty-five—which is hardly being in one's childhood."

"I'd have guessed you as nearer eighteen," Prince said, draping his right arm gently across her bare shoulder, almost as if by accident. Suddenly she pressed against him and lifted her parted lips. It was a very long kiss. She did not resist when his hand slipped down through the low-necked dress and groped for her breasts, only half cupped in a wispy brassiere.

"*Danke*," said Prince, after this totally unexpected embrace.

Saskia said with mock gravity, "That's German, Commander, a language I do not admire." She quivered as his fingers flicked across a taut nipple. "It has not been a long war, yet for us it has

144

already lasted an eternity. All the young men have gone away. Did you not notice this as you looked around?"

"Yes," Prince said. "I noticed. Of course, there's always van Dekker. He's young enough."

"And Pieter is also my first cousin," she pointed out.

"I wouldn't have reckoned that cousinship matters all that much."

"It does to me," said Saskia, "even if it doesn't count with royalty. Pieter is a bore. Besides, he is almost twelve years older than I am."

Prince tightened his hold on her yielding flesh. "Hell, baby, I'm damned near his age, myself."

"But you are *not* a bore, Commander." She pulled free of his grasp so that she could confront him directly. "You are the kind of man who is very attractive to women. There is a certain—how do you say?—masculine chemistry which one finds intriguing. When you get to Australia, some day, you should be very much occupied."

"Australia!" Prince scoffed. "With MacArthur mired down in Bataan, and us defending a myth called the Malay Barrier, Australia might as well be the moon."

"It was merely an idea," Saskia said, "a stupid jest, knowing that the Australian women suffer as we do, from a lack of suitable young men. Most of ours went home to defend Holland, and now they're either dead or imprisoned. Theirs are fighting in strange places like Tobruk and El Alamein."

"You *do* follow the war, don't you?" Prince said admiringly.

"Yes." Saskia flashed him a rueful smile. "What else is there for me? The Resident keeps a great map in his study, on which he marks the Nazis' progress with little black pins. Lately, of course, he has added yellow pins to show where the Japanese are. He lets me watch him place the pins, and sometimes he permits me to read the dispatches upon which this information is based."

"That sounds like a pretty exciting sport." Prince yawned.

"But not very encouraging, everything considered."

For a moment he glowered across the stretch of black water toward the ships of his paltry command. They struck him as being even less impressive than he had imagined they would from this height: dimly lit by the faint moonray, with wisps of smoke rising from their quadruple stacks. He made a mental note to find out why they smoked so damned much. At night it didn't matter so much. But by day those dark streaks would be a dead giveaway to the enemy. Maybe he could do nothing about it. After all, they were old and badly out of condition. But with Slattery's expert help, he'd sure as hell try to cut down on these telltale emissions.

"You are thinking bad thoughts?"

Prince turned back to the girl, his scowl diminishing as he discerned the provocative moue of her carmined lips.

"Yes," he admitted. "They were bad thoughts, about those lousy ships of mine, which seem to have given everybody around here such false hopes."

"You are not happy with your destroyers?"

"That's right."

"And you, personally, have certain fears—about yourself as well as your ships?"

Prince's expression hardened. "You *do* read minds, miss."

"The name," she whispered, "is Saskia. Not 'miss' or even *juffrouw*, as you'd say it in Dutch." She lay back against the wooden bench, her batik dress rising up along her rounded legs as she did so. "We do not have a great amount of time, Commander, for that which we both so obviously desire. . . ."

When they returned to the Residency, the dancing had faltered to a desultory finish, and the guests were beginning to depart. The Beaver was the first to greet them. He eyed Saskia's rumpled batik gown appraisingly, grinned at Prince and said, "His Excellency asked me to find you a few minutes ago. I've been looking all over the place for you, old cock, except—" his voice dropped low so that only Prince could hear him—"where I damned well knew you were, you lucky bastard."

"What's up?"

"The frigging jungle telegraph has sent word there are eight Jap Bettys heading our way."

"Okay," said Prince. "Let's get rolling." He touched Saskia's smooth arm. "We'll have to pull our ships out of the harbor and scatter 'em at sea. But we'll be back. I promise."

"Please," she murmured. "I do very much wish to see you again."

"Aren't you ticketed for Surabaya if transportation arrives?"

"Yes."

"We'll probably be there, too, eventually."

"That," said Saskia, "is something for which I shall pray with all my heart."

"Goodbye," he said, trying to make the stark word sound like a caress without alerting the Resident, who was bearing down on them fast, to their new relationship.

"*Dag*," she whispered. "Or *au revoir*, as the French express it so beautifully . . . and so hopefully."

His Excellency grumbled, "I gather you have been informed of the situation, Commander."

"Yes, sir."

"We have notified your ships about this impending attack."

"Good." Prince looked at his wrist watch. "I'd appreciate it if you'd instruct them all—including *Gray Eagle*—to be ready to clear the harbor in fifteen minutes, as soon as I get aboard *Davidson*."

"It shall be done," said the Resident.

As the flagship's whaleboat lurched through the darkness, pounding against a rising swell, Prince could sense the weather change, caused by an inversion layer of cool air settling down

147

over the surface heat, a quick upbuilding of fog and perhaps along with this rapid change a session of high seas.

The Beaver felt it, too. "We're all damned lucky," he said, "although you seem to have the lion's share where the *femmes* are concerned. Mine was a powdery little creature who insisted on dancing the *schottische*, a decent enough exercise if you can sustain two-fourths time all evening, but hardly what I had in mind. Then she invited me in for high tea at sixteen hundred hours tomorrow, as if there wasn't a bloody war going on." The Beaver unleashed one of his enormous snorts. "What I mean is, this Christly awful weather may prove a godsend yet."

Davidson was already starting to slide forward through the murky harbor, gathering speed, as Prince and the Beaver bounded up the ladder. They left the whaleboat moored at the buoy. There was no time to lower lines from the davits and hoist it aboard.

Lieutenant Rodney had the bridge watch. He glanced briefly at Prince. "Good party?"

"Tolerable."

"Pity it had to bust up so soon."

"More of a pity," said Prince enigmatically, "than you might imagine, young fella."

The luminous hands on the flagship's bridge clock showed a few minutes after midnight. From the place where he had taken up his stance on the starboard wing, Prince could physically feel the fog coming in and almost hear it giving off a faint susurrus, like rustling gray taffeta. It had a dank, salty smell. And the bomber's moon, thankfully, had succumbed to this increasingly low-hung blanket, leaving the night as pitch-black as a widow's weeds.

Davidson was the last of the five vessels to sortie from the harbor, close on the unseen heels of *Gray Eagle*, with which Prince kept in contact via TBS radiophone.

"Just keep heading east," he counseled the supply ship's captain. "If this fog holds, we're in clover. But if it lifts and the moon gives those bastards enough light, we'll have trouble. In that case you'll be on your own—unless we can furnish you a little AA protection, which isn't too likely."

After consulting the shrouded map in the charthouse below the bridge, Prince returned to the TBS.

"Calling all ships of DesDiv Eleven," he bellowed into the transmitter. "Maintain course oh-four-five until further notice, speed twelve knots. We'll rendezvous in two hours—oh-two-fifteen—at Point Able. That's one hundred seventeen degrees, thirty minutes west longitude, one degree south latitude, precisely."

"What if we can't get a decent bearing in this weather?" *Mc-Graw* wanted to know.

Prince recognized Koch's schoolmasterly voice. "Then try for visual contact at daybreak," he said, "somewhere along the same course." He added a sarcastic inquiry: "Any better suggestions, Mr. Koch?"

"Negative," said *McGraw*'s skipper curtly. "Over and out." Koch's crisp *out* made it plain he didn't give a damn for his superior's taunt and that as far as he was concerned, Prince was entirely on his own now as ringmaster of this sorry show.

The Beaver, standing alongside Prince, said quietly, "I think you're overcompensating, old chap. Don't get the wind up."

Prince shot him a cold glance. "That's easy enough for you to say, mister, because you have no responsibility. You're super-cargo, remember?"

"Not exactly," the Beaver responded, parting his beard in a gap-toothed grin. "I'm more—shall we say—your Dutch uncle."

Luck held with them.

For most of the night the skies remained heavily overcast, and at dawn DesDiv 11 managed to straggle back into a semblance of formation, minus *Gray Eagle*, which was unable to maintain the twelve knots Prince had decreed. At 0530, with visibility about three miles, they altered course for Balikpapan and revved up to twenty-five knots. *Gray Eagle*, contacted by TBS a half hour later, was told to proceed independently, but not (repeat *not*) to re-enter the harbor until they signaled that the coast was hygienically clean of enemy planes.

"We're going in to top off on fuel," Prince told her captain, "and stand by for a possible follow-up try by the Japs, who might get their second wind."

"Still Point Able for our rendezvous in event of trouble?" *Gray Eagle* asked.

"Affirmative."

By 0700 the division was moored once more in the roadstead. Prince turned his functions over to Rodney, who in turn relinquished them to Lieutenant Hagen, with Prince's approval. Since the gunnery officer had been catnapping most of the night alongside his director platform, he was in relatively fresh shape to handle the minimal bridge duties during the process of refueling from the oil barges.

After a sleepless night, Prince dragged himself off the bunk at 0800, and pressed the buzzer which signaled the captain's messenger. There was a ten-minute delay, enough to annoy Prince, even as he utilized the time to wash and shave in the infinitesimally small washbasin above which was fastened a bent metallic mirror. The image that leered back at him came in two parts, like those good-guy bad-guy photo montages the tabloid papers were so fond of creating whenever a murderer or kidnaper was arrested, demonstrating that the left (or was it the right?) side of a man's face displayed the worst aspects of his character, if any.

When the messenger, a youthful, raven-haired seaman second, whose swarthy face still bore traces of juvenile acne, finally appeared, Prince growled, "What took you so long, son? I'd like some coffee. Black. And *muy pronto*."

"I was eating breakfast, sir, and didn't hear the buzzer right away."

"But you're supposed to be on fulltime duty for me, aren't you? After this take your goddamned tea and crumpets on the bridge."

The boy flushed. "That's right, sir. But nobody figured you'd be getting up and wantin' coffee so early. Lieutenant Rodney's still sacked out."

The inference was unmistakable. Commander Prince had come aboard last night, slightly stoned from the fancydan party he'd attended, and had even seemed a little tipsy during the earlier part of their dash to sea. So while the cat slept it off, safely in port, the enlisted mice could take things easier for a welcome change.

Prince's coffee arrived within five minutes. Aware that the messenger, whose name was Falcone, had sprinted all the way down, then back up the trio of steep ladders to the bridge from the wardroom, he sought to ameliorate his criticism of the lad's earlier dereliction.

"It's damned good java," he remarked. "Just right. Hot as Hades, and just as black."

"Glad you enjoy it, sir," said Falcone briefly, refusing to be placated even by so lordly a maestro as the divisional commander.

Prince shrugged as the messenger left. Okay. If the son-of-a-bitch couldn't accept a deserved chewing out, followed by a handsome implied apology, to hell with him. He'd have to learn. Either that, or get relocated in some job less enviable than serving as the boss's valet, such as an engineering watch. He sipped his coffee slowly, in connoisseur fashion, before donning a set of fresh khakis.

When he went below for a spot of late chow, Prince found the Beaver, red-eyed and frowzy as usual, regaling a handful of j.o.'s with an apocryphal yarn about the war's greatest hero, thus far, a Limey soldier who had made the supreme sacrifice for

King and Country under circumstances that boggled the mind. Tom Rand, Peter Blue and Carl Virtue were attending his story with skeptical grins, yet appreciatively, as if savoring an interlude that helped bridge just one more painful gap in their bored young lives.

"These laddies," explained the Beaver solemnly, while Prince ordered bacon and eggs, "have been grousing over minor sufferings like echo sounders that funk out at seven thousand yards, or can't distinguish shrimps from submarines . . . and torpedoes which broach and won't explode on contact, or ash-can depth charges that sink like rocks, with just about as much explosive power. I'm just trying to buck 'em up a wee bit with this account of a chap who experienced *real* troubles, all due to his possession of certain faculties that set him apart from his fellows. It's quite a thrilling tale, old boy, so maybe I'd better recap it for you."

It seems (said Beaver) that there was a certain lance corporal in His Majesty's forces, one Arbuthnot Simms, a creature of formidable physique, blessed (so the medics averred) with the keenest eyesight, sharpest ears, fastest legs, greatest tactile sense, loudest voice and most attuned nose that had ever come within their professional ken. Early in the European phase of the war, during a hedgerow skirmish, Simms had sped so far ahead of his platoon that he came under heavy machine-gun fire and lost both legs.

This might have discouraged a man of lesser stature. But not Lance Corporal Simms, who sought and got, because of his marvelous touch, a delicate assignment defusing dud bombs. Unfortunately, even he was unable to cope with a faulty 500-pounder that had dropped from a Stuka over Belgium, during the agonizing British retreat toward Dunkirk. The resultant explosion cost him both his arms.

Thereupon Simms was rated, by any proper definition, a total basket case.

Yet the gallant blighter persisted. He volunteered as an air-raid spotter, detailed to an area which was deficient in radar, only to become blinded when a Jerry bomber laid an egg too close to his tower. But Simms still had his superlative ears, so he stayed on spotter duty, *listening* for the sound of approaching Nazi planes. Then ill-fortune struck again, in the form of yet another Stuka near miss, which shattered both his eardrums.

But did this indefatigable bugger quit?

Never, exclaimed the Beaver, not on your life!

Lance Corporal Simms owned that monumental Cyrano de Bergerac of a nose, remember? At his insistence, doubtless impressed by the fact that the NCO's trumpet voice was uninhibited as ever, the desperate British command permitted him to stand anti-chemical warfare guard, with orders to sniff out the first indications of German poison gas on the beleaguered front, and yell out an alarm.

Unhappily, Simms was stationed in the midst of the British Army's own chemical cannister dump, which was inadvertently shelled by a BEF howitzer. In a trice the poor fellow's superior sense of smell evaporated, along with his foghorn voice.

Nevertheless (the Beaver went on) this valorous non-com wouldn't give up. Somehow, by using the stumps of his elbows to inscribe a message on the very sands of Dunkirk, Simms made it known that he still wished to be of some use—searching out hidden minefields. Manpower had become so scarce by then that the high command consented to let the redoubtable lance corporal crawl on what remained of his arms and legs, like some prehistoric mud creature not yet equipped for traveling upon dry land, ahead of the evacuating troops.

On the ultimate day of Dunkirk, he did indeed locate an emplanted Nazi mine, albeit a small one, which normally might have wounded a soldier without killing him, if he were nimble enough to leap aside when it blew. Regrettably, Simms, being unable to roll away very fast, much less jump, caught the full brunt of the devilish device.

"Posthumously," concluded the Beaver, "Lance Corporal

Arbuthnot Simms was awarded the Victoria Cross, George Cross, Order of the Bath, Order of Merit, Order of St. Michael and St. George, Royal Victorian Order, OBE, DSO and—by special permission of the Viceroy himself—the Order of the Indian Empire. The French came through with their bloody old Croix, of course, which His Majesty personally presented along with all the others to Simms' mother, a charwoman at a hotel not far removed from Buckingham Palace."

Prince shoved aside his plate.

"That," he growled, "is a damned idiotic breakfast story."

"Ah," breathed the Beaver, "but it's a splendid morale booster. Shows what a chap with a bit of *élan* can accomplish if he puts his mind to it." He grinned evilly. "Also shows these young gentlemen here what war *can* be like, ashore, and helps keep their jolly peckers up as they consider their relatively easy lot."

On his way back up to the bridge, Prince saw that the native bumboats were already peddling their wares: *bananen, sinaasappel* (oranges) and succulent *meleons*. Temporarily off-duty sailors and even a few officers, he observed with a disapproving frown, were flipping silver coins at the bumboaters, who in turn heaved the desired fruit up toward *Davidson*'s low-lying main deck.

It all seemed so utterly peaceful, like something that might have been happening around one of those great white-painted tourist liners that used to visit Manila.

But it wasn't.

The fog had completely lifted by now. And, still unbeknownst to DesDiv 11 or to the officials at Balikpapan, a flight of twelve Japanese Bettys was winging southeastward from Brunei, bound for the hapless Dutch town, seeking to accomplish what they had failed to do the previous night.

The Residency wouldn't receive its warning along the crude jungle air-raid alert system for another fifteen minutes.

PART III

6

"Blooded—and Bloodied"

GENERAL QUARTERS SOUNDED at 0917. From his comfortable canvas-upholstered chair on the bridge, where he was leisurely inhaling an after-breakfast cigarette, Prince heard the klaxon's intermittent bleat and then the metallic noise of pounding feet as the men dashed for their action stations. He glanced shoreward at the row of multicolored flags which fluttered from a tall staff on the Residency's well-watered, manicured lawn.

"Air raid imminent," they warned.

Prince turned to his own signalman. "See if we can reach the Dutch by TBS. Ask 'em *how* imminent." To Lieutenant Rodney, who had the bridge watch, he said, "Regardless, we've got to get the hell out of here. Run up the immediate-departure hoist —and make it 'urgent.' "

Lieutenant Commander van Dekker's voice responded on the Dutch headquarters' TBS. He seemed rather shaken.

"Somehow," he said, "a flight of *verdammen* Bettys managed to penetrate our distant-warning defenses by flying at extreme high altitude. They're due any moment."

"We're going to sortie at once," said Prince. "You'll have to put off your cruise with us till another time."

"A launch is standing by," van Dekker said hopefully. "I could hurry."

"Not as fast as we can, Commander. We've already cast off, and we're starting to move."

Davidson led the pack through the entrance in the breakwater, closely followed by *McGraw, Travers* and *Vincent*. All four had their three-inch antiaircraft rifles trained skyward on their fantails, despite the rooster's plume of foam that seemed to envelop them as the division gathered speed; and the machine-gun crews in each ship were busily draping extra webbed loops of .30-caliber bullets over convenient rails for instant use. Hand-fed, these outmoded guns were a nautical world away from the newer Oerlikons with which these four-pipers' sisters had been refitted for the Atlantic war. The 20-millimeter Oerlikon automatics could project 450 rounds per minute up to ranges of 4,000 yards or better. But these despised popguns had only a fraction of that speed and range and even less of the Oerlikon's accuracy. As for the ineffable AA tail gun, groused Lieutenant Hagen, it had been fused for planes flying at 150 knots, whereas even the slowest bomber in the Jap arsenal could rev up faster than that.

Their supply vessel, *Gray Eagle*, loomed on the horizon, her disused boilers belching smudge, as DesDiv 11 cleared the harbor. Still striving to make port after her fruitless all-night run, the clumsy old bucket was out of TBS range. So Prince had Rand raise her on the short-wave radio.

"Reverse course" was the command, sent in plain language with no effort to employ code, which would have taken too long, while serving as an empty gesture at best. "Prepare to take evasive maneuvers. And belay that smoke."

Even as the message crackled out from the communications cubicle below the bridge, Prince knew the futility of what he had ordered. *Gray Eagle*, unlike the fleeter-footed tin cans, would be a sitting duck when the Japs arrived, wriggle and twist as her skipper might strive with her ancient hull, inadequate engines and too small rudder. The destroyers were vulnerable enough as it was, for all their thirty-six knots at 32,000 shaft horsepower. This morning their originally designed propulsion meant no more than a draftsman's twenty-year-old dream. They'd be lucky to generate the twenty-five knots he had ordained the night before. Maybe they could manage a hull-banging thirty. But that was absolute tops.

Unlike the previous night, moreover, the weather was near perfect. From the truck of *Davidson*'s aftermast the battle flag, ordered raised by Prince as they left Balikpapan, fluttered in the twenty-four-knot breeze the division had by now attained, its red and white stripes rippling like wavelets on a small lake. Off to the southeast, Prince observed without much enthusiasm, lay the inevitable trade-wind cloudbank. It could mean anything. It might burgeon into a thunderstorm, if they were lucky, or simply remain there, ivory-hued, inert, like a sprawling mountain chain.

Because the Japs controlled the Asian land areas where most of the storms germinated, only a card-carrying prophet could determine what their cumulus cluster portended.

Clouds, nonetheless, *did* speak a certain language, if one read them carefully; Prince tried to recall some of the lessons he'd learned in his Academy meteorological course. Their degrees of moisture, temperature, movement, all carried a special significance. But for the moment his only random recollection was that an English meteorologist named Luke Howard had given clouds their names in 1803, which persisted to this day: cirrus, cirrocumulus, stratus, cumulo-nimbus, and even such exotic nomenclature as altostratus translucidus. What mattered now was whether the trade-wind cumuli would, through some miraculous good fortune, metamorphose into cumulo-nimbus, the harbinger of thunderstorms.

Prince turned to Beaver. "What d'you think?" He pointed across the bridge shield toward the faraway mass.

"If we had a chaplain aboard," said the Briton, "I'd get him starting to pray for rain." He unleashed a postprandial belch. "But we haven't. I'm afraid this is a very godless crew, old chap. So we'll just have to let nature take her course. But I would suggest heading for that charming bit of scud."

Prince spoke over his shoulder to Rodney. "Hoist a course-change signal. We're veering to one-forty." That was roughly south-southeast.

"And *Gray Eagle?*"

"Get her on the TBS, if she's come within range, and tell her to make for those clouds." Prince again indicated the towering cumulus formation.

"Yes, sir." Rodney issued crisp instructions to the wheelman, to the signalman, then picked up the TBS mike. "Can you hear me, *Mama Mia?* Come in."

Each ship of DesDiv 11 had her own code designation. *Gray Eagle*'s was obvious for two reasons: she was indeed the division's mother, providing whatever sustenance was available for their survival under their lonely, disfranchised condition; and her skipper's name was Commander Aldo Mancini, Italian born and an up-from-the-ranks mustang like the ill-fated R4D pilot, Lieutenant Dawkins, who was recovering from his injuries in *Mama Mia*'s sick bay.

Davidson's cognomen was Big Shot, also for obvious reasons, since she normally flew the divisional commander's pennant. This telltale strip of blue cotton could, of course, be hauled down when an engagement impended, to make the flagship less conspicuous. When Prince had ordered all four vessels to break out their oversized battle ensigns, he had also directed that his personal flag be lowered and replaced by *Davidson*'s commission pennant. Noting this, the Beaver made an uncomplimentary grumping noise deep in his throat but had offered no comment.

McGraw was Mick. Also obvious. *Travers* was called Dusty; *Vincent* was Tiger.

"I read you five-by-five," said *Gray Eagle*'s TBS. It was her captain speaking in his slightly Italianate accent. "What's the word?"

Rodney told him.

"Roger," said Mancini. "Over and out."

The way Mama Mia's skipper pronounced this standard cut-off phrase made it sound like a valedictory.

At 0943 the Japanese planes intercepted the fleeing destroyers. Somewhere along the way they had lost two of their original dozen. But the ten that remained were a formidable sight as they barreled straight for DesDiv 11, flying at medium altitude over the peaceful blue sea like an echelon of migrant geese. In the stark morning sunlight of Borneo, the twin-engined bombers loomed big, black and ugly as sin. Designated in the official recognition handbook as Mitsubishi Zero 1, the Betty was cigar-shaped, almost midwinged, with a rounded nose and a machine-gun stinger in its tail. There were bulges along each of its flanks from which protruded more guns. It could achieve a top speed of 200 knots, 50 more than the old four-pipers' AA guns were geared to handle, and possessed both horizontal and dive-bombing capabilities.

When the Japs had approached within a few miles of the racing destroyers, which had fanned out into a wildly zigzagging dispersal pattern, Prince could discern the red circles on the fuselages, their meatball bloodiness enhanced by the white squares that surrounded them.

It was clear that the onrushing Bettys had orders to concentrate on the largest, slowest and clumsiest of their targets. They made straight for *Gray Eagle*, ignoring the tin cans for the moment, leveling themselves for the assault on the smoke-belching supply ship. For once Prince didn't curse *Gray Eagle*'s untidy habit. Instead, he felt like mouthing a silent prayer, but couldn't think of suitable words. Then he walked to where Rodney stood near the wheel, staring at the incipient slaughter through his high-powered binoculars. At least six miles of open water intervened between the tender and her brood. There wasn't a chance in hell that DesDiv 11 could reach her soon enough to be of assistance, even at the thirty knots the destroyers had finally attained, considering the Japs' overwhelming superiority and the four-pipers' lack of AA potential.

Prince was about to issue orders to belay zigzagging and make for the distant cloudbank with all possible speed when he caught the Beaver's speculative glance.

"You think we should try to lend *Gray Eagle* a hand?" Prince demanded rather than asked, already knowing what the reply would be.

"I'm merely the supercargo," the Beaver reminded him. "But if it were my choice, I'd give it the old Oxonian try."

"It'd be futile," Prince said, "and it would leave us wide open to the goddamned Nips."

"That," said the Beaver, "strikes me as one of your primary obligations in this bloody war—making futile gestures. We British have been doing it for years, in places like Narvik and Crete."

Bombs had already begun to burst around *Gray Eagle*. Although the Bettys were unleashing their loads from a scant 6,000 feet, they seemed to have trouble in finding their mark. White splashes pocked the roiled sea around the supply ship, but none had yet come closer than a couple of hundred yards.

"We can be bloody well glad those buggers aren't Nazi Stukas," the Beaver said. "Otherwise they'd have already finished the job and started after us."

Prince tapped Rodney's shoulder.

"Signal course change for *Gray Eagle*," he said. "We'll see if we can siphon off some Nip fire."

"Yes, sir."

By TBS and flag hoist, the other three destroyers got their instructions. They wheeled sharply, almost as if they had been awaiting this move, and proceeded toward the tender, which was plowing cumbersome circles in her desperate attempt to elude the enemy bombs.

Before DesDiv 11 had covered half the distance to the mother ship, the Japs finally found their aim. Two 500-pound bombs fell simultaneously upon *Gray Eagle*, one exploding near her fantail and carrying away her rudder, the other just forward of the bridge. Viewed from four miles away, it was evident that the explosion had swept sternward, demolishing a large portion of the ungainly vessel's boxlike superstructure.

Rodney, Prince and the Beaver had their binoculars trained on the doomed ship. The exec muttered, "That blast must've killed everybody on the bridge."

There was no need to comment on Rodney's remark. He was echoing the obvious, putting their combined thoughts into useless words.

When DesDiv 11 was within two miles of her, *Gray Eagle* gave up the ghost under a literal hail of 500-pounders, riddled from stem to stern with bomb bursts that ripped off her skin, degutted her 8,900-ton corpse, then spewed her iron entrails into the quietly recipient waters of Makassar Strait. A final explosion split the ancient craft in half almost exactly at mid-section, and these twin segments sank like thrown rocks.

Yet the four destroyers remained on collision course with the place where *Gray Eagle* had vanished, toward a spot in the calm sea which was marked only by a series of bubbles and a few bits of wooden debris.

"Prepare to take aboard survivors," *Davidson* messaged.

But there were none. All hands had gone down with their blazing ship, either trapped below or killed in the holocaust that engulfed her shattered deck.

Having attempted the impossible and failed, DesDiv 11 was even farther withdrawn from the unmistakably developing storm front, now a good twenty miles to the east. Meanwhile the Japs had regrouped into a menacing echelon and were bearing down on the destroyers.

Prince called in a voice that he strove to make brusquely confident, "Tell the division to scatter and take necessary evasive action, while keeping generally on a course for those clouds."

He resisted an impulse to tell the Beaver what damned fools they'd made of themselves, with this suicidal attempt to aid a ship that had clearly been doomed from the start. Given the same circumstances, he knew the bearded idiot would doubtless give the same counsel again. Instead, Prince allowed himself the luxury of one last guilty thought before he turned his full attention to the wheeling enemy aerial formation: Lieutenant Commander Roger Thornburg would never return to the flagship; so he, Custis Hensley Morgan Prince, must henceforth serve both as *Davidson*'s captain and DesDiv 11's leader, a dual responsibility which he had already found nerve-wracking to the point of sheer, unadulterated fright. He wondered if the others suspected how he felt. Rodney probably didn't. But the Beaver —the goddamned, grinning, self-sufficient Beaver—was regarding him as if he were some strange insect impaled on a specimen board, not yet entirely classified, although fairly well established as to its general characteristics, none of which was especially charming, even for an entomologist.

The Beaver said matter-of-factly: "We'd better get braced for about forty minutes of unshirted hell, old boy, before we reach the shelter of yonder squall."

Prince gave him a glance which he hoped was impassive. He moved across the bridge to the engineering-room voice tube, blew into it and called for Slattery. "You there, Slats?"

"In person, Commander."

"What's our shaft horsepower?"

"Twenty-two frigging thousand."

164

"Can you crank up any more?"

An instant of silence followed Prince's question. Then Slattery said dubiously, "Not unless you want to risk a blown boiler, sir."

Prince peered back at the oncoming planes. "We'll have to chance it, Slats. Pour on all you've got."

"Yes, sir."

Snapping shut the tube, Prince turned his gaze briefly toward the fantail, where Lieutenant Hagen was supervising the AA battery. Then he scanned the four machine-gun teams: one located above the rear superstructure which also housed the torpedo shop; two on either side of the No. 2 funnel; and one just aft of the forward main rifle, that impotent four-inch weapon which wouldn't elevate more than forty-five degrees.

At 32 knots *Davidson*'s stern was vibrating like the tin can for which she had been so scornfully nicknamed, a garbage can filled with sharp rocks that threatened to burst through her flimsy sides. Hagen had already started pot-shooting at the nearest Betty, which was slant-diving toward them with its own machine guns firing. From this distance, perhaps 4,000 feet, the Jap's guns seemed merely to be flickering harmlessly, like Roman candles you buy in a cheap Fourth of July assortment.

But the bombs were real enough.

The Betty laid a stick of them just astern of the flagship, where they raised gouts of creamy water a dozen times the height of *Davidson*'s five-foot rooster-tail wake. Rodney called to the chief quartermaster who had the wheel, telling him to increase his zigzag pattern.

The first Betty swept overhead, then another and another, but still *Davidson* remained unscathed.

The Beaver exulted above the intermittent *crump-crump* of the near misses and the noise of Hagen's popgun: "You know, old cock, there's a saying that no ship is ever lost until her skipper thinks so. Just keep those good thoughts coming."

"Thanks," Prince said shortly, "I will."

Meanwhile the others were absorbing their share of the Japs' attention. Apparently the enemy flight commander had decided to divide his strength, allocating two Bettys each to *Davidson, McGraw* and *Vincent* and a full quartet to the remaining escapee, *Travers*, which had fallen well astern of the raddled formation. She appeared to be having engine trouble. Prince estimated her advance at less than twenty-five knots, and *Travers* was visibly losing speed.

But, unlike the ill-starred effort to succor *Gray Eagle*, there was no slowing down to assist the straggler. In a last-minute TBS conference before leaving Balikpapan, it had been decided that any wounded destroyer would have to look out for herself. The main objective was saving the bulk of the division, so those who remained might live to fight another day.

Unless they reached the asylum of the squall, there would be no survivors, Prince told himself bleakly. He swung his binoculars toward the Alpine cloud mass. Its cumulus base had turned noticeably darker, from clean white to pale blue and finally to a darkly dirty gray. But the apex shone bright with snow crystals. Once these began falling into the jumbled interior of what now had become a cumulo-nimbus formation, they would touch off the thunderstorm for which DesDiv 11 was desperately hoping. The heated lower air would surge upward, electricity would generate and no plane could possibly dare to plumb its turbulent depths.

Below, on the sea's surface, the division would be enveloped in lifesaving gloom.

The fleeter-footed DesDiv 11 trio was midway to this squall line, with about twenty minutes intervening between them and temporary safety, when it was obvious that the Japanese leader had developed some second thoughts about his tactics. The six Bettys which had been attacking *Davidson, McGraw* and *Vincent*, with minimal results—a bent plate or two as they continued to outmaneuver the astonishingly inaccurate bombers—

abruptly broke off the duel and retired in a body toward *Travers*.

Rodney posed a soundless question with his eyes, but Prince shook his head.

"You know the drill," he snapped. "Stay on course for those goddamned clouds."

"Yes, sir."

The Beaver waggled his ursine head sorrowfully. "In this case, old boy, you're dead right. Better three ships than none." He sighed. "We had the same rule for stragglers. Bloody awful tough. But there's no other way."

They watched with a sense of detached anguish as the Japs began methodically and cold-bloodedly to work over the luckless *Travers*. Prince tried to imagine how Lieutenant Commander Sam Pierce, the closemouthed sundowner who had taken such a vast pride in running a taut ship, felt now about his crippled tin can. Like the others he had ordered flank speed on his engine-room telegraph. But then something had gone wrong, appallingly wrong, for when *Travers*' r.p.m. needle reached the point which indicated her screws were producing the requisite thirty knots, it faltered and began to curve downward. Pierce would not have taken kindly to the engineer's report of a faulty boiler, even though its failure was the result of a near miss whose concussion had shaken loose its creaky brick fire walls. So there he was, probably stomping about on his exposed bridge, cursing, with his vaunted destroyer limping along at fourteen knots—and six more enemy bombers roaring at him to reinforce the four that were already giving *Travers* an excessively bad time.

Pierce did what the Book ordained: he unleashed a thick blanket of smoke from his fantail pots, in an effort to provide some man-made cover, through which he could intermittently weave while the Japs expended their bombs. Below decks, *Travers*' crew would be wrestling ammo into the handling rooms, which were almost bare, now, after a half hour of steady yet futile firing with her four-inch rifles. Pierce had ordered these weapons, which were designed for surface battles, into action when the disdainful Bettys began to make low-altitude runs against his lagging vessel.

Meanwhile *Travers'* single AA gun had been shooting steadily and with amazing accuracy at the enemy planes ever since they came within its limited range. One of the Bettys, venturing too close, caught a three-inch projectile squarely in a fuel tank. It exploded with a noise that was audible across the several miles of sea that divided the cripple from her departing mates. Moments later, from his vantage point on the flagship bridge, Prince saw the AA gun go dead.

What had happened?

The Beaver supplied the likeliest answer: "Poor bastard's recoil system must've messed up, with all the overheating it's undergone. Those pistols weren't made for prolonged firing, you know."

Prince knew. And the knowledge gave him no comfort whatsoever, for when the Bettys returned, *Davidson's* lone AA rifle would have to sustain them. Or else.

Travers kept up the unequal fight with her four .30-caliber machine guns. By a miracle, she managed to bag another incautious Betty, which had flat-hatted fifty feet over her main truck after dropping a pair of bombs along the starboard side. The flagship's observers, those on her main deck, those on the bridge, along with others who were waiting at their weapons for the Japs to come back, unleashed a vast, simultaneous cheer. Even Prince joined them, forgoing the dignity he deemed so necessary as their divisional commander, unabashedly applauding *Travers'* dogged heroics.

But the stricken ship's luck had finally played out. As the low-flying Betty windmilled into the sea, one of the bombs she had dropped tore a ragged hole in *Travers'* side, near the engine room. The huzzahs aboard *Davidson* turned into groans as

Travers slushed to a halt, her propulsion system a shambles. What few survivors remained in the superheated machinery compartments below shut off the boilers and came scrambling topside.

Travers, Prince could discern clearly, was taking water through her riven stern and settling fast. He could envision Pierce, angry at whatever treacherous fates that had condemned his precious command, shouting for his first lieutenant and damage-control officer. (On *Davidson* this would be Peter Blue, in whom Prince had scant confidence, despite the youngster's reputation as a chap who'd learned his hazardous trade well.) There would be no encouraging news for Pierce. Lying almost inert in the water, pitching helplessly, *Travers* was a goner. No alternative remained but to abandon ship, an order which Pierce would willingly have sacrificed his right arm to avoid issuing.

Perhaps he debated within himself too long. Perhaps he was dead. God only knew. For an unconscionably long time, it seemed to Prince, *Travers* delayed lowering her whaleboats and life rafts, and when some sign of this action became visible through the binoculars to Prince's aching eyes, it was too late. The Bettys were swarming over the destroyer's carcass like a pack of hyenas, tearing away at the mangled wreckage with their explosive teeth. A few men were seen leaping off the uptilted foredeck, frantically swimming away from the carnage. But then the Bettys circled back, as *Travers* slowly sank, and deliberately finished them off with machine-gun fire.

It would have been worse than useless for DesDiv 11's remaining ships to retrace their course. No possibility of helping *Travers*' crew existed, because neither *Travers* nor her crew existed, as even the Beaver had to admit grimly. *Sauve qui peut . . .*

What remained was to preserve the other destroyers by slipping into the cloudbank, which by now had dropped menacingly to a few hundred feet of the graying sea. Within ten minutes they were, indeed, securely inside this natural sanctuary that extended, as best as Prince could estimate after a hasty TBS conference with his fellow skippers, for a good twenty-odd miles. This should be ample for them to maneuver at ease, while the Japs milled around outside until their fuel ran low, forcing the bombers to head back to their northern Borneo base.

Prince waited almost an hour before venturing beyond the cloud cover. The Bettys were nowhere in sight. So he told Rand to run up the signal hoist that sent the division on a straight course for Balikpapan and to reinforce these visual instructions by TBS.

In the interim he composed a message for Asiatic Fleet headquarters at Surabaya. His hand was shaky as he wrote, Prince knew, and moist with cold sweat.

"Attacked at 0945 by ten Jap Bettys at latitude 2 degrees, 20 minutes south, longitude 118 degrees east," he scribbled on the dispatch pad. "During 40-minute action shot down two bombers but regret to announce loss of *Travers* to enemy action."

Prince shoved it at Rand, who had remained topside during the brief encounter. "Mark it urgent and top secret," he said.

Rand read the missive as he descended the ladder to the radio room. It occurred to him that the commander might at least have granted *Travers* credit for the Nip bombers. As it now read, any one of DesDiv 11's four-pipers, including *Davidson* herself, might claim the honors. In fact, by inference, that was precisely what Prince had done, leaving the notion that the flagship was the deadliest marksman of them all. But what the hell. Regardless of who received the plaudits, exchanging one irreplaceable destroyer for two lousy bombers—of which the Japs had an inexhaustible supply—was a piss-poor bargain any way you looked at it, with faint glory for whoever grabbed the laurels, whether illicitly or not.

Chief Yeoman Bream had stayed in the radio shack this

whole time, decoding the Pacific and Asiatic Fleet circuit traffic that kept flowing in, unstoppable, rain or shine, battle or no battle. He was singularly unmoved for a man who had been forced to listen while *Davidson*'s guns converted the miniature cabin into a sort of reverberating steel drum, much more so than the radioman who sat at the shortwave, wearing his sound-proofing headset.

When Rand handed him the scrawled sheet, Bream perused it carefully. He glanced up.

"This is all of it?" he asked. "Nothing more to follow?"

"The works," Rand assured him.

Bream smiled knowingly. "Okay, if that's how the commander wants it."

Quite plainly, Bream had reached the same conclusion, Rand thought, that Prince was trying to salvage something out of the debacle—a debacle that wasn't a debacle—truthfully, if you considered the circumstances, one that required no alibis whatsoever.

The reply to Prince's message came long before the division reached port. It was crisp and to the point.

"Continue assigned search-and-destroy operations in upper Makassar Strait. Rumors of possible amphibious attack against Balikpapan. Keep remaining destroyers operating as a group. Enter harbor only when absolutely necessary to replenish fuel. Further orders will be forthcoming as situation clarifies."

As the days passed it became evident that the Japanese were taking their own devilish sweet time about administering the *coup de grâce* to Balikpapan. The Old Man was spouting veritable geysers of instructions from Surabaya, where he had gone by submarine the morning after Prince himself departed Manila. A few antique river gunboats, some minesweepers, tugs and a half dozen PTs had remained in Manila harbor to lend assistance to MacArthur's Bataan-trapped army. This was strictly a delaying business, though, aimed at slowing down the Nips, while the defenders hoped against hope for some meaningful aid from the outside world.

As he read the endless stream of intelligence from Surabaya and Corregidor, the Beaver spoke admiringly of those expendable naval units.

"If Singapore had such an assortment of small craft," he told Prince, "Malaya might hold out for a while. But it doesn't. So it won't."

What little remained of December evaporated quickly, and January wore on, while DesDiv 11's three destroyers went about their assigned duties, unimpeded by Jap aircraft, who were otherwise engaged for reasons nobody could fathom, although this respite was welcome. It was monotonous, seemingly pointless work: patrolling, always patrolling by day and night. The after-dark missions were better, as far as Prince was concerned, than daylight cruises in the blistering heat of a relentless sun. At night the division, spaced a dozen miles apart, fanned northward through Makassar Strait, never quite venturing into the widening mouth of the Celebes Sea, beneath a great serene bell of blue-black skies where the constellations flamed like Christmas candles.

Occasionally they would make cautious contact with a friendly submarine recharging her batteries on the surface after the sun went down. And the news was always the same: the Japs lying doggo for some inexplicable reason, gathering strength, perhaps, for the main thrust southward. The enemy had forced the British out of upper Sarawak. By January 6 they walked ashore unimpeded at Brunei Bay; and five days later they clinched their pincers tightly upon that whole strategic territory, 400 rugged miles from Balikpapan as the bomber flies. In the second week of January the rampant foe had begun to protect his eastern defenses by steaming down through the Celebes Sea to capture Menado peninsula at the nether end of Celebes Island itself, and to occupy Tarakan on Borneo's northeast coast.

Now they were within 300 air miles of Balikpapan, their real goal, with its vast petroleum resources.

At ABDA headquarters in Surabaya, the Allies argued and pleaded their individual cases. Saving Singapore and thus the accesses to the Indian Ocean was all-important to the British, whose entire "fleet" consisted of the heavy cruiser *Exeter,* light cruisers *Hobart* and *Perth* and three destroyers. Of these, all but *Hobart* were marked for destruction, although the ABDA debaters never dreamed of such calamity at this moment of relative euphoria.

The Dutch saw only the imperilment of their rich colonies, especially Java and Sumatra, from which they had reaped a fat living for more than 300 years and which were the only home that almost 500,000 Dutch settlers had ever known. Their contribution was a trifle more impressive than Britain's, though it was still no great shakes. The Dutch counted one heavy cruiser, *Zuyder Zee,* two lights, *Noorden* and *Volendam,* seven destroyers and sixteen submarines of varying degrees of decrepitude. Only *Volendam* was destined to survive among the surface ships before March ended.

Both the Americans and the Aussies viewed the situation with long-ranged realism, having earlier decided that the Japs could not be halted for the immediate present. Their conclusion: in some fashion the enemy had to be kept from probing so deeply into the southwest Pacific that the Allies would lose the bases that were absolutely essential to the slow, but necessary, uphill climb after their strength had been rebuilt, perhaps years later. Tommy Hart had considerably more muscle to back up his contentions: the heavy cruiser *Houston*; light cruisers *Boise* and *Marblehead*; three destroyer divisions originally numbering four ships each, but now one short, thanks to the loss of *Travers*; a patrol aircraft wing; a respectable submarine contingent; plus the only viable service force of oilers, repair vessels and tenders in the vast area capable of moving to the assistance of fuel-hungry or combat-damaged units which couldn't make it unaided to Surabaya. Nine of these, including *Houston* and eight others, would die in the ensuing spring engagements with the Japanese.

So it went during those few relatively quiet weeks, a microcosm of the erstwhile "phony war" in Europe that was no longer a matter for derisive retrospection, the entire continent having fallen prey to Hitler.

Prince began to feel more at ease, less inclined to dread the unknown that might be crouching just beyond the horizon. He enjoyed the final glimmering of the sunsets as DesDiv 11 scouted along the Borneo headlands, the dark land mass like a recumbent woman, fructile and full of generous curves. It was possible, then, to imagine a whole universe at peace, with all its planets in harmony. He savored the wonderful loneliness of it, in this tenuous interval of peace, until the inevitable truth poured over him like a lava flow—that he was in command of these three absurd ships, and *that* was a special loneliness which he found difficult to endure. At such a moment the night breeze, stage-whispering past the bridgehead, seemed to carry a message for his secret ear, as he sat quietly on his swivel chair. With minimal imagination he could hear the distant roll of heavy gunfire and glimpse flashes from the rifles of the warring squadrons.

He saw Saskia only once during those unproductive weeks. They met briefly on the quay while *Davidson* was being refueled from the harbor barges. At her insistence Lieutenant Commander van Dekker had fetched Saskia there so that she could tell Prince personally that, God willing, a PBY lent by the Americans would take the Dutch officials' wives and dependents from Balikpapan to Surabaya at dawn next day.

"Maybe," Prince said without much conviction, "we'll have a reunion in Java."

"It would be a real one," Saskia whispered. "Worth waiting for."

But not dying for, Prince told himself. Not even this succulent, available Saskia, with all her marvelous expertise, was worth a man's life. Then he visibly shook his head. That was a damned fool thought. Saskia had nothing to do with whether he survived or perished. And it *would* be good to renew this delectable association, now that Mari was gone forever and Gwyneth Dean was certain to become a Japanese prisoner. Or worse. How did a man parse out a creature like Saskia? She was neither an ordinary little high-born tramp nor a compulsive nympho. In their earlier brief encounter she had been as genuine as a spring rain, and as pervasive, with her limpid eyes and her abrupt yet gentle closing around him, like one of those purple sea anemones when it is disturbed in its tide-pool nest by a probing finger.

After he said goodbye to Saskia, and she had entered van Dekker's staff car for the ride back up the hill, Prince stood for an instant, watching the sedan's wake, before he went for a walk on the beach. It struck him that there were levels of survival; and as he strolled along the sand, he brooded upon this mystery, which seemed exemplified by the strutting seabirds that fled at his clumsy approach. To them, he was the fearful Unknown. Yet, like himself, they were linked irrevocably to the same unfathomable sea that guided his own destiny as a naval officer. Pelicans and helldivers, the aerial ones; terns and ducks, the submarine ones; gulls, the scavengers that arrived after the killing had stopped; and the smaller beach fowl, eking out a precarious existence amongst all these larger creatures.

More and more, only half conscious of what he was doing, Prince delegated his shipboard command authority to the Beaver, who accepted it gracefully and without comment. The Briton was virtually brevetted as *Davidson*'s skipper. This didn't displease Lieutenant Rodney, who found his own executive-officer chores sufficiently exacting, seeking impossible answers to the thousand and one ills that plagued the flagship's various departments, from inadequate gunnery facilities to dwindling food supplies.

So DesDiv 11 patrolled, refueled and patrolled again. Unlike Commander Pryor, his predecessor, Prince was unable to husband his thin red line, taking out two for a forty-eight-hour prowl, while leaving the other pair of tin cans behind for rest and recreation. As the Beaver said, they were getting uncomfortably close to the Ten Little Indians syndrome: down to three ships now, and Christ only knew when the next Jap assault would lop off another four-piper.

On their brief interludes at Balikpapan, the fantail of each destroyer was officially designated as "ashore." This meant that the men could quaff gallons of excellent Heineken beer which the grateful Dutch sent out to them in super-generous quantity, when you remembered that when this supply was gone, there'd be no more. But, then, Balikpapan doubtless wouldn't exist any longer either, so it became a sort of beer-guzzling race against the inevitable.

At first, when he learned of this custom, which had originated with the lenient Pryor, Prince was inclined to call a halt to it, as an impediment to the stern discipline he felt the division would require when it finally went into battle.

The Beaver helped change his mind.

"You toffs don't even have the British right to a tot of rum," he reminded Prince.

"True enough," Prince admitted reluctantly. "Josephus Daniels knocked it off in nineteen twelve. He figured drinking fouled up a man's efficiency."

"It can," said the Beaver. "It does. But so do hangovers, and there's nothing in your naval law that precludes even an admiral making a night of it and waking up with a split skull." He paused ruminatively. "One wonders, doesn't one, how many brass hats had hangovers on the morning of last December seventh or eighth, depending on which side of the bloody date line they inhabited?"

Prince didn't reply. But if he'd been forced to make an estimate, he would have guessed a hell of a lot of officers' minds were a bit blurry in those ugly post-dawn hours when the enemy struck. He had only to recall the Army air group's wingding at the Manila Hotel on the night before to know that the Beaver was right.

"His Majesty's warships have had their morale-purpose grog since seventeen thirty-one," the Beaver prodded. "Great stuff. We call it 'Nelson's Blood.' "

"Okay," said Prince wearily. "We'll continue with the goddamned happy hour."

On January 19, long after nightfall, a U.S. submarine stalking Makassar Strait stumbled upon a Dutch "K" class sub. They warily swapped recognition signals and eased within earshot of each other. Each had earlier spotted Nip destroyers heading southward in the strait, well above Balikpapan, yet providing a fairly sound indicator that the Japs were getting braced for something big. That something, both skippers agreed, could only be the long-overdue amphibious try against Balikpapan itself. It also meant that the enemy had solidified his hold on the other northern Borneo beachheads in record time—ten days, to be exact.

Seizing Tarakan, above the coveted oil center, apparently was such a simple business that the foe had advanced his timetable by several weeks. Or so the wizards at Surabaya concluded, after receiving the word from the two submarines.

Prince got his instructions on January 3, during a refueling layover. They read flatly: "Japanese convoy departing Tarakan for probable Balikpapan invasion effort. Interpose DesDiv 11 between enemy and objective. Your immediate support will be four submarines. Have ordered DesDiv 10 to join you soonest along with cruiser *Marblehead*. Good hunting and good luck."

He shoved the message at the Beaver.

"The others will already have received this," he said. "But

tell the poor bastards to finish topping off as fast as possible. I want us out of here—" he consulted his wrist watch—"by sixteen hundred. That's fifty-five minutes."

The Beaver nodded. Then he tapped the dispatch with a broken fingernail. "Damned decent of Surabaya to offer reinforcements at this late date. DesDiv Ten has almost double the distance to travel as that Nip convoy. And even figuring on their relative rates of speed, the Japs will be within our striking range long before those lads arrive—since we'll be heading north."

"I know," Prince gloomed. "Oh, how frigging well I know! Especially if they wait for *Marblehead*. That old sea hag has one of her turbines out of commission, Surabaya says, and she can only crank up fifteen knots."

"What about your other cruiser—*Boise?*"

Prince uttered a mirthless laugh. "She's temporarily laid up after hitting an uncharted coral head somewhere in Sape Strait. You can scratch her for a week or so."

Either the ABDA command was tardy in passing the word to DesDiv 11 or the Japs were quicker than had been anticipated. That same evening, as the three destroyers were hustling northeastward, hoping to intercept the convoy where Makassar Strait narrowed about halfway between Tarakan and Balikpapan, one of the four support submarines encountered the enemy's lead ships. These comprised five transports laden with work gangs, escorted by two Nip destroyers, already navigating the bottleneck barely 200 miles above Balikpapan.

The American sub moved in fast, at periscope depth, and loosed a spread from her forward tubes at a dark shape. For a welcome change, the too often unreliable torpedoes exploded on contact, and their victim blew up with a magnificent roar. The sub's skipper got off a hurried dispatch before diving to escape the onrushing Japanese tin cans.

"Sighted enemy force," he radioed, "sank one transport."

From their 600-mile-distant haven at Surabaya, night-flying

Catalinas gave the next account of the enemy's southward passage. Behind the advance body, said the PBYs, streamed sixteen transports lightly protected by three patrol boats. A Catalina equipped with wing bombs made a miraculous direct hit on one of the two frontal transports. The unlucky vessel began to burn furiously and must (exulted the PBY pilot) be considered a complete loss, even if she didn't founder.

All this radio traffic was monitored by DesDiv 11, which by now was halfway to the strait's gap, about 100 miles from Balikpapan. Thus it was that Prince, from *Davidson*'s bridge, was unable either to see the flames from the wounded Jap ships or the vast conflagration at Balikpapan itself, where the Resident had decided the time had finally come to trigger the destruction of his isolated town's oil tanks. Nor did Prince know that the Resident, a far tougher man than he would have imagined, had also called for an air strike by Java-based Dutch bombers after he'd safely herded the populace into their prearranged inland shadow city.

At this point Makassar Strait was almost 200 miles wide, a formidable area for three radarless destroyers to patrol at night, even though they had a rough idea of the enemy's likeliest course—arrow-straight, Prince assumed, because of the Japs' disdain for the puny challenge they anticipated from the decimated Yankee division. Like the optimistic Americans, enemy commanders were apt to put the best construction on intelligence from their aerial missions; and the Bettys which had dispatched *Travers* the day after Christmas had overestimated their accomplishments by some 400 percent. DesDiv 11 was no longer in existence, they avowed. So the nearest threat to a Balikpapan amphibious assault would have to come from DesDiv 10, which was too far away for any serious concern in the early hours of January 24, when they expected to drop anchor off Balikpapan.

This euphoric acceptance of the Bettys' inflated report might also have been one of the reasons why the Jap bombers hadn't bothered to return to the town, preferring, rather, to await the ultimate moment of invasion. The great Halsey himself, three years later, would make such a miscalculation, one that almost led to disaster, based on his carrier aviators' overly exuberant reports in the early stages of the battle for Leyte Gulf.

Prince's original view that the enemy would make directly for Balikpapan might have been correct in the first instance, but no longer. The successful submarine attack, followed so closely by the Catalina's chance blow, persuaded the Japanese admiral in command of the expedition to adopt a more circuitous route, hugging close to the undulant Celebes coastline, before cutting sharply to the right toward his objective.

When the Beaver suggested this might happen, Prince brusquely riposted that he take care of *Davidson*'s needs and leave tactical decisions to the divisional commander.

"Aye, aye, sir," growled the Beaver. "Just thought I'd bring up the possibility in case it hadn't occurred to you, old cock."

"It had," Prince said, "and I've rejected it. The Japs have a proven habit of never changing their minds once they're made up, even when things start going sour. They try to bull it through. We'll stay on this direct-interception course. *Comprenez?*"

The Beaver sighed. "*Je comprends très bien, mon capitaine.*"

At the outset of their sweep north there had been a full moon, a phenomenon of ambivalent interest to Prince as he saw it slither through the intermittent cloudbanks like a child playing hide-and-seek with a jack-o'-lantern. The Beaver, using the enlisted men's argot, which he had come to enjoy hugely, also termed this a "mixed frigging blessing." *Davidson*'s chief lookout, perched in his main-mast crow's nest seventy-five feet above the deck, had a frequent clean sweep of the horizon through his

7 x 50 binoculars. He took in the area under observation five degrees at a time, scrutinizing each segment closely before swinging to the next sector. Such was Navy doctrine. You never let your gaze wander aimlessly across the entire field of vision, but concentrated eyes, mind and viscera on that one small portion, always seeking some prime objective: an enemy ship, or an aircraft, or a whole list of things running the gamut from shoals to periscope wakes to discolored water, which might mean anything.

When an object was sighted, the spotter called out its identity, bearing and range in a loud, clear voice.

Prince kept waiting for the lookout's cry of "Ships dead ahead, thirty-five thousand," give or take a few thousand yards.

None came.

Once a twin-engined seaplane swung low across the division's starboard beam, whereupon the four-pipers' trio of AA guns promptly trained upon it. But the pilot flashed a quick recognition, and in a brief interval of full moonglow Prince recognized it as a PBY.

"Ask him what he's seen," Prince ordered his signalman.

Davidson's blinker light flickered even as the Catalina was continuing its own message.

"Jap convoy traversing Makassar Strait approximately fifty miles south of here. Would estimate enemy within one-hour range of Balikpapan at present speed of twelve knots . . ."

The PBY finished its report and banked sharply, plainly bent on returning to its reconnaissance mission against the Japanese who had so successfully eluded DesDiv 11. And so humiliatingly, Prince raged, his inward anger heightened by the fact that the Beaver had guessed the foe's intent so correctly, whereas he had been so utterly, damnably wrong.

But the Beaver, self-contained as usual, cloaked whatever impulse he might have felt to say "I told you so" behind a simple twitch of his shoulders. He looked at Prince expectantly.

"Signal reverse course for the division. And see if Slattery has a couple more knots up his greasy sleeve."

"Right-o," the Beaver acknowledged.

Through the engine-room tube, Slattery sounded doubtful but game. They were absorbing water into the bilges through a cracked seam, he reported; and from what he figured, this new southwestern course would take them into a damned sight heavier seas than they'd been encountering most of the night. That might cause real trouble before they reached their goal.

Prince summoned Ensign Blue. "Line up a five-man detail and go below," he said. "Keep an eye on that leak—and any others you find. Let me know exactly how bad they are, also whether we can risk a flank-speed run to Balikpapan. Consult with Slats."

"Yes, sir."

The Beaver nodded approvingly. "That's eminently sound, old crock. But I'd urge that we err on the side of non-caution if we have to." He held up his right arm so that the luminous dial of his wrist watch glinted faintly. "Time passeth."

"Thanks for the advice," Prince snapped. "I'll bear it in mind."

It was 0115. At best DesDiv 11 would close Balikpapan two hours after the Japs' arrival, hopefully while the convoy was still sorting itself out after groping through the Dutch minefields and before the enemy could begin unloading his transports for an amphibious assault on the thinly protected town.

As Slattery had guessed, and Krebs, the navigator, had known, the weather was indeed thickening. Less than thirty minutes after the destroyers wheeled around, retracing their arrow-straight compass course for the threatened base, they encountered frontal seas that burst over their foredecks with such force that one of *Davidson*'s bridge windows shattered, and even her metal spray shields bent under the immense hydraulic thrust.

The crow's-nest lookout announced visibility at less than a half mile. Every deck hand sought fragile shelter behind gun tubs, the galley shack and the after torpedo shop. On the bridge, those assigned to watching from the exposed wings crept inside, wet and miserable, for brief wring-out periods before emerging to try again to pierce the gloom with their streaming binoculars.

Prince occupied his chair, silent, inwardly fuming and, he knew from the amorphous lump that had begun to germinate deep in his gut, once again preparing to taste the sour bile of fear. To make matters worse, all likelihood of surprise was gone. They must now come to grips with an enemy who, having escaped detection, would doubtless be menacingly ready for the belated Americans. What had started as an exercise in hit-run tactics, he told himself dourly, had degenerated into a ridiculous situation where the lambs led themselves to slaughter. Three little lambs named *Davidson, McGraw* and *Vincent*, carrying thirty-six torpedoes apiece, enough for three spreads from their twelve tubes, and a handful of four-inch guns whose ammunition was already at a perilously low ebb.

He tried to remember what the skippers had told him about their shell supply. Then he tried to forget.

At 0200, restless, nerves jangling, Prince swung himself down the ladder to Krebs' charthouse for a quick smoke. He found the Beaver huddled over the plotting board with the navigator, discussing in muted tones the off chance of contacting the Japs before their originally estimated time of 0315. For one thing, the head winds had abated slightly, and the division was averaging a decent twenty-four knots, occasionally touching twenty-seven, in its southward race. Lieutenant Hagen no longer bellowed with frustrate rage now that the seas had eased and his precious forward guns weren't being doused every few minutes by the waves that crashed across *Davidson*'s knife-sharp bow.

If the Beaver was correct, it would mean that DesDiv 11 would have to tangle with the Nips alone, since DesDiv 10 would be hours late arriving on the scene. Prince had a momentary urge to order his three ships to slow down, hold back, so that they could meet the enemy with more than double their present pitiful strength.

But the Beaver's boundless enthusiasm dissuaded him.

"Let's hammer," the Briton urged in a platitudinous fashion that increased Prince's distaste for this stubborn man who had, somehow, appointed himself as the division leader's unofficial conscience, "while the bloody iron's still red. If we wait, Balikpapan's had it."

"And if we don't wait," Prince countered, "probably we've had it."

"That," observed the Beaver, "is exactly our problem, old sod, what we were invented for. So there's no other QED possible for this one. I say, press on."

Ensign Rand had quietly joined them, with a decoded message clutched in his hand.

"DesDiv Ten?" Prince asked.

"Negative, sir. Some fresh poop from our Catalinas."

"Bad news?"

"Very."

Prince accepted the dispatch. "Enemy support force sighted near Balikpapan. One light cruiser probably flagship plus nine destroyers several minesweeps and subchasers. Would anticipate their arrival on target approximately same time as main amphibious group now estimated at 14 transports with two destroyers as screen."

He let the Beaver and Krebs read it together under the dim goose-necked lamp that was bolted to the chart table.

"Still want to play 'Anvil Chorus' all by our goddamned lonesome?" he demanded.

The Beaver's expression was oppressively grim. "We've got no choice. I'd vote yes."

"This isn't a democracy," Prince said. "I cast the only vote that counts."

"So how d'you mark your ballot, old boy?"

Prince shut his eyes briefly and appeared to be engaged in deep thought. The odds were horrible. It was no longer a turkey shoot, DesDiv 11 versus an array of lightly protected Jap transports, but a forlorn charge against a foe that outnumbered them better than four to one, with a cruiser suddenly added to their other woes. Prince would have liked to ponder this immense problem, forever if possible, until it automatically took care of itself and somehow went away. As he knew from his nautical history, sea battles were too often matters for flash decisions and chain-lightning responses. He preferred the reflective rather than the reflexive approach, with conclusions hammered out— not on the Beaver's hypothetical anvil but deliberately, painstakingly, after weighing all the alternatives.

Once committed to battle, there was no further room for hesitation, for meditating, except for what little you could arrange in advance over a damp chart; and advance arrangements, like those that preceded an aborted wedding, couldn't be depended on.

Prince considered the PBY's dismal findings. Nine Jap destroyers added to the pair that was herding the convoy made eleven, each armed with the vaunted Nipponese type 93, model 1 torpedoes, which had rightly been nicknamed "Long Lances" by Americans who had encountered them: fast, hot-running, deadly accurate. Naval intelligence documents averred that these torpedoes could travel at almost fifty knots over an incredible distance of ten miles. Oxygen-fueled, they carried a half ton of high explosive, twice the payload of the whimsically unreliable U.S. Mark XV fish.

He opened his tired eyes.

"There's still an hour remaining," Prince said. "We'll ask Surabaya for instructions."

But Fleet headquarters, from its privileged sanctuary 500 miles away, was just as implacable as the Beaver. The word returned quickly. "Attack." That was all the Old Man said. Period. Over and out. With neither invocation nor benediction. For a split-second Prince actually hated the admiral for abandoning him to this disastrous predicament, which should have been so clear to as wise and high-placed a personage as Cinc-Asiatic.

Nevertheless he flashed the curt order to *McGraw* and *Vincent*, which were following the flagship in close formation. Then he told Rodney to have *Davidson*'s lone pharmacist's mate, who was more used to doling out anti-venereal prophylactics than binding up wounds, to set up his surgical shop in the officers' wardroom, with Bream and Marcus as his assistants. At this juncture, both the yeoman and the former GHQ seaman-driver were excess baggage, grudgingly available for such unfamiliar extra duty.

Morphine syrettes were distributed to all hands, for self-administration in the event a man was wounded, unable to obtain prompt medical assistance and suffering intolerable pain.

By 0230 DesDiv 11 had achieved a bone-jarring twenty-nine knots. In the clearing weather, with the moonglow once more a bright reality, their rooster-tail wakes boiled five feet high. Periodically, an engine-room slavey would pop out of the tiny circular hatch which led to the inferno below for a snatch of fresh air.

Beside Prince's swivel chair, the chief quartermaster was steering a plumb-line, straight-on course, his gaze divided between the luminous binnacle whose needle pointed to a steady 210 degrees and the darkness ahead. *Davidson* had no gyro-compass, which would have mechanically compensated for the stress of wind and current, so the CQM had to conduct his navigation with what was known as "seaman's eye," an amalgam of inherent skill, intuition and feel, which only the best helmsmen ever attained.

Prince offered up a silent prayer of thanks for the graying

chief's know-how. He himself, he realized, couldn't have kept *Davidson* on such a course if his worthless life depended on it. Which was also ironic, Prince thought, since the CQM's perfection at the wheel was manifestly cutting down the elapsed time before these three antique tin cans would fire their guns at an enemy for the first—and perhaps only—occasion in their long, uneventful careers.

At 0245 Prince ordered General Quarters.

For a few moments *Davidson* seemed to be in the throes of utter confusion as the klaxon goose-honked the alarm. But it was an ordered confusion. During the flagship's dwindling days of peace, the late Lieutenant Commander Thornburg had trained his crew thoroughly. Now each specialist bent to the task assigned him in businesslike fashion, training torpedo tubes outboard, elevating the main battery to its ultimate forty-five degrees for maximum range, removing the canvas covers from the muzzles of the four-inch rifles and the protective shields from the torpedo directors, making certain that bullet clips were emplaced in the AA guns, donning life jackets, rechecking the red and green levers of the depth charges in case the Japs' formidable armada included submarines.

The condemned man, Prince thought grimly, has now eaten his hearty breakfast, belly-filling but hardly a meal to be relished.

There would be a torpedo run against the enemy, who, he hoped without much conviction, might yet be caught unawares. This was a tricky affair. DesDiv 11 had drilled endlessly in night operations, but always against targets that didn't shoot back. He recalled an academic discussion at Newport, during his placidly enjoyable War College days, about how long a destroyer might survive in a night engagement. Something less than an eager bride's virginity, the coolly efficient tutor had said: perhaps ten minutes, if you really pressed the assault against an overwhelming force. For that was the destroyer's role,

187

to be expendable as a maidenhead, so that the Big Boys thundering a few miles behind them could finish off the job with relative ease, thanks to their eight- and sixteen-inch rifles.

After a hurried powwow with the Beaver, Prince read over the radiotelephone his final mandate to *McGraw* and *Vincent* at 0250. The phraseology was the Briton's, and so was the spirit, although Prince was privately gratified that his own voice rang out with such authority, however spurious, as he dictated the words into the mike.

"We will make a torpedo attack on the Nip transports disregarding enemy warships. Withhold gunfire until all fish are expended. Push attack to utmost. After engagement proceed to rendezvous point Able, which is latitude three degrees south, one hundred eighteen degrees east. Godspeed you and the damned torpedoes."

Just under the horizon, Balikpapan was a mass of flame that flared against the western night sky like a demoniac pyrotechnic display. The doughty Resident had done his job well, making sure that the oilfield and refineries destruction was complete. The old Hudson bombers and Brewster fighters out of Surabaya struck shortly after dark. From the onrushing DesDiv 11's bridges one thing was certain: the great clots of oily fire along the waterfront would create a splendid backdrop to the drama which was about to ensue. The Americans could slip in from the enemy's blind side and make their initial run against the sharply silhouetted transports, an advantage which neither Prince nor the Beaver had anticipated.

With less than twenty minutes remaining before they reached their objective, all was in readiness. Jungle-survival gear had been distributed, in the event *Davidson*'s demise occurred close enough to shore for her crew to swim to dry land. There'd be a hellishly tough jungle hike for those who made it, a couple of hundred miles to the lower end of Borneo, where they might safely signal for seaborne help. The Beaver, who professed to have some expertise in such matters, recommended that each officer carry a supply of fish hooks and lines, quinine pills, razor blades, a pocket compass and sheath knife.

Almost gaily, like actors readying themselves for a grand entrance at stage center, they complied. Only Prince demurred.

"I feel," he said, after they had arranged the gear in their pockets and waistbands, "like a goddamned idiot. It's so frigging futile."

"Maybe," said the Beaver. "But it could also save our bloody asses. We'll still be in command. And this silly impedimenta is for the crew's use, too. Remember? Officers look after their subordinates. Your Book, old chap, ordains it the same as ours."

"Very well."

Prince turned to observe the rapidly approaching coastline through his night glasses. The stench of burning crude oil was pervasive, snuffing out even the abnormal smells of the overheated destroyer's engines as the shore breeze carried the fumes to them from fifteen miles away.

Suddenly the crow's-nest lookout bellowed a warning.

"Enemy ship eight degrees to port, distance four thousand yards." A pause, then the lookout appended an unauthorized comment: "And she's a godawful big bastard, too!"

Even as he spoke, the Japanese vessel, which Prince guessed to be the cruiser flagship *Naga*, flashed a green-blinkered challenge.

"Change course a shade to starboard," advised the Beaver, "and ignore the blighter."

"That's what I had in mind," Prince replied stiffly.

But the helmsman, still true to his instinct while listening to his commander's talk, had already swung *Davidson*'s wheel hard right. The rest of the division followed dutifully in her moonlit wake. The Jap vanished into the void without pursuing his inquiry.

Moments later the division burst through the thickening

smoke pall, less than five miles from the harbor entrance, to find the entire array of enemy transports and supply ships anchored fore and aft, like decoys tethered near a duck blind.

"Holy Mother of God," breathed the Beaver. "What absolutely smashing luck."

All of DesDiv 11's rehearsals had been based on runs against a fast-moving foe. This was too good to be true. Yet there they lay, at least a dozen vulnerable Nip vessels, waiting to be bagged.

DesDiv 11 drove at a slight angle toward the outboard line of supply vessels, four in all, with torpedo batteries trained to starboard: eighteen individual fish ready in their cosmolined mounts, awaiting the crisp order from each ship's gunnery officer to launch.

In the van, *Davidson* was the first to let fly. Brute Savage, astride the controls, fired a spread of three as the flagship tore past the nearest target. None of the torpedoes connected, because of the tremendous speed at which *Davidson* was traveling and the inordinately close range. Savage had six seconds to compute his fix. That wasn't enough.

So the Beaver brought the four-piper a fraction to port, gave Savage a few more seconds to re-estimate the range, which by now had closed to less than 1,000 yards, and *Davidson* unleashed another three fish. The result was still negative.

Aft, *McGraw* and *Vincent* had joined the melée. Something exploded in the murk as *McGraw*'s initial spread found its mark. It was a splendid blast that must have caught the Jap in her ammo-laden hold.

By now, though, DesDiv 11 had passed beyond the moored vessels. Prince ordered a quick reverse course that would take his trio between the double line of enemy ships on their return sweep.

"Where are the goddamned Nip tin cans?" he demanded of nobody in particular.

The Beaver shrugged. "All bollixed up, I assume. Maybe they figured us for a pack of subs."

That seemed to be the most logical answer. In the alternate incandescence of the burning supply vessel and the darkness that fell abruptly whenever a cloud of oil smoke from the shoreside fires engulfed them, those few who realized the truth—that they were under attack by Yank destroyers—began shooting at random. More often than not, their shells struck their own ships.

To compound the enemy's egregious error, the Nip admiral took his full squadron of destroyers, any one of which would have been more than a match for a DesDiv 11 four-piper, back out into Makassar Strait. He was among those convinced that the mysterious assault came from submarines. He wanted to find these triply accursed Americans and sink them before they destroyed his entire amphibious fleet.

As they traversed the narrow aisle between the hapless Japs, *Davidson, McGraw* and *Vincent* began expending their limited remaining torpedoes with more finesse, greater deliberation.

Davidson's third spread was successful. Her victim was so close that the concussive back-blast from the exploding fish left the dozen officers and men on the flagship's bridge momentarily stunned and almost blinded.

When he could see again, Prince looked back. *McGraw* and *Vincent* were launching their torpedoes both to port and starboard, with extraordinary results. In the chaos surrounding them, the precise nature of their targets was impossible to ascertain, for weaving amongst the larger Jap ships were the subchasers, left behind by the bemused admiral as he led his destroyers seaward.

By the time DesDiv 11 finished its march through the crazily milling enemy, Prince had counted four more explosions, which he would eventually list as transports or supply vessels, for a total of six. A half dozen smaller blasts, he concluded, spelled the demise of the Jap patrol craft.

Now came the moment for gunfire. With all their torpedoes gone, the three destroyers again reversed course and cruised swiftly along the ragged offshore row of battered enemy ships, aiming at targets of opportunity. How much damage this inflicted, Prince could only guess. But he planned to compose an impressive score when, as and if DesDiv 11 managed to escape southward after the incredible adventure ended.

It occurred to him, then, that they were involved in the first U.S. naval battle in the Far East during this century. Admiral Dewey had last engaged the foe at Manila forty-four years earlier.

In the excitement, with each unit of DesDiv 11 operating on her own, the established game of follow-the-leader was out of the question. *Davidson* hauled northeastward, *McGraw* started due east. And *Vincent*, bringing up the rear, had lost all track of her consorts and was heading south. Security forbade use of the TBS. So the three ships continued to scatter, aware that the bemused Japanese admiral would sooner or later come to his senses and race back to seek whatever revenge he could upon the audacious Americans.

Buoyed up, elated beyond his wildest imaginings, Prince ordered one last pass at the enemy, between the inboard line and Balikpapan itself. For once the Beaver urged caution. But Prince ignored his counsel.

"We've got to head south to regroup at dawn," he argued, springing off his chair. "Might as well have a final fling at these friggers. It'll be like swatting flies."

"Your baby," acknowledged the Beaver compliantly. "Just thought we'd reached the end of our string. No torpedoes left. Just popguns."

So *Davidson* resumed the charge, her four-inch rifles blasting away at dark shapes which loomed up intermittently in the murk, and all the while rattling along at twenty-five knots. She was dangerously close to shore when the Beaver ordered an abrupt ninety-degree course to port. The unexpected swerve tumbled Prince to the slippery deck, at almost the same instant that a Jap shell struck her, by the extremest of lucky chances, near the bow. When Prince struggled to his feet, sputtering angrily, he found that three members of the No. 1 gun crew had been wounded. None was badly hurt; but, as they later discovered, these were the only DesDiv 11 casualties sustained during the whole extraordinary encounter.

Nonetheless, the random enemy shot touched off a series of minor fires around the exposed weapon, which began charring the .30-caliber machine-gun ammo boxes. These were quickly heaved overboard and the injured men carried below for the tender ministrations of the pharmacist's mate and his two amateurish assistants. Called topside for the emergency, Ensign Blue extinguished the fires promptly before serious damage was done.

Main battery No. 1 was ready for action again. But its own supply of four-inch shells stood at a dangerously low ebb.

From the initial sighting until *Davidson,* playing it alone, undertook her final run past the disorganized enemy file, DesDiv 11 had been in action less than an hour. In his super-euphoric condition, Prince found himself whistling to the accompaniment of the flagship's engine-room blowers, which created a high, plaintive whine in the soft night breeze, as Slats Slattery squeezed out the last ounce of steam he could from the overburdened boilers. It was no longer a question of safety. The commander wanted speed, and by God he'd get it—maybe thirty knots—even if it meant sending *Davidson* sky-high at her own suicidal hands.

By 0410, after working over a Jap transport at the nether end of the raddled formation, and having received news from Lieutenant Hagen that they had about reached the potato-throwing stage of their ammo supplies, Prince reluctantly ordered the unequal duel broken off.

"Ease her down to twenty knots," he told Slattery through the voice tube. To the Beaver he said, "We'll head southwest and join the rest of the division at Point Able around dawn."

This pre-selected rendezvous lay more than three quarters of the way down Makassar Strait. Here they were scheduled to pick up DesDiv 10, in the event that further combined operations against the Japs were indicated. It was some 380 miles north of the latter's temporary home port of Sumbawa, in the Lesser Sunda Islands. Between Point Able and the Sundas stretched the eastern reaches of the Java Sea, soon to become one of the most tragic battle arenas of modern naval history.

DesDiv 11 had chalked up a substantial tactical victory, Prince knew, although he was sanguine enough to realize that, at best, it could only be considered a brief holding action. For the enemy, stung by the impertinent Americans, would surely regroup in short order and proceed as planned against the ABDA forces guarding the mythical Malay Barrier.

Moreover, despite the havoc wrought among its amphibious attackers, Balikpapan had not been saved. The burned-out city would be occupied at daybreak, about the time the two destroyer divisions made contact. Later, when he'd had a chance to confer with Lieutenant Commanders Koch and Horton, Prince would officially report to the Old Man that six Nip vessels were struck by one or more torpedoes, that a number of others were undoubtedly hit, although these strikes went unobserved in the confusion of the moment, and that "all these torpedoed Japanese ships were so seriously damaged as to conclude they must be counted as total losses."

It could reasonably be assumed that nine Nip vessels, including at least one destroyer, went down that night, he opined.

Prince added jubilantly that the surface gun crews "could hardly restrain themselves for the final torpedoes to be expended so they could take a hand in the proceedings." They had, he noted, been eager for the opportunity to lash back at an enemy whom they had only seen from the skies, and whose aerial bombs had been forced meekly to absorb without retaliating to any degree of real effectiveness.

The Beaver was somewhat less optimistic, suggesting that Prince scale down his estimate. "My experience has been," he said, "that a good rule of thumb is to cut in half whatever you figure you've scored, after the excitement wears off next day."

But Prince was adamant. They'd seen what happened. The statistics would stand. And so they did—until six years had passed, the war was over, and interviews with the erstwhile enemy made it plain that the actual Japanese losses were four transports out of the original sixteen (not counting those sunk by the U.S. submarine and the Catalina flying boats), one small-ish patrol craft eliminated and a handful of other ships left injured but in repairable condition.

Yet DesDiv 11 was now, as the Beaver proclaimed in his foghorn voice, properly blooded and even a little bloodied.

Davidson's off-duty officers, too exhausted despite their exhilaration to enjoy the powdered eggs and bacon prepared for them by the almost comatose wardroom cook, raised their coffee mugs in a toast to Prince and the Beaver.

"To our new commanders!"

Prince responded graciously: "Thank you, gentlemen. And now back to work. We're not out of the goddamned woods yet."

For the remaining fifty minutes before first light, *Davidson* fled along her assigned course. All hands kept anxious watch astern, whence the Jap reconnaissance planes would doubtless come in search of the Yankee marauders. Prince held his ship at General Quarters, guns manned, their crews fed in hasty shifts from the bountiful soup cauldron that bubbled in the deckhouse galley between the destroyer's towering pair of forward and after stacks.

But the enemy never came.

"Nursing their wounds," said the Beaver. "Or doing what we did originally, looking for us where we aren't."

195

Prince grumbled, "You could've gone all night without bringing that up, you cynical bastard."

"Terribly sorry." The Beaver grinned evilly. "It just slipped out." His grin widened. "Hell, old cock, that small error, which I can readily understand, doesn't hold a ruddy candle alongside the abysmally bad judgment which our noble friend, the Nip admiral, displayed. He's got to be the stupidest flag officer since old Rojdestvensky lost the Russian imperial fleet to Togo at Tsushima in nineteen-five."

"Togo was a Jap, too," Prince pointed out.

"Which simply shows, my friend, how times can change. But let's not count on all of the Mikado's admirals being this inept."

At 0515 they sighted *McGraw* and *Vincent*. Ten minutes later DesDiv 10 hove into view, each of her four destroyers flying "Well Done!" hoists at their signal yardarms.

From *McGraw* came a brief question on the TBS. Koch wanted to know what was he supposed to do with Lieutenant Commander van Dekker, the Dutch liaison officer, who had become extremely restive—and who seemed to think that, somehow, he'd let his side down by not swimming ashore at Balikpapan to take it on the chin with the rest of his compatriots.

"Inform Mr. van Dekker," said Prince, "that whither we go, he goeth. Over and out."

The *whither* message wasn't long in coming. CincAsiatic's instruction arrived as the ships' gongs tolled four bells, at the stroke of 0600.

"DesDivs 10 and 11 proceed immediately with *Marblehead* to Surabaya. For ComDesDiv 11 our heartiest congratulations for a splendid night's work."

Prince made a mental note to file a copy of this missive with his personal papers. It would make fine postwar reading for his children, if he ever had any, and it bolstered his already inflated ego to the bursting point. Suddenly he felt invincible, indomitable, perhaps even immortal, the commander of ships that couldn't be sunk, which would sail on and on forever, to victories that would live in naval annals for all time.

But this soaring mood passed almost as quickly as it had come upon him, leaving in its stead a curious sense of depression. Because Prince was aware that the battle from which he had emerged so gloriously was a freakish thing, a happenstance, which might never be duplicated. He had been terrified at first, when the attack began; then, caught up in the headiness of unmistakable victory, he had felt brave as a mating lion.

And now he knew that he was not brave at all.

7

"A Job Remains to Be Undone"

SLOWLY, IN PRECISE FORMATION, the two destroyer divisions entered the narrowing waters that stretched between the shelter of Madura Island and Java's northeast seacoast, at the western end of which sprawled Surabaya, the imperfect Dutch equivalent of the great British naval base of Singapore. It was 400 statute miles from the Netherlands East Indies' capital of Batavia. But it might as well have been a million. Each city, under the mounting Japanese threat, was on its own now, save for whatever air support might be exchanged, which was a paltry minimum at best, even when you threw in the defenses of other inland provincial centers like Bandung and Djokjakarta.

DesDiv 11 paced the small sea parade.

For Prince, as DesDiv 10's commander had graciously signaled, deserved this honor, owing to his accomplishments at Balikpapan. *Davidson* would be the only ship to dock, to receive whatever official welcoming was planned, thence proceeding to the fitting yard to have her minor wounds healed. The other six four-pipers would remain anchored in mid-harbor, awaiting orders, while their skippers came ashore by whaleboat.

Close abaft a huffing little escort tug, DesDiv 11 led the Americans through the Dutch-strewn minefield toward Surabaya harbor. From his place on *Davidson*'s port bridge wing, glasses trained on the approaching wharfing site, Prince could perceive a white-uniformed line-up and the glint of tropical sunlight off the polished instruments of a brass band. As they drew nearer, he saw that the Old Man himself was there, standing aloof from the others of his staff, holding something small and boxlike in his right hand.

It was early morning, no later than 0700. They had fled southward during the dark hours, so as to navigate the lozenge-shaped Maduran Strait just before dawn light, thus minimizing the chances of any possible Nip aerial assault. Such an attack, although very much in the tactical cards, hadn't as yet been attempted by the enemy, who seemed content to consolidate each new conquest before he struck again, like a python leisurely ingesting a swallowed piglet in the hot jungle sun. The Japs were maddeningly deliberate. This calculated disregard for firebrand action only served to heighten ABDA's apprehensions as January waned. The enemy ruled both sides of the South China Sea, from Malaya to Borneo; and now he indisputably controlled Makassar Strait, far to the west, below the virtually occupied Philippines.

Therefore the Japanese possessed the keys to all three gateways to the Java Sea, which would become the final battleground in defense of the Malay Barrier.

The Beaver unobtrusively retired to the opposite wing of the twenty-four-foot-wide navigation bridge from where Prince stood vigil, to let Lieutenant Rodney handle the delicate business of warping *Davidson* alongside the pier. It would be more appropriate, he felt, for a Yank exec to be seen publicly in charge of the maneuver rather than an upstart Britisher. For whatever reason, his own solitude, or some unexpressed knowledge that berthing a 314-foot destroyer in strange waters was beyond his staff-trained expertise, Prince hadn't offered to take a hand in the proceedings.

While the mooring lines were still being passed from dock to ship, the band launched into "Anchors Aweigh." The welcoming party moved closer.

As soon as the hawsers were made fast and the cleated gangway swung into place, Prince strode through a small knot of *Davidson*'s officers, who stood aside respectfully while he left the quarter-deck. They allowed him ample time to descend before they followed him ashore.

Prince saluted the Old Man smartly.

The admiral permitted himself one of his infrequent frosty smiles. "That was a pretty damned good show at Balikpapan," he said.

"We might have done better," Prince admitted candidly. "But it was a question of losing everything and not accomplishing much more than we did if we hung around."

"I know," said the admiral. "You had no choice."

Prince cast the Old Man a sharp glance, to discern whether he was being quietly sarcastic. But this didn't seem to be the case. The admiral had accepted the facts of life as they existed: three destroyers, confronted by an overwhelming Jap force, withdrawing after they'd achieved all they could within their limited abilities. So here they were, *Davidson, McGraw* and *Vincent,* the former slightly mauled, yet ready for another go at the enemy. When you weighed the alternative—a suicidal stand by DesDiv 11 which wouldn't have forestalled the inevitable loss of Balikpapan anyhow—Prince's decision to pull out was eminently reasonable. Besides, the Old Man was never one to weep futile tears over spilled milk. He could get mad as Hades, and you'd better not overturn your glass more than once. But if the action taken had provable logic behind it, he would back you to the everlasting hilt.

The chief of staff ambled up. He introduced a number of

British, Dutch and Aussie brass to Prince and the Beaver, while the junior officers from *Davidson* and those of the ABDA staff commingled briefly.

At length the boats from the other destroyers were piped alongside the gangways. Lieutenant Commanders Perry, Koch and Naylor emerged first above the scarred timbers of the main wharf. After them came the commander and the captains of DesDiv 10, who were still courteously deferring to the heroes of the hour.

The Old Man's new personal aide, who turned out to be Pokey Benson, whispered to Prince: "Line up your skippers. The Boss has some nice little baubles for you buckaroos."

"Right," said Prince, beckoning to Koch and Broad Tail.

Ramrod straight, they stood before the admiral while he made his presentations. To Commander Custis H. M. Prince, USN, went the Silver Star for extraordinary gallantry in ordering his badly outnumbered force against a vastly superior enemy, thereby sinking at least six transports, possibly sinking one destroyer and seriously damaging an undetermined number of other Japanese vessels. All this, the citation read, being above and beyond the call of duty, as well as in the finest tradition of the naval service.

As the Old Man pinned the medal to Prince's shirt front he muttered, "You've passed your first test, young fella. But there's a damned sight worse to come."

"Yes, sir." Prince assumed his best straightforward look, taking extra care to shake the Old Man's gnarled hand with unusual firmness. "I understand." He did, too, and the knowledge that he understood the admiral's stark implications proved highly unsettling as he stepped aside for the other honorees.

Lieutenant Commanders Perry Koch and Horton Naylor received Bronze Stars for having pressed home a successful attack as commanding officers of DesDiv 11, their conduct also being above and beyond, etc., etc., etc.

The admiral told Prince: "You can have today off, Commander, while our people take over *Davidson* for repairs. I expect her back on the line within twenty-four hours."

"Yes, sir."

Pokey Benson moved in. "Normally we'd put you up at the Oranje Hotel, which is the best in town, although that's not saying much. But the Oranje's overflowing with high-class refugees. So we've found a spot for you at the Dutch officers' club, which is worse."

"After the last few weeks," said Prince, "anything sounds good."

"As for you, Commander Monk . . ." Benson turned to the Beaver.

"Don't worry about me," the Briton said. "I've got a dozen matters to attend to. And I'm sure one of my beloved countrymen will be delighted to shelter me, until we see what's what about my future."

Pokey seemed relieved. "Good. At any event, the boss wants both of you to attend the Fleet staff meeting at oh-eight-hundred tomorrow here at the base." He gave Prince a meaningful look. "That's eight bells, friend, right on the proboscis."

"I read you," said Prince, "loud and clear."

Prince slept a full ten hours in his room at the scrofulous O.C. When he finally shook himself awake, he lay for a while on the mildewed sheets, his left leg astride the cotton-shrouded bolster that was supposed to make it easier to capture a bit of nonexistent cool air and thus ease the nocturnal sweating. This fat, round, elongated pillow was called a Dutch wife. It felt like one, or, at any rate, as Prince imagined a Dutch wife would feel, lying supine and compliant, awaiting her *mahn's* pleasure.

He looked at his wrist watch. Damned near seven o'clock. The tropical sunset had almost run its swift course. The room was losing some of its barren ugliness as twilight waned.

Sometime during his lengthy slumber a Javanese servant had brought two green bottles of Heineken's, which he had placed on a cigarette-burned table near the bed. There was a glass but no opener. Prince exited through a gap in the mosquito netting and fumbled in the pockets of his trousers, which he had flung with unwonted carelessness over the back of the room's solitary straight chair. He found a stray Philippine peso. This he placed on the table, allowing it to protrude slightly over the side; then, holding the coin firmly flat with his left hand, he opened one of the bottles by thrusting the cap hard against the exposed edge of the dollar-sized peso. It was a neat trick, which he'd learned from the Beaver after many unsuccessful tries and at the expense of several bruised fingers.

The Heineken's was warm. But it tasted rich and good, and it partially slaked a thirst which, when he had first come alive, seemed unquenchable.

Bottle in hand, Prince walked across to the open window. The rattan blinds had been raised. Through the gloom, past the alley which ran beside his room, he could glimpse the outlines of the city and see the dim blue lights of the few motorized vehicles that were allowed to travel after dark. They appeared to be military or governmental rather than civilian. It was highly unlikely that the taxicabs would be permitted abroad at night, a circumstance that further complicated the prospects of his establishing a rendezvous with Saskia, even if he could find her.

Ruminatively, he rubbed a hand across his chin and felt the day's growth of beard stubble. At the very least he might as well start with a morale-boosting shave, he thought, turning back toward the table where the Javanese houseboy had also deposited a candle for critical emergencies. Twice, as he hacked away at his face in the flickering light of the small taper, which gave him a ghostly image in the cracked mirror, he managed to cut himself, on the right cheek and beneath his chin. He stanched the flow of blood with bits of grayish toilet paper, remembering as he did so an adage he'd picked up during a prewar cruise: the harder a nation's currency, the softer its bathroom tissue. Quite plainly, the Netherlands East Indies' finances were in terrible shape.

There was no shower. A waist-high cistern, filled with brackish water, with a tin scoop floating on its surface, provided the sole facilities. So Prince took an unsatisfactory sluice bath, which neither cleaned nor cooled him. Afterward he dried himself as best he could with a moldy towel and anointed his heat-rashed body with after-shave cologne. It stung like hell. But it also provided a base for the baby talc that would give him a few glorious moments of relief.

Then Prince leisurely dressed and strolled through the club compound to the mosquelike main foyer. Several officers, some American, British and Australian, were lolling about in wicker chairs, quaffing beer while they idly slapped at mosquitoes. Dinner wouldn't be served for another half hour, he was told by the inevitably white-clad Javanese dragoman who presided behind the reception desk.

"I don't believe I'll be eating here," said Prince. "What I'm really looking for is information about a girl I know. She came from Balikpapan a couple of weeks ago."

The dragoman shrugged blade-thin shoulders. "Many females have come to Surabaya from many places. White ones. Chinese. Javanese women from the countryside. It would be difficult to find any special one, I think." His obsidian eyes glistened. "But if you wish a girl, *overste,* certain arrangements can be made . . ."

"No thanks," Prince said. "Not yet, anyhow."

He ordered up a beer and joined the listless group on the mosaic-tiled patio. This was the first real opportunity he'd had to inspect the club's commons room. It had inverted U-shaped archways, and its ceiling boasted a concentric circled decor composed of strange naked goddesses strolling hand in hand, surrounded by fat cherubims. Corrugated tin eaves, like those of a Victorian railway station, caught the slatting rain that arrived, also like a faithful Victorian train, regularly at noon each day. From the thirty-foot-high salon extended dark passageways, with waist-high teak paneling, smelling of sweat and mildew like a tanktown YMCA. These led to the interior rooms, which were deemed somewhat less desirable than the outdoor cottage complexes. A romantic might have regarded the club as derivative Maugham, although just beyond it loomed the oddly naval architecture of Surabaya that featured buildings with superstructures, bridges, funnels and parapets, remindful of old-fashioned dreadnaughts.

Most of the talk around him ran to the dire shortages which confronted those unfortunate enough to be condemned to this benighted hole.

"God help the friggin Japs if they ever bomb the brewery," somebody drawled. "Then it'll be time to end this bloody fracas."

Prince noticed that one of the red-faced Aussies, a lieutenant commander, was grinning at him. He smiled back in comradely fashion.

"You must've been caught up in a fair dinkum scrap, mate."

Prince suddenly remembered that he'd forgotten to remove the toilet paper from his cuts. "These," he explained, "are honorable wounds, acquired while shaving by candlelight."

The Aussie nodded. "Occupational hazard hereabouts. You'll soon enough master the technique. Or maybe grow a beard."

"My outfit already has one fellow with a full beard," said Prince. "Two could be rather confusing."

The Aussie leaned over confidentially. "I overheard your little confab with the boy just now. This girl you're questing after, is she the social type?"

"Sort of. Her cousin was the Dutch naval liaison officer with our destroyer division, and her father's in civil service."

"In that event," the Aussie said, "I'd suggest you give the Simpanische Societeit a bit of surveillance. It's a private club.

But they allow us guest privileges. What remains of Surabaya's upper crust usually hangs out there, although the food isn't much better than the swill they serve here." He took a long pull at his Heineken's. "Personally, I can't stand the bloody trap. But you might find your dolly at the Simp. Turn left as you leave. It's only a block down the main drag."

"Thanks."

Prince finished his beer and went out into the partially moon-lit evening. As he neared the club, which sat well back from the street beneath a grove of magnolias, he could hear a stringed orchestra playing "My Blue Heaven." Not well. But considerably better than the Balikpapan Residency's pick-up ensemble had been able to cope with similar Yankee tunes.

A portly Dutch doorman greeted him at the massive entrance.

"Your name, sir?"

"I'm Commander Prince—"

The doorman interrupted: "Ah, the destroyer hero. I read about you in this afternoon's paper. We are deeply honored." He stood aside. "Please come in, Commander, and I shall intro-duce you to our president."

"Dank U," Prince replied, demonstrating his gratitude for this recognition of his celebrity status by doling out one of the few Dutch phrases he'd picked up in Balikpapan.

In its heyday, as recently as two months before, Simpanische Societeit had been an elegant Victorian palace where the women wore their best gowns, the military their miniature medals on the breast pockets of dinner jackets and the diplomats their crimson shirt sashes. Now it was a social hodgepodge. With some reluctance, its members had voted to permit the temporary intrusion of foreign officers of field grade or above—that is, army majors and naval lieutenant commanders. This none too welcome influx had succeeded in draining off most of the club's supply of potables, to the point where the Simp (as the irreverent newcomers dubbed it) was reduced to ordinary beer, like any common tavern, and a severely rationed amount of Bols gin.

Because of his unexpected fame, Prince was accorded the full guest-of-the-house treatment, which meant, as at Balikpapan on the night he'd met Saskia, a never-ending succession of pink gin cuplets passed along to him by native waiters, while the Dutch stood by, eagerly attending his every word.

Prince had quickly determined that Saskia wasn't there, although a portly man in a white dinner jacket said he knew her father and would relay the information that the commander was most anxious to renew this charming acquaintanceship. If Prince were fortunate, the lovely *juffrouw* might arrive at the club well before closing time. The white dinner-jacketed Samaritan had a car, an after-dark permit, and a driver. He would send his chauffeur to pick her up.

Saskia arrived a half hour later, escorted through the social club's diverse array of drinkers, diners and talkers by the maestro in the white tuxedo jacket. He delivered her to Prince in the manner of an entrepreneur who had just concluded a million-dollar deal, proudly, with tremendous *éclat*. A table had been especially reserved for the commander and his lady, he announced, and the very best that the establishment's depleted larder could provide was theirs for the asking.

"I would have been here sooner," Saskia explained, "but this happened so suddenly that I was not—how you say?—quite presentable. Besides," she added, "the driver went first to the apartment which had been assigned to my parents. I do not live with them."

"Why?" Prince asked.

"It was already overcrowded, this apartment, so I preferred to join the other single girls from Balikpapan in a dormitory on the other side of town. We are engaged in defense activities, at the hospitals, the factories where bullets are made, or even learning to use firearms. A bus picks us up each morning."

"What is your particular job?"

"Firearms."

Prince scrutinized her across the table. Despite Saskia's deceptive plumpness, which betrayed the baby-fat look of a Sonya Henie, she had a daintiness, a delicate air, which made it impossible for him to imagine her aiming a rifle with intent to kill. Yet he saw a toughness in her blue eyes that he had not observed before, and the small palm held clasped in his was unmistakably callused.

"You're not kidding," he said admiringly. "It's for real."

"Yes, Prince. For real, just as what you are doing is both genuine and very deadly."

"But tonight we'll resist our military impulses, right?"

He could see Saskia's dimpled cheeks turn a degree pinker in the candlelight. "My impulses with you," she whispered, "are never military."

"There might be only tonight," he said. "My ship took a hit at Balikpapan. But they'll have her repaired tomorrow. Then it's back to business."

"Where are you staying, Prince?"

He told her. Saskia laughed softly. "Cousin van Dekker is also there. He complains bitterly about its lack of ambience."

"It's no palace. But my stall has a nice, private rear entrance, so I won't have to disturb the front-desk clerk when I return."

"That is good," Saskia said, "because two can be as mouselike as one, can they not?"

His grip tightened on her hand. "You'll come?"

"Of course. You didn't think that I merely wished to exchange pleasantries at the Simp. This is an exceedingly dull place, filled with dull people, who tend to blame everyone but themselves for what has happened. After we dine, let us go to your . . . 'stall,' didn't you call it?"

"That was pure euphemism," Prince said. "Van Dekker's right. It lacks a certain ambience, which not even three-inch cockroaches or gecko lizards can quite supply."

Halfway to the officers' club, at the intersection of the main street and an alleyway which appeared to lead nowhere, they were delayed by a throng of Javanese gathered around an old man whose trishaw had just been broadsided by a motorcar. The automobile driver paused only long enough to make sure he hadn't killed the small vehicle's owner before he sped away. Tears streaming down his withered face, the old man stared at the battered trishaw, muttering something in his native tongue, mournfully, but without rancor. He continued to sob quietly as he squatted on the curb.

"What did he say?" Prince wanted to know.

Saskia was fumbling in her purse. "He weeps for his broken wheels, for perfection destroyed." She handed the old man a one-guilder note. "Take this," she said, "and have your machine restored to its original perfection. It has not been damaged beyond repair."

The old man accepted the gift hesitantly, as if the bit of paper currency might abruptly vanish in a puff of smoke and Saskia along with it.

"*Dank U zeer,*" he muttered. "The officer's *vrouw* is too kind."

"*Niets te danken.*" Saskia turned to Prince. "He thinks I am your wife."

"Don't disillusion the poor devil. He's got enough trouble already."

The crowd around the shattered trishaw had begun to disperse, except for a few persons who remained behind, helping the old man gather up his cargo, a loosely bundled assortment of sweet potatoes and cassavas.

"What will he do with that mess?" Prince asked.

"His friends will carry the melons and the potatoes to his home," Saskia said, "if he has a home. Otherwise he will be taken to a safe place until his trishaw can be fixed. There is a brotherly feeling among the Javanese poor which transcends belief."

Prince took her arm as they stepped across the intersection, which was still wet from the inevitable midday shower.

"Before you came," he remarked, "one of the people at the Simp, a fellow wearing a whole chestful of military ribbons, was talking about how the Javanese were more apt to fight among themselves than for the Dutch."

"You must have been listening to Colonel Heemskerk. He is a retired army officer with some rather definite ideas on many issues, especially politics. He suspects all politicians, and he believes that the Javanese variety is the worst."

"Are they?"

"It's entirely a matter of degree," Saskia replied. "After all, they have more to be political about, haven't they? Freedom, for example . . ."

Prince had expected a sentry challenge when they started down the pathway toward the club's rear cottages. But none came. They entered his room undetected, then paused just inside the door, bodies locked in a taut embrace. Saskia strained against Prince's lean frame, kissing him with openmouthed hunger as his hands clasped her amazing buttocks through the thin silken dress. They released each other reluctantly.

At that tingling instant Prince felt sexually invincible, just as during the climax of the Balikpapan battle he had experienced a kind of immortality which mere shells and torpedoes could never penetrate.

He lit the candle stub on the bedside table. Noticing the lone bottle of Heineken's, he said wryly, "That's all I can offer as a nightcap, dear child."

"I do not need a nightcap," Saskia murmured. She smiled up at him. "But if you have a shower, Prince, that would be most agreeable. Our dormitory lacks certain minor essentials. We wash in bowls filled from pitchers at a muddy well."

Solemnly, carrying the guttering candle, he led her into the bathroom and beckoned toward the cistern.

"That is the shower."

"Heavenly!"

Prince balanced the saucer on the rim of the toilet bowl.

"Should I explain how this do-it-yourself affair works?" Saskia shook her head negatively. "Okay. I'll bug out while you clean up," he said. "Holler when you're through, and I'll show you the rest of the suite."

"That is not what I meant, Prince," she said.

"What do you mean?"

"I wish," Saskia answered without embarrassment, "for you to help me bathe."

"Madam's gentleman-in-waiting is ready," he said, grinning. "Shall we commence by disrobing Her Ladyship?"

"That is customary."

He unzipped her dress and raised it easily over her head. She bent over, released her brassiere, slipped out of her brief panties and kicked her pumps across the dank floor, in the general direction of the bedroom. Naked, shoeless, standing as tall as she could beside him, she was less than shoulder-high to Prince. He noted appreciatively that she was a true blonde, downy as a thrush.

Prince reached for the tin scoop.

"Be careful of my hair," Saskia warned. "My appointment with the coiffeur isn't until next Wednesday."

She uttered a girlish shriek as the water splashed across her shoulders and onto her jutting breasts. But Prince kept pouring, relentless, until she was drenched. Then he took a washcloth and began to soap her meticulously, beginning at the nape of her slender neck, working slowly downward, past her bosom and gently convex belly.

"I think," said Saskia, "that I can finish."

"Madame is displeased with my services?"

"Not at all. You make a splendid lady's maid-in-waiting. But there are certain things I must do for myself."

He gathered up her clothes from the washbasin, where she had casually tossed them, and left the bathroom. By now his own uniform was thoroughly soaked. As best he could, after undressing, he arranged the damp garments over the chair, which he had placed near the unscreened window. He wiped the dust from the sill and laid Saskia's dainty apparel across it. This was, he mused wryly, one hell of a lot different from Gwyneth Dean's perfumed boudoir. The random notion sobered him for an instant. He tried to exorcise from his tired mind any further thoughts of Gwyneth's plight, trapped in Manila, maybe a prisoner of the Japs, subject to Christ only knew what indignities from the sex-hungry soldiery.

Prince was already in bed when Saskia slipped through the mosquito netting like a vagrant ghost. She had used a liberal portion of his after-shave cologne, he noted. Moist, yet surprisingly cool, she crept close to him.

"You may," she said, "cast that damned Dutch wife aside. We shall not be needing her."

Next morning, quite early, the Javanese messboy trotted into the room, skillfully balancing a tray on his fezzed head, on which were arrayed a teapot, two cups and four slices of toast. He seemed unconcerned by Saskia's presence. It was obvious, from the contents of the tray, that he had earlier peered through the blinds, seen her there, before preparing this *petit déjeuner à deux* like a faithful palace retainer.

They ate their modest breakfast in bed, sitting naked in the half-light that filtered through the bamboo slats, and then made love once more.

When they had finished, lying back on the damp sheets, exhausted, replete, Prince glanced at his watch. It was seven-thirty.

"Holy Christ!" He sprang out of the rumpled bed. "I've got

exactly thirty minutes to get dressed, find a cab and make it to the base—before the Old Man flays me alive."

He extracted his last fresh uniform from the seabag and dressed hurriedly. Saskia had made no move to leave the bed. She held out her arms.

"One final kiss, Prince, before you go."

He brushed her lips lightly. "So long, baby."

"Dag," she whispered. *"Tot ziens."*

"What does that mean?"

"Goodbye . . . until the next time."

Prince nodded gravely. "Like *au revoir?"*

"Yes."

He kissed her again, feeling her tongue soft against his, and stood up to leave. A fine cowardly bastard he was, the parfit gentil knyght, hieing himself knavishly back to a war which he hated and feared so much it brought a bitter taste to his mouth, and all the while trying to do it with such panache that nobody, especially those foredoomed females, would ever suspect what really went on behind that goddamned insouciant façade of his.

Then Prince shut the unlockable door noiselessly and left, making a mental memorandum to have something done about his laundry. Judging from the abominable quality of the tea he concocted, the Javanese houseboy might be a damned sight better washing clothes than brewing oolong and pekoe, if Prince were to keep this room for romantic purposes.

The Old Man greeted him with less coolness than Prince had anticipated. In fact, he gave Pokey Benson a mild chewing out for having failed to send a car to the club so that Prince wouldn't have to rely on Surabaya's notoriously inadequate taxicab system. The skippers from both destroyer divisions were already present, seated in a tight half circle near the admiral's desk, with DesDiv 10's commander slightly to the fore. The Beaver, Prince noticed, was positioned among DesDiv 11's contingent. Behind the Old

Man, also in straight-backed chair, were arranged the remnants of the staff he'd brought along from the Philippines.

The admiral acted weary, although his pinkish countenance remained unlined and his pale-blue eyes gleamed as fiercely as ever as he swept his gaze around the assembled officers.

Prince could sense a difference in the atmosphere, too, from the earlier sessions they had held in Manila. No longer existed that forced optimism which had prevailed before the attack. Instead, there was an almost tangible feeling of muted grimness —not despondency, however—in the face of a task that damned well had to be done, or at least attempted. The Old Man epitomized this spirit, with his quietly stern voice and his implacable personal deportment.

"You gentlemen," he said, gesturing from his swivel chair at the destroyer captains and their two leaders, "are newcomers to this mare's nest. Perhaps I'd better bring you up to date on what's happening. Or," he amended dryly, "what *isn't* happening."

DesDiv 10's commander nodded. "We'd appreciate that, sir. We've been pretty well cut off from the outside world."

The admiral gave a derisive chuckle. "We're all cut off from that 'outside world,' Commander Long. That's precisely what I intend to discuss."

"Yes, sir."

What followed, in the Old Man's dry-bone discourse, was a candid appraisal of just where they stood today, in this first week of February, *anno Domini* 1942. The Japs were maddeningly deliberate, as they could well afford to be, landing on undefended beachheads, building their airfields, leisurely regrouping for their strike. As a postwar historian, Samuel Eliot Morison, expressed it years later, the admiral compared the enemy's methods to those of an octopus, which concentrated on strangling many small points instead of expending its total strength on some vital organ of its prey.

Unfortunately, ABDA was an ideal setup for this Nip strategy. The interests of its individual components differed widely, and its haughty commanders were too often heedless of one another's views, like the comic cowpoke who leaped on his horse and rode off in all directions. Yet this was no time for comedy. It was a moment of intense anguish for those who understood the true nature of their problem, as did the Old Man.

Despite their overwhelming superiority, the Japs continued to ease southward gingerly, not yet certain that the Far East had really been abandoned by the Washington brass in favor of an all-out European effort. They remained always intact behind their land-based air cover, or beneath their carrier umbrellas. For their part, the Allies had no carriers and not enough land-based planes to shake loose the enemy's tightening grasp. Thus each new Japanese move was approximately 400 air miles. Even the least brilliant ABDA planner could step off these expectable advances on the charts that hung in the huge, airless map room and estimate with dividers and compass where the next blow would probably fall.

The Old Man's opinion leaned toward a Nip invasion of the southwest tip of Celebes Island, in the vicinity of Makassar Town, and thence into Bali and Timor islands, which hung like diamonds from a necklace, ready for the taking by a light-fingered foe.

But the Dutch, who had seniority and the dubious right of ownership, since this comprised their richest remaining real estate, differed with the admiral. *Nee,* said they, which was an outright No, as flatly intransigent as the Russians' *nyet.* They proposed to waste valuable troops, including an Aussie battalion and some irreplaceable Hudson bombers, on a fruitless adventure to Ambon Island, far to the east, midway between the Molucca and Bandu seas. The Old Man had snorted that the Nips couldn't care less about Ambon right now, although this land spit did lie athwart their easternmost passage to Java. Makassar was the key, the battleground, he insisted.

So ABDA was a nightmare for any orderly minded personnel chart-maker.

The Beaver leaned over and whispered to Prince, "Even the floggin' name sounds like a baby's mewl." Prince acknowledged this sally with a rictus grin worthy of a week-old corpse.

Its domain theoretically extended from Burma to the Philippines. Below ABDA proper stretched the ANZAC (Australia–New Zealand) zone, commanded by an American admiral based in Sydney, who also controlled the sweepings—New Guinea, the Solomons and the Fiji Islands—which seemed much too far away to interest the Japs in the foreseeable future.

Although what remained of his fleet was based at Surabaya, the Old Man spent most of his working hours at Bandung, eighty miles inland from Batavia, coordinating with Field Marshal Sir Archibald Wavell, who was then over-all commander of the whole complex. This supreme GHQ was about 300 miles— slightly less than the magical Jap leapfrog measurement—from the naval base. Prince wondered why the admiral preferred it that way. Probably, he surmised, because the poor guy was aging fast, tired and disillusioned with the never-ending squabbles among his ABDA counterparts.

If *Hakko Ichiu* meant fetching the world's presumed eight corners under one monstrous Japanese roof (Nippon's basic foreign policy since 1931), then ABDA was where the rough-hewn four quarters of the Allied endeavor gathered to argue, plan and endlessly revise their strategy. Always, it had to be accepted, with the uncomfortable awareness that they were, designedly, condemned by those faraway bigwigs in Whitehall, No. 10 Downing Street, the fugitive Dutch royal mansion in London, the White House and the War and Navy Departments in Washington, D.C., to push back the tide. King Canute couldn't do it. Nor could they; and the Old Man damned well knew it.

General Wavell was a consummate gentleman, something of a compromiser, to be sure, a warrior who had tasted defeat. He and Tommy Hart got along splendidly.

But the Royal Netherlands Navy commander, Vice Admiral C. E. L. Helfrich, a plump, bald, surprisingly hard-driving officer, was a constant thorn in the Old Man's leathery side. He also performed as the Indies' Minister of Marine. This gave him a special and rather bothersome civil-service status that he didn't hesitate to flaunt on occasions. The Dutch were inordinately proud of their three light cruisers, seven destroyers and sixteen submarines, which they intended to employ in their own stubborn fashion.

The Americans had scant choice but to state their objections as cogently as possible, then string along when the final decisions were made, usually against their better judgment.

Determined to stop the Japs *before* they could invade Java, Helfrich won Wavell's grudging approval, largely because the British general remembered with gratitude how the Dutch had aided him at Singapore with subs, aircraft and troops which they might well have used elsewhere. Thus began a series of will-o'-the-wisp romps, usually with pick-up forces and no sign on the strategic horizon of the combined armada that the Old Man rated as an imperative if they were to inflict any real damage on the enemy.

Moreover, Hart believed the Indies were already lost, for all practical purposes, and that ABDA should withdraw to Australia. So they compromised by stationing a couple of U.S. tenders at Tjilatjap, halfway up Java's southern coast. There these ships sat at anchor, too far away to be of much immediate use, in a damp, rodential, insect-infested harbor which their crews labeled the crummiest unfrigging port in the whole frigging world.

Helfrich, whenever he was stung by the Old Man's arguments for a better blend of operations, huffily declaimed that his submarines had sunk more Jap shipping since December 7 than the entire American air, surface and undersea effort put together. This was true enough. But the Dutch had enjoyed the privilege of ranging free during December and January, while Hart's pseudo-fleet had to fight alongside MacArthur in the Philippines' lost cause.

After DesDiv 11's vaunted success at Balikpapan, the Dutch admiral chortled that his point was now proved: the enemy *could* be defeated at gunpoint.

The Old Man retorted: "Fine. Why didn't we combine our forces then—and finish the job?"

"It wasn't the appropriate time to put our eggs in one basket," said Helfrich.

"Is it ever?" Hart snapped.

All of which, the Old Man told his staffers and their engrossed destroyermen guests, brought the situation up to date. As a matter of cold fact, this very weekend they would have to make another half-baked try at blocking the Japs with a splintered force, consisting of the heavy cruiser *Zuyder Zee* and the light cruiser *Volendam* under Rear Admiral Jules F. W. G. Kuyper, RNN; the U.S. heavy cruiser *Houston* and an archaic American four-stack light cruiser; plus two four-unit destroyer divisions, one Dutch, one Yank. Why? Because Helfrich had chosen this particular juncture to waste his principal task force in chasing down a fallacious report that the Japs were massing in Karimat Strait, far to the northwest.

Aerial reconnaissance had reported a Nip convoy of twenty transports, three cruisers and several tin cans heading south along the western Celebes coast.

The Old Man agreed that the foe's objective was undoubtedly Makassar Town. But he made no secret of his doubts about sending out a detachment which, at best, barely equaled the Japs in number. Yet he had no choice. "Estimated departure date," he informed his audience, "has been set for midnight

218

Wednesday." He glanced at Prince. "I've designated DesDiv Eleven for our share of the screening job, since you've had the experience. We'll give you *LeBaron* from DesDiv Ten to flesh out your division. Sorry. But it leaves you only twenty-four hours to phase her into your line-up before Kuyper's ETD."

With that, the conference broke up.

When Prince revisited his room at the Dutch officers' club, briefly, to collect his belongings, he found a penciled note from Saskia: "Do not be afraid, my Prince, that I have designs on you, or that I wish to become your *vrouw* or even *dienstmeisje*. Namely, wife or housemaid. But I did launder your soiled linen. It seemed the least I could do in repayment for such a lovely evening." She had scribbled a telephone number as a P.S. "Call me when you can."

The underwear and uniforms were hanging neatly from a line which Saskia had borrowed from the club's stores. They were still damp. But he folded each garment with his usual care and stowed them in his seabag.

At the front desk he told the manager he might be coming back on short notice, so please keep the room in his name.

That, Prince was assured, would be done. Nothing was too good for the brave captain who had so valorously beaten back the enemy. Prince thanked him and crawled back into the moth-eaten sedan which Pokey Benson had, with belated remembrance, provided for his temporary convenience.

"The navy yard," he instructed the driver. "Wherever they've got *Davidson* tied up."

"Aye, aye, sir."

Almost from the outset the venture was a four-star snafu. The only bright spot proved to be *LeBaron*'s ability to blend herself into DesDiv 11's scheme of things. Her skipper, who had been a class behind Prince at the academy, was himself ticketed for divisional command soon, so he made a special effort to comply.

He had just received his third stripe. His name was Roswell Hogg. Everybody called him Piggy, behind his back if they were inferiors, to his face if they were his peers.

Yet Piggy held no vast admiration for Prince, whom he regarded, as did so many others, as a posturer whose professional skills had never been tested on the high seas. True. That affair at Balikpapan looked nice on the record. But Piggy, whose division hadn't arrived in time for the fracas, was beginning to believe some of the malicious gossip that was making the rounds, to the effect that DesDiv 11 could have done a damned sight better if its commander had pressed home the charge with greater vigor.

Admiral Kuyper, an officer with a deserved reputation for bravery, assembled his striking force at Bunda Roads, off Madura, punctually at 0000 hours, with orders to fan out into submarine-evasive formation once they passed the lighthouse at the island's eastern tip.

He voice-messaged his ragtag assemblage, both in English and Dutch: "Enemy transports will be attacked and destroyed in night attack."

Brilliant, thought Prince, as he listened to the orders, and so loftily simple. It was like the Word of the Lord, a mandate from on high, with no options. Not even the customary "good luck" postscript.

The Beaver said, "Confident devil, isn't he?"

Prince grunted, "If confident is the right word."

They were arranged in a diamond-shaped cruising pattern, with Kuyper's flagship, *Zuyder Zee,* in the van and the other three cruisers churning along a half mile apart, with *Volendam* bringing up the rear. Split into pairs, DesDiv 11 watchdogged the flanks of the thin line; the four Dutch destroyers protected the rear, alert for hostile subs. *Davidson* and *McGraw* drew the starboard watch, nearest to any potential foe. Kuyper set a straight route for Makassar Town, slightly north of east, apparently disdainful of the unpleasant fact that his task group would be traversing most of the Java Sea in the bright light of day.

They had advanced less than a third of the way across this dangerously wide-open span when, shortly after 0930, a patrolling American PBY flashed a warning that it had sighted three dozen Japanese bombers headed for Surabaya. These Nells had taken off, radioed the Catalina, from the Nips' fresh-built field at Kendari on the Celebes coast opposite Kuyper's goal. Their mission would mark the first enemy blow at the Dutch naval base. It could also signal the beginning of the end, particularly should Makassar Town, a solid 200 miles closer to Surabaya, be added to the Japs' airfield roster.

Nells were, if anything, more deadly than the Bettys with which DesDiv 11 had jousted a month earlier. Twin-engined, they were flown by Japanese naval pilots, who had more combat expertise and could be expected to press home an attack with more vigor than the Nip army jockeys who rode the less flexible Bettys.

Prince felt that cold familiar visceral queasiness, which indicated that he'd passed his latent fear level and would now have to start fighting back against stark terror. He would lose the struggle, of course, although he must somehow prevent the inner defeat from showing on his jaw-clenched face.

Swallowing hard, Prince stared aft, across *Davidson*'s jumbled deck, toward the fading mountains of Bali and Lombok. They were almost obscured by low-lying cloud masses. But unlike the day he'd lost *Travers,* these clouds were too far away to afford any hope of shelter. The sky was a brazen kiln.

He called for Lieutenant Hagen. The saturnine gunnery officer arrived on the double, wearing his flak helmet, beneath which were visible the inevitable wisps of coppery blond hair.

"Yes, sir?" Hagen's voice was as cool as his bottle-green eyes. Prince envied the man's patent lack of self-concern for the peril that was thundering down upon them. "Any special instructions, Commander?"

Prince shook his head. "No. I just wanted to make sure you've got everything in shape. That's all." He tried a grin. "Admiral Kuyper has issued the same orders I gave last month. It's every ship for herself when the Nells arrive."

"Naturally," said Hagen, turning briskly on his heel to resume his post at the midship gunnery controls. "Anything else?"

"No."

As the eight vessels scattered like marbles kicked by a disgruntled schoolboy, Prince wondered again if this was the proper maneuver. They had discussed such tactics often at War College, calmly, with owlish wisdom based more on pure theory than what scant knowledge the British had been able to contribute from their encounters with Nazi planes. One theoretician, who subsequently was proved correct, suggested that the only solution would be to increase the warships' AA armament by at least thrice the number of guns they presently carried and then hold circular formation intact, much as the pioneers had grouped their covered wagons, for a greater concentration of firepower. But others argued that since this rearming would be a long-drawn-out business, they'd best stick to their singular defense routine, in hopes an aerial enemy would split into smaller, more vulnerable segments.

Besides, the widely separated ships could twist and turn at will, with no danger of collisions.

So much for dead theory.

It was time now for the real thing.

Staring toward the east through his 7 x 50 binoculars, the Beaver sighted them first: thirty-six bombers divided into four echelons of nine each, soaring with meticulous grace at about 15,000 feet. It was evident that their flight commander, upon advice from Kendari, had changed his plans. Kuyper's unprotected squadron was too juicy a morsel to pass up even for a first-time blow at Surabaya—which would be bereft of any significant shipping anyhow, what with Helfrich's units hunting for wild ducks hundreds of miles to the west and the British patrolling the sea lanes to Singapore.

Inside of ten minutes, the Nells launched their bombing runs, impeded only by a quartet of Catalinas that had shadowed them from Celebes Island with more courage than good sense. During their pursuit the PBYs had kept a safe distance. Now they went on the attack, like stiff old collies clumsily charging a pack of young fighting bulldogs. Within minutes, the importunate flying boats were reduced to flaming mid-air debris by the Nells' turret guns, before they could inflict any damage of their own. Prince watched, ashen-faced, as they exploded, one after another, in the azure waters of the Java Sea.

Nine of the Japs suddenly cut away from the leisurely moving flight and boresighted in on *Zuyder Zee* and *Marblehead,* which had led the original formation. Because of their lack of radar and the brevity of the warning, both cruisers were fairly close together. *Marblehead* caught the brunt of the initial assault from the Nells, which had flattened out at less than 14,000 feet, traveling at 150 knots in an elongated V-wedge.

Through his glasses Prince saw dark smoke belching from the American cruiser's four stacks as her captain ordered her six idle boilers lit so that she could exceed the twenty-five knots she was presently turning up. But it would take almost a half hour for the twenty-year-old *Marblehead* to reach her rated speed of thirty-five knots, if indeed she could attain that, considering her befouled bottom and general disrepair after all her tropical months on station.

To his vast surprise, Prince found himself engaged in what had become purely a spectator sport. The enemy, it was plain, had no intention of wasting valuable bombs on the eight agile destroyers when they had these fat, tempting cruisers in their cross-haired sights.

From his unexpectedly safe vantage, Prince tried to picture himself on *Marblehead*'s navigation bridge, which wouldn't be much different than *Davidson*'s, except for its larger size and number of personnel involved. He sought to envision how the cruiser captain would be reacting, to derive a lesson from what he both imagined and actually saw across a mile of strangely untroubled water.

Marblehead had suddenly veered sharply to port, just as the Nells reached the stage where they would most likely drop their eggs, seeking to deflect their aerial salvo before the Japs could adjust to her maneuver. She also stepped up her pace.

The enemy planes zoomed harmlessly overhead. No bombs emerged from their dun-colored bellies.

Once again *Marblehead* swerved, and once again the foiled Japs showed remarkable aplomb by not pulling their triggers.

But on the third pass, perhaps fathoming a method in the cruiser's zigzag pattern, they placed seven bombs alongside her port forequarter. Only seven? Prince had counted the splashes, numbly wondering why the enemy didn't throw everything into the attack. The Nells had descended to 10,000 feet. For one of them this was a fatal error. A lucky shot from one of *Marblehead*'s three-inch AA rifles sent it pinwheeling into the sea, where it blew up like the hapless PBYs. A small victory. But it evoked wild applause from the onlookers who crowded *Davidson*'s bridge and portside.

Then a second Nell was winged by the cruiser's sharpshooting gunners. Spewing flame, it deliberately barreled toward the gyrating target, its pilot grimly intent on crashing amidships in one last burst of *bushido* glory. But a veritable wall of .50-caliber machine-gun fire deflected the Nell, and it, too, careened into the voracious sea.

Marblehead's luck gave out shortly before 1030, after she had lasted through an incredible forty minutes of attack by the nine Jap planes.

Seven more Nells reinforced this less than successful first flight. Disregarding the cruiser's desperate AA barrage, they laid a stick of contact explosive HE bombs neatly across her midsection. Later Prince would learn from those who survived that one of the bombs penetrated the thin deck, gutted the sick bay, the wardroom and half of the nearby officers' country. From his position on *Davidson*'s bridge wing, Prince could see flames erupting through the jagged cavity created by this direct hit. Then another HE bomb, scarcely missing *Marblehead*'s sharp prow, blew in a section of forward plates and caused her to start taking water. The speed at which the stricken cruiser was traveling added to the damage. Within minutes she had begun to lower her proud head, like a sacrificial bull at the end of a hopeless duel with a champion matador.

Prince flinched visibly. But his involuntary gesture went unnoticed. The bullfight simile occurred to him even as *Marblehead* absorbed yet another lethal blow, this time on her stern, which froze her rudder in a hard-left position. Inconsequentially, he recalled having watched such a match in Barcelona years ago, along with a group of midshipmen. It had been a gory, unequal affair, in which the bull never had a chance; but the bloodthirsty crowd had cheered like crazy. Prince left before it was over. Like the naval engagement now under way, bullfighting was a brutal exercise, in his judgment, and one for which he had no stomach.

Listing heavily to starboard, pocked with fires from stem to fantail, *Marblehead* was helplessly drawing tight circles on the gentle surface wavelets. Nonetheless, her captain continued to respond to the departing Nells, who had turned their attention to *Zuyder Zee* in the belief that the American cruiser was mortally wounded and thus unworthy of further assault.

The Dutch flagship's AA weaponry controls were put out of commission when a string of four bombs enfiladed her stack area.

Next came *Houston*'s turn. Her marksmanship, as always, was excellent. Three Nells went down under the heavy cruiser's blasting. But finally, in this uneven contest, she absorbed a direct hit on the broad expanse of her main deck, which demolished the eight-inch after-turret and slaughtered more than fifty men, including the ammo handlers deep in the ship's bowels, who were crisped by the powerful blast.

Still under full steering control, *Houston* moved alongside *Marblehead*.

Prince heard her skipper talking to the four-piper cruiser's commander on TBS. It was a remarkably quiet dialogue, despite the hellish sights and sounds that engulfed both of them.

"Do you need some help, Robbie?"

"Negative," responded the unruffled voice of *Marblehead*'s Captain A. G. Robinson. "We'll manage."

"Are you sure?"

"Absolutely. You've got your own troubles, mister."

"Very well. Then we're going to make for Bali Strait," said *Houston*'s Captain A. H. Rooks.

Prince, listening, marveled at Robinson's aplomb. *Marblehead*'s plight seemed beyond redemption. Her rudder jammed, she was still describing circles in the blue waters. Off to the south, a darkling squall line had grown perceptibly, offering some small chance for cover; but it was a damnably long haul away. If he'd been Robinson, thought Prince, he probably would have suggested that *Houston* stick around just in case.

The Jap bombers had finally expended all their eggs. Confident that they had sent two Allied cruisers to the shallow bottom of the Java Sea, while severely pummeling two others, they turned their disdainful meatballed tails for Kendari. In scant moments they were swallowed up in the high cloudbank.

Guided by her twin propellers, with her broken rudder angled almost directly aft by the damage-control crew, *Marblehead* a half hour later was pronounced able to chart a reasonably straight course. Admiral Kuyper ordered his shattered formation to head directly for Lombok Strait, which separated Bali and Lombok Island itself, with *Zuyder Zee,* the relatively unscathed *Volendam* and the eight destroyers as guardians for the cripple.

When Kuyper requested aerial cover from Surabaya, he was promised that GHQ would do what it could. But there wasn't much optimism in this naval headquarters response. Proceed to Tjilatjap, said ABDA, because Surabaya no longer enjoyed sanctuary from Nip bombers. It was implied, but not spoken, that the failure of Kuyper's mission would soon mean an influx of Japs into Makassar Town, a closer airfield, and a daily round of aerial Hades for the nakedly exposed repair base.

As they regrouped for their snail-paced southward passage, Prince suddenly felt physically ill, nauseated, and he contemplated for a wild moment the likelihood that he might have to vomit over *Davidson*'s slatternly gray side. Then the feeling subsided. What had just happened, terrible as it was, was only a foretaste of the immediate future. He wondered dully if he could ever screw up his nerve to go through with it again.

8

"Theirs Not to Reason Why"

TJILATJAP DIDN'T EVEN SHOW on the list of the East Indies' seventeen major cities, although it lay athwart a narrow-gauge railway between the historic Buddhist princedom of Djokjakarta and the farmlands of Bandung, providing the only refuge for combat shipping on Java's undulant southern coast. At that, it was a miserable excuse for a seaport, entered through a twisting channel, with an attenuated harbor where poorly charted reefs and shoals had mangled many an unwary vessel. There was generally a queue of ships anchored in the deeper mid-sector, waiting to be offloaded or resupplied. Tjilatjap was, in short, a homecoming mariner's nightmare.

Nevertheless, with Surabaya so closely threatened, it would have to suffice.

Admiral Hart flew down from Bandung, where he had been huddling again with Marshal Wavell, to confer with Kuyper, once the unfortunate Dutchman brought his cripples and their watchdogs into relative safety. The Old Man hadn't taken kindly to Kuyper's retreat. Cast in the John Paul Jones mold, he would have continued toward Makassar Town after the Nip planes departed and made a stab at breaking up the enemy amphibious landing. But political issues had to be considered; and to revoke the Dutchman's command at this point might further endanger the tenuous relationships that existed at ABDA's highest level. Moreover, as his forces continued to be whittled away, Kuyper became less bold, more cautious.

The Old Man found scant comfort at Tjilatjap, where, he groused, the accent should be on the last syllable. *Jap!* Firsthand inspection assured him that *Marblehead* required a full-scale overhaul, if she could be rendered fit for the journey to the nearest British base with suitable facilities, Ceylon, more than 3,000 statute miles of westward steaming. Somehow they lifted the ancient cruiser partially into a floating drydock and fixed a crude patch under her perforated bow. She left by week's end in company of one of the two invaluable American tenders.

Houston's triple rear battery of eight-inch rifles was a complete wreck, never to be fired again. But the Old Man figured she was two thirds better than nothing and only twelve years old to boot, which put her among the most modern Allied warships in Asian waters.

Zuyder Zee could be restored to reasonable shape. *Volendam* needed only minor patchwork. And the eight destroyers, thank merciful heaven, were as pristine as they'd ever be, in view of their general decrepitude, a factor caused by age rather than pummeling by the enemy.

When the Old Man clambered aboard *Davidson,* according Prince the rare compliment of a visit from a senior officer, his first words were: "I see you've been lucky again, Commander."

"Yes, sir." Prince felt uncomfortable under the admiral's arctic stare. "Mainly because the Japs didn't pay us much attention."

"I know," said the Old Man. "More's the pity. If they'd gone after some of the little boys, maybe we'd be in a better shape today."

"Yes, sir."

What else could Prince say? DesDiv 11 didn't have a magic magnet to attract the enemy bombs away from the big boys. It was simply how the hand was dealt. Of course, he might have offered as his opinion that Kuyper's task force should have left *Marblehead* behind and pressed on to Celebes Island. But he didn't. It would have sounded both fatuous and untrue, because he had been in total agreement with the Dutchman that caution under those circumstances was the better part of valor.

As matters presently stood, Hart's own Asiatic Fleet consisted of the injured *Houston,* the light cruiser *Boise,* eleven destroyers, twenty-five submarines and five oilers and supply vessels scattered from hell to breakfast, convoying, scouting, standing ready for mothering duties whenever the need arose.

As commander of Allied naval forces (ABDAfloat), the Old Man could also count on one heavy and two light British cruisers, plus three Royal Navy destroyers. The Aussies offered HMAS *Hobart,* a light cruiser. Even with her three main afterguns gone, *Houston* was as powerful as *Exeter,* the British heavy. This had played an important part in Hart's judgment to keep her available.

The Dutch under Admiral Helfrich contributed three light cruisers, including the somewhat battered *Zuyder Zee,* seven destroyers and fifteen overaged subs.

Not, grumped the Old Man, a very prepossessing lot when you reckoned what the Japanese had on tap in the southwest Pacific: aircraft carriers, battleships, cruisers galore, and at least treble the Allied complement of destroyers.

"I'd say," he observed dourly, for Prince's benefit as a divisional chief, "that the Nips have us outweighed about ten to one. What's worse, they have the advantage of being on the attack, while we can only watch, wait and try to counter them."

Prince summoned up the temerity to ask, "Where do you reckon they'll strike next, sir?"

"Perhaps Sumatra." The Old Man squinted at the mountainous western horizon. "That's where the oil is."

In this estimate, the commander of ABDAfloat was right on the button, and there was little that the truncated Allies could do about it. Two enemy convoys exited Camranh Bay, in Vietnam, bearing south through the China Sea for Palembang, the petroleum capital of Sumatra. Once more the dismal job fell to Admiral Kuyper to interpose his meager force between this valuable target and the greatest amphibious assemblage ever put together by the foe. He went courageously enough, despite the certainty that he'd never have a chance, with his outclassed Dutch, British and Aussie cruisers and six Yank tin cans.

For once, *Davidson* was dropped from the line-up. Her undersides were so befouled with tropical growths and sludge that the Old Man kept her behind for a quick cleaning. *McGraw* and *Vincent* were added to DesDiv 10.

Prince went ashore to the staff headquarters which Hart had temporarily established in Tjilatjap, to lend a hand in planning future operations. This, he discovered, consisted mainly of trying to outguess the Japs, a futile game at best, less rewarding and by no means as precise as Twenty Questions.

For the next couple of days, however, they mainly huddled around the communications shack, listening to reports from the hapless Kuyper. One of his destroyers had driven headlong into a coral head the first night out; and then the Nip reconnaissance planes arrived. Soon afterward, Kuyper's "striking force," as it was grandly called, came under aerial assault from carrier planes, bent on wiping it out before the Jap convoy dropped anchor off Palembang.

Through some miracle the Allied contingent escaped destruction. Two DesDiv 10 four-pipers were near-missed. But that was all.

Again Kuyper pleaded for fighter cover. Again there was none forthcoming. Well aware that history might brand him a coward, he turned back toward Sunda Strait, between Sumatra and Java, to save his paltry command. Simultaneously, the Dutch began laying waste their petroleum facilities in this area. DesDiv 10, perilously low on oil, underwent an emergency refueling at a tiny hamlet near the strait's northern entrance. Then all hands fled south of the mythical, indefensible Malay Barrier, back to Tjilatjap.

That same day, on February 15, supposedly impregnable Singapore fell.

The Old Man personally plucked the black pin from the wall chart, which had signified British possession of the island, and jabbed a yellow one in its place.

On February 16, Hart himself gave up the struggle with his politico-naval opponents in the Dutch hierarchy, weary of explaining why the United States couldn't dispatch additional aircraft to the doomed Indies, tired of urging greater ABDA aggressive action against the enemy, and none too secretly advocating withdrawal to Australia.

With the Old Man's abrupt departure, for "ill health" reasons, Admiral Helfrich took over. And immediately he learned what Hart had discovered the hard way over the months: ABDA was a monstrosity, beset by jealousies, language blocks and a predilection on the part of its several commanders to forsake useful combined operations and proceed alone, without reference to the so-called Supreme Command.

Disaster multiplied upon disaster.

First the Allies sought to replenish Timor, a large lizard-shaped island that lay between the main Indies chain and northern Australia, with manpower and planes. But the Japs drove them back without much trouble, like a farmer brushing flies off a horse's back.

Next the rampant enemy had the unmitigated gall—plus the immeasurable strength—to send a four-carrier force into the

Timor Sea itself. Supported by two battleships and three heavy cruisers, this was the largest armada the Japanese had dispatched against a pre-selected target since December 7. Their goal was the Australian seaport of Darwin, a sleepy, sun-baked cluster of tin-roofed cottages and warehouses, which in recent weeks had become the key Allied supply point south of Surabaya.

For years, what happened that February morning would be remembered Down Under as "Australia's Pearl Harbor."

Two Aussie transports and a pair of U.S. troopships were presumably in snug harbor, unloading the soldiers who hadn't been able to reach Timor. An American four-piper and an aircraft tender were also anchored in Darwin, along with an assortment of Canadian and Norwegian shipping. Almost a score of unwary vessels in all, tethered in the roadstead beneath a cloudless sky.

By the time the Nip dive bombers finished their leisurely job, impeded only slightly by a few U.S. Army P-40s, a dozen vessels had been sunk, eighteen irreplaceable Allied planes wrecked, the town's lone airport rendered temporarily unusable and Darwin itself left in shambles. Its population fled for fear of a return Nip engagement.

But the foe was supremely content with his day's work. For all practical purposes, Darwin had ceased to exist as a viable base. Nothing worthwhile remained between the tottering Indies, Java in particular, and Australia's populated east coast.

Her fouled bottom cleaned, her guns refurbished, her storeroom as well stocked as Tjilatjap's limited resources would allow, *Davidson* went back on the firing line at about the same time that Darwin was being deleted from the active list of supply stations.

Even Prince knew that the latest operation brainstormed by the overworked staff of Admiral Kuyper was, like the two which had preceded it, undoubtedly marked for failure. Forty-eight hours earlier the Japs had stealthily put ashore a small detachment at Bali, a scant 100 crow's-flight miles from Surabaya. Yet the landing should have come as no vast surprise to ABDA, whose intelligence had been bleating warnings about such an invasion for the past ten days, to little avail.

Since its abortive attempt to interdict the Palembang invasion, the Dutch-commanded fleet had dispersed from southern Sumatra to Surabaya. Pulling it together posed a massive, perhaps impossible chore. Nevertheless Kuyper was determined to manage this, somehow, after a series of conferences at his own headquarters in Tjilatjap. Bali, he believed, could still be saved. All that was required, decreed the admiral, was a determined assault on the enemy convoy now en route to reinforce the troops who so thinly occupied the beautiful island of bare-breasted females and their tiny singsong men.

Kuyper reached this fateful decision on the morning of February 18.

In his unofficial liaison role, Prince stood by, stonily, while the Dutchman traced the three-pronged effort that must be made to regroup an adequate striking team in Bandung Strait. As he listened, small droplets of cold sweat trickled down Prince's tanned forehead, and his insides began to roil involuntarily. Perhaps, he thought, he'd caught a fever in this hellish place. Dengue. Or something worse, like the dreaded blackwater, which caused a man to piss purple.

If so, he'd be in no physical shape to command DesDiv 11 on Kuyper's insane expedition. Prince resolved to visit the base hospital as soon as the conference ended. There was no reason why the Beaver couldn't assume his duties. And, Prince thought mordantly, probably win that gaudy Yank medal he'd wanted so long, to hang alongside his bloody DSO.

But the Aussie medic who examined him a half hour later was a cold-eyed bastard, seemingly able to peer into Prince's

234

psyche like a human X-ray machine. He pronounced him fit as a fiddle. Except for a slight touch of guts-a-crook, doubtless from eating native shellfish, the commander was in fair dinkum shape.

"I never touch those goddamned oysters," Prince protested. "What's my temperature?"

"A safe hundred degrees," the doctor assured him. "Nothing to worry about." He gave Prince a slantwise grin. "Now get out there and murder the little bastards, cobber!"

"Thanks," Prince said stonily. "I'll try to sink one for you."

"Thank *you*," said the medic, with an elaborate humility that couldn't have been genuine. "We chaps who're condemned to stay here salute you ruddy sailormen. It's not easy to squat idly on our duffs while you wash all the dirty dishes."

"No," Prince said, "I guess it isn't."

They were scheduled to sail at midnight. This witching hour, Prince mused bitterly, must hold some mystical meaning for the Dutch admiral. He himself called together DesDiv 11's skippers, Perry Koch, Broad Tail Horton and, in their dual roles as exec-captains, Lieutenant Rodney and the Beaver. They seated themselves around the baize-covered wardroom table as they had so long ago, waiting for Prince to deliver the Word on the Word.

Some scared ensign, scuttling out of his superiors' way at the last instant, had forgotten to switch off the short-wave radio. It was, as usual, tuned to Tokyo Rose. And, as usual, she was playing Cassandra to the hilt, between snatches of the latest home-front songs.

"One of the favorites of your lovely wives and girl friends— and of the civilian men who are lolling in peaceful luxury while you risk your lives in a worthless cause—is this rousing little ditty. Listen!" commanded Tokyo Rose.

It came on hard, raucous, full of hand-clapping: something called "Deep in the Heart of Texas," where the stars at night were big and bright.

"Wouldn't you," asked Rose brightly, "just love to be back there, fellows, 'Deep in the Heart of Texas'? I'm sure Admiral Nimitz would, because he's a true Texan. And let's never forget —he relieved Admiral Kimmel after Pearl Harbor."

Then she played "They're Either Too Young or Too Old" and "Don't Sit under the Apple Tree," neither of which was calculated to uplift the morale of a sailor whose only contact with his absent sweetheart was an occasional letter that managed to struggle through the tangled morass of Fleet Post Office mail to the Far East.

"Oh, by the way," Tokyo Rose added dulcetly, as the music faded, "for those of you destined shortly for battle in Bandung Strait . . . my deepest sympathy to your prospective widows and orphans."

Prince whirled upon Bream, who was preparing to record the proceedings. "Turn that infernal caterwauling off!"

"Yes, sir." Bream got indolently to his feet. "She does have a most uncanny way of outguessing our movements, doesn't she, Commander?"

"Uncanny, hell. This frigging village is crawling with more spies than cockroaches. Not that they're needed, with the Japs owning the skies, watching us like goddamned hawks."

Prince buckled down to business.

Kuyper would take his flagship *Zuyder Zee, Noorden* and nine destroyers, six Dutch and DesDiv 11's three, eastward along the big island's lower coast to the strait's southern entrance. There they would be joined by *Volendam* out of Surabaya and by DesDiv 10, which was still en route from Sumatra, having detoured to the north rather than returning to Tjilatjap, as did her two excess four-pipers, *McGraw* and *Vincent*. This was, Prince acknowledged, an extremely delicate, close-timed affair, especially since an additional third echelon had been ordered by the Dutch admiral—five torpedo boats to polish off any Nip cripples and do the final sweep-up chores.

Ideally, DesDiv 10 and *Volendam* would attack first, moving in at twenty-five knots from Taefel Hoek, a rocky cape on Bali's southeast corner. Two hours later, Kuyper's main strike force would close in to administer the *coup de grâce,* then depart, leaving the PTs to their vulture pickings over the Jap remains.

As best the ABDA scout planes could discern, the Japanese convoy was escorted by three cruisers and an indeterminate number of destroyers.

Once more, on paper, this seemed a fantastic stroke of good fortune. For a change the Allies should outnumber their enemy.

Exactly why Kuyper chose to split his command in such a fashion Prince couldn't satisfactorily explain, either to himself or to his captains. The Dutchman's last instructions, he said, were that those who arrived first—or at all—were to tangle with the Nip convoy, even if the entire force of three cruisers, thirteen tin cans and the PT quintet failed to make their projected rendezvous for whatever reason. There were to be no slip-ups, no retreat. Kuyper was still smarting from the Old Man's implied criticism of his costly reluctance to press home the Celebes operation and more recently his fruitless Sumatran excursion. On that regard, the Old Man was more outspokenly critical, downright acid in his remarks, as he made it abundantly clear that a strong offense was the heart and soul of a successful defense.

"Remember," Prince said, concluding the session, "we move out at zero hour. I'd advise you to check over those harbor charts again. They aren't worth much. But we'll be traveling at twenty knots when we hit the outer passage, and I'd hate to see DesDiv Eleven reduced to two ships."

The destroyermen left. So did Rodney and the Beaver, presumably to do their master's bidding and bone up on Tjilatjap's thorny waterways.

Only Prince and Bream remained. The chief yeoman, who had finished his shorthand notes, was deliberately stalling until the wardroom cleared so that he could make some sort of Breamish pitch. Prince waited. It wasn't long in coming.

"You don't need me in *Davidson*," Bream said flatly. "I'm strictly excess baggage among the communicator types. There's no correspondence to handle, and it'll be weeks before we get a chance to file our battle reports."

"So what do you propose?"

"That you cut me a set of orders to ANZAC headquarters in Sydney."

Prince gave him an incredulous look. "You must be off your ever-lovin' rocker, Bream. Nobody's quitting this area now."

"Except a few bigwigs," Bream countered, "and the walking wounded."

"Of which you're neither."

"Let me explain what I have in mind." The chief yeoman sounded very patient, very understanding, as he detailed his scheme, the way a bright young salesman might cajole a singularly obtuse department supervisor out of a better route. "We both know that ABDA's had it, that it's about finished as a combat entity. I'd bet good money that you're going to pull through, Commander, because you've a knack for covering your bases." Prince scowled, started to say something, but Bream rushed on. "If you send me to Australia for reassignment, I've got enough friends down there to locate me at GHQ. Most likely you'll also wind up in Sydney, with or without *Davidson*. When you do, I'll be on hand, ready to keep an eye on promising requests for three-stripers—because we yeomen see correspondence even before it reaches the captains and the admirals."

"I know," Prince said dryly. "And you're a special expert in this house-espionage trade."

"True," Bream admitted, as if accepting a deserved accolade. "I make it my business to keep on top of the news."

What the chief said, Prince privately had to concede, made pragmatic sense. A smart yeoman, strategically placed, might prove damned useful one day. His presence at ANZAC naval headquarters could mean the difference between a back-water supply base command, more detested sea duty, or returning to the assignment for which he really craved, on some hot-shot command staff where the potential honors were many and the dangers minimal.

"All right," Prince said abruptly, "we'll do it. Fix 'em up so you can go ashore this evening."

"Thank you, sir." Bream smiled his cool gratitude. "You won't regret it."

"But how will you get to Sydney?"

"They're starting to deadhead supply planes to Darwin, now that the airfield has been repaired. I can always hitch a ride. From there it's a cinch to move along to Brisbane and Sydney —provided I've got legit orders."

"Yours won't be legitimate," said Prince, "because we're by-passing CincAsiatic."

Bream's pale-blue eyes narrowed. He drummed delicate fingers on his shorthand pad. "Hell, Commander, with things as screwed up as they are, who'll give a hollow hoot whether they're endorsed or not? This is an emergency situation. The ANZAC people will understand."

"What about your friend? What's his name—Marcus?"

"Oh, Peter's happy as a clam, sir. All he dreams of nowadays is steering twelve hundred tons of great, big, beautiful pig iron."

"That's not very loyal," Prince grunted, "referring to *Davidson* as a hunk of pig iron."

"My loyalty, Commander, encompasses people, not things."

They sortied at the stroke of the designated hour. DesDiv 11 took the lead, closely followed by *Zuyder Zee* and *Noorden,* with the six Netherlands destroyers bringing up the rear. But as the last of the force was clearing the tricky harbor mouth, a Dutch tin can managed to stray slightly off course and plow headlong into a reef. She hung there, irrevocably trapped, while the others disappeared into the night. Prince heard the excited gabble of foreign voices on *Davidson*'s bridge TBS; and soon the clarification came in stilted English.

"We have lost *Kalberer*. Regardless, we shall proceed."

Viewed from the seaward side, there are hospitable and unhospitable shores, as you strain at them through your binoculars, seeking some movement, some index, to a hidden enemy's proximity. Had *Davidson* been a cruise ship, white-sided, staffed by obsequious stewards, echoing to the sounds of soft-stringed music, what its crew observed from this nether extension of the Indian Ocean would have extracted *Ohs* and *Ahs* from its appreciative passengers. The sweeping, charging surf, as it broke against the coral reefs of eastern Java, was lovely in the tropical starlight. But *Davidson* was not a pleasure liner. Thus her men, while agreeing that the passing tableau was undoubtedly beautiful, in a romantic sense, knew the mendacious fiction of its beauty. You might imagine that safety beckoned from those half-hidden beaches; but it was like a Kafkaesque dream, not quite valid, nor yet entirely unreal either.

All this Prince understood, not in specific terms, but intuitively, as he peered for what seemed hours through his night glasses. The standard naval 7 x 50 issue for officers was a heavy piece of hardware, weighing several pounds, and clasping them to your face for a protracted period caused more than eyestrain. Your biceps first began to ache, then resisted the deadweight of the binoculars. It was, Prince thought, a small enough exercise in endurance, one which had to be borne, although damned insignificant alongside of Slattery's labors in the engineering Black Hole, or even the problems that confronted Hagen, perched precariously astride a railing on his exposed gunnery platform, twenty feet above where Prince sat in his armchair.

Prince wondered how Nelson and Wellington could have found such glory in war. Little glory existed in *this* miserable campaign, because it was a lost cause from its inception. Except for that dreadful kind which came posthumously to those who sacrificed themselves on a forgotten, faraway altar, whatever glory ensued went to the shore-bound high brass. Or so the sea-going types believed. Nor could there be that deep, personal satisfaction which Nelson and Wellington derived from their great deeds. Hell. Their lordships—the admiral and the general—played games with great fleets and mighty armies, yet always on familiar territory, in full knowledge that the resources of their countries stood firmly behind them. Out here? Nothing. The Americans, the Dutch and—yes—the British inheritors of the Nelsonian tradition were forgotten rejects of a futile war.

Prince instinctively felt for the sheath knife he always wore in his webbed khaki belt when at sea. Once again, he reminded himself contemptuously, he was play-acting. Like the .45 Colt automatic which hung against his right hip, it was a relic of the days when you might anticipate a sudden coming to close quarters with an enemy frigate, the heave of a grappling hook and the command to repel boarders.

They had cleared Tjilatjap's minefields and were gradually swinging to course-110, which would haul them clear of the coastal shoals. To curb his restlessness, Prince made a brisk tour of the darkened ship, chatting briefly with the men who stood watch at their guns and torpedoes, checking the radio shack, sampling the omnipresent soup kettle, even crawling down the hand-blistering ladder to Slattery's demoniac engineering realm. There he found Slats explaining, for the fortieth time, the uses of the Navy's diaphragm gas mask.

"If you forget to tear off that little piece of adhesive tape on the back," the engineering officer was saying, "you won't get any air through the vents." He made a gagging sound and snapped his fingers. "You'll smother like that!"

Gas attacks were a hypothetical horror aboard every naval vessel. To date, they had never been employed in sea warfare.

241

But there was always a first time; and, after Pearl Harbor, the Allies figured the enemy was capable of anything. Poison gas could render a ship useless before her crew got the vents shut. Interior spaces, like Slattery's murderously hot boiler rooms, would be especially vulnerable.

As he prowled the decks, gulping the fresh, hot, humid air, Prince checked the bulkhead hatches. One of them, leading to the wardroom, was open several inches. A glimmer of blue light emerged from the small aperture. He went inside, slammed the steel door shut and dogged it securely.

Ensign Virtue was sitting alone at the table, softly playing his accursed harmonica.

Prince glared at him. "Didn't you know that hatch was open?" he demanded.

Virtue's rendition of "When the Lights Go on Again All Over the World," an unfortunate choice, spluttered to a cacophonic halt.

"No, sir."

"Well, it was!" Prince stalked toward the galley for a cup of coffee. "The goddamned weatherdeck looked like Forty-second Street and Broadway during a whores' convention."

"Sorry, sir."

Prince moodily sipped his black coffee. When he finished he said in a calmer tone, "This excursion fleet has enough troubles, son, without adding to 'em through our own foolishness."

"Yes, sir." The assistant engineering officer betrayed an appropriate measure of contrition. "I guess I was in too much of a hurry, trying to catch a little rest before I go back to that friggin' Black Hole of Calcutta."

Once more on the bridge, Prince glanced aft to see how the rest of the formation was faring. On his way up he barked his shins on the ladder that led to the charthouse, acquiring a painful bruise. Ladder chancres, these were termed in caustic naval parlance. He rubbed them morosely. Although the stars were gleaming with incredible brilliance, *McGraw,* second in line, was a formless blob in the velvety blackness, discernible mainly because of the blue battle lights on her truck and her faintly phosphorescent wake. The flamin' Southern Cross, as the Beaver would have designated it, was at its flamin' best.

All eleven ships stood at Condition Two, a degree of readiness that allowed their crews a modicum of relaxation during the night, since their encounter with the enemy wouldn't occur for almost twenty-four hours.

Prince stared abaft, then at the arching heavens. A lingering cloud hung luminescent, well above the horizon. The stars gave it the shape of a long-necked, predatory bird, poised there silently, as if waiting to plunge down upon its prey. Beneath the monstrous cloud Kuyper's formation seemed insignificant, almost motionless.

For the rest of that night and during the daylight hours, Kuyper's two cruisers and nine destroyers steamed in stately procession, alternating between twenty and twenty-five knots so as to reach the Japs' beachhead at exactly the right instant, two hours after *Volendam* and the DesDiv 10 four-pipers had finished their gunfire-and-torpedo attacks. The seas were calm, the southeast wind easy, and only a mild offshore swell caused the old four-pipers to wallow slightly as they skirted Java's lower shores in an intermittent zigzag pattern.

At one point in the early morning, Broad Tail Horton signaled that he had a torpedo running "hot" in his number-three tube mount. He wanted to ease off to ten knots while his gunnery people located the internal ailment that was heating up the pent fish. Otherwise *Vincent* might wind up with a misfire, or even an explosion, when the battle joined.

Prince gave him a grudging affirmative.

"But make it snappy," he commanded over their TBS channel.

"Okay, boss."

That was hardly the response a mere destroyer skipper gave his division commander. Brash. Overly familiar. Yet it was expectable of Broad Tail, a man who would wear a rope in place of a regulation belt. Prince was glad that the language wall separating the Dutch from the Americans kept this Yankee-style insubordination among friends. Kuyper's TBS would respond only when DesDiv 11 specifically asked for an English-speaking message relayer. The Beaver derided this arrangement as "trying to glue a goddamn plaster patch over the Tower of Babel."

Vincent quickly dropped astern, was lost to sight for an hour, then came barreling back into her proper place in the vanguard at thirty knots.

"Trouble's fixed," Broad Tail called.

"Good," responded Prince. "Let's hope we don't have any more."

The Beaver shook his head sadly. "Yon sailor is a stout fella," he said, "literally and potentially. You ought to pat him on the fanny to show your appreciation."

"He did his job," Prince snapped. "Which is what he's so highly paid for. Why praise him for that?"

Shrugging, the Beaver turned back to his silent contemplation of the lush Javanese coast.

By nightfall Kuyper's force had rounded the big island's eastern tip and started across the widest thirty-mile stretch of Bali Strait. A deceptive aura of tranquility pervaded the squadron. Bathed in the sunset afterglow, Bali itself was as beautiful as its name. Prince overheard the machine-gun crew forward of the bridge swapping ribald jokes about how its pink-tipped peaks looked exactly like the Balinese maidens' renowned breasts—firm, yet velvety soft, outthrust and provocative.

They had stopped zigzagging an hour earlier. Throughout the long day only one plane was sighted, too far away to be identified as friend or foe; either it failed to see the Allied formation or, having glimpsed it, raced away to make a report. A Dutch destroyer caught a sounding on what it believed was a submarine. This engendered a certain amount of confused signal hoistings and dashing about, until Admiral Kuyper was convinced that his tin can had more likely picked up a porpoise on its sonar than a Jap sub.

Sonar was, at best, a tricky gadget, reliant upon "echo-ranging" and the skill of the listener who sought to determine the range and bearing of the presumed enemy submersible. It was better than the World War I hydrophonic gismos, though, which couldn't even distinguish between subsea and surface propeller noises and which invariably failed the distance test. Nevertheless, the new electronic gear, developed by the hard-pressed British after the Nazis commenced their unrestricted submarine warfare, was fairly accurate—once you separated the chirpings of shrimp from the pinging noise of a veritable U-boat.

The Dutch destroyer rolled a couple of ashcans over its fantail, just in case, waited for them to explode 100 feet below the surface, and then rejoined her teammates after no telltale debris or oil slicks appeared.

It was now 2200, ten P.M., and the initial strike was preparing to engage the foe off the tiny Balinese village of Sanur, whose sugar-white beaches fronted on Badung Strait, across from a cluster of small islets. At this point the passage was barely ten miles wide, Prince observed on Lieutenant Krebs' chart, and much too tight for decent maneuvering, if they found themselves in a bind with an unexpectedly superior Nip force.

Eleven minutes later *Volendam* radioed that it had established contact with the enemy. DesDiv 10's commander followed with a laconic message: "One Maru and a pair of dog-dogs. Seems like the rest of the geese have flown north for the summer."

But even this minuscule Japanese amphibious group proved

a lot harder to counter than to count. *Volendam* instituted proceedings at 2215, with a broadside salvo from its main battery. Undaunted, the Nips immediately lit up the dulcet sky with star shells, aimed searchlights impudently at the Dutch cruiser and blasted back with their own five-inch rifles. *Volendam* had missed. But the two enemy destroyers, savagely protecting the single transport like mother terriers, managed to pink her on the stern.

DesDiv 10 promptly belched out a smoke screen, into which the five Allied ships plunged at twenty-eight knots. When the lead destroyer emerged a few minutes later, her yardarm spotters announced that the *Maru* was trying to escape to the northeast, with a Jap tin can close alongside her.

Two of DesDiv 10's four-pipers, gathering speed to outflank the enemy on the portside nearest the shore, simultaneously let fly with a barrage of four-inch gunfire and a double spread of torpedoes. They were rewarded by seeing orange flames erupt from the transport.

This euphoria was short-lived, though, because a lucky fish from the Nip escort caught one of the destroyers squarely amidships. She was Piggy Hogg's *LeBaron*. She slewed to a halt, mortally stricken, her engine room flooded. Within a dozen minutes she sank. With her went Piggy's heady dreams of divisional glory.

DesDiv 10's remaining ships now flung themselves bodily at the two Nip tin cans, each of which was newer and better armed than their four-piper opponents. *Volendam*, meanwhile, acting under prescribed orders, continued up through Badung Strait, taking with her the only six-inch guns capable of outsparring the Japs' surface batteries. Her mission was to avoid tangling with the main enemy flotilla, somewhere in the vicinity of Lombok Island.

Murderous, accurate fire from the enemy split DesDiv 10 into a ragged threesome and precluded their following the Dutch cruiser northward. All of them had expended their starboard torpedoes. So the DesDiv 10 survivors wheeled to fetch their portside tubes into action, in the constricted space that remained between them, the foe and the encroaching islets off Bali.

Two of the Yanks made smoke to allow the third to start her run. She unleashed all six fish. But nothing happened. The Jap destroyer raced on, spewing shells, as the faulty torpedoes ran too deeply or dudded out.

So DesDiv 10, badly mauled, unable to rejoin *Volendam*, elected to hightail it south toward Kuyper's advancing contingent. They sought the larger force as a protective shield against their retirement into Surabaya, where all three would need extensive repairs. For once they got a break. Both Nip destroyers, unexpectedly entrapped in the thick residual smoke screen, began shooting at each other, under the blithe assumption they had American warships in their beclouded sights.

Thus, ignominiously, concluded the first phase of the plan which was designed to pulverize the enemy's brash Balinese expedition.

From their narrowing range, the eleven ships of the second wave had heard the sounds of cannonading, seen the flares and audited the welter of plain-language messages among the four-pipers of DesDiv 10. Abruptly, for Prince, any semblance of gay adventure, such as it was, including a preplanned victory parade against an outnumbered foe, no longer pertained. It was an abysmally screwed-up operation, plagued by confused signals from Kuyper in *Zuyder Zee*, and with a sense of futility overpowering him, where at least some confidence had existed before, owing to their presumed superiority in numbers.

Then word came from *Zuyder Zee* that the bulk of the Japanese combatant vessels, along with their convoy, were reported driving north, well beyond their original beachhead, to await a more propitious moment for invasion. It was Kuyper's estimate that the enemy would have to match his progress to that of the troopships, perhaps twelve knots, and that a determined effort by the Allied forces could overtake them before they escaped into the Java Sea. So he ordered flank speed.

For DesDiv 11 this meant a jarring thirty-two knots.

Slattery accepted the bad news philosophically.

"If you see something catapulting up through the main deck," he said, "that'll be me, propelled by a burst boiler."

"When you start having real pain, let me know," Prince said.

"Hell," said Slats, "I ache all over. It can't get any worse."

"Stay in the buggy."

"Where else?" retorted the engineering officer.

Prince stalked back from the voice tube to his canvas-covered chair. He'd have nothing to do for at least two hours while they attempted to close intercept the three Nip cruisers, their destroyer screen, the convoy and whatever other tin cans the enemy admiral had managed to salvage from the encounter with DesDiv 10. It was almost midnight. A peculiar mist had shrouded Bali's coastline. Depending upon how far this haze extended seaward, Prince thought gloomily, the Nips might get an unexpected break. They could proceed close to shore, on the fringe of this semi-fog, while the Allies steamed in full clarity of the star-spangled night, silhouetted like cardboard targets in a Coney Island shooting gallery.

Moreover the waves had risen perceptibly, and *Davidson* was starting to buck in her maverick bronco fashion. This familiar, unpleasant motion overlaid a patina of distinct physical discomfort on Prince's growing spiritual malaise.

Seaman Peter Marcus held the wheel. Proud as a peacock, he'd just commenced his two-hour watch at the helm. All things being equal, he would not be relieved by the chief quartermaster until shortly before the enemy was sighted. Prince resented Marcus' evident delight in handling the 1,200-ton four-piper and the man's feckless disregard for what he was guiding them into.

At 0120, cautiously rising to periscope depth, the U.S. submarine which had earlier revealed the Japs' northward withdrawal semisurfaced long enough to inventory the Japanese force. As nearly as the sub's skipper could make out, it consisted of one heavy cruiser, two lights, at least seven destroyers—and six partly offloaded transports.

He let the Nips continue northward until a relatively safe stretch of open sea lay between his submarine and the enemy before he hoisted his antenna and tapped out Kuyper's call letters. By then it was 0135. The Allies had closed to within a dozen miles of the foe, still traveling at thirty-odd knots.

Kuyper took the information with typical phlegmatic calm, although he was seriously disturbed at the sub's account. His pair of light cruisers, he knew, were already outgunned by their Japanese opposite numbers. Confronted by the unanticipated presence of an enemy heavy, with her eight-inch main battery, he was at a distinct disadvantage for any long-range sparring.

The only chance of evening these potentially calamitous odds lay in a torpedo charge by his nine destroyers. No. Make that six. He must keep three of them as a rear guard, in the dire event that the cavalry assault failed and he had to retire. This covering trio, he decided, must be Dutch.

"DesDiv 11," came the flagship's curt order via TBS, "plus destroyers *Zeeland*, *Haarlem* and *Dordrecht*, will execute a torpedo attack at 0200. DesDiv 11 will lead. Targets will be three enemy cruisers with particular concentration on a heavy cruiser sighted by friendly submarine. Cannot emphasize too strongly the urgency of this maneuver. Success of our mission depends upon it."

Prince studied the unwelcome decree for an instant, after which he silently handed it to the Beaver.

The bridge clock now showed 0145.

Immediately upon receipt of their mandate, the division had sprung noisily to General Quarters. In this condition of total readiness, a ship became as secure from the intrusion of seawater gushing through pierced plates as her nautical designers could contrive. Every horizontal deck hatch, every vertical door leading from outside or inside compartments was dogged tight shut, their rubber gaskets pressed flat against the interstices to prevent any leakage. Portholes were equally protected, locked behind metal shields. As *Davidson*'s GQ klaxon bleated, Ensign Blue, whose first-lieutenant duties gave him primary damage control responsibility, and Ensign Virtue, the junior engineer, made a fast round of the four-piper, each with gimlet-eyed detail, to double-check every aperture. When they were finally satisfied, *Davidson* had been transformed into a series of watertight cubicles, each sealed off from its adjoining compartments, so that no single enemy shell could cause a disastrous inundation, although inhabitants of any flooded area were irrevocably doomed.

To be sure, if *Davidson* were unfortunate enough to catch a full broadside which holed her in a number of spots simultaneously, this system might well fail. Like all else devised by man, nothing was infallible; and *Davidson*, along with her sister ships, was very old, very brittle and exceedingly vulnerable. Meanwhile, she breathed through a few vents that led to her villainously hot engine rooms as she slipped through the darkness toward the hidden enemy, like a cutthroat in the night.

Peter Blue remained below with his work gang, ready to patch up broached bulkheads, fight flames, repair broken power lines. Carl Virtue went back to his detested duty station, to assist Lieutenant Hagen in monitoring the dials that recorded boiler pressures, revolutions of the ship's 100-foot drive shafts and all the other ingredients which made for swift passage through the mounting seas. It was damned uncomfortable below. The relative airlessness, combined with *Davidson*'s intensified pitch-and-roll, converted the engineering compartment into a sort of undulant hell.

Now the Dutch threesome, *Zeeland*, *Haarlem* and *Dordrecht*, came huffing up from the squadron's tail to add venom to its fanged head. As Prince had anticipated, Bali was cloaked in a faint mist, which extended several miles seaward. Beyond doubt, the Japs, whose proven nautical shrewdness had changed the Allies' original scorn ("they steal our plans, copy them wrong, and when they launch their goddamned ships, the bastards turn turtle") into grudging respect, would take full advantage of this meteorological boon. They would be barely perceivable, if at all, in the infernal haze, whereas the six destroyers must operate in the clear during their hazardous charge.

Prince eyed the clock again. Ten minutes to zero hour.

The ill-assorted sextet had reached a point marked X on Krebs' chart, almost north of Nusa Besar, largest of the three islets off the Bali coast. The map showed a slight indentation in the main island's shoreline which added a couple of miles to the shrouded area where the enemy was located. As closely as Prince could figure, DesDiv 11 and her Dutch consorts would have a five-mile run through the gleaming night before they made contact with the Nip cruisers.

Then the relentless minute hand of the bridge clock touched twelve.

All six destroyers, waiting on the TBS circuit, heard Prince's peremptory command at the same instant: "Attack!"

Their pace quickened from the twenty knots to which Des-Div 11 had slowed to let the Dutch tin cans form up, to thirty-two. After a hurried consultation with the Beaver and Rodney, who still accepted the former's brevetted captaincy with good grace, reverting quietly to his designated job as exec, Prince returned to the TBS mike.

"We'll make a dead-on approach," he decreed, "then swing hard right for a portside torpedo spread. Acknowledge."

His five subordinates responded at once, two with clipped Yankee affirmatives, three with guttural Hollander *ya's*.

"And keep in close formation," Prince added. "I don't want anybody crossing our own damned *T*—and getting clobbered by a friendly fish."

Again the affirmatives and the *ya's*.

Prince affixed a pair of rubber eye protectors to his binoculars. At the critical apex of their run, shortly before they triggered the torpedoes, the tin cans would be blasting away with their paltry main batteries. But even four-inch rifles dealt a tremendous concussive impact at the moment of firing.

The other officers on the bridge followed suit: the Beaver; Rodney; Krebs, who had forsaken his sweaty charthouse since he'd done everything that could be done navigationally to ready the formation for the attack; and young Tom Rand, who felt equally free to leave his now silent radio room. Communication henceforth would be handled by TBS.

Less than a quarter of the way to their target Prince saw a pair of ships—huge and formidable in the mist—blinking green-colored signals at each other. He couldn't read Japanese. But it was painfully apparent that the Nips were aware of their approach and had adopted appropriate defensive postures. The third enemy cruiser wasn't in sight, although Prince knew she was in the vicinity somewhere, with her weapons trained on the terrier pack that was scampering toward them across the white-capped waters of Badung Strait.

At 8,000 yards the Japanese opened up.

They could have started their barrage sooner, Prince knew, but they had probably waited, on the off chance the destroyers wouldn't spot them in the foggy darkness. Eight thousand yards for a six-inch gun was virtually point-blank. For a heavy cruiser's eight-inch rifles, it was like shooting ducks from the banks of a midget mill pond.

Prince discovered that his teeth were so tightly clenched that it required a distinct effort to unlock them. He glanced at the Beaver, who was leaning against the starboard bridge wing. The insouciant bastard had an unlit cigarette dangling loosely between his lips. It loomed absurdly white among the whiskery growth that covered his Malta battle scars. As white, Prince abruptly realized, as the knuckles of his own hands, gripping the spray-moistened steel rail.

The first enemy salvo burst like skyrockets, incandescent, over the racing formation. These were star shells. They stripped the last vestiges of security from the attackers, leaving them naked as a fan dancer just before the final curtain fell. Unlike the burlesque stripper, though, the tin cans could expect no sudden blackout. They would remain there, still naked, under the hostile audience's bold gaze.

Near misses straddled *Davidson* as she continued toward the foe.

A quarter mile astern, *McGraw* drew the first direct hit, on her foredeck. Luckily, thought Prince, it missed her bridge and her torpedoes.

Ten seconds later, with the range now down to 7,000 yards, *Davidson* caught one near her midships galley. The blast effect was immense. Prince, who had long since left his chair, was momentarily stunned, shaken to his knees. When his head cleared, he briefly counted *Davidson*'s blessings: there'd be no more soup kettle, but the fish were still intact on their mounts abaft the four slim funnels.

That was all that counted now. Getting close enough to these deadly behemoths to unleash their torpedoes. The destroyers plunged on, oblivious to the increasingly accurate enemy cannonading, with their own pitiful weaponry spitting like a string of Chinese firecrackers, and with about as much effect on the thick-skinned cruisers.

At 5,000 yards Prince yelled through the TBS for a ninety-degree turn to starboard. Three of his command obeyed instantly. The two others, *Vincent* and *Haarlem*, sought valiantly

253

to comply. But both had been damaged, their steering gear ripped, so their response was sluggish.

Nonetheless *Davidson* persisted, with her supportive strength now reduced by a grievous one-third.

Had he been in supreme command, Prince would have ordered an about face and gotten the hell out of there. They were in a totally impossible predicament, trapped under the guns of three ruthless cruisers, already nagged by the Nips' escorting destroyers, yet still a thousand yards from the optimum launch point for their unreliable alcohol-fueled fish.

But Prince wasn't in supreme command. He was finally that non-person he had always feared he would become—a cog, a pawn, in a game directed from afar by somebody else.

He felt almost grateful when the Beaver ambled over to join him on the portside of the exposed bridge. Even the sweaty smell of the man gave him a certain comfort at that moment; and the Briton's fierce countenance, behind its rufous beard, wore the look of a Moses about to deliver up the original Ten Commandments.

Suddenly *Davidson* was wracked by a colossal explosion, caused by a shell that had burst upon her out of the smoke-filled gloom as if from nowhere. None of the bridge watchers had heard the freight-train rumble of the projectile. It simply happened. The blast occurred twenty feet forward of the superstructure, obliterating *Davidson*'s No. 1 gun, hurling steel shards aft like shrapnel and bits of bodies in all directions.

Prince was knocked off his feet. Still dazed, he pulled himself upright by gripping a nearby stanchion and stared around at the carnage that surrounded him on the shattered bridge.

Seaman Marcus, who had been steering the flagship so proudly a few hours earlier, lay draped across the rail, his clothing stripped away, bleeding like a butchered sow. Prince noted with mute horror that Marcus had been brutally decapitated. The chief quartermaster was guiding *Davidson* with his left hand. His other arm had been severed at the elbow. And Tom Rand, that putative author of the Great American Novel, was sprawled like a rag doll tossed aside by a careless child against the bulkhead which separated the open bridge from the captain's sea cabin. He, too, was dead.

But the Beaver, along with Rodney and Krebs, had survived. He gripped Prince's shoulder, giving him a vigorous shake.

"We're damned near inside the cruiser's closest gunnery range," he shouted above the tumult of lesser detonations that succeeded the initial discharge. "Don't you think it's time to toss the friggin' fish overboard?"

Prince nodded.

His brain wasn't functioning properly, for some idiot reason, and he was conscious of a cold chill gnawing through his body, coursing up from his toes to his aching head. Involuntarily, he passed his hands over his vital parts, to discover whether he'd been wounded. But he was physically whole.

Then he realized that Hagen, the gunnery officer, must have been killed, too, when the first Jap shell struck the galley. So he ordered the bridge-talker to reach Brute Savage, Hagen's assistant, on the intercom.

"Tell him to fire his spread," he muttered.

"Sir?"

In a louder, firmer tone, Prince repeated: "Have him fire the goddamned fish!"

The Beaver said, "We'd better send the quartermaster below, if he can make it under his own steam. That arm's got to be tourniquetted."

Having overheard him, the wheelsman mumbled, "I'm afraid you're right, Commander."

"Can you manage without help?"

"Yes, sir."

"Very well." The Beaver turned to Rodney. "It's a bit irregular, Lieutenant, but the conn's all yours, personally."

Rodney smiled faintly. None of the four remaining enlisted men on the riddled bridge had any steering experience. Besides, they had other important duties: signaling, phone-talking to the various ship's departments, running messages.

Rodney smiled faintly, understanding. "Aye, aye, sir." He moved into the rubber-slotted place which the quartermaster had vacated and grasped the brass-rimmed wheel. It was slimy with fresh blood, too slippery, Rodney found, for dependable steering. The Beaver saw the problem and briskly cleansed the helm with his enormous bandanna.

"Okay now?"

Rodney's vestigial smile seemed to have become permanently etched on his freckled countenance, although there was no element of humor in it, and his disarming plumpness had somehow hardened. As he stood at the wheel, the exec looked like a piece of khaki-draped granite.

When Brute Savage triggered *Davidson*'s six-fish spread, the flagship was within 4,000 yards of the leading Jap cruiser. In the thickening mist, only partially alleviated by the star shells the enemy had lobbed in their direction, the cruiser loomed as huge and menacing as the fabled eighteen-inch-gun battle wagons the Nips were reputed to have under construction. On the depleted bridge, Prince waited, tense with anticipation and rigidly concealed fear, for the results of this initial launch. If they were driving through the sea at their top speed, the fish should strike within four minutes. *If*. Also, if they ever reached their target, didn't swerve because of some error in their complex mechanism, or do the less than unexpected—run too shallow or too deep. The torpedoes discharged like fishbones stuck in a giant's throat, to be ejected only by a gargantuan cough.

Prince darted a glance across the torn decking at Tom Rand, who lay where he had fallen. There had been no time to remove the dead bodies, and none had suggested it. Rand's eyes were open, and they appeared to be regarding the living occupants of the bridge with curious interest. Looking into Rand's unscarred face, Prince observed that the habitual carbon circles which crescented the communicator's upper cheeks were darker than ever, as if death were more fatiguing than life to this perpetually wearied youngster.

Four minutes passed like an eternity.

But nothing happened.

Prince waited another sixty seconds before he issued his instructions to the talker. "Tell Mr. Savage to fire the next round." To the Beaver he said, "As soon as the fish let loose, we'd better start hauling ass before we run smack into that goddamned cruiser."

"I'd suggest," said the Briton, "a fast reverse course so we can expend our starboard torpedoes before we quit this charming area."

Prince's jaw tightened. Once again he had to fight to unclench his aching teeth. Inanely, he wished he were a cigar smoker so that he could have something to bite down on in his terror and frustration. Hagen always chewed a stogey to help absorb the shock of the four-inch guns. But Hagen was dead now, for all the earthly good those flogging cigars had done him.

Close behind *Davidson*, under Lieutenant Commander Koch's cool guidance, *McGraw* had better luck—given the miserable torpedoes' deficiencies, you had to assume a large measure of luck along with the skill involved—with his first spread. His assigned target was the No. 2 enemy cruiser. One of *McGraw*'s fish caught her near the waterline, slightly aft of her flared bow, and bored a visible hole in the Nip's two-inch plating.

All four Allied destroyers were, as the Beaver predicted, too near for the Japs to employ their heavy main batteries. But five-inch quick fire was erupting all around them.

At long last, unconscionably late, it seemed to Prince, the distant Dutch cruisers had opened up with their own big weapons. *Zuyder Zee*'s eight-inch shells passed so close overhead that the crews on the tin cans' decks automatically ducked. The six-inch projectiles hurled by *Noorden* and *Volendam* came even nearer to the crouching men. As yet, Admiral Kuyper's cruisers hadn't found the range, because of their antiquated fire-control systems. By the time they did, Prince thought grimly, it wouldn't matter much to the survivors of DesDiv 11 and the three Dutch dog-dogs anyhow. They'd probably all be trampled into oblivion by the thundering Japanese herd.

Zeeland and *Dordrecht,* having passed the injured *Vincent* and *Haarlem,* were positioned for their torpedo attack against the Jap's two light cruisers. In the rapidly generating melée, Prince was only vaguely aware that they had pulled close by and that their opening salvos had seriously hurt the foe.

But the Nips weren't content to sit doggo and take a pounding. Their own destroyer escort had finally come alive after a surprising period of inactivity.

Davidson found herself assailed from both sides: the larger enemy ships blasting away with their secondary batteries, the destroyers with their five-inchers and, to Prince's sudden anguish, with their long-lanced fish.

Tormented, twisting, striving to elude this latest threat, *Davidson* was maneuvering in dangerous proximity to the Balinese coastline. She was making about twenty-five knots as she swung around 180 degrees to fetch her starboard torpedoes into play. In the process, she narrowly missed colliding with one of the Jap destroyers. But that near disaster had the immediate effect of throwing the Nip off balance, so the foe's torpedoes whished harmlessly past the American vessel's low-slung fantail. Scant minutes later Prince saw them burst against a coral reef, exploding and making the hideous night brighter.

Without bothering for orders, Brute Savage got rid of his fish. One of them miraculously ran true and pierced the Japanese heavy near her stern. It apparently deranged the mammoth cruiser's steering apparatus, for the wounded ship began to swing out of the strangely tight battle formation, heading westward and away from combat.

But the two light cruisers, including the second in line which had been stabbed by *McGraw*'s accurate spread, continued to concentrate on *Davidson,* as if acting under some prearranged tactic of picking the attackers off one by one, beginning with the lead four-piper.

Prince issued the "cease fire" command and ordered his talker to have the searchlight doused.

"We're bugging out," he informed the Beaver succinctly.

"Agreed." The Briton nodded his ursine head in undisguised sadness. "We've no bloody choice, mate."

Yet the flagship could not elude the probing beams of the enemy's searchlights, try as she might. Moreover, the Japanese marksmanship was improving, and the bridge survivors felt, rather than heard, the continued effects of the devastating barrages.

His face ashen, the talker suddenly relayed the news that the steering engine room had been struck by a five-inch shell. Skin-searing leaks from shattered steam pipes below had forced the three-inch AA rifle crew away from its position on the semi-submerged fantail.

Prince called out in a voice that sounded to him like that of a man speaking from an incredible distance: "Tell Mr. Savage to secure his torpedo mounts, then go aft to close off those steam pipes. We'll have to go to emergency steering with the manual tiller, now that power's been lost. That'll be his responsibility, too."

"Okay, sir." The talker repeated the order. "Mr. Savage says he's already on his way."

Thus, guided by the crude physical handling of Brute Savage's team, plus the AA gun crew, *Davidson* started to draw astern of the enemy while still being harassed by the Nip destroyer. She was unpleasantly close to shore, near enough for Prince to catch intermittent glimpses of surf beating upon coral reefs, even without the use of his padded binoculars. So he directed another course change, due south, and without much optimism asked Savage whether the raddled vessel had any more knots up her sleeve.

"Negative," said Savage. "I'm afraid we're losing one boiler as it is. We'll be damned lucky to hold twenty-five knots."

"Do what you can, mister."

"Yes, sir." Like the divisional commander's, Savage's voice had a faraway quality about it, unreal, almost inhuman. "We're giving it all we've got."

Davidson's departure did not go unnoticed. The Jap cruisers administered a few last rounds from their main batteries, now that the range had widened, and she was unexpectedly assailed by an enemy patrol craft which sped along her starboard flank, machine-gunning as it whirled past. More casualties were telephoned to the talker from the midships quarter, near the davitted whaleboat. The launch itself was badly shot up, and a chance .50-caliber bullet neatly cut through her forward lines. Prince ordered the boat jettisoned.

Then the enemy's attention turned upon the remaining destroyers and upon the rapidly approaching *Zuyder Zee* and *Noorden*.

Looking back for the first time in more than twenty minutes, Prince saw that two of the Nip cruisers were burning in several places. Their destroyer guards were too busy protecting the larger ships, he concluded, to bother themselves further with *Davidson*, which they were obviously prepared to write off as a total loss.

From various parts of the ship came doleful reports of extensive damage, relayed to Prince, the Beaver and Rodney, who was himself wounded in the right shoulder, although he refused to go below and have his jagged cut treated. A new talker stood close to the wheel, wearing the gory headset of his predecessor, holding an equally bloodied mike in his unsteady hand. The original talker was sprawled against the after bulkhead, near Tom Rand, whence he had been flung by the force of the Jap patrol boat's .50-caliber fire that had stitched a vertical row of holes from his left hip upward to his right forehead.

Unlike the dead Rand, who continued to stare at his living mates with glazed brown eyes, the talker lay with one eye shut, the other obliterated by an m.g. bullet.

At first Prince thought that his flagship's injuries were chiefly those of which he had already been informed, overt things he had personally seen amidships and on the No. 1 gun, and the blast from the steering engine room. But he was wrong. Terribly wrong.

Shipboard damage can have a chain-reactive effect. So it was with *Davidson*. From Slattery came word that the explosion aft had not only holed her below the waterline but had also sprung the starboard shaft out of line, requiring him to halt the engine that drove it, cutting *Davidson*'s speed in half. In fact, said Slats, they were having the devil's own time trying to stanch the flow before the water began seeping through the less than watertight doors. What was now only an annoying seepage could turn into a veritable flood, Slats said, if those goddamned rusty doors gave, as well they might under the mounting pressure.

"The Blue Peter," he added in a voice stripped of emotion, "got trapped in that frigging compartment with the eleven men he took along to repair the leak."

"Any chance they're alive?" Prince relayed.

"None," said Slats.

"What about steering?"

"By God's grace," said Slattery, "they managed to get the steering lines unfouled. I think we can rig up a makeshift arrangement in the after crew's quarters."

"Keep on it," Prince said unnecessarily, not intending his

message to be transmitted. It wasn't. Even in his state of semi-shock, the talker could distinguish a rhetorical command from the real McCoy.

Further depressing intelligence came from the sonar room. Its electrical supply had been knocked out of commission by a five-inch Nip shell. They'd gone to storage-battery power, but the underwater detection chief sure as hell couldn't guarantee the commander any reliable results unless some Nip sub they might be tracking came within awfully close range. Maybe so close there'd be hardly any warning at all. Over, sir, and out.

Beyond this, Prince soon learned, *Davidson* had sustained numerous small yet potentially lethal punctures from near-miss fragments along her entire portside. Damage-control personnel, under a CPO in Peter Blue's permanent absence, was doing their utmost to plug them with mattresses, blankets and whatever else was handy.

Then Slattery returned to the intercom.

"We've just lost Carl Virtue," he said tonelessly. The No. 2 boiler blew while he was directing repairs. Scalded to death. So were six other guys.

Here the dismal litany finally ended: *Davidson*, a critically wounded craft, almost a hulk, steering uncertainly by manual control, traveling at twelve knots on one engine that might conk out at any moment, absorbing tons of water through more than a dozen holes in her dented hull; four of her ten officers killed; forty-seven of her 186 enlisted men and noncoms dead; more than thirty injured, some superficially, some perhaps fatally, since adequate medical care was quite impossible.

Among the dead, Prince learned, was Falcone, his messenger, who had also caught a Nip patrol-boat bullet as he was carrying a handwritten message from Krebs to the Beaver. As soon as *Davidson* reversed course, close to the Balinese shore, Krebs had scuttled back to his tin-walled charthouse to plot the best possible route along the island's sketchily mapped coast.

The Beaver pried loose a bit of paper from Falcone's lifeless hand where he was spread-eagled at the base of the pelorus, a device which provided bearings on objects that lay ahead, or aft to port and starboard.

"Follow course one eighty, due south, while I figure this out," was the navigator's admonition.

To complicate Krebs' efforts even more, *Davidson*'s chronometers had been jostled about so severely during the shelling that none of them worked properly. As a result, navigational star sightings were little more than educated guesses.

Krebs' verdict meant veering directly away from the sheltering shore and back into the teeth of the battle, if the Japanese decided to pursue the issue.

"We can't do it," said Prince.

The Beaver emitted a disapproving belch. "No ruddy alternative, old cod. Not while we're on this half-arsed emergency steering. Unless you want to chance running aground."

Prince was about to remind the Briton that he, as divisional commander, held the ultimate decision. But he didn't. For it suddenly occurred to him that his proper domain was DesDiv 11, or whatever remained of that hapless assortment of four-pipers, whereas the Beaver ruled this single unit, no longer a supernumerary but in full control of *Davidson*'s individual movements. That *de facto* relationship had been tacitly established, to be sure, but the Beaver was indeed the skipper. Therefore Prince, who had willingly enough eschewed the double duties of captaincy and divisional commander, must not overrule him.

If he continued to observe the strict letter of the Navy's hallowed Book, he couldn't even give the order to abandon ship —which he had seriously considered as the tally of *Davidson*'s enormous troubles continued to mount up.

Fortunately, the enemy appeared content to leave matters as they prevailed for the nonce—a sort of Mexican standoff.

The Japs had managed to establish a minor beachhead on Bali, where the indolent natives would offer little resistance, if any, and which they would reinforce at their leisure, after calling in the carriers that were hovering somewhere in the Banda Sea, well to the east. Besides, two of their cruisers and one of their destroyers had taken a mauling, so the Nip admiral evinced no immediate desire to tangle with Kuyper's relatively unscratched trio. As he headed north through Badung Strait for the open sea, with the Dutch squadron in hot pursuit, there was a brief skirmish at long range, after which the fleeter-paced foe passed out of sight over the dim horizon.

The three crippled tin cans, *Davidson, Vincent* and *Haarlem*, promptly received instructions from Kuyper to proceed for Surabaya in company with *McGraw, Zeeland* and *Dordrecht*, whose damage was minimal. Only at the big Javanese base could *Davidson*'s hurts be repaired. She required major surgery, which would entail a lengthy stay in drydock.

For this, Prince was secretly glad. Within weeks, perhaps days, the remnants of ABDA's combined fleet would have to face the Japs again, woefully outnumbered, like Christian martyrs thrown to the Roman lions, in one last attempt to save Java. It would be a forlorn, useless battle, in the best naval tradition, the grisly epilogue to the history of a cause that was lost from its inception. Prince also felt a certain guiltiness as he contemplated his own immunity from this inevitable carnage. But relief overrode shame.

So they headed for home the long way around, circumnavigating Bali's southern coast, up through the western narrows between it and Java, thence into the Maduran Straits to Surabaya itself. The other course along the northern side of Bali would have been much shorter. But nobody knew for certain where the Japs might be lurking. And the six destroyers, confined to *Davidson*'s limping twelve knots, were told to take no chances.

"If you imagine Surabaya's going to be a rest cure," the Beaver growled to Prince, "I'd suggest retooling the jolly old brain cells. I'll wager the Nippers will be bombing the floggin' place before the week's out."

"Why do you reckon I'm counting on a 'rest cure'?" Prince demanded coldly.

But the Beaver only grinned his unlovely gap-toothed grin, leaving Prince to guess, once again, whether the telepathic bastard had divined his craven maunderings. The Beaver, he knew, would scornfully label him a paper-shuffling beach wallah— God's lowest creature in the nautical hierarchy.

Dawn was breaking as they slowly shaped their new course. The brightening sky to the east, where the night's disasters had taken place, gradually assumed the color of old, pale-pink coral, the sort you find in costly necklaces, not the deadly greenish-white sort of which the nearby reefs were constructed by the quadrillion calcified skeletons of minuscule sea animals. The warmish breeze, soughing across their starboard quarter, had dropped to a scant force 0-1, and the surface was tide-pool calm. With the gentle breeze came the odor of frangipangi, hibiscus, gardenia and orchids, which grew in wild profusion along Bali's magnificent shoreline.

Such fortuitous weather, Prince assured himself, had to be a harbinger of good fortune. Somehow they would make it.

But for the surviving officers and men of *Davidson*, this wasn't the hour for relishing temporal joys. The dead must be gathered up, those who weren't drowned behind the after bulkheads, and sewn into canvas sacks. Unless the weather turned unexpectedly bad, thus further impeding their painful advance, these bodies could await a decent burial in the fertile, foreign soil of Java. If the winds and sea rose, well, then they'd have to toss the poor buggers over the side, after a few perfunctory remarks by Commander Prince, who wasn't at all sure whether there was a Bible aboard the flagship since she didn't rate a doctor to tend the wounded, much less an accredited chaplain.

In addition, there remained the far greater task of keeping *Davidson* afloat, as well as ambulant, for her exhausted repair crews. Thanks to their unremitting labors, and perhaps to the good fortune which Prince had perceived in the gorgeous dawn, they succeeded. The sea water inside *Davidson*'s breached hull was held at a constant level, neither rising nor falling, as the bilge pumps ran smoking hot. Electrical power kept firm. And all other vital functions continued to operate with reasonable efficiency.

Twenty-five hours later the six destroyers crept into the Surabayan roadstead. *Davidson* was ushered straight into drydock.

9

"Whosoever Shall Strike His Colors"

EMPLACING THE 1,240-ton *Davidson* into the floating drydock
was an exacting, worrisome, exasperating business, overseen by
an elderly U.S. naval captain in oil-smeared khakis. He introduced himself to Prince as Franklin Bradshaw—"call me Brad,
son, and belay the ceremonials"—a foul-mouthed EDO (engineering duty only) officer whose assignment was restoring
ABDA's cripples to some semblance of fighting shape. He
looked big and ornery enough for the job.

The drydock itself was capable of hoisting 15,000 tons of
deadweight through the simplistic process of letting the visitant
ship drift through her open stern, then pumping out the water,
until the patient lay high and dry in her steel womb. Most of
the workers were Javanese, supervised at their chores by an in-
different, hard-visaged Dutch foreman. They went about their
tasks lackadaisically, Prince noted with something akin to surprised shock, as he watched the proceedings from a site high on
the drydock's bow.

Captain Bradshaw sensed Prince's concern. "Hell, Commander, just wait'll tomorrow."

"Tomorrow?"

"Sure. It's Sunday. None of these bastards will show up, Christians and Moslems alike. So we've got to make goddamn certain they finish positioning your tin can before quitting time today."

"Jesus," Prince breathed. "And with the war right at their bloody doorstep!"

"That's the problem," said Bradshaw. "We've already had a couple of token air raids by the Japs. Scared 'em shitless." He scratched the beard stubble on his chin. "Even before the raids the natives weren't the world's best friggin' roustabouts. This happens to be a commercial dock, which further complicates matters. Sometimes I have the feeling they couldn't care less . . ." Bradshaw's last sentence dwindled off into ironic silence.

As Prince stood moodily staring down at the emptying dry-dock, he remembered an article in Navy Regulations which markedly decreased his concern for the clumsy nature of these proceedings. The Book stated it very succinctly: "When a ship operating under her own power is being drydocked, the commanding officer shall be fully responsible for [her] safety until the extremity of the ship first to enter the drydock reaches the dock sill and the ship is pointed fair for entering . . ."

Davidson had cleared that uncompromising hurdle. Now she was Bradshaw's baby. Before this, he couldn't have sloughed off the blame for a misstep onto either the Beaver or Rodney, for he, Prince, would be recognized as his ship's skipper, regardless of any informal arrangements made with the Englishman, or the fact that the exec could have taken over after Lieutenant Commander Thornburg's death.

Moreover, despite his messily treated wounds, which demanded immediate attention at the fleet hospital, Rodney had other duties of immense importance at this nadir of *Davidson*'s ill-starred career. The Book was equally specific on that issue.

"Maintain high morale within the command," said another NavRegs article, probably written by somebody who'd never heard a shot fired in anger. "The discipline, welfare, and privileges of the individuals of the command shall be a chief concern of the executive officer . . ."

Davidson's battered hull slowly settled into an upright position on the keel blocks. In waist-deep water, the diminutive brown men began to brace the four-piper with an assortment of four-by-fours, castoff telephone poles and what appeared to be palm logs, to keep her steady during the surgery which Bradshaw hoped to commence next day—using an American naval work force in lieu of the mendaciously Sabbath-minded regular gang.

Bradshaw suddenly yelled at the foreman, "You guys haven't put enough shoring around that bucket. Get more braces. Wooden spatulas, oboes, toothpicks—anything that'll do the trick."

The Dutchman glowered at him. "We're doing the best we can, Captain. But oversized shorings are in short supply."

The Javanese, who had stopped to listen appreciatively to this discourse, went back to their duties, more relaxed than ever. An hour passed.

It was evident, during this stage of the tricky proceedings, that *Davidson* might be in serious trouble. The drydock was designed for fairly large cargo ships, thrice her size, so that an inordinate number of timbers were required to truss her securely against any swells that might develop during the night in the broad harbor. Because of the destroyer's slim thirty-four-foot beam, these timbers had to be extraordinarily long. But no more were available. What resulted was a jerrybuilt affair, which caused Bradshaw to shake his head angrily.

"It won't work!" he roared at the Dutch foreman.

"Sorry, *mijnheer*," said the Dutchman, with no sorrow in his bland voice. "We've used up all our materials."

At this juncture only a few feet of water remained in the bottom of the drydock. *Davidson*, perched uneasily on the blocks, showed unmistakable signs of slippage in the final moments before the dock was fully emptied. Slowly, agonizingly, she started to heel toward her port side as the inadequate shorings gave way, splintering like the toothpicks which Bradshaw had so sarcastically demanded earlier.

With an abrupt lurch, *Davidson* careened against the drydock bulkhead and came to rest at a forty-degree angle, like a tired animal reclining in the shade of a jungle tree. Only the heap of broken spars kept her from collapsing entirely.

From her canted bridge the Beaver shouted through the engine-room tube to Slattery: "Cut off all boilers, mister, and button up your watertight doors again."

"What's happened?" asked the indefatigable Slats. "An earthquake?"

"Worse," snarled the Beaver. "We've been jolly well buggered by human stupidity."

He clapped the voice tube shut and glanced up at Prince, shrugging his mammoth shoulders in mute disgust.

Bradshaw ordered a wooden brow slung between *Davidson*'s uptilted starboard quarter-deck and the drydock. What remained of her crew climbed up the steep slope, lugging their seabags: the hale, the walking wounded, the strongest of the noninjured carrying the worst hurt in improvised blanket-stretchers.

When the Beaver and Rodney reached the place where Prince stood with Bradshaw, the captain said, "I'll order an armed guard in the drydock, to keep the locals from looting your ship blind. Meanwhile, since she's obviously uninhabitable, we'll find bunks for the crew somewhere ashore. As for you gentlemen," he added wryly, "there's always the Dutch officers' club—until the wizards of ABDA decide how to redistribute the wealth, in case *Davidson* proves unsalvageable."

He brooded at the ruined four-piper. Then he concluded: "Personally, from what I read in your dispatches, Commander, and from what I've just seen, I'd guess that Surabaya has neither the facilities nor the equipment necessary to put her back into proper combat readiness. Maybe we can get one engine and one shaft operable. If so, ABDA might order you to Ceylon or Australia, whichever proves more feasible, now that the Japs are swarming down on us like horse flies in turd country."

"And if not?" asked Prince.

Bradshaw grimaced. "Then we'll blow her up."

Under Krebs' temporary leadership, the crew was ferried to the camp set up on a nearby depot grounds yard for homeless casuals. The other officers accompanied Bradshaw to the main pier in his chuffing whaleboat. But this time there were no brass bands, no admiral's staff to greet them, for the Old Man had long since quit Java, and the real welcome had been postponed until Kuyper's cruiser detachment returned next day.

Prince was about to enter Bradshaw's decrepit sedan, along with the Beaver, Rodney, Savage and Slattery, when a dust-covered jeep came bounding around the nearby warehouse. It braked to a halt beside them. Lieutenant Commander van Dekker was at the wheel, wearing a thundercloud look on his ascetic face. Beside him sat Saskia. Unlike her cousin, she was smiling radiantly at Prince.

"Come with us," she invited.

"Yes," van Dekker said in a surly tone, "please do. Saskia insists upon it."

Prince threw his own seabag, which had been fetched to him by some anonymous seaman who had replaced the slain Falcone as the captain's messenger, into the back seat.

He grinned. "I accept your kind invitation."

Before the sedan and jeep parted company, Prince told the Beaver to have yard communications send a message to *McGraw* and *Vincent*, asking that Lieutenant Commanders Koch and Horton meet him at the officers' club at 1600. By then, four P.M., he hoped to have some word about future duties from the U.S. brass at ABDA's advance echelon. It was now shortly past noon. He intended to drop by ABDA's advance headquarters to formalize DesDiv 11's arrival, find out whether they had any word from the main GHQ at Bandung, then grab a bit of lunch at the Simpanische Societiet with Saskia and van Dekker before registering at the goddamned O.C.

"Wilco," said the Beaver, appraising the girl with mock-lechery through narrow green eyes. "We'll rendezvous as instructed. Now you kiddies have a delightful time and try to forget our little troubles for a while."

"Java's troubles," van Dekker responded, in a voice that dripped venom, "are not ones that can be lightly dismissed."

"I wasn't," purred the Beaver, "thinking about you, Leftenant Commander—*ect*ually."

The senior officer of ABDAfloat's skeletal advance headquarters at the Surabaya navy yard was a three-striper, whom Prince recognized vaguely as being a couple of classes ahead of him at the Academy, a beefy blue-jowled fellow named Percival. Under the less than inscrutable nomenclature for midshipmen, he had drawn the nickname of Percy, although he played fullback on the Annapolis football team of 1924-25 and thus hardly deserved such a lace-kerchiefed handle. Percy looked pooped as hell as he scowled up from his temporary plywood desk in an attic office which many years earlier had been a sail loft for Dutch square riggers plying the Indies trade. Then his rough-hewn face relaxed into a semblance of a smile.

"Oh, it's you, Prince," he said.

"You were expecting General MacArthur?"

"Hardly. He still seems to be a trifle tied up on Bataan."
Percy's smile faded. "Perhaps I should've come down to the
dock to meet you. But it wouldn't have served any useful purpose, since Brad had things in hand, anyhow, especially with
this flow of traffic from Bandung." He passed his hand across
a stack of dispatches.

Prince observed that Percy, who had been rated as a remarkably cool customer in his younger days, had gnawed all his
fingernails down to the quick. An ashtray was filled with the
stubs of at least two dozen cigarettes, and Percy was chain-
lighting a fresh one off the butt of yet another.

In one corner of the shabby, dim-lit room were a pair of army
cots, bedding unmade, mute evidence that Percy and his single
yeoman ("my staff," he explained saturninely) did most of
their sleeping here, now that the bombing had begun. This
wasn't, Prince reflected, the sort of *pukka sahib* backwater billet
about which the Beaver had always been so scornful.

"What's the scoop?" asked Prince.

"Totally ungood. The Nippers have gathered four cruisers,
two of them heavies, and fifteen tin cans for a go at Java itself.
They've got a back-up force of four battleships, five carriers,
two heavy cruisers, six lights and twenty-three destroyers. All
guarding the biggest convoy that's ever been assembled in these
parts—fifty-six transports."

Prince managed to convert a shudder into a nominal shrug.
"Sounds like standard operating procedure."

"It's standard, all right," said Percy. "Even the pigheaded
Dutchman's reaction follows the usual script."

"How?"

"Our brass, along with the British, want to pull out. They
know the game's over. Only the Dutch are determined to fight
to the last ship—and man." Percy also shrugged. But his gesture was a mighty expression of distaste. "British ground forces

273

have evacuated Java. Our B-seventeens have all left, and so have most of the transport planes and ground crews."

"So who's running ABDA?"

"The Dutch, of course, who else?" Percy said in a voice that suggested Prince must be some sort of Mongoloid idiot to ask such a stupid question. "Helfrich has the wheel all to himself. He's got a handful of our fighter planes and some beat-up Aussie craft, thirty-one in all, plus what few ships that are left. Most of 'em are cripples. But they're still ABDAfloat," he added derisively. "Still the official, brave, busted-ass, thin red line." Percy stared mordantly through the screenless window of his top-floor office. "Java! Look at it. Rice paddies, palm trees and stinking canals. Our guys find it goddamned hard to imagine they're defending the good old U. S. of A., especially with the Javanese themselves making it plain they have no intention of battling to the bitter end, like their Dutch bosses."

"What's the word from Washington?"

"Nothing's changed," Percy said tonelessly. "Not a flogging thing. Secretary Knox broadcast last night that the Nazis have to be licked first, after which we'll deal with the Japs. That was the gist of it. Kee-rap!"

"So where do we go from here?" Prince demanded. "I mean right now."

Percy made a visible effort to collect his thoughts, while at the same time arranging a set of dispatches on the splintery desk. "You're to assign *Vincent* to DesDiv Ten, get *McGraw* patched up as fast as possible and try to make *Davidson* seaworthy enough for a trip to God knows where. Except for stand-by emergency crews, all your people have been reassigned to Des-Div Ten. Both officers and men. We've absorbed some pretty rough casualty losses throughout the whole force."

"I'd already assumed that," Prince said, "and so did Captain Bradshaw. But I'm talking about the Big Picture."

"Oh," Percy rumbled, "that."

"Who's going to do what to whom and precisely how?"

"Helfrich wants to try a final stab at the Nips. Since nobody's around to argue with him at his level, he's gotten his way. Admiral Kuyper's due here for refueling around dawn tomorrow, as you know. They'll give him everything we own, including *Houston, Perth* and *Exeter* to reinforce *Zuyder Zee* and *Noorden,* and a gaggle of tin-can geese. Eleven of 'em. Yank, British and Dutch." Again Percy uttered an explosive "kee-rap" and lit a new cigarette. "Hell, you know how it is first hand. They'll have to play the whole damned exercise by ear, because Kuyper hasn't a dog's chance of working out an operational plan at this late date. And his communications are as snafued as ever, with no mutual signal code for tactical maneuvers. This time, though, they've really latched on to a brilliant idea."

"So?"

"Kuyper will relay his signals from *Zuyder Zee* to *Houston,* where a Dutch liaison officer will translate 'em into English for transmittal over TBS to the other English-speaking ships." Percy grinned fiendishly. "Your young friend from Balikpapan —what's his name? van Dekker—has been bugging the hell out of me for a combat billet. Now he's got one."

"You mean van Dekker will go in *Houston* as communications liaison?"

"Exactly."

Much to his amazement, Prince actually felt sorry for the eager young Dutchman.

"Has van Dekker been told about his job?"

Percy shook his head. "Negative, fella. I thought you'd be the logical guy to break the news. Being such an admirer of his charmin' female cousin and all that sort of rot."

"Thanks a bundle."

"Forget it," Percy said graciously. "And incidentally, while we're still on the subject of reassignments, you'd probably like to know what they've got in mind for your fair white corpus."

"I would." Prince waited for the blow to fall. "What've they decided?"

"Well," said Percy, "it apparently wasn't easy. We're out of desdivs for gents of your august rank, and ABDA headquarters at Bandung doesn't amount to much more than burial grounds any longer. Still, they've concluded it would be a salubrious idea to bring you across the mountains for a little chat—along with Commander Monk—about how bad affairs look from close up." Prince's expression perceptibly darkened as Percy added, "They're giving you twenty-four hours first to attend to *Davidson*, to make sure she's either finished or capable of minimum repairs. If it's the latter, Rodney can take her to whatever major dockyard the brass chooses. If it's the former, you're expected to guarantee that your gallant flagship is properly set for self-immolation—you know, explosive charges, et cetera, et cetera, so she'll never fall into Jap hands."

"If *Davidson*'s a total loss," Prince asked, "why all the fuss about this scorched-earth policy?"

"I guess ABDA had developed a peculiar respect for the little bastards' ability to mend busted toys," Percy said. "They want to be abso-bloody-lutely positive. That's all."

"Isn't Bradshaw capable of handling it?"

"Plenty. But he's got a million other things on his mind. So *Davidson*'s destruction—assuming it has to happen—is strictly your baby."

In the brief period that he'd been away from Surabaya, the once hustling seaport had become almost a ghost town, Prince observed as they drove toward the Simp. Goats browsed in the scrubby field around an unfinished Moslem temple, whose onion-shaped dome gleamed like molten gold in the broiling midday sun. Traffic was virtually nonexistent, and the pedicabs had disappeared. The city exuded a distinct aura of helplessness, even doom. Yet despite all this there existed a certain fatalism among the remaining populace. Most of the natives had scattered to the countryside in fear of the massive Japanese bombing, which, they understood from gossip freely passed in the waterfront coffeehouses, was bound to come soon. When it did, it wouldn't be the light-fingered stuff they'd felt thus far, but hundreds of tons of HE raining down from the heavens like some kind of devilish manna.

Hanging low in the brazen sky was a pallid sliver of daytime moon. As he caught sight of it, Prince had a vagrant, chauvinistic thought, which took him back to his boyhood in Province Beach, Virginia, where blacks had waited on MaMa's boardinghouse tables. The legend was, he recalled, that Negroes didn't have moons on their fingernails. He'd find himself covertly peering at the servants' hands, to learn the truth of the matter; and even aboard *Davidson* he would rather guiltily snatch a glance at the wardroom attendants' fingers, still wondering. Not that such nonsense mattered. The blacks aboard the four-piper had fought well, once they were summoned from their humble galleys to help man the weaponry, better than many of the whites who held regular topside stations. They fought with a kind of stoic courage that made Prince envious, considering the forlornness of their lot, now, and later when they left the service. They were among the dead who had fallen beside *Davidson*'s No. 1 mount and in the exposed m.g. tubs during the Balinese battle.

Suddenly, illogically, this seemed the opportune moment to inform van Dekker of his communications duties aboard *Houston*.

Prince gave it to him straight. The Dutch lieutenant commander listened in silence while he piloted the jeep past the barricades which had already been erected at principal intersections against the time when the island's defense forces would engage in hand-to-hand combat with the Jap invaders.

Then van Dekker said calmly, "Where is *Houston* now, sir?"

A strangely respectful note had crept into his voice. He was no longer the contemptuous youngster who'd given Prince such arrogant shrift at the wharfside a half hour earlier, but a junior member of the Team.

"She's expected at the fueling dock in the outer roadstead about the same time Admiral Kuyper arrives with his task group. They've sent her up from Tanjong Priok."

"In that event," said van Dekker, "I shall leave you and Saskia at the Simp and make my preparations for joining her."

Prince looked surprised. "Hell, it won't take you that long to throw a few items into a ditty bag. Why not stay for lunch? Might be the last decent meal you'll eat for a damned long while."

The Dutchman replied, "I wish to consult with my friends at headquarters, study their charts and learn what I can about this coming operation."

"You won't learn anything," said Prince, "except the fact that Kuyper has blanket orders to stop the Nips. Period. There's been no chance to iron out the details. It's strictly an *ad lib* affair."

"All the more reason, Commander, why I should like to examine those charts. For all its immensity, the Java Sea is an area filled with much menace. Shoals. Tiny islets. Many places where a ship could be lost. Perhaps I could be of some assistance to *Houston* in that regard, too."

"I'm quite sure," said Prince with genuine sincerity, "that Captain Rooks will appreciate it."

The jeep pulled into the driveway of the Simp, and van Dekker waited for them to disembark. His face was quite solemn. He kissed Saskia on her left cheek, very sedately, and gave her shoulder a quick embrace.

"Dag," he said quietly.

Saskia's eyes were glistening with tears. *"Tot ziens,"* she whispered.

After van Dekker sped away, they walked slowly into the

club's verdant dining patio, hand in hand, like young lovers. Only a few luncheon guests were seated at the wrought-iron tables. Prince selected a spot as far removed as possible from the other guests. He wanted to talk, privately, about some matters that lay heavily on his tired mind, things which Saskia might understand but others would not, especially those here at the Simp: the hardheaded, implacable, resist-to-the-end burghers to whom Java was almost as much home as Holland itself.

Prince knew he could be utterly candid with Saskia, even to the extent of confessing to her his never-ending sense of terror by day and night, his unfitness for the grinding duties allocated him, his unspoken desire to obtain a staff sanctuary for the rest of the war.

Once, when they had gone for a short drive in a borrowed car, before he left for the tragic battle off Bali, Prince had explained this to Saskia. Instead of remonstrating or seeking artificially to bolster his courage with meaningless words, she had cradled his close-cropped, prematurely graying head against her soft breasts, crooning softly, like a mother comforting a frightened child.

Prince remained in her perfumed embrace, listening to the small waves lapping against the corniche where they had parked on a promontory beyond the Surabaya naval station. Then, both silent, they heard the sound of gulls and curlews, wheeling above the inshore marshes, and what might have been an expatriate thrush caroling from a bush near the edge of the strait. It was a good place. They were fortunate to have it, even for these fleeting instants, for that kind of privacy, of aloneness, had become a rare commodity in a world at war. They could spend an hour here, or even a precious few minutes, knowing that this time span was the equivalent of much more—a day, perhaps—in some impersonal public place. Nights were the best, when the moon shone and the brighter stars pierced the velvet draperies of the blue-black sky.

To be sure, there was always Prince's room at the officers' club. They went there often, but it wasn't the same, being more clandestine, furtive and less romantic, even though they could make wild, uninhibited love in the dank darkness.

Now, surrounded by the shabby gentility of the Simpanische Societiet, he again confessed his inadequacy, which was all the more intensified by the verve with which van Dekker had dashed off to join Kuyper's condemned squadron.

"I, too, am habitually afraid," said Saskia.

"Balls! Nobody else in the world could feel the way I do," Prince said dourly. "Like a kid ready to wet his britches."

She smiled at his deliberate crudeness. "Yet you go where you're told."

"Sure. Because I'm more afraid *not* to go than I am to stay. The alternative is worse."

"Being shamed before your peers?"

"I guess that's about it."

"Perhaps," Saskia said, "you are braver than you imagine."

"It's a hell of a way to have to prove it," he growled. "Take the goddamned Beaver. He's made of rock, or iron, or something just as impermeable. The bastard never flinches. He hasn't a scared bone in his whole ugly body."

"Certain people are born that way," Saskia said. "They have something in their genes that dispels the fears the rest of us mortals must live with." She added gravely, "Possibly this is not an attribute at all, but a lack. I think a man who never experienced fear would frighten me. He would be rather inhuman."

"Well," said Prince, "you should feel very safe when I'm around."

"I do. Very, very safe, my darling."

He wanted to pursue the matter, to talk of heroism and cowardice, to wonder aloud in Saskia's comforting presence why he'd become a naval officer at all. Hell. If he had disregarded MaMa and worked his way through some jerkwater college, he'd have been thirty-five when the war started. Plenty old enough to have avoided the draft; and now he would be reveling in those lovely stateside pleasures which Tokyo Rose was always detailing.

Saskia asked, "Why are you so silent?"

He stared at her for a moment. "You plan to stay here in Java, don't you?"

"Yes."

"So you'll wind up in a concentration camp."

"If I'm not killed," Saskia said. "I do not intend to surrender meekly. None of us do."

Prince pretended not to have heard this. "When it's over, and we've finally won, and they've set the Dutch free, do you think the Netherlands East Indies will ever be the same?"

"No. If I live through it, then I shall return to Amsterdam, where it won't be the same, either. Nothing will ever be the same, Prince."

"Why?"

"Here the natives will take over. Our colonial rulers have misconceived their ambitions for too long. We've underestimated their pride, thinking of them merely as Little People to be ordered about—whose souls are as small as their bodies. But this isn't so."

With that the topic seemed exhausted. They ate their sparse meal in silence. When they had finished, Prince said, "I've called a meeting of my commanders—all two of them—at four o'clock. It shouldn't last more than a couple of hours. Will you join me for cocktails here around six?"

"Please," Saskia replied, "yes."

"And then to the delectable haven of my O.C. digs?"

"That, too," she agreed, "for not much time remains."

Prince returned to his delectable haven and entered the mean little room, wondering why the devil he'd given it such a euphemistic coloration, even in jest. It looked rattier than ever. Before he hit the sack for a couple of hours of overdue sleep he told the Javanese houseboy to rouse him at three-forty-five.

When he finally awakened, his watch showed four-fifteen. The goddamned gook had, naturally, forgotten to carry out the simplest of orders. But as Prince was pulling on his greasy, wrinkled trousers, the servant padded in on his bare feet, carrying a mist-cold bottle of Heineken's on a tin tray.

"The commander was sleeping so soundly," he apologized, "that I did not wish to disturb him."

Prince accepted the beer and the apology without comment.

"You'll find a group of American naval officers in the patio lounge. Oh, yes, and one British three-striper with a red beard. Tell them I'll be there in a couple of minutes. *Begrijpt U mij?*"

The houseboy grinned his appreciation of the Yankee's clumsy attempt at Dutch, which he understood better than English, although less well than his own Javanese patois.

"Yes, Commander, I understand."

He departed, still wearing a broad betel-stained grin, as Prince finished dressing. Before leaving, Prince splashed water over his face from the rancid cistern and debated briefly whether he should shave. Then he decided to hell with it, since he was a half hour late already.

Crowded into a corner at the patio for whatever security this slight isolation provided on the wide-open verandah, were Des-Div 11's two remaining skippers, Koch and Horton, and *Davidson*'s surviving officers, Rodney, Slattery, Krebs and Savage. All of them seemed to be listening, entranced, to another yarn in the Beaver's unduplicated repertoire of bawdy tales. Rodney's arm had been neatly bandaged and placed in a khaki sling.

Prince caught only the tag line in the Beaver's protracted joke, so he did not join in the general laughter.

"Class dismissed," he said. "Now we'll talk shop."

Unmincingly, he relayed what Commander Percival had told him at ABDAfloat's advance headquarters. Tomorrow afternoon, late, he and the Beaver would fly over to Bandung to talk with the big brass, leaving Rodney and five crewmen to keep a weather eye on *Davidson*'s repairs. This was, Prince had to admit to himself, narrowing the twenty-four-hour deadline. But he saw no need to wait over an extra night, since the yard workers wouldn't be doing anything after dark anyhow, floodlights being forbidden now that the air raids had started.

The other flagship officers and men would report for reassignment to Commander Percival, who should have their new postings on hand by midmorning.

Van Dekker, still visiting his friends at the Dutch GHQ, had promised that transportation would be provided in front of the O.C. at 0800.

"Or earlier," Prince said, "if trouble breaks."

"Trouble, sir?" asked Brute Savage.

"Like a bombing by the Nips. There are reports of enemy carriers somewhere in the Java Sea. Christ knows what they're apt to try—or when."

"Yes, sir." Savage relaxed into his usual unflappable silent self, seated with his long legs drawn up under his chair, like an angular Buddha.

Koch took his instructions with similar aplomb. Rejoining DesDiv 10 was getting to be old hat for *McGraw*. As for Broad Tail Horton, he reported that *Vincent* mightn't be as badly damaged as they had originally reckoned. With some extra effort she could be rendered—as the Book said—"in all respects ready for sea, prepared to proceed on duty assigned" by the following nightfall.

"Maybe not in *all* respects," Broad Tail added grimly, "but enough so we can carry our own weight in a scrap."

"Good," said Prince. "Kuyper's going to need every blasted gun that's available, and then some." He briefly outlined the preposterous plan for stopping the Japs with cruisers *Houston, Perth, Exeter, Zuyder Zee* and *Noorden*, plus the few destroyers still relatively intact. "It sounds wild. But that's how it is, gentlemen."

"Now that we've heard the good news," said Koch in his dry, pedantic voice, "what's the bad?"

"You've got the full pitch, Ole Pare. There's nothing more."

"In that case, I think I'll shove off. Kuyper's the kind of joker who'd wake up at midnight—and decide it's time to haul anchor."

"He's not due back till morning."

"Wait not, want not," intoned Koch, rising to his feet. "What about you, Broad Tail?"

"I'll string along, too. *Vincent* could at least help stave off an invasion."

They walked toward the steps that led to the asphalt driveway, chatting earnestly together, and began the long wait for the taxicab the doorman had called for them.

The Beaver, who had downed the last of his Heineken's, impassively watched them go. He emitted a farewell belch. "It is, I suspect, time for us bereft types to get down to some serious drinking." Then he shouted at the white-jacketed waiter hovering near the bamboo bar. *"Kom hier!* The Javanese pattered across the mosaic-covered porch. "What's the whiskey situation in this royal establishment?"

The waiter shrugged his incomprehension. But an American officer seated with still another batch of potential replacements called from the adjacent table, "They're out of Scotch, Commander. All that's left is a weird concoction from Australia which tastes like a cross between bad bourbon and good hemlock."

"Sounds delectable," the Beaver opined. "I shall—as you Yanks say—spring for first round. If we survive, Prince can buy the next."

When the whiskey arrived, it proved to be as vile as the informative American had predicted. Nonetheless the Beaver, in an unwontedly sober mood, hoisted his glass in a toast: "To our fallen comrades, God rest their souls."

Saskia met him an hour later. Prince was already tipsy from the beer and the poisonous Aussie booze, but the girl made no mention of his condition, even helping guide him to their usual secluded table. He ordered champagne. Much to their surprise, a magnum of Bollinger '29, one of the world's best, was available. Perhaps, thought Prince, Saskia's beauty or his residual reputation as a hero had impelled the management to delve into its Very Special Reserves. More likely, he decided morosely, it was the former. At this desperate stage, anybody who sailed against the overwhelming Jap fleet was a ruddy hero; but beauty such as Saskia possessed, deep-down beauty, was vouchsafed to very few women.

He listened quietly while she described her afternoon of drilling with Lee Enfield rifles in the town square.

"We have become quite proficient. My marksmanship has been pronounced *zeer goede* by the instructor."

Prince nodded unsmilingly. The thought of a thousand Saskias, armed with those wretched weapons, was not amusing. They wouldn't last five minutes against a determined Jap landing party.

He pushed away his fruit-tart dessert. "Let's get the hell out of here," he said harshly, "and go to my room."

Saskia concealed her surprise at his abrupt change of mood. "As you wish."

Both of them, entering the grubby chamber at the rear of the O.C., knew without voicing the thought aloud that this would probably be their last night together for a long, long while. Perhaps forever. The likelihood that either would survive struck Prince as being extremely remote, if not impossible. Yet for some curious reason the poltroon attitude he had displayed during their luncheon conversation was gone, now, leaving in its place something that was neither courage nor cowardice, but a kind of lethargic submissiveness to the fateful events which were crowding upon them both.

Still without speaking, they undressed in the darkened room, not bothering to light the candle, and went immediately to bed. Slowly, his irrelevant anger gone, Prince drew her naked body against his.

For the first time in his life he heard himself tell a woman, "I love you," knowing that he genuinely meant it.

"And I love you," she whispered.

He took her gently at first, until her response became more passionate, and they reached their violent climax together. That night they did not sleep. Instead, they rested, eyes wide open to the moonglow which poured through the slatted window, until they were ready for more lovemaking.

"Suppose," Prince asked softly at some unknown moment of an indeterminate predawn hour, "you have a baby?"

Saskia nestled closer. "I have pondered this often," she said, "and the thought of bearing your child gives me great pleasure."

He gazed into her smiling face, incredulous, as she interwove her small moist body around his own hard six-foot frame.

"But God only knows where I'd be if it happened," Prince demurred.

"No matter." Saskia's face was beatific in the dim light. "We would join you, our child and I, when the war ends." She paused, then added almost shyly, "If you still wanted me."

"Christ," he muttered, "I'd want you, anytime, anywhere, and always."

The sound of sirens brought them rudely awake. With the ululant wail came also the noise of distant bombing. Prince brushed aside the mosquito netting and leaped from the bed. He rushed to the door and stepped outside. The dawn breeze felt chill against his sweat-drenched body, but he disregarded it as

286

he sought to determine the origin of the explosions. Then he returned to Saskia, who had also slipped from the bed and was rapidly dressing.

"It's got to be the Japs," he said, "bombing the goddamned harbor."

He flung himself into his clothes. Side by side they ran along the tangled garden pathway to the patio. It did not occur to them that their ill-kept secret was, by this simple act, thoroughly cast into the open. Nor would they have cared. In a few moments they were joined at the club's entrance by the Beaver, Krebs, Rodney, Slattery and van Dekker.

The latter evinced no annoyance or surprise at finding his cousin and Prince together at this unseemly hour.

"My jeep," he said bluntly, "can hold only six persons."

Saskia nodded. "I understand, Pieter. I shall make my own way back to my duty station."

"I'm sorry," van Dekker added.

"Don't be," she pleaded. "Just hurry."

With the Dutchman at the wheel, the overcrowded vehicle raced away, down the O.C. drive, two-wheeling onto the semi-deserted main thoroughfare, and thence along a beeline course for the naval station. As they approached nearer, they saw great gouts of black smoke rising from the stricken yard. Soon the acrid reek of burning oil engulfed them.

They found Bradshaw at the pierhead, preparing to descend into his whaleboat for the short trip across the fuming harbor to the anchored drydock in which *Davidson* lay.

"Come along," he offered, "but make it snappy."

So Prince, the Beaver, Rodney, Krebs and Slattery joined him. Van Dekker tossed them a hasty collective salute before spinning the jeep around to head for the outer roadstead where Kuyper's flagship, *Zuyder Zee* was due within the hour. The Dutch force had made contact earlier than expected with the American and British cruisers and, owing to the expectation of still more Jap air raids, had directed them to proceed at flank speed toward the fueling depot.

"This time around," Bradshaw said, "the bastards used carrier planes. It's the first such strike. And it means we can expect visits every hour on the hour, if that's what pleases 'em."

Although the attack had been a hit-and-run affair, enough enemy aircraft had participated to give the ships moored in Surabaya harbor a thorough working over. *Vincent*, already wounded, had been sunk. With her, said the bleary-eyed salvage captain, went most of her crew, including Lieutenant Commander Horton. The injured Dutch destroyer *Haarlem* had also been sent to the shallow bottom of the landlocked bay. *McGraw* had sustained some topside damage. But she was still seaworthy, said Bradshaw, and had gotten under way to join DesDiv 10 as part of Kuyper's mini-armada.

There was no opportunity to lament these losses, either of ships or boon companions like Broad Tail Horton. Too much work remained to be done.

In the smoky confusion of the raid the Japs had mistaken the drydock for a capital ship. She had absorbed cruel punishment, yet stayed alive, after a fashion, although she was clearly in a precarious position. Around her clustered an assortment of small craft and barges which, under Bradshaw's orders, were busily offloading everything remotely useful from *Davidson*'s reclining hull, which also had taken a further pounding. Portable gear went first, including dry stores, fresh foodstuffs, radio spares, tools, small arms and ammunition. With the captain prodding them mercilessly, the native work crews next removed the echo-ranging devices, TBS radio and short-wave receivers, deck guns—all except the three operable four-inch main battery rifles. These were too heavy to lift without a crane, and the drydock's hoist had been among the casualties of the Nip attack.

"Nothing to lose sleep over," Prince remarked bitterly. "They make a nice, loud noise. But they aren't worth a hoot against planes, because they can't elevate past forty-five degrees. And when you run into anything bigger than a sampan, they're about as effective as a busted slingshot."

"So," said Bradshaw, "they'll be blown up along with every-thing else that's left aboard—torpedo tubes, propulsive equipment, the ship herself."

"Today?" asked Prince.

"Whenever the Big Brass passes the word."

Quietly, determinedly, the indefatigible captain thereupon plunged ahead with his preparations to send *Davidson* to King-dom Come upon instruction from ABDA at Bandung. There was, he conceded, an off chance that the four-piper might be rendered fit for duty again. But it was exceedingly remote. The Javanese artisans were so unnerved by the latest air raid and so aware that others would inevitably follow that they could no longer be relied upon for any consistent work. To ready *Davidson* for a long voyage to an Indian Ocean port was undoubtedly beyond their limited capability, Bradshaw concluded sadly, and therefore beyond his, too.

"We'll handle the demolition detail ourselves," the captain said. "I'd rather not let this particular cat out of the bag. Not yet, anyhow."

"Why?" Prince asked.

"In case we get an unexpected respite from the friggin' Nips, which allows us to proceed with repairs."

"But you just said—" Prince began.

Bradshaw shut him off brusquely. "I was discussing the like-liest possibility. Even a tired old man can dream."

Prince gave the captain a wondering look. Bradshaw's face, neck, arms and hands were the color of burnt barbecue meat, after his many trips below to supervise the task of stripping *Davidson*. Now this incredible fellow openly admitted to hoping that DesDiv 11's prostrate flagship might yet be pulmotored back into some semblance of life. Prince had remained topside during the whole endeavor, issuing commands when necessary, but letting the captain carry the brunt of the job. He shook his immaculate head. Dedicated antique types like Bradshaw, he supposed, preferred to dream of slim-hulled destroyers rather than slim-hipped damsels. To them a ship really was a *she*.

The captain was amplifying his last statement: "Besides, once those shoreside buggers figure we've given up the ghost, it'll just serve to panic 'em that much more. So we'll keep this quiet. Savvy?"

"Affirmative," said Prince. "I read you five-by-five."

The Beaver, who had been serving below with Bradshaw, smoothed his beard. It was a redundant gesture. The rufous growth was already plastered flat against his scarred face with sweat and grease.

"You're absolutely right, Captain," he said. "From what I've seen, our friends seem to be funking out rather rapidly. Not that I blame the poor devils, considering what they've got left to fight with."

After the bumboats and barges had departed, laden to the gunwales with *Davidson*'s gear, Bradshaw went calmly about his deadly business, with the four Americans and the Beaver following his crisp instructions like docile coolies. They strung electric leads to a half-dozen areas throughout the destroyer, with special attention to the engine rooms, and attached explosives to the end of each wire. Only the final connections were left unhooked. Carefully, with a patience that belied his exasperation with the multiplicity of circumstances beyond his control, Bradshaw explained in detail how these were to be joined to the lead-ins.

"It's my basic responsibility," he said, "but Christ only knows whether I'll be around when the moment comes to throw the switch." He surveyed his four companions. "Or any of us, for that matter. But if we each understand how to handle the chore, then the odds are six-to-one improved. Correct?"

Prince answered for all of them. "Naturally, sir."

"Have you got the drill fixed in your minds?" Bradshaw persisted.

"Yes, sir," said Rodney.

The others nodded their assent. It was a simple enough procedure, Prince thought, which hardly required all this precise foo-fa-raw from a retreaded EDO captain. Nevertheless, to satisfy the old coot that they comprehended, and perhaps out of belated pity for his obvious utter exhaustion, Prince soothed him with a promise that he had nothing to worry about.

"Commander Monk and I have to run up to Bandung," he said. "But we'll be back soon. In the meantime Lieutenant Rodney is in charge. He's a bright guy. So are Slattery and Krebs. Especially Slats," he added, not unkindly, "because this fat bastard holds a wizard's degree in mechanics. He's the genius who kept *Davidson* going when it looked as if we'd had it for sure at Bali."

"All right," Bradshaw acknowledged grudgingly. "But in case I'm knocked off in a raid, and anything goes wrong, I'll come back and haunt you—so help me Hannah!"

"Depend on us," said Prince.

"Very well." The captain knuckled his smarting eyes. "Incidentally, when you get to ABDA headquarters, give it to those jokers straight, will you? No weaseling. No beating around the goddamned bush. If you think this place is a shambles now, wait till we've had a few more Jap calling cards dropped on us."

Even Admiral Kuyper had received orders to bypass the stricken base, and told to move immediately against a large Japanese task force somewhere east of Bawean Island, with his four cruisers, a handful of British destroyers, DesDiv 10 and the Dutch tin cans.

Van Dekker had been delivered to *Houston* in a fast patrol boat. So all was well, from the bilingual communications standpoint.

Prince tried unsuccessfully to erase Saskia from his mind, as they climbed the spindly ladder into the fat-bellied fuselage of the plane, an Aussie-built version of the American Lockheed twin-engined bomber. Sitting in the left-hand command seat was the pilot. He had no assistant.

"Just you two cobbers?" he asked.

"Check," said Prince. "One Yank, one Limey."

With a casual flick of his hand, the pilot signaled the ground crew to remove the wheel chocks, and the Hudson started waddling down the runway. Taking off, it climbed steeply, and within minutes Surabaya was well behind them. Below, the rice paddies were already giving way to the foothills of the 10,000-foot peaks that lined their due-west course to Bandung. As at Manila, ages ago, Prince's final glimpse of the Dutch base was a dwindling pall of dark smoke.

There was no need to gild any lilies, Prince and the Beaver discovered shortly after they landed at Bandung and were escorted to the GHQ presided over by the Dutch naval chief, Admiral Helfrich. Nobody at ABDA held any illusions, even though Helfrich himself persisted in his belief that the Netherlands East Indies should—and must—be defended to the last man, woman or child.

A squat, grim-visaged officer, Helfrich asked a variety of questions. He listened gravely as either the American or the Briton replied. They were intelligent queries, not *pro forma* ones, because the Dutchman seemed honestly anxious to learn exactly how ABDA's ships fared in close combat with the Japanese—where they excelled and where they failed.

The Beaver's answers were the most explicit. "I'll save Commander Prince the embarrassment of having to respond to those matters. He fought his destroyer well. But, like most of our Allied vessels, the *Davidson*-class four-pipers are old, undergunned and inferior in virtually every way to their opposite numbers in the enemy's fleet. The same goes for our cruisers, sir. And I needn't remind you that our air cover is almost nil."

"No," said Helfrich grimly, "you needn't. Admiral Kuyper has requested aerial support for his present mission. He has already come under attack by Japanese bombers. Fortunately, our ships thus far have escaped without serious damage." He spread his small hands in a way that reminded Prince of a beggar seeking alms. "We have eight Brewster fighters and less than a dozen dive bombers in service at Surabaya. The decision has been made to employ these against the Japanese transports."

At Helfrich's invitation, Prince and the Beaver went into the ABDA operations room, a sprawling complex the size of a king's ceremonial chamber, which overlooked the marketplace of the handsome inland city. From below, through the screened windows, Prince could hear the inevitable sounds of sidewalk hawkers, shouting their wares, and he caught the pungent odor of overripe tropical fruit. Like the native inhabitants of Surabaya before the air raids, Bandung's populace seemed determined to live out their remaining days in normal fashion, ignoring the omnipresent fact of war, and then perhaps strive to retain this same normality after the Japs came. But unlike Surabaya, their city possessed little of military value worth bombing. It stood in the midst of lush, highly cultivated country. As the *Pacific Islands Year Book* remarked in its 1942 edition (released before the Asian war began): "It presents a magnificent view of ordered beauty."

Regrettably, the huge room crowded with the Allies' joint operational staff offered no such pleasant and orderly vista.

A single glance at the charts hanging from its walls spelled out the story of chain-reacting disaster. An equally brief scanning of the drawn countenances of the officers who sat at their desks pondering dispatches, or who were huddled over plotting boards, doodling aimlessly with sharpened pencils and dividers, gave Prince an immediate sense of dire futility.

Somebody offered him a mug of black coffee. He accepted it gratefully. The scalding liquid felt good as it traveled toward his queasy stomach.

The battle into which Kuyper had steamed so gallantly lasted precisely eight hours, from four P.M. until midnight. It ended

293

in predictable catastrophe, which neither Helfrich nor his American and British counterparts, Vice Admiral W. A. Glassford and Rear Admiral A. F. E. Palliser, had any power to forestall, once the die was cast at the Dutch leader's insistence.

On Helfrich's desk lay a message sent him the previous day by Kuyper, whose ships had been scouring Java's north coast for forty-eight hours, ready to break up the anticipated enemy landing.

"Personnel have this afternoon reached the point of exhaustion," it said bluntly. "Request permission to enter Surabaya for rest and refueling."

This plea, of course, had to be denied when two reconnoitering Allied submarines and a lone seaplane radioed that the Japs had concentrated their amphibious fleet near Bawean Island for the invasion of the Malay Barrier's cornerstone, Java.

Almost contemptuously, aware that the Allied force was largely composed of cripples, the Nip admiral guarding the convoy did not bother to summon reinforcements. Thus, numerically, it might have appeared that the two opponents were evenly matched.

While the troop-laden transports moved north out of danger, the Jap warships hastened southward along a direct interception route. Every move which Kuyper made was known to the enemy commander, for Nip scoutcraft shadowed him at every zigzag turn. Down the sealanes, straight as a flight of homing mallards, sped the Japanese Covering Group: two heavy cruisers, two lights, eighteen destroyers.

Less than an hour after having been turned away from Surabaya, the Allies encountered the foe, driving toward the southwest in two echelons. *Zuyder Zee*, in the van, started firing her eight-inch forward batteries at 28,000 yards. So did the leading Nip heavy, which had the immense advantage of three gunfire spotting planes. Yet during the initial clash *Zuyder Zee* was hit by only one shell, a dud at that, which penetrated her auxiliary engine room.

With unflagging zeal, Kuyper continued to press northwest-ward, aiming for his assigned goal, the transports.

So the Jap admiral interposed a light cruiser and a squadron of swift, modern destroyers athwart the Allies' forward com-ponent. They raced across choppy waters at full throttle, plainly intent on crossing Kuyper's *T,* while leveling a torpedo attack.

By the sheerest chance, one of the Nip heavies at this awk-ward moment managed to drop an HE shell directly on *Exeter's* afterdeck. It was no dud. It exploded in a powder chamber, causing the British cruiser to slew to port, out of what until then had been a reasonably firm line.

Those ships immediately behind her, without waiting for van Dekker's relayed word from *Zuyder Zee* via *Houston,* also turned left. This inadvertent maneuver laid the Allies' broad-side to the onrushing enemy destroyers. Nevertheless only one Dutch tin can was sunk.

Like a wagon-train master, Kuyper raced his flagship around the milling throng, struggling to reassemble them into a sem-blance of proper formation. *Perth* laid down a smoke screen to protect the severely wounded *Exeter,* which was nearest the advancing Japs, then took up station aft of *Zuyder Zee.*

But the Combined Striking Force, as Kuyper's small band was grandiosely named, never regained its original order. Coun-terattacking in a valiant effort to save *Exeter,* the three British destroyers came under murderous fire from the enemy's cruisers. One was sunk by a hail of shells.

As darkness fell, Kuyper decided to retire under the protec-tion of the American destroyers, who kept the foe temporarily at a respectful distance with a long-range torpedo assault. His withdrawal was only a diversion, however, for the ensuing signal from *Zuyder Zee* sent the Allied survivors back on a collision course with the Nip troop ships.

This was a brave, tragic, fatal error.

As Kuyper's reduced force headed north, a swarm of Jap bombers zoomed overhead, releasing magnesium flares, which illuminated his ships like bull's-eyes in a shooting gallery. Indeed, those few square miles of the Java Sea were just that: a shooting gallery with flesh-and-blood targets, photographed and grotesquely overexposed.

One British destroyer, her guns useless, aflame, was finally abandoned by her crew.

To compound this incredible confusion, Kuyper, in guiding his battered group westward along the Java coast for a try at the transports if they attempted a landing, stumbled into a minefield laid earlier in the day by a Dutch team which had failed to inform the beleaguered admiral.

That cost him another British destroyer.

Still, with his four cruisers and his pitiful assortment of tin cans, Kuyper plunged on. Shortly before midnight a pair of Jap heavy cruisers hove into indistinct view some 8,000 yards distant on the Allies' port. It was a thoroughly unequal duel at such short range, made even worse by an enemy torpedo charge which administered fatal blows to both *Zuyder Zee* and *Noorden*.

Before his blazing flagship went down, the heroic Kuyper sent word to *Houston* to lead *Perth* and whatever destroyers remained into Batavia. For safety's sake they took separate courses toward the Dutch capital's harbor of Tanjong Priok.

Shortly after one A.M. *Houston* felt that she was far enough away from the Japanese to radio the doleful news to Helfrich: half of the Allied force destroyed, its admiral lost, and not a single Nip vessel sunk. Moreover, the unscathed convoy was even now advancing toward its scheduled beachhead on northern Java.

Nobody went to his quarters that night, nor the next day, while Helfrich debated what he must do. Prince stood by uncertainly, chilled despite the sodden heat, as the Dutchman argued stubbornly with Glassford and Palliser. What few ships he had left were divided between Surabaya, where *Exeter* had gone with DesDiv 10 to nurse her injuries, and Tanjong Priok.

Reluctantly, Helfrich approved dispatching the American four-piper division to Australia. Koch, in *McGraw,* received orders to help the sole remaining British destroyer escort *Exeter* to the Indian Ocean haven of Ceylon. It was agreed that the Java Sea was too risky a place for any Allied ship now, with the rampant Japs in full cry. Because the operational experts believed the foe had put a stranglehold on Bali, and as a result closed the straits between that island and Surabaya, they elected to send not only the crippled *Exeter* but the two relatively healthy survivors, *Houston* and *Perth,* around the western tip of Java, through Sunda Strait. The latter were told to make Tjilatjap their base.

This was, like so many other recent edicts, a cataclysmic mistake, one that would seal the Allies' fate in the Netherlands East Indies.

Unbeknownst to the ABDA commanders at Bandung, who no longer enjoyed the advices of long-range intelligence, the Japs had barricaded Sunda Strait with a mighty task force—assembled to protect their biggest amphibious operation to date.

Houston and *Perth* were murdered at approximately midnight on February 28. Next day, not having received word of this latest disaster, *Exeter* and her two escorting destroyers ran headlong into a potent enemy force midway during their swing through the Java Sea. All three were sunk.

Prince listened distractedly as Helfrich announced these dismal tidings in a sepulchral voice. It seemed impossible that the disdainfully cool Perry Koch was dead, *McGraw* gone and only *Davidson* left out of DesDiv 11's original quartet. For a full five minutes he leaned against the window, eyes closed, trying to reconcile himself to what had happened.

Then he turned his attention back to the oblong table at which the three naval chieftains were sitting, smoking and endeavoring to pick their way through the dilemma that confronted them. They were admirals without fleets. All that remained, it seemed to Prince, was to see what the generals without armies would recommend, particularly in the face of fresh news that a Nip carrier group was on the loose between southern Java and Australia, obviously bent on interdicting any attempt by the Allies to assist the Indies from Down Under.

Opening the discussion with a candid appraisal of the hopelessness of their plight, Glassford gave it as his solemn opinion that they should get the hell out of Java—soonest.

Admiral Helfrich looked stunned for a moment. He coughed and carefully wiped the spittle from his beard-stubbled chin before he spoke.

"I must decline," he said quietly, "to accept your recommendation. I must continue resistance as long as I have ships that can fight. I have already ordered a greater concentration of submarines against the enemy in the Java Sea. The enemy will make another attempt to land tonight near Rembang. He may succeed—but I shall attack the next wave of transports."

When the Dutchman finally paused, Palliser declared: "Then I must say to you as the Senior British Naval Officer in this area that my instructions from the Admiralty are to withdraw His Majesty's ships from Java when resistance will serve no further useful purpose." He hesitated a split-second, but plunged on before Helfrich could interrupt. "That time, in my judgment, has come. Therefore I feel it my duty to order my ships to India at once, and this I propose to do."

"You realize," the Dutch admiral snapped, "that you are under my orders?"

"I do, of course," said Palliser. "But in this vital matter I cannot do other than my duty as I see it."

Helfrich played his trump card. "You know what I lent to the British when Malaya was threatened, all of my fighting fleet— my cruisers, my destroyers, my submarines, my air—all of it was placed at your disposal for operation as you saw fit. In doing so we suffered grave losses. Furthermore, you did not hold Malaya. Singapore is now in the hands of the enemy. You failed. I think the wisest course now is to let me continue to handle this situation and save Java."

But Palliser was unmoved. In a voice depleted of all emotion he said simply, "I cannot alter my position."

"Will you delay one hour?" asked Helfrich, "until I see the governor general and inform him what you intend to do?"

"I cannot delay any longer. Every minute counts now."

"And you," asked Helfrich, turning to Admiral Glassford, "what do you intend to do?"

"My instructions are to report to you for duty," the American replied stonily. "Any orders you give will be obeyed at once. I wish to say to you, however, that I concur without reservation in the advice given you by your chief of staff." Glancing at the Briton, he added, "I am to retire on Australia by order of my Commander in Chief if necessary to abandon Java. But that is for you to decide."

Helfrich let a long moment pass before he stood up, taller than life size, with his palms pressed flat against the tabletop.

"Very well then, Admiral Palliser," he said in a low voice which Prince had to strain to hear, "you may issue any instructions you wish to His Majesty's ships. Admiral Glassford, you will *order* your ships to Australia."*

With the Beaver close behind, Prince went out into the blistering autumnal sunlight, where even the palm trees appeared to be withering in the pitiless glare, and the unwatered turf around GHQ had burned an ugly brown.

Glassford, said Prince, had offered them a choice: accompanying him to Exmouth Gulf, in northwestern Australia, or flying down to Sydney with a few other Americans ticketed to join MacArthur, whose departure from Corregidor was expected at any moment.

* This slightly edited conversation, as recounted in the Glassford Report, pp. 58-60, was taken from Samuel Eliot Morison's *The Rising Sun in the Pacific*, pp. 376-77, third in his magnificent 15-volume semi-official "History of United States Naval Operations in World War II."

The Beaver mulled this over for a few moments. Then he said, "We've got a third alternative, old boy."

"We have?" Prince acted surprised.

"Yes. We could return to Surabaya and lend our chaps a hand in seeing to it that *Davidson* is properly disposed of."

"Hell! Between Bradshaw and Rodney, there's ample talent to handle that detail."

"Speaking for myself," said the Beaver, "I should hate to have it on my conscience if anything went wrong."

"What could?"

"The way the Nippers are bombing Surabaya, I can think of a dozen eventualities, such as either or both of those fellows getting knocked off. If it's Bradshaw, all you'd have left is a two-striper who doesn't carry much clout with the bloody Dutch."

Prince pondered this somewhat longer than the Beaver had weighed the choices of Exmouth Gulf, Sydney or Surabaya. *Davidson* wasn't really his baby, but a sort of stepchild; or, to phrase it in nautical terms, merely the vehicle that carried his divisional command burgee. As the flagship's senior surviving officer, Rodney held the prime responsibility for her destruction. Prince's obligation to *Davidson* was a proxy matter, one that he didn't intend to exercise. Not now. Not while there was such a golden opportunity to leave this island, under Admiral Glassford's honorable aegis, and make his way to safety. He had already decided on Sydney, where Chief Yeoman Bream presumably was on the lookout for a decent shoreside billet suitable to his special talents. With MacArthur on the scene, there would be plenty of staffwork for certain. What he had decided upon was realistic; but realism can also mask cowardice, he knew, and often does.

"We'll send word to Bradshaw and Rodney to blow the goddamned ship," he growled, "as soon as we get to Tjilatjap tomorrow."

"Is that final?"

"Affirmative."

The Beaver's bearded lips compressed. "Very well, mister, but please let the record show that your humble servant does not—repeat not—concur."

Prince didn't reply. Instead, he stalked back into the defunct ABDA headquarters, where the admirals without fleets and the generals without armies were somberly ironing out the details of their exodus.

Four Catalinas were summoned, one pair from Surabaya and the other from Broome, midway between bombed-out Darwin and Exmouth Gulf. They were due at Tjilatjap next day. The two admirals and their staffs left Bandung in automobiles for the long drive to the last Javanese coastal city still free from Nip aerial assaults.

That same morning after their terminal conference, Helfrich himself boarded a Dutch naval plane for Ceylon.

Prince and the Beaver rode in a car jammed with middle-grade American officers. It was a rugged trip along a twisting mountain road, much of it after dark, when they had to proceed with minimal headlighting for fear a stray Nip reconnaissance plane would spot them and leap to the natural conclusion that the Allies were evacuating.

More bad news awaited the escaping ABDA personnel at Tjilatjap, least of which was the fact that one of the PBYs had been forced back to Broome with a conked-out engine. The three that floated like oversized ducks on the deceptively untroubled harbor couldn't handle all of the officers, men and necessary equipment which must be removed from Java to Exmouth Gulf and Sydney. So Glassford ordained that a U.S. submarine would act as an additional getaway vessel, along with a few merchant ships thinly protected by an array of old Yangtze River gunboats and a couple of small British corvettes, whose combined firepower wouldn't have deterred the least destroyer in the Japanese navy.

For the Sydney-bound group, a nondescript DC-3 transport plane, flown by a Dutch pilot, would have to suffice.

But the worst news was that Surabaya's latest bombing had cost the lives of Captain Bradshaw, the salvage expert, and Commander Percival, the American liaison officer. They were in the latter's topside headquarters, debating how best to aim the handful of ships still in the great port toward dubious safety, when enemy carrier planes suddenly appeared at low level over the almost deserted city. There was no time to run downstairs to the bomb shelter.

By some vagary of chance, Percival's yeoman escaped with minor shrapnel wounds. His name was signed to the message which a Tjilatjap communicator handed to Prince soon after the motor convoy straggled into the south-coast base.

"Regret to inform you," read the dispatch sent to Admiral Glassford, with ComDesDiv 11 as information addressee, "that Captain Bradshaw, Commander Percival and undetermined number of shipyard ratings were killed in air raid. All vessels except destroyer *Davidson* have departed Surabaya. Lieutenant Rodney, executive officer of *Davidson*, requests instructions on disposition of his ship now immobilized in drydock. He urges prompt reply in view of precarious nature of crisis and fact that most of his men have also been killed in attack."

In conformity with time-honored custom, Prince relayed the sheet of tissue to the Beaver, who perused it without visible emotion, also as usual.

The Briton gave his companion a long, searching look, which bespoke his thoughts more clearly than any words might have done. Prince understood. The Beaver was silently reiterating what he had said at Bandung: They should have taken that last opportunity to fly back to Surabaya and made certain beyond all doubt that *Davidson* was given a decent burial, so that her mangled corpse wouldn't just lie there and rot.

"Radio Lieutenant Rodney," Prince muttered, "to execute immediately the demolition of his ship."

PART IV

10

"Winter of Discontent"

IN THE UNCERTAIN March of 1942, even though he flew the proud flag designating him Commander Allied Forces Southwest Pacific (ComSouWesPac) from his Sydney headquarters, Admiral Herbert F. Leary's naval larder was almost bare. He had the six destroyers which fled the carnage along the Malay Barrier, two gunboats, twenty-one long-range fleet submarines and five antique S-type subs, built in the post-World War I period that had spawned *Davidson,* displacing 800 tons each and incapable of much more than close-in defensive patrolling.

Later that spring, after General MacArthur arrived, his successor would acquire three Australian cruisers as the backbone of an amphibious team for reinforcing New Guinea.

When Prince reported to ComSouWesPac's GHQ, he found Chief Yeoman Elliot Bream awaiting him at the front door, like an honor guard of sideboys, with an ironically pleased smile on his patrician face as he rendered an elaborate salute.

Observing Prince's surprised look, Bream drawled, "The desk clerk at the Australia Hotel is a friend of mine. I asked him to ring me up when you left for headquarters."

Prince returned the salute in a negligent manner.

"Your friend," he said, "hardly strikes me as the kind of fellow who'd cotton to a mere American."

Bream's smile escalated into a self-satisfied smirk.

"Hell, Commander, you can't be choosy these days. Shanley's a useful sort. I slip him a quid every so often to find me a stash in the Australia, so that I'll have a place to romance some delicious chick who's just dying to be picked up in the Snake Pit."

"Snake Pit?"

"That," said Bream, "is the hotel's main promenade. Believe me, sir, it's the world's happiest hunting ground."

"I'll file away that intelligence for future reference," Prince grunted. "Now, what's the word on my assignment, if any?"

"Oh, that's all been taken care of," Bream said complacently. "I'm Captain Brannigan's special man Friday. He's in charge of operations. When I told him I'd worked for a desdiv commander, he instructed me to sign you up as one of his assistants —till something better turns up."

"Sounds excellent," said Prince. "Congratulations. Now let's go meet my new boss."

"Right-o!"

As they mounted a flight of steps to the second-floor office which housed Brannigan's meager operational setup, with the yeoman nimbly in the lead, Prince speculated for the hundredth time on Bream's amazing ability to produce on what seemed to be impossible promises and his shrewd eye for delicate details—like meeting him at GHQ. It was positively uncanny. Bream, he decided, must have a special, direct pipeline to the Almighty or to the Devil himself, whichever one ruled a man's wartime destiny. God or Satan. It didn't really matter, although you had to admit it was damned convenient.

As Prince had pretty much expected, Brannigan was a weathered no-nonsense Irishman, with a corncob pipe clamped between stained teeth. Not a MacArthurian corncob, but the kind you could buy for a shilling at any Sydney tobacco shop, modeled after the famed Missouri meerschaum. Brannigan puffed at it constantly. Thus his rapidly balding head was surmounted by a perpetual halo of pale, acrid smoke.

"Delighted to have you aboard," he said without rising. But he leaned across his desk to shake Prince's hand, with a powerful grip that was remindful of the Beaver's bearlike clasp. "We haven't much to work with yet, but we've been promised more soon. Meanwhile, it's an interesting game, playing tag with the Japs and trying not to get caught."

Brannigan jerked his thumb toward the inevitable wall chart. Prince studied it briefly. A few blue pins which represented ComSouWesPac's ships were scattered from Exmouth Gulf all the way around Australia to Brisbane, with way points at Perth and Fremantle on the continent's southwest extremity.

"We've had some rather hairy moments," Brannigan went on. "Not long ago a Nip midget sub sneaked into the harbor and polished off a couple of merchantmen. But we nailed the little bastard." He paused. "You might be interested in our basic orders from the Washington moguls."

"Yes, sir," said Prince. "I would. Very much."

"They're quite simple. We're committed to 'hold the key military regions of Australia for bases of future offensives against the Japanese homeland and to check further enemy conquests.'" Brannigan propelled a disdainful volley of smoke in the general direction of the chart. "MacArthur's due here any time. Then we'll move up to Brisbane, I imagine, to be closer to our jump-off place for New Guinea."

Prince gave the map a closer scrutiny.

Several yellow pins showed where the Japanese had occupied the strategic port of Rabaul, on the northeast tip of New Britain, a good-sized satellite island just above New Guinea. Other yellow pins were affixed to the upper reaches of the latter island itself, across the Owen Stanley Range from Port Moresby, now tenaciously held by an Australian brigade. It was, Prince privately conceded, the usual unremittingly black picture, with no tones of white or even gray. Nevertheless he was content, for the moment at least, to be a deputy mover-of-pieces in this abysmal chess game, rather than a helpless pawn. If the proper time came, when he could manage it without transgressing the unwritten code against officers fraternizing with enlistees, he'd have to buy Bream a drink.

Two, in fact, or perhaps a whole goddamned bottleful.

During the weeks before MacArthur reached Australia by PT boat and Flying Fortress, there wasn't a great deal for Prince to do. He checked into GHQ at eight A.M. each day, doodled with fleet directives and dispatches, moved a smattering of pins on the wall chart, lunched in leisurely fashion at the staff mess, then generally left early for the hotel. Brannigan didn't seem to mind these midafternoon departures.

"Let me know where you'll be," he said occasionally, "in case I need you in a hurry."

Prince got the uncomfortable feeling that the operations captain regarded him the way he himself had once considered the Beaver, as supercargo to be dropped off, sometime, somewhere, when it was convenient—that Prince, in effect, was a bird-of-passage, serviceable enough for the nonce but of limited permanent value.

To exorcise these apprehensions, Prince became an habitué of the Snake Pit, paid his quiddish tribute to Shanley, the saturnine desk clerk, romped with the accessible women who frequented this perfumed foyer, and made the rounds of Sydney's bars. He and the Beaver, who had found temporary duty with the British liaison office, arranged a night-on, night-off schedule for the use of the hotel room, rather like a port-and-starboard watch bill aboard ship, to avoid embarrassing confrontations. It was quite possible, Prince soon discovered, to find a girl on his off nights who either lived in an apartment of her own or who knew a convenient friend with quarters available for the "evening," as such periods of dalliance were euphemistically termed.

Letters from MaMa had finally caught up with him, too, and he found them sufficiently boring to take his mind off his troubles at odd moments. They were banal and spuriously hopeful. He answered in the same vein, always wondering if his replies would ever reach her at Province Beach, Virginia, via San Francisco's harried Fleet Post Office.

Yes, said MaMa, the boarding house had become a mecca for naval officers craving a bit of respite from their arduous duties at Annapolis or Washington. She had fixed it up rather elegantly. (As a shack-job joint, he supposed, a sort of junior-grade Australia Hotel.)

Affairs, wrote Prince in response, were progressing nicely in this part of the globe. He was no longer at sea but held a responsible job with ComSouWesPac, which could lead to loftier things.

A couple of nights before MacArthur's arrival at Melbourne on March 18 Prince unexpectedly ran into Lieutenant Rodney, late of the USS *Davidson*, in a popular King's Road saloon just around the corner from the hotel. The former exec was hunched over a green bottle of Tasmanian bitter, oblivious to his surroundings, alone at a corner table. As usual, Prince was accompanied by a chattering, gaudily made-up Aussie girl.

He guided her across the room to where Rodney sat.

"By Christ," Prince exclaimed, "it's good to see you, Mike!"

Rodney did not display the expected amount of enthusiasm at this extraordinary chance encounter. Nonetheless he did get to his feet, painfully, and stretched out his left hand. His right arm was still in a sling, and he seemed to be experiencing some difficulty with one of his legs.

309

"Hello, Commander."

Prince tried a lighter-veined approach. "Why so pale and wan, fond lover?"

"That's how I want it," Rodney replied ungraciously. "But grab a couple of chairs, anyway." He studiously avoided the avid gaze of Prince's date and failed to append a *sir* to his grudging invitation.

"May I present Miss Barnes," said Prince, passing over the erstwhile exec's churlishness. "Meg, this is Lieutenant Michael Rodney."

It occurred to Prince that he didn't know whether Margaret Barnes was a Miss or a Mrs. A lot of Aussie sheilas lately had been leaving their wedding rings at home when they went out for an evening on the town. Meg was busty, boisterous and falsely blond. But she was more fun to be with than most of the others he'd chosen at random from the Snake Pit's female stag line. Some of them tended to become sad, even lachrymose, before the night was over. Some expected money. All Meg ever wanted was a jolly good time, which included ample to eat and drink, and then a fast roll in the hay, with no questions asked and no post-coital recriminations afterward.

Prince noted that Rodney's crewcut had grown into a sort of unkempt shag rug. The two-striper would be only twenty-eight, but he looked forty, older than Prince and more worn.

They didn't have much to say until the beers came. Rodney continued to toy with his jug of bitter. He appeared disinclined toward small talk, lost in his own thoughts, which, judging from his grim countenance, weren't especially pleasant ones.

Then Prince asked, "How did you manage to get out, fella?"

"Same way most of the others did," said Rodney. "Hitch-hiked from Surabaya on an empty tanker, got torpedoed during our try at running Torres Strait between Cape York and New Guinea, made it by life raft to some piss-ant atoll where we were picked up by a cruising S-boat. Like that."

"Sounds rugged."

"It was."

Prince waited, hoping Rodney would volunteer some information on what had happened to *Davidson*. But the lieutenant relapsed into the brooding silence that was so unlike the erstwhile Rodney, who'd been a hearty creature full of mirth and wild practical jokes.

So Prince took the initial plunge. "What about the ship?"

"Do you really want to know, Commander?"

"Certainly."

By way of answer Rodney reached into his hip pocket with his good arm and pulled out a folded sheaf of legal-sized yellow scratch-pad sheets. He gave the packet to Prince, who unfolded it carefully, and with pursed lips began to read what the exec had handwritten. Rodney's penmanship was rounded, boyish and quite legible. This was a draft of his official report on events in Surabaya harbor that hectic morning. Each paragraph, in accordance with proper style, was numbered, and the language was precise navalese.

CONFIDENTIAL

11 March 1942

From: Lieutenant Michael Rodney, U.S. Navy

To: Commander, ALLIED NAVAL FORCES, SOUTHWEST PACIFIC.

Subject: USS *Davidson,* destruction of.

1. In compliance with orders received from ComDesDiv 11, who was then at Tjilatjap, on 2 March I proceeded by whaleboat to the floating drydock to complete the destruction of USS *Davidson.*

2. Certain enlisted personnel from *Davidson* were already on board when I arrived: DARRYL, Howard K., Chief Machinist's Mate, USN; HECKER, John R., Torpedoman 1st class, USN; ROBERTS, O.R. TM3c, USN; and WERNER, Olaf P., Seaman 2nd class, USN. Three other ratings reported shortly thereafter: ADKINS, R.J., Chief

Electrician's Mate, USN; RIGGIO, A.A., Quartermaster 2nd class, USN; and WISEMAN, Sidney P., Gunner's Mate, 3rd class, USN.

3. Captain Franklin Bradshaw, who originally directed the emplacement of explosives in *Davidson,* had been killed at 1750 the previous day during an enemy air raid, along with Commander L.J. Percival, liaison for ABDAfloat at Surabaya. It was then made known to me that I was the senior U.S. officer present at this time.

4. *Davidson* was lying in approximately the same position as when she was left on February 23, on her port bilge with a list of 40 degrees, and her bow entirely off the keel blocks. The bow of the drydock itself was well above water. There was no indication that efforts had been taken toward righting the dock. Yard authorities informed me that almost constant air raids had so diminished the effectiveness of the work force that virtually nothing could be accomplished. They had hoped to secure steel shores on the dock's starboard side, pump it dry, so as to gain access to the damaged destroyer. This was never done.

5. Moreover, it became readily apparent that the drydock containing *Davidson,* having sustained numerous other bomb hits during the night and early morning hours, was in imminent danger of capsizing. Portions of both the dock and the ship were burning when I reached the scene. *Davidson*'s No. 1 engine room had been badly damaged, her forecastle awash, and all interior spaces from amidship forward were flooded.

6. DARRYL, CMM, and HECKER, TMM1c, perceiving the situation, exhibited commendable initiative prior to my arrival, by detonating the explosive charges installed in the lower sound compartment. Unlike several other lead-ins from the bridge, these had not short-circuited, and there were definite sounds of explosions, although we were unable to ascertain actual results. Subsequently, we found it impractical to install additional charges, except for an 80-pound arrangement in the after ammunition handling room, which was the closest unflooded area to the keel. This also exploded when activated. We were prevented from determining the exact degree of damage because of increased flooding below. It was my expectation that the depth charge locker and after magazines would detonate, but I had no way of knowing if this actually took place.

6. Upon our departure from the drydock, it was therefore assumed that *Davidson*'s condition had rendered her of no potential use to the enemy.

Prince refolded the papers and handed them back to their author. "Are you positive about the last paragraph?" he asked.

Shrugging his deceptively soft-fleshed shoulders, Rodney said, "Hell, Commander, I'm not sure about anything. That's why I weasel-worded the goddamned conclusion. I assume the crate's done for. But I wouldn't make book on it." He lifted his beer glass and took a long, thirsty drag of the potent brew. "For a couple of days before I got your message, all sorts of scuttlebutt was going around. You know. Wild rumors about sabotage by the Javanese work gangs, maybe even their sneaking out to the drydock to unhook our explosives wiring. There wasn't enough time to check out all the circuits. We just had to cross our fingers and pull the bloody trigger . . ." He stopped talking and directed his full attention to carefully refilling his tumbler.

Prince muttered reflectively, "Jesus, I wish I *knew*, that's all."

"That's my thinking, likewise, Commander," said Rodney. "But I did my best."

"Of course." Prince's voice was placative. "You had a rough go."

"It would have helped," Rodney said, "to have received support from somebody higher up. Perhaps we'd have been given more manpower, gotten a better job done."

"I had no choice," Prince said uncertainly. "I was under orders to leave."

Rodney impaled him with a glance that was twenty degrees colder than the Tasmanian bitter. "Sure," he said in a tone heavy with disbelief. "Everybody had his orders."

"We're going to put you up for a Silver Star, now that you're back," Prince said. "Glad it doesn't have to be posthumous."

"Thanks a bundle—sir."

313

Clumsily, knowing precisely what Rodney implied, Prince asked him if he'd like to join them for a bit of pub-hopping. Meg had a girl friend who would be just perfect for the exec's morale-boosting purposes.

"Sorry," said Rodney, "but I've a bus to catch for MOB-two in fifteen minutes." Twisting the knife deeper, he added, "And I want to write a letter home to my wife."

Prince watched him leave. MOB stood for Mobile Officers Base. The No. 2 designated it as the second such pool established at Sydney for unassigned rankers. The Beaver doubtless would have called MOB 2 a repple-depple, the old Limey slang for replacement depot. Once again Prince caught himself fervently wishing he had whatever it was that Rodney possessed, which had made the exec so capable of facing down the world's problems, even if it only meant dashing off a love letter to a wife who was waiting for him in Coronado, California, with two plump kids. Prince turned toward the girl at his side. Her over-carmined lips parted in a provocative smile. He observed that Meg had one incisor missing and that heavy rouge covered a multitude of tiny pimples on her cheeks.

"Come along," he said curtly. "I'll take you home, and then I'm going to hit the sack—alone for a change."

"Home?" she protested. "Why, it's hardly eight o'clock."

"I know," Prince agreed, "but all of a sudden I've had it."

April came. With it, in mid-coastal Australia's gorgeous autumn, the isolated Allies learned the bitter truth that their far-off masters, President Roosevelt and Prime Minister Churchill, had decreed an Atlantic First policy. The Pacific would be a holding operation until Hitler was crushed. And how long would this take? Neither God nor MacArthur, who seemed interchangeable at times, apparently could provide a solution to that riddle.

Most of the Aussie fighting men were locked in the African campaign. MacArthur was supreme commander, as a result, of a single inadequately prepared U.S. division, an assortment of obsolescent aircraft and a "navy" that numbered neither carriers nor battleships. The American division was the one which had been dispatched in haste from San Francisco after the enemy attack on the Philippines. Originally intended to relieve pressure on those islands, it was rerouted to Australia when the Japs took possession of the sea lanes.

Nonetheless, he moved his GHQ to Brisbane and began laying plans to advance even farther north to Port Moresby, well west along the Papuan peninsula of New Guinea.

Prince left Sydney without regret. He had become bored with its fleshpots and its sheilas. Conquests were *too* easy. Life there was depressingly unreal, after more than a month, except for the R-and-R types who were looking for such carnal pleasures and hadn't any spare time to waste in ferreting them out. The Beaver went along, too, for everything was going north now.

Still in his role as quasi-assistant to ComSouWesPac's operations officer, Prince continued to shift pins on a chart which encompassed the whole western Pacific. During this inverse Australian fall, which would soon enough lead to his personal winter of discontent, he went about his paltry chores, managing to develop a routine that satisfied his minimal physical and psychic needs.

Brisbane itself was a handsome, neatly laid-out city of some 300,000 souls, not counting the naval and military forces that jammed its available hotel and roominghouse spaces. Its undulant river broadened into a fine deep-dredged harbor fourteen miles east, where ample wharfage was available to handle the trickle of thinly convoyed supplies from the United States. Behind the city, sharp-toothed against the western skies, rose the formidable Great Dividing Range, which separated the humid coast from the barren outback. There was generally a mild southeast trade wind blowing, to ease the discomfort, especially at night.

Prince took to walking Brisbane's placid streets in the blackouts, beneath the flame trees which reared up like dark ghosts on moonless evenings, before returning to his Victorian hotel for a late supper. The Queen's was a remarkable three-story structure, all white gingerbread and wooden latticework. But it pleased him and reminded him a little of MaMa's *déclassé* mansion back home. He finally had a room to himself, the Beaver having at long last moved in with a group of Royal Navy officers at a much smaller hotel—for, as he elegantly phrased it, a "refresher course in how to behave like a bloody Limey instead of a goddamned Yank." Their digs were a block down the street from The Queen's. Lieutenant Rodney remained stubbornly at MOB 2, although Prince had offered to find him a spot in his hotel. The advantage, said Prince, was that hotels could serve booze after normal pub hours.

"The guys out there in the boondocks," Rodney protested, "seem more my kind. But thanks anyhow."

He did, however, accept Prince's aid in obtaining a subordinate billet in ComSouWesPac's burgeoning operations department. The Beaver visited GHQ often, as liaison between the nonexistent British forces and the slowly evolving U.S. naval detachment. Thus the three of them, willy nilly, saw considerable of each other.

"We're a sort of Last Man's Club," the Beaver observed one night at dinner, "survivors of the *Davidson,* bound together until death do us part."

"Hell of a prospect," Prince grunted.

Rodney said nothing. His rotund frame had thinned out perceptibly, although he had returned to his crewcut hair style, which belied his young-old face. The untrammeled grin that had been the exec's happy trade mark aboard their four-pipe flagship came seldom now, even when the Beaver was at his outrageous, bawdy, pecker-upping best. Mostly when Rodney smiled it was an ironic, derisive, even contemptuous grimace, as if he were privy to occult secrets denied others. Prince got the uncomfortable feeling that Rodney was aiming these odd looks at him, like a Maxim-silenced rifle, for reasons he could not fathom, try as he might.

They threw a welcome-home bash for the Beaver after the Coral Sea battle. By some crafty means known only to himself, the Briton had wangled his way aboard HMAS *Hobart,* an Aussie cruiser assigned to guard one of the American carriers, as an official observer for His Majesty's Navy. That night he was brimful of raucous tales about modern sea-war tactics.

"We never laid eyes on the little bastards' ships," said the Beaver. "Only their buggerly aircraft. It was the craziest game of blind man's buff I've ever experienced. Sparring at long range— maybe a hundred miles or so—after feeling for 'em in the darkness." He took his usual thorax-wetting drag at The Queen's vile whiskey. "What a devilish queer way to conduct a naval battle."

Surprisingly, Rodney responded to this before Prince could express his own views on the matter.

"Our thrashing around in the Java Sea," he said, "wasn't real warfare. Hell, airplanes will ultimately win this thing, along with subs. But the day of slugging it out toe to toe with surface ships has gone the way of square-rigged sailing ships."

Prince mused: "I wonder. It's apt to be a matter of exactly what kind of action you stumble into. Someday we'll have the stuff to start amphibious operations of our own. Then what? Won't the Japs have to break it up? Planes alone can't turn the trick."

"You'll see," said Rodney, unconvinced.

Much later, much drunker, they parted company, and Prince walked up the creaking stairs to his solitary room on the top floor. As usual, for no particular reason, he was dog-tired. Yet he almost wished the Beaver was there, sharing these musty quarters, so that he wouldn't have to struggle through still another night, alone with his dreary thoughts—and culpable memories—without someone to discuss them with.

What concerned Prince the most was that damnable, enigmatic, equivocal Paragraph 6 in Rodney's official account of *Davidson*'s destruction. Beyond question, the exec himself couldn't swear on the proverbial stack of Bibles that the flagship had been "rendered of no potential use to the enemy." He had been forced to evacuate on the last vessel out, yet less cravenly than Prince, since he had remained until the agonizing final moment to carry on with his assigned duty.

In the small, dead hours of the night Prince would awaken in a cold sweat, despite the eighty-degree heat, with the old seismic sensation in his gut, wondering whether the Japs had been able to patch *Davidson* together again. Certainly they would have ample opportunity to accomplish the job, if the four-piper had stayed relatively intact in her floating cocoon. There were no Allied air raids to hinder them, and he could envisage the Nip engineers, not caring a whit for the niceties, lashing the natives into a frenzy of activity in the ruptured dry-dock.

Prince's gravest worry, when he stopped to consider it, was not so much the possibility that the enemy would make some marginal use of *Davidson*—for surely she could never be restored to full battle readiness—but that the fact of her Lazarus-like restoration might become public knowledge. He could already picture in his tormented mind's eye the sly side glances of his staff companions if the Word leaked out, and hear what they would be whispering behind their hands at the O.C. Things like: "I've always had a feeling about that fellow. . . . No follow-through. . . . If he'd done what he should've done, and given the kid a hand, maybe his ship wouldn't have developed a case of slant-eye."

Another nightmare assailed him, too, the remembrance of Captain Bradshaw, grim-faced, minatory, declaring that he'd come back and haunt Prince if anything went wrong with the flagship's demolition.

The Beaver found Prince reading Melville's *Moby Dick* one evening when he dropped by for a drink. He gave the volume an inquisitive glance.

"Strange book for you to be browsing, old chap."

"Why so?" Prince asked, irritated and a little nonplussed. He poured a drink for the Beaver. "Have you ever read *Moby Dick?*"

"Bloody well near memorized it once, for some damned reason, possibly pure discipline. And came near losing my mind trying to figure out what it all meant."

"And your conclusions?" Prince wanted to know.

"Same as anybody else with half a brain comes away with—that Ahab was combatting an evil that can't be comprehended, which overcomes him in the end. He was a maniac, you know, surrounded by religious men of all kinds . . . and always Ishmael there listening, watching and remembering." The Beaver lifted the book and riffled through its pages. "Then you have those who figure that Ahab wanted to strip off humanity's mask and discover the reality that was hidden behind it. I can't buy that, though. Ahab had a quest, like an Arthurian knight, a dragon to slay, the great white whale against which he bore a special grudge. Maybe that's oversimplifying it. But I don't believe so."

Prince noted that the Beaver's expression had become even more quizzical.

"I ask again, why the surprise at finding me reading *Moby Dick?*"

"Maybe it's the timing," said the Beaver, "or a certain assortment of intriguing possibilities."

"Such as?"

"Seeking guidelines, old boy, a way out."

"Of what?"

"Of whatever it is you find yourself trapped in."

"I wasn't aware," said Prince with a trace of hauteur, "that I was 'trapped' by anything."

"Nobody ever is—until the trap closes around him."

In June came the Battle of Midway, fought more than half an ocean away from Brisbane, with the bulk of the Japanese fleet under Commander-in-Chief Isoroku Yamamoto throwing itself against the presumably inferior Americans, while at the same time another sizable force pounded the Aleutians prior to landings on a trio of fog-shrouded islands. Once the Yankees were defeated, the Nips would move into Midway atoll with consummate ease.

It was a beautiful plan.

But it failed because of the coolly calculated response of Admiral Nimitz from his GHQ high in the Aiea hills above Pearl Harbor, where the *Arizona* still lay at her open dockside grave; and the equally cold coverage of his tactical leaders, Rear Admirals Raymond A. Spruance and Robert A. Theobald. Moreover, the U.S. Navy was continuing to crack the enemy's code, so Yamamoto, despite his overwhelming power, was unable to repeat the surprise assault he had leveled against Pearl Harbor barely six months earlier.

The carrier *Yorktown*'s Coral Sea wounds were hastily bound up. *Hornet* and *Enterprise* joined her. On June 2, in the summer seas north of Midway, Spruance was ready with three fast carriers, seven heavy cruisers, a light AA cruiser, fifteen destroyers, plus a nineteen-unit submarine screen.

Land-based on the coral spit of Midway itself stood Navy PBYs, hastily converted into clumsy combat craft by fitting torpedoes beneath their flat wings; Marine fighters and scout bombers; a sparse handful of Army Air Force B-17 Fortresses.

The odds against Spruance seemed fantastically impossible: four large carriers, all veterans of the devastating sneak raid on Pearl Harbor; a light carrier and two seaplane carriers, seven battleships, including *Haruna,* which gallant Captain Colin Kelly had definitely not sunk off the Philippines; and *Yamato,* at 64,000 tons the mightiest warship ever constructed, with a main battery of nine 18-inch rifles; along with four heavy and five light cruisers, forty-four destroyers, sixteen submarines and assorted auxiliaries. Behind this huge Midway contingent trudged a dozen troop-laden transports.

Far to the north near the Aleutians, Admiral Theobald cast his own outnumbered pieces against the enemy with cautious skill. His only air cover came from a diverse collection of land-based planes. He had five cruisers and four destroyers, with six subs as advance guards. Fog hampered the operations of both opposing forces, although the Japs managed a couple of less than crippling aerial blows at Dutch Harbor from their two carriers.

But they did place troops on bleak little Attu and Kiska islands.

From the instant a Navy Catalina spotted six Japanese ships in close formation 700 miles southwest of Midway, early on June 3, events progressed inexorably from bad to worse to disastrous for the foe.

As in the Coral Sea battle, none of the opposing surface ships ever glimpsed each other. The Nips were unable to exercise their tremendous firepower. It was an air engagement from start to finish, over an excruciating period of five days. Midway was attacked; but its planes were conveniently gone, seeking out the enemy. Although they absorbed heavy losses, it was in honorable combat. They were not ignominiously grounded, as on December 7.

In his reported conclusions, Admiral Nimitz later would declare, almost wistfully, that more assiduous pursuit by scout planes, improved communications, and a follow-up strike when the beaten Japs withdrew might well have destroyed almost the entire enemy fleet. Nevertheless, all four of the major Nip carriers, *Akagi, Hiryu, Kaga* and *Soryu,* were sunk, along with a heavy cruiser. Japan lost 322 planes and 3,500 men, among them more than 100 of their best pilots. American casualties included *Yorktown* (which Nimitz believed could have been saved through more efficient damage-control efforts), one destroyer, 150 aircraft, 307 men.

When the battle was over, the white-haired Pacific Fleet commander remarked: "Perhaps we can be forgiven if we claim that we are about midway to our objective."

This wasn't quite true, of course, as the anxiously listening staff at MacArthur's Brisbane GHQ knew. It was still only 1942. Leagues and leagues of blue water, and millions of bloody acres of enemy-held real estate, remained to be brought under control and captured. But the United States *had* won a tremendous victory at a moment when national morale was perilously low. The time had come, MacArthur told his assembled officers, to go on the offensive.

Glumly, from his back-row vantage point in the crowded operations room, Prince thought again of the philosopher Zeno, who "proved" you couldn't get there from here, because you were always *midway* from one point to another as you proceeded.

Meanwhile the planners at Imperial General Headquarters in Tokyo were reshaping their ideas, too, in the light of this catastrophe. No longer could there be an easy, triumphant sweep southward to New Caledonia, the Fijis and Samoa. Now they must find a way to buttress their attenuated front, especially in the southwestern Pacific, where the Allies appeared ready to dish up something nasty.

Between the Equator and the 10th latitudinal parallel south lay the impending battleground: New Guinea, New Britain and the Solomons—the latter a chain of islands first sighted by Spain's Don Alvaro Mendana in 1567. His lordship was, as usual, hunting for gold. Instead, he stumbled across these hot, humid malarial lands, which he promptly dubbed "King Solomon's Isles," to give his discovery more class for the peasants —and for his monarch—back home. During their uneventful history, the Solomons passed through several imperial hands. After World War I the British ruled them as a protectorate. Between such strangely named islands as Vella Lavella, Kolombangari, Rendova, Choiseul and Guadalcanal ran New Georgia Sound, almost 400 miles long from its northern entrance at the lower tip of Bougainville to the nether end of Guadalcanal. Its widest stretch was only fifty miles across; its narrowest, barely twenty-five.

This waterway would not be known much longer as New Georgia Sound. Soon it would be nicknamed the Slot. Along its twisting course would be fought some of the fiercest surface battles of World War II. The Tokyo Express would use it to ferry Nip reinforcements; and one of its bloodiest sectors would become known as Iron Bottom Bay, because so many ships went down there.

Perhaps the Japanese foresaw this after Midway.

At any rate, the Nips had already occupied the Solomons in May, after the Australians withdrew what they scornfully called their pipsqueak "Gilbert and Sullivan Army," following several months of aerial pounding from enemy bases in New Britain. At first the Japs were content to set up shop in Tulagi, the Solomons' ramshackle capital, mainly for seaplane uses. But then, as June waned, they sent a convoy into Guadalcanal, equipped with laborers, technicians and machinery, to construct an airfield.

This did not go unnoticed by the Allies.

In Washington it was decided to erect a counter-base at Efate, in the equally torrid New Hebrides, about 600 miles south of the enemy's fast-growing stronghold. Admiral King masterminded this initial arrangement, then proposed a more daring venture—the first real Allied offensive in the Pacific since the dismal days of December.

The well-trained First Marine Division would—by God and by Ernest Jesus King—make an amphibious landing on Guadalcanal and Tulagi!

Prince, who had come to view himself as the eternal kibitzer, the man on the fringe of events, perused the interchange of dispatches that flashed between Brisbane, Pearl Harbor and Washington. Both Nimitz and MacArthur craved jurisdiction over the far-flung area. MacArthur said he could seize Rabaul, the key Jap establishment, in one grand swoop if he were vouchsafed the Pacific Fleet and the Marines.

On the other hand, Nimitz argued against exposing his still slender fleet and his single combat-ready division to an enemy bastion which could be reached only through some of the most dangerous and least charted waters of the world. He opted for a more gradual approach. He agreed with King.

Washington had to resolve the dilemma.

The Pacific Fleet command would undertake the job—and to this end, Nimitz was given sway over everything east of the 159th parallel. Operation Watchtower was scheduled for August 7.

Like most of mortal man's plans, even the best of them, Watchtower was hardly an unqualified success in its earlier stages. It soon earned the opprobrious epithet Operation Shoestring, which adhered long after its original commander had departed and Admiral William F. Halsey took over the frail reins on October 18.

The original expeditionary fleet convened at sea late in July, near the British Fijis, having arrived there from New Zealand, Australia, New Caledonia, Hawaii and California. It ran through a so-so amphibious assault trial, then headed for Guadalcanal, that simmering lozenge-shaped island which was to hold world attention, military and civilian, for almost twelve lethal months. Storm fronts gave Watchtower the initial advantage of surprise, for this wing-walking weather kept the Jap scout planes grounded.

So the Marines landed—but failed, despite their hallowed legend, to get the situation immediately well in hand.

Savage fights ensued in the volcanic jungles and on the seas surrounding Guadalcanal. Once the support ships had to withdraw and leave the embattled leathernecks to their own tenuous devices. On August 9 came the Battle of Savo Island, a few miles north of the 'Canal. Result: three U.S. cruisers sunk in a wild night imbroglio; an Aussie cruiser so badly damaged that she had to be dispatched next day by an American destroyer; some 1,000 crewmen killed.

Then the Japs moved their own chess pieces.

Down from Truk in the Carolines they swarmed, with warships and transports, aimed at replenishing their outnumbered insular detachments. *Enterprise* was mauled in an encounter with a Nip carrier task force and rushed to Noumea for patchwork repairs. In September, off the Shortland Islands, the U.S. carrier *Wasp* met her doom; the new battleship *North Carolina* caught a torpedo that holed her so badly she was sent back to Pearl for major surgery; and another precious tin can went down. In the second week of October, after enemy battlewagons had leveled a devastating barrage against Henderson Field, the renamed air base originally built by the Japs, was fought the Battle of Cape Esperance.

This was billed as a victory for the Allies. It wasn't, really, because reports of Nip losses in that debatable night engagement were considerably inflated. Yet it bolstered spirits—briefly.

Enter Halsey. Bull or Stud to his friends. Wild Bill to the newsmen who delighted so in chronicling his audacious sweeps across the broad Pacific.

He was handed the job of saving Guadalcanal, and then conquering this foul bit of terrain, at the lowest ebb in Allied fortunes. The Marine commander believed he was getting insufficient help from Allied seagoing forces; the latter's chieftain claimed the general should have been more aggressive in pushing back the foe.

In his tiny Flag quarters aboard an ancient supply ship in Noumea harbor, Halsey asked Marine General A. A. Vandegrift: "Are we going to evacuate or hold?"

And Vandegrift promptly replied: "I can hold," adding, "but I've got to have more active support than I've been getting."

To which Halsey responded succinctly: "All right, Van. Go on back. I'll promise you everything I've got."

He kept his word, even as the Japs touched off their campaign to recapture Henderson Field a week later.

Admiral Yamamoto, he of the brilliant Pearl Harbor attack and the debacle at Midway, sent a carrier force down from Truk. They collided with two U.S. carrier teams, led by the hastily repaired *Enterprise* and *Hornet,* off the Santa Cruz Islands. Again it was a Pyrrhic victory for the Nips, although *Hornet* was destroyed and another American tin can sunk. Yet it cost the Japanese 100 planes, the Americans seventy-four, at a time when the U.S. industry was gearing up its immense aircraft and shipbuilding effort and pilot training was in full swing.

While all this was going on, capturing the headlines and thrilling war-weary Australians as well as Americans who were still fairly new to the home-front rigors of global conflict, Halsey and his top staffers elected to pay an impromptu visit to MacArthur's Brisbane GHQ. Their announced purpose was to establish credentials with their opposite numbers in SouWesPac, and to redefine the curious geographical apportionment of their two areas.

It was early November by then. Brisbane had never been lovelier. Spring showers had refreshed its myriad of parks and gardens, and the sunsets were glorious above the Great Dividing Range, more brightly crimson, even, than the blazing flame trees themselves.

Prince joined the operational conferences, generally listening, rarely summoned to speak, as the eager-beaver young Halsey-men discussed strategy and tactics with the well-worn Mac-Arthurites. There was a boundless enthusiasm apparent among these officers in starched khaki who had flown from New Caledonia, even though they knew (and vociferously affirmed) that a battle of enormous consequences was shaping up near Guadalcanal itself, where the Japs were reliably reported to be readying a last-ditch effort to reinforce the menaced island.

This was the high-water mark of the Tokyo Express, they said. Until recently, the Yanks had held sway over the approaches to Iron Bottom Bay during daylight hours, offloading precious cargoes under cover of Henderson Field's busy fighters. After nightfall, however, the game changed abruptly, with Allied cargo vessels withdrawing to offshore safety and the Nips charging down the Slot with fast troop-carrying destroyers and cruisers. They would fire off a few rounds to keep the Marines pinned down, drop soldiers ashore, before retiring northward again.

"Damned annoying," groused one of Halsey's senior operations officers. "Something to be stamped out like a cockroach when the right time arrives."

Prince, as one of the few ComSouWesPac staffers who had been through the Java mill, screwed up his courage to ask, "When *is* the right time, Captain?"

"Soon."

"Do you have the necessary hardware?"

The Halseyman smiled. "You should know, Commander, of all people, that we never have enough hardware. But we're a lot better off than Tommy Hart ever was. In fact, we don't invoke God and the proverbial long-handled spoon as often as we used to. Sure, the shoestring is still knotted together in a few weak spots. But it's holding. And we intend to see that it holds."

Prince glanced around at the visiting officers. They seemed to have been cut from the same tough mold as their dashing boss-admiral: broad-shouldered, gung-ho, broadly grinning when the mood struck them, which was often. Suddenly he envied them. He wished he could join this close-knit group, who were so different from any of the others he'd lately been associated with, so victory-confident despite the cruel punishment they had absorbed, and the patent fact that Guadalcanal was far from being a *fait accompli*.

He suspected they wouldn't take kindly to outsiders.

That night Prince invited several of them to be his guests for dinner at The Queen's. They accepted graciously, for their immediate work had been completed; and tomorrow at dawn they would return to their Quonset hut cantonment at Noumea, to begin preparations for the final derailment of the Tokyo Express.

The Beaver joined Prince's party. He was, he announced jubilantly, about to become His Majesty's liaison with Halsey at ComSoPac headquarters, an activist billet that suited his pugnacious nature far more than sitting on his bloody arse at Brisbane, waiting for something significant to happen, if ever.

That made five of them around the damasked table in the high-beamed, candlelit old dining hall. In honor of the occasion the management had dredged up a stringed trio, bad enough, yet infinitely better than those who had tortured the Anglo-American wartime melodies in Manila, Balikpapan and Surabaya. They still played "The Last Time I Saw Paris," while the uniformed audience sang the lyrics; but they also favored "When the Lights Go on Again All Over the World," and, with a gallantry reserved for a respected foe, "Lili Marlene."

The meal itself was expectedly mediocre, centering on overcooked mutton. But there was a tolerable red wine from southern Australia and a fiery brandy from God only knew where to top off the strong black coffee.

Immediately after dinner, the Beaver rose heavily to his feet and announced that he would sally forth to produce a covey of sheilas to lighten an otherwise boresome evening. None of the Halseymen dissented.

When he had departed, the visitors tried to explain to Prince why ComSoPac was finally getting affairs in shape after months of ineffectual dawdling.

"The old Man," said the communications two-striper, meaning Halsey, "has put us all into the same uniforms. He threatens to stencil *ComSoPac* on the seat of the pants of any son-of-a-bitch who doesn't shape up."

But soon they verged from such mundane issues as tactics, morale and discipline and sought to outyarn each other with stories of the weird events which happened regularly within the sprawling confines of their island-dotted, mainly oceanic domain.

For instance, there was this pilot whose scout bomber had been pinked by a Jap shell, yet who made it safely to a white-sanded beach on an idyllic islet which, to this day, he refused to identify. The native women, reported the pilot, following his rescue by a PBY which dropped a raft offshore, were all Dorothy Lamours, albeit a trifle dusky. But willing. Anxious to please. Fetching him coconuts, breadfruit, guavas and mangoes till the goddamn stuff stuck out of his ears.

There was also the time that Halsey's son got shot down, and the Old Man carried on as usual, ordering up no special search efforts, until the kid was found in due course.

There was . . .

It went on and on, interminably, until the two-stripe communicator was reminded of something which had everybody at ComSoPac wondering What the Hell. Doubtless the news, as yet unverified, fell into Top Secret category. But he knew that Commander Prince would keep it quiet, particularly as the matter at hand might well concern a little item out of his own recent past.

"One of our reconnaissance Catalinas," said the lieutenant, "was on a mission to hell and gone in the Bougainville precinct when he caught a glimpse of this—this thing."

Prince waited, holding his breath, for what he would have given anything to forestall.

"It was a three-piper," the Halseyman went on, "with a typical Nip tripod mast forward. The Number One stack was raked backward, too, the way those little friggers have a way of doing. But she was flush-decked. And her two rear funnels hadn't changed a bit. If we're to believe the Cat's pilot, this was a rebuilt American four-piper."

"Why the doubts?" Prince inquired in a low voice.

"Because the PBY pilot had to dive for cloud cover a couple of seconds after he first caught sight of this crazy-looking crate, to escape a Jap Zero. When he emerged again, the tin can was out of sight to the north, beyond range. Besides, from fifteen thousand feet, he never got a real chance to study her in silhouette, to be absolutely certain."

One of the guests, a logistics three-striper, stared at Prince for an embarrassingly long moment.

"We haven't had any real, live, living four-stackers captured in this man's war," he said. "So that's ruled out. But there was a tin can in drydock at Surabaya, as I recall vaguely, when the Japs moved in."

"Sure," the communicator agreed, "but she was supposed to 've been blown up. Hell. I read the dispatch from the exec who'd been left in charge of demolition."

The logistics officer continued to survey Prince with his frigid eyes.

"Weren't you the commander of DesDiv Eleven?"

"Yes."

"And wasn't *Davidson* that ship in drydock?"

"Since you obviously know," snapped Prince, "why bother to ask?"

"Just wanted to refresh my flagging memory, that's all."

The other two Halseymen now focused their full attention on Prince, with a kind of appalled wonderment in their gaze, as if he'd suddenly sprouted horns.

"Wasn't the exec's message correct?" the communicator wanted to know. "Didn't *Davidson* blow?"

"Goddamn it," Prince flared, "how can I be positive? I wasn't even there!"

"Oh." The lieutenant fell briefly silent. "I see."

But Prince was aware that the youngster didn't see. Nor would anyone else ever see. He had failed to complete a job that rightfully was his, try as he might to slough off responsibility after the dreadful fact; and now he must face up to the consequences.

I I

"Every Ahab Must Have His Ishmael"

IT WAS PERHAPS ONLY NATURAL that Chief Yeoman Bream should happen across the very assignment for which Prince had been subconsciously questing, urgently desiring, yet privately fearing for the past week. Both of them were standing overnight operations watch at ComSouWesPac headquarters, Bream on duty at the electric decoding machine keys, Prince uneasily slumbering on the office cot, too warm beneath its Conestoga wagon-topped mosquito net.

Nothing much was happening in the immediate Australian area. A few submarine sightings of minor enemy feintlike movements. Reports from the handful of reconnaissance planes which flew along the Great Barrier Reef toward New Guinea, then swung left to scout the Arafura Sea sector which led to Jap-held Timor. But that was about it. Almost all the ambulant combat stock had been sent to Halsey in SoPac, for use in the engagement that everyone knew was pending—and damned soon—off Guadalcanal itself.

So most of the short-wave traffic, aside from these routine search missions, involved Top Secret crypto-translations of Japanese plans for their offensive aimed at relieving the hemmed-in Nips on Guadalcanal. As always, Admiral Yamamoto was carrying the strategic ball from his behemothic flagship, *Yamato*, anchored at Truk. Thus far, as the first week of November came to its dreary end, the mercurial enemy genius appeared ready to commit anywhere from two to four battle wagons, possibly a half dozen cruisers of varying displacement and an incredible number of destroyers.

There was a certain aura of desperation about the messages which Bream decoded that night, occasioned by the fact that the Japs had learned of imminent U.S. ground reinforcements and of President Roosevelt's personal orders that Halsey was to get more cruisers, tin cans and subs, along with bombers and fighters from both Hawaii and Australia. Nonetheless, although Halsey had managed to scrape up another 6,000 marines and dogfaces from his sparse exterior defenses, the Allies were still outnumbered on the main embattled island of Guadalcanal.

Now, advised the Imperial Japanese Headquarters in the Carolines, their gallant men would be augmented by 13,500 troops, shortly to be brought southward in eleven transports. Thus the great battle began to take form.

At 0200, two hours after midnight, Bream awakened Prince, who had finally managed to drift off into a sodden sleep. Nothing could be done about the Jap's natterings until the intelligence people sorted them out in the morning; and their tenor, to be perfectly candid about it, hadn't changed much, anyhow. Just the fleshing-in of a few more details, a tightening of the enemy's schedule, an increased sense of something closing in.

"Here's a message you probably ought to see, Commander," Bream said.

Prince yawned. "What's so all-fired important?"

By way of reply, Bream thrust the dispatch into his hand. It was not lengthy. Addressed to ComSouWesPac from ComSoPac, it simply requested the "immediate return" of USS *Shearcross*, a destroyer which had been undergoing refurbishing at Sydney, whether or not post-repair trials had been completed. ComSouWesPac was further asked, in politest navalese, to provide a temporary captain and executive officer for *Shearcross* to oversee the 1,100-mile ferrying journey to Noumea, where they would be replaced by a full-time skipper, exec and gunnery officer, all of whom had been killed in recent combat.

Prince retained the radiogram for a long moment before he spoke. Small sparklets flashed from the Academy ring on his left hand which held the message flimsy. The unshaded light was harsh. It made Prince's face unwontedly harsh, too, and somehow this same harshness crept into his voice.

"Why wake me up for this kind of piss-ant thing, Chief?"

Bream gave him a steady, unfazed glance as he retrieved the missive.

"It struck me, sir, that *Shearcross* might be just what you've been waiting for."

Well aware of what Bream meant, Prince relapsed into brooding silence, trying to sort out his confused thoughts. Goddamned Bream! The sly, omniscient bastard, with his amazing connections, probably knew everything there was to know about his former boss's plummet into quasi-disgrace, into the kind of limbo which wasn't total disrepute, though it came close enough to the real thing to be rough as hell for the man on the indefensible receiving end. Coventry, the British services called it: ostracism for having failed egregiously in line of duty. Yet what had happened to Prince wasn't all that drastic. True. He had come to accept with a pained smile such jolly questions as "What's the latest scam on the good old *Davidson-maru*, fella?" Or: "Understand your former flag bucket's drawn the rice-and-copra run out of Saigon. Pretty sad state of affairs, isn't it?"

And once he'd heard, without evincing notice that he had heard, a couple of his ex-classmates sarcastically evaluating somebody who managed to "go from padroon to poltroon in one easy generation."

His early career sins of staff-induced hauteur and disdain were coming back at him now, in full measure, to be paid with the bitter coin of quiet withdrawal from the society of his peers. Only the Beaver stayed with him, behaving as if nothing untoward had ever happened. He was willing to drink publicly with Prince, or to visit him in his hotel cubicle for a private libation.

Yes. And Bream, too, judging from the yeoman's readiness to assist his former commander at certain critical junctures. Like this excruciating instance. Bream understood that Prince had to get the devil out of Brisbane, away from a hostile milieu, into something entirely different. The only answer, as Prince himself had to agree, was a return to combat.

To Bream he finally said, "Lay this message aside, will you? I'll deliver it personally to Captain Brannigan in the morning."

With an enigmatic smile the yeoman replied, "Affirmative, sir. I think that's a fine idea."

"Do you really, Bream?"

"Yes, sir. Positively four-oh." He paused before adding in a burst of surprising frankness: "Especially as a cure for one's bruised psyche."

Prince could have lashed out at this impertinence which transgressed even the loose-knit bounds that had become established between him and Bream. Yet he didn't. Instead, after a split-second's hesitation, he said seriously, "Yes, fella. I guess you've got it pegged right on the button."

Promptly at 0800 Captain Brannigan came stomping up the creaky wooden steps to the operations floor. He went directly to his splintery desk, shouted for a cup of black java, filled his malodorous corncob pipe, lit it, and reached for the overnight file. Prince waited until the craggy four-striper had finished digesting the messages fastened to the clipboard before he approached him with ComSoPac's order for *Shearcross*.

He offered it to Brannigan without a word, feeling as he did so for all the world like a dog tendering a stick toward his master to be thrown in a game of chase-and-fetch.

The captain scanned it quickly. Then he scowled across the desk at Prince, who stood at rigid attention.

"Why in Tophet are you giving this routine business such special treatment?" he demanded.

"Because," said Prince, "I'm applying for the job, sir."

Brannigan's fierce blue eyes returned to the dispatch. He glanced up again, more puzzled than angry. "You want to act as ferryboat captain for a goddamned tin can?"

"Yes, sir."

"And after that you'd like to stay with Bill Halsey's gang?"

"Yes, sir."

The operations chief rubbed his splayed nose with the corn-cob bowl, as if seeking an inspiration from the pipe's rough caress. "There are plenty of other good men around, Commander, who'd give their right nuts for this chore, you know. Both balls, probably."

"I know, sir."

"Besides, it's not even a *good* job. It's tailor-made for some old has-been like myself—an excuse to get him part way home."

Prince inched closer to Brannigan's desk. There was a placative note in his usually crisp voice. "I'd hardly call ComSou-WesPac's operations officer a has-been, sir. But in case you haven't noticed it, I happen to be just that. A has-been. Maybe a trifle premature, but a has-been nevertheless." He let a fraction of a minute pass. Then: "Besides, you were right the first time. I'd like to join Admiral Halsey. This wouldn't be a one-way ticket back to the States—I hope."

Brannigan tossed down his pipe and ran both hands over his balding skull, like a man in the throes of comic desperation, although there was nothing farcical in his grim expression.

"For the life of me, Commander, I don't know why I should do it." Prince felt ready to collapse onto his starched khaki knees, to plead his case, when Brannigan continued: "But I'm going to give you those goddamned orders."

Prince exhaled audibly. "Thank you, sir."

As he moved toward the open stairwell, Brannigan called out, "Pick your own exec, mister. For openers I'd suggest young Rodney."

"He's precisely the man I plan to ask, Captain."

"Well, then don't just *ask* him. Tell him it's orders from ComSouWesPac. He needs a change of venue, too, I suspect. There's precious little chance of a fair trial around here for either of you . . . although you personally seem to be the principal culprit of the piece."

Prince halted at the door. "I accept that responsibility, sir. Fully and without any reservation."

"Good. Now get the hell out of here before I come to my senses and change my senile mind."

The Beaver was at The Queen's, dawdling over a breakfast of kippers and eggs, when Prince returned from GHQ. It was the latter's habit, before retiring after an all-night vigil (whether or not he'd catnapped during the boresome watch), to drink a cup of Ceylon tea, prepared English-style with hot milk and sugar. The Beaver knew this. So he obviously had been awaiting Prince's arrival.

"You're deuced late," he grumbled. "It's bloody well nine o'clock. Do they pay you blokes for working overtime?"

"Considering my confounded charity status," said Prince, "hardly."

"So what kept you, old boy?"

"Answering help-wanted advertisements. Looking for better employment."

"And you found it?"

"Affirmative."

337

Prince sat down across from the Beaver, who was blowing lustily into his own teacup. The fumes which wafted over the small table smelled unmistakably of the rum with which the Briton had laced his portion. The Beaver intercepted Prince's disapproving glance.

"I realize the hour is early for me, although late for you," he said elaborately. "But I, too, am celebrating a fresh assignment. Damned good spot, too. Besides, I operate on the time-honored theory that one should never allow water on his skin or down his throat. That's why I always carry a silver flask of this stuff, which, if you were to ask me, is slightly less villainous than Australian whiskey. And one never knows when the traditional tot o' rum will go astray. One prepares for these evil contingencies." The Beaver, having cooled the tea-and-rum to his liking and taken a generous swig, inquired, "What's *your* new job?"

Prince told him.

"By God," the Beaver ejaculated, "whether it's coincidence, telepathy or pure witchcraft, blessed if you and I won't be winding up at the same place."

"So?"

"Because, old cock, I've been tapped to be His Majesty's naval representative with Admiral Halsey, on ComSoPac staff. My associates here have already started calling me the most peripatetic liaison jockey since Noah."

"Congratulations," said Prince. "At any rate, you've latched onto a fairly permanent billet this time. I imagine Halsey's going to be around for quite a while—a damned sight longer than Tommy Hart was, certainly."

"What sort of craft is this *Shearcross?*"

"Reasonably modern, I understand, certainly not a four-piper like *Davidson*. Apparently she caught it bad in one of those Solomons cat-and-dog fights. That's about the size of it. Hell, what do I care, really?" Prince frowned down at the tea which the waiter had just brought. "Mine's strictly a one-shot arrangement anyhow. After that, Christ only knows. Maybe harbormaster at Samoa, if I'm lucky."

"How soon are you leaving?"

"On the noon shuttle flight to Sydney."

"I mean for Noumea."

"My orders read 'proceed immediately.' That would be to-morrow morning at the latest, I figure."

"Good-oh. If you don't mind too much, I'll tag along. Even a rebuilt tin can is better than some unseaworthy Aussie air-plane. And this way, I'll see a lot more of the scenery."

"Fix it up with ComSouWesPac's travel agency," said Prince, "and you've got yourself a deal."

"Consider it done." The Beaver tossed off his rum-laced tea. "While I'm at headquarters, if you want, I'll pick up a dossier on this *Shearcross* vessel. Might be interesting to learn a bit more about her."

Prince said, "Fine idea," wishing he'd thought of it when he was talking with Captain Brannigan. It was stupid of him not to have cared more about his forthcoming command, even though it was such a transient affair. Anything could happen in a 1,000-mile passage across the Coral Sea in this November of 1942. Anything. From a torpedoing to a sneak air raid by some far-ranging Nip bomber.

"When you're at headquarters, I'll be rounding up Mike Rodney. He's going along as acting exec," Prince said.

"Great. Rodney's a stout fella," said the Beaver. "Very stout, physically and intestinally."

Lieutenant Rodney took no convincing. Prince located him by telephone at MOB 2, where he was enjoying a half day off, and gave him the word without embellishment. Once ebullient, Rodney had turned strangely quiet in the past few months. Yet his reply came loud and clear, 5-by-5, when Prince described their brief mission.

"Hell, Commander, you're frigging well right I want to leave this pesthole. If you'd told me we were towing a bargeload of crap to Noumea, I'd have jumped at the chance."

Prince laughed mirthlessly. "My command will dissolve automatically when we reach our destination. But I can't see any reason why you shouldn't rate orders to remain as exec. For what it's worth, I'll do everything within my power to have 'em keep you on."

"Thanks, sir."

"Don't thank me," Prince said gruffly. "Just consider it as a sort of down payment on an overdue debt."

As they flew southward along Australia's verdant coastal belt, they perused the file which the Beaver had obtained from Sou-WesPac logistics.

USS *Shearcross* was a *Mahan*-class destroyer, class of '33, but refurbished in the summer of '41, shortly before the Pearl Harbor blitz. In fact, she had been one of the escorts for *Saratoga*, when the old carrier was sent racing to bolster the Pacific Fleet's shattered forces after December 7. Fully burdened, she displaced 2,100 tons and measured 341 by 35 feet. Her top-rated speed was thirty-six knots.

Comparing *Davidson*'s paltry equipage to *Shearcross*' array of weapons and electronic gear was like viewing a Model-T Ford alongside a Packard convertible. After her overhaul at Sydney, *Shearcross* would have, besides her normal main battery of four 5-inch, .38-caliber rifles, which were semiautomatic and geared for surface or antiaircraft action, a pair of the new twin 40-millimeter Bofors-type AA guns and four 20-millimeter Oerlikons. The Bofors could spew 160 projectiles per minute, with a workable range of almost 3,000 yards. As for the smaller Oerlikons, they blasted away at the amazing rate of 450 rounds a minute and had a range of more than 4,000 yards.

But it was the modernized five-inchers that delighted Prince, the Beaver and Rodney most. They were able to hurl fifty-plus pound shells 18,000 yards, and their skyward maximum when pressed into AA service was damned near six miles. Given a well-trained eleven-man crew, each of these five-inch cannon could fire better than twenty rounds every sixty seconds.

There were, of course, the usual ten twenty-one-inch torpedo tubes, armed, Prince trusted, with something better than those ineffably limp tin fish with which *Davidson* had gone into battle.

Shearcross, they found, had been severely mauled in mid-September, in a chance encounter with an I-class Jap sub during the enemy's determined effort to halt U.S. expansion into the Solomons. She had been towed to Noumea for emergency repairs, then sent under her own steam to Sydney.

Part of her upgrading was installation of radar, both search and gunnery, along with the best ECM (electric coding machine) apparatus available.

Near the tail end of SouWesPac's logistical report on *Shearcross*, it was curtly recorded that the destroyer had lost not only her captain, exec and gunnery officer in the disaster which occurred so suddenly but a large portion of her crew as well. As a result, she would sail for Noumea almost 100 men shy of her normal 250-member complement.

"We're fortunate," said Prince, "that they don't expect us to fire any of these new guns in anger. There won't be enough men aboard to handle a battery of crossbows, much less those fancy gismos."

Rodney peered up from his set of orders. "Nevertheless," he pointed out, "we're supposed to try 'em on for size before we report to ComSoPac—and 'undertake maximum speed trials of subject vessel,' namely *Shearcross*."

"Simply rehearsing," Prince assured him. "Not even full-dress, at that."

"Should be jolly good fun," said the Beaver. "My recollection of a five-inch rifle crew, which groweth dim since I joined you four-piper buggers, is that it requires roughly the following: gun captain, sight-setter, pointer, fuse-setter, trainer, spade man, hot-case man, powder man, ram operator, sight checker —and a merry bank of blokes to pass the ammo up from the handling room below."

"As you say," Prince agreed, "it sounds like jolly good fun."

Going aboard *Shearcross* late that afternoon was like a re-prise of Prince's initiation to his DesDiv 11 flagship, except that he was joining a ship whose company would know him only cursorily, whose personal loyalty he felt no overwhelming urge to woo. The destroyer was anchored in the roadstead a half mile off the navy-yard entrance, at the seaward extremity of Sydney itself, gently rolling in the slight tide swell.

A perspiring coxswain swung up the ladder from the whale-boat with Prince's seabag. The Beaver and Rodney came close at his heels, behind their own luggage bearers. Because the shut-tle plane, as usual, had been tardy in taking off, dusk was already falling as the whaleboat returned to shore. Prince focused his heavy-browed eyes on the junior officer-of-the-deck, a warrant boatswain in khakis. Even in the gathering darkness, sweat patches showed on the wiry little man's shirt. He had acknowl-edged the boarding parties' salutes perfunctorily.

"You are Commander Prince, sir?"

"Who else?" Aware, then, that the boatswain had probably put in a devilish hard day helping get *Shearcross* in order for her temporary skipper, he abruptly changed his tone. "Sorry, mister. Didn't mean to be rude."

This was a surprising admission for a three-striper to make to a warrant ranker. The boatswain blinked, and his dour expres-sion softened.

"Gee, sir, I didn't notice . . ."

The hell he didn't, thought Prince. But the apology had its effect. On their way to the wardroom, the JOD fell into a talkative mood, proudly explaining all the wondrous new gadgetry which had been festooned onto *Shearcross*, in the manner of a master surgeon exhibiting a set of before-and-after face-lift pictures of some aging woman who had suddenly come radiantly alive again under his magic touch. The revamped destroyer even smelled good, Prince decided, clean, wholesome, without that noxious excrement of ancient oil, rotting food and lived-in staleness which had always permeated *Davidson*.

The small procession edged carefully around the quintuple pairs of torpedo tubes and the two lofty stacks, toward officers' country, then paused before the door leading from the main deck to the wardroom. The boatswain expertly spun the wheel which unlocked the barrier, after noting aloud that Lieutenant Folkes, the navigator, was uncommon fussy about darkening ship. He ordered total blackout, with smoking lamps doused on all weather decks a half hour before sundown. Mr. Folkes, the boatswain implied discreetly, was a very cautious man, especially since he'd become the senior surviving officer among *Shearcross'* original ten.

They stepped into Stygian gloom as the door closed, making a compressed-air sound as it swung against the watertight coaming, and the wheel spun again, automatically switching on naked light bulbs over the standard green baize-covered wardroom table.

Four officers looked up inquisitively as Prince led his group into the broad chamber, which seemed like a castle hall in contrast to a four-piper's constricted dining-living space. Two of them had been playing cribbage; a third was drafting what obviously constituted an official report; the fourth was sipping coffee from a handleless mug, warily, in the manner of someone sampling a new and possibly lethal beverage.

The officer with the pen arose hastily. He wore the tarnished double bars of lieutenancy.

"Welcome aboard, Commander."

"Thanks." Prince eyed him critically. "You must be Lieutenant Folkes."

"Yes, sir. Jeremy Folkes. Navigator."

"I know."

For a fellow who had presumably been enjoying R-and-R for seven weeks, while the yard buckaroos patched up his ship, Folkes appeared remarkably tired. Almost as weary, in fact, as the worn-out gentry of DesDiv 11 when Prince had first met them. Then the thought crossed Prince's mind that, perhaps, *Shearcross'* stay in Sydney hadn't provided her crew with such a bed of roses after all. It was entirely possible, in view of the general shorthandedness of labor throughout Australia, that Folkes & Co. had been forced to work manually alongside the yard mechanics to restore their destroyer to her pristine fighting shape—or better. In truth, they had done just that, he learned. Battles were battles, as Folkes dutifully recorded.

By the time the Negro mess attendants, clad in dungarees instead of their usual clean whites, had finished serving dinner, the officers had eaten, and the wardroom was again cleared, Prince had gained a hazy impression of these youngsters who ran *Shearcross'* various departments. He made no attempt to pry into their past records or to search out any biographical tidbits. The destroyer's passage to Noumea would take slightly more than fifty-two hours, he reckoned, even allowing for the delay occasioned by gunnery practice. He planned to average twenty-five knots on a beeline course for the commodious, sheltered harbor capital on the southwest coast of French New Caledonia, so there would be scant opportunity or necessity for socializing.

In order of their seniority, *Shearcross'* officers included:

Lieutenant Jeremy Folkes, USN, about twenty-six, which made him very senior-in-grade. He was squat, darkly hirsute and somber-miened. Prince attributed the latter to Folkes' disappointment at not having received instant promotion to exec, a spot for which he undoubtedly felt entitled as well as qualified. He'd been seasoned in battle. And he had served as top aide to the lieutenant commander who skippered *Shearcross* from Noumea to Sydney. This two-and-a-half-striper was long gone to another job. But Folkes' burning desire for the executive officer billet remained unabated.

Lieutenant Samuel Coleridge Taylor, USN, probably twenty-five, the ship's engineer. Unlike the rubicund Slats Slattery, he was as pale as a ghost, thin, a dark-eyed Virginian; and Prince made much of their both having come from that sovereign state, although often it seemed that half the Navy derived either from Virginia or Texas.

Lieutenant (jg) Herbert Standish, USN, also in the twenty-five-year range, the communicator. He was the damp, nervous sort, with thinning red hair. (Why, mused Prince, did red-haired men always tend toward baldness?) Plainly, Standish was bursting to relay the latest poop about ComSoPac's gathering armada, but Prince kept him under leash until a more opportune moment came for talking strategy.

Lieutenant (jg) Carleton Franks, USN, maybe twenty-four, the first lieutenant. He gave the impression of being ice-calm, determined, without the boyishness of the late Peter Blue. He was tall, muscular, built like an offensive football end. His most striking feature was an immense shock of crisp, curly black hair.

Ensign Manuel de Carlo, USNR, in his earliest twenties, the assistant engineer. He'd been graduated as a naval V-12 reservist from some obscure New England college. It surprised Prince to find a commissioned *latino* on board, although he reluctantly supposed that anything went in wartime; and he noted with some amusement that de Carlo, in demeanor and appearance, could have been Yeoman Bream's Castilian cousin, if such were possible.

Ensign Barrett O'Brien, USN, also in his beginning twenties,

345

torpedo chief and assistant to the slain gunnery officer. He was short, randy-looking, with overlong blond hair. O'Brien, it became quickly apparent, was inclined to be quippish, a conscious Irish buffoon, thus carrying out the tradition that every ship's company must have its court jester.

And, of course, *Warrant Boatswain Henry Hamilton*, USN, who had met Prince's trio on the quarter-deck. He was in his mid-thirties, an up-from-the-ranks mustang like Eric Hagen, who served variously as supplies procurer and assistant damage-control officer to Franks. Despite his ferrety looks, Hamilton was warmly regarded by his fellows as a dedicated type who would do anything, anytime, to keep *Shearcross* well fed and alive.

None of the seven destroyermen gave the vaguest hint that they had ever heard of Prince's Surabayan troubles involving the non-loss and subsequent miraculous revival of his flagship, *Davidson*, as a unit of the Imperial Japanese Navy. He watched and listened attentively, while they chatted over their after-dinner coffee, for some hint that his ignominious reputation had spread this far south. But none came, yet.

Lieutenant Standish finally found his chance to tell the assembled ten, among whom were Rodney and the Beaver, what seemed to be brewing at ComSoPac. Prince learned little he did not already know, except that as of today, Sunday, November 8, the Nips had at last launched their move southward, on the heels of the fast destroyers and cruisers which carried fresh troops to bolster the Mikado's beleaguered garrison on western Guadalcanal. A PT out of Tulagi had damaged a Jap tin can in the Slot, and a minesweeper managed to sink an enemy sub off San Cristobal. Mainly, though, in the Solomons vicinity, it was still the calm before the storm, an interval dedicated to battening down the hatches, securing loose fittings, bracing for the blow.

Prince rose from the table just as the brass ship's clock on the wardroom bulkhead was striking four bells. Ten P.M.

346

The others immediately followed suit.

"We've let the noncoms handle the duty detail long enough," announced Prince. "Some of you gentlemen have watches to stand, and the rest—like myself—ought to hit the sack early." He scrutinized his wrist watch, verifying the hour. "Our estimated departure time is oh-five hundred. I'd like to make it right on the button. Roger?"

There was a chorus of "Affirmatives" as *Shearcross'* officers left for their various stations or to their staterooms.

Prince turned to Folkes. "Will you stick around a few minutes, Lieutenant, for a brief powwow with Mr. Rodney, Commander Monk and myself?"

"Certainly, sir."

Succinctly, Prince outlined his plan for the journey to Noumea. They would conduct flank speed trials as soon as *Shearcross* was well clear of Sydney harbor. These should take around six hours, he judged, after which they would top off the afternoon by trying out both the new and the rebored weaponry.

"This means," said Prince, "that Monday will be a pretty rugged workday. But you'll have Tuesday and part of Wednesday to relax a bit, before joining whichever outfit Admiral Halsey decides needs your talents."

Folkes nodded. After a moment he spoke in a tone that wavered somewhere between uneasy diffidence and grave concern. "We're rather like orphans, you know, sir, living in a foundling home. It's not going to be easy, taking on our third CO in less than two months." He paused again. "Plus a brand-new exec."

"I understand quite well," Prince said. "I went through much the same thing with DesDiv Eleven, only I was housemaster, you might say. It's not easy. In fact, it's damned hard to adjust in a hurry."

"I've read the reports on DesDiv Eleven," Folkes said.

"You have?" Prince showed his surprise. "All of 'em?"

"Yes, sir."

"Right down to the bitter end?"

"The whole history," said Folkes, "including what happened in that drydock in Surabaya." Rodney opened his mouth to speak, perhaps in defense of Prince, who continued to regard the navigator in a somewhat bewildered fashion. But Folkes went on: "I've also heard the scuttlebutt from Brisbane. And I want you to know, sir, that neither I nor the other officers aboard this ship feel any qualms about having you as our captain."

"Well," Prince said dryly, "it's only for a few non-combatant days at worst."

"That's not the point, sir."

"What is?"

"Hell," Folkes burst out, "a man is faced with a decision—as you were—and he has to take a reading in his own mind before he acts. Maybe he doesn't do the right thing. Maybe he does. But if he chooses wrong, he shouldn't have to hang by his thumbs for it. Especially after what you went through at Balikpapan and Bali."

"You are a remarkably ·considerate, tactful young fellow," said Prince. "A lot of people don't own up to your brand of compassion. At this late date I goddamned well regret not going back to Surabaya to lend Rodney, here, a hand. Not that it would have helped. But it might. So I didn't, and I guess I'll have to live with that failure the rest of my life."

Neither Rodney nor the Beaver offered any comment as Prince's self-castigation dwindled into an almost palpable, taut silence. To them, knowing him as they did, it was akin to over-hearing a priest's confrontation with a sinner in the confessional box. Prince was patently sincere. His words had emerged effort-lessly, as if he were achieving an overdue *katharsis*, which eased his spirits and exorcised the pent-up demons that had plagued him for so long.

"Anyhow," said Folkes, a bit awkwardly, "I just thought you ought to know how we feel."

"Thanks, Lieutenant."

Folkes left.

Prince looked steadily at Rodney and the Beaver, his face drained of emotion. "Sorry to have exposed you to this public unburdening of my soul," he said. "But suddenly it seemed the appropriate time to get the infernal business off my chest."

The Beaver laid his vast right arm over Prince's slim shoulder. "You did fine, old cock. Clears the bloody air. Sets the record straight." He glanced toward Rodney. "Agreed, Leftenant?"

"Agreed, Commander."

He and Prince solemnly clasped hands.

"Now," said the Beaver, "let's follow our hardhearted master's orders and turn in."

Before he could go, Prince stopped him. "One favor, fella."

"Name it."

"We're short a gunnery officer. I doubt like hell if that kid, O'Brien, can hold down the detail alone. Will you take over as temporary keeper of all those magnificent new HE baubles?"

"Consider it done," the Beaver rumbled. "Remember, I've had a modicum of experience with Oerlikons and Bofors in the Mediterranean."

"Which is why I asked," Prince said. "Plus the fact, you old bastard, that I've belatedly come to regard you as my resident Dutch uncle." He turned to Rodney. "Need any help in your area?"

"Negative, sir. *Shearcross* is bigger, faster and a damned sight better than *Davidson*. But she's still a destroyer. I'll manage all right."

"Bear in mind," Prince added, "that brother Folkes also hankers for this exec billet."

"I'm aware of that, sir. Less than three days is an awfully short period to prove that I can handle this duty. So I guess we'll just have to see."

In his cabin, Prince could hear the Beaver's loud rhythmic

349

snoring, which cut around the bulkhead and across the narrow companionway. Before the war, *Shearcross* boasted such fripperies as blue canvas curtains embellished with white anchors that screened stateroom doors and served as partial soundproofing. Now she had none. Like all the other fighting ships of the fleet, even her interior paint had been scraped away until she gleamed dully, with the sheen of well-scoured kitchenware. *Shearcross* was as utilitarian in her own deadly way as a stiletto: a fine, plain, workmanlike stiletto that is best wielded in dark cul-de-sacs, where the user can strike fast without being clearly seen by his victim, and then escape into the alleyways of the night.

Prince sat on his bunk to remove his well-worn jodhpur boots, peeled off his socks, trousers and shirt, and then painfully stretched out, full length, on the hard mattress. He couldn't sleep. But he knew that the Brobdingnagian noises emanating from the Beaver's nearby room were not the real cause of his insomnia. Something inside himself, ticking like a time bomb, was keeping him awake.

He wondered, then, if he would ever sleep again. Because the demons had not been driven out. They were still present, and they would remain so long as a hermaphroditic monstrosity once named *Davidson* was plying the oceans under the red-and-white emblem of the Rising Sun.

Shearcross slipped her moorings at 0457, three minutes early, and gingerly picked her way through the ferryboats and small craft which dotted the harbor, evading the booms and anti-submarine nets that guarded Sydney's winding egress to the sea. Red-eyed, unshaven, fatigued, Prince had reveilled at 0300 to supervise their departure. He was glad that the destroyer was moored offshore. Warping a 2,100-ton vessel away from dockside was something he had never yet been called upon to do, and already he was worrying about bringing her smartly along-side a wharf in Noumea, if that's what ComSoPac wanted.

By 0800 Prince decided they were ready for speed trials.

The Coral Sea was in one of her nicer moods, deceptively calm, with minimal swell and two-foot rollers that approached *Shearcross* head on, but evenly spaced. Of all the world's great waters, the Coral Sea, thus denoted for her myriads of polyped islets, reefs and uncharted shoals, could be the most hazardous at times. She was a massive entity, restless, never completely still, seemingly with a life of her own. She was prone to sudden hurricanes and to generating unbearable musty heat across her span, which extended from New Guinea on the north to the blustery Tasman Sea on the south, below which spread New Zealand; her waves lapped Australia on the west and on the east that string of subtropical islands which stretched upward from New Caledonia to the Bismarck Archipelago. To those who habitually sailed the Coral Sea, she was like an unpredictable friend, often lovely to know but much too frequently an angry creature of homicidal whims.

At that moment *Shearcross* was a lonely dot on the azure surface. No other ship lay within view. Only the limitless horizon surrounded her, marked by trade-wind clouds and the darker shade of the arching skies.

"True, blue Monday," remarked the Beaver, appreciatively snuffling the fresh air as he surveyed the peaceful scene. "Literally."

"Let's hope it stays this salubrious," Prince said as he went to the voice tube to raise Lieutenant Taylor, the engineering officer. "Everything set down there?"

"Copacetic, sir," came Taylor's prompt reply, in a thin tone that equated with his wraithlike features.

"Good. Let's get with it."

"Yes, sir."

Prince made a sudden decision: "I think I'll crawl down and

kibitz while you're bringing her up to—what is it?—forty thousand shaft horsepower?"

"Make that forty-two thousand eight hundred," said Taylor proudly. "Plus whatever else we can drag out of her glowing guts."

As Prince swung down the interior ladder, he called up to the bridge, "Take over, Mr. Rodney. See you in a little while, if I don't get toasted too brown in Taylor's oven."

During his descent to the bowels of the destroyer, Prince kept asking himself: Why? It had been so dulcetly pleasant on the bridge, occupying a chair that was even more elegantly padded than his old flagship's command throne, ready to pronounce judgment on the engine room's performance. His one experience in *Davidson*'s hellish propulsion spaces had been, he believed, enough for a normal lifetime. Yet here he was behaving like a veteran captain who expected to hold his command for a couple of years, rather than a Johnny-go-quickly on a pick-up mission.

There was no answer, actually, except that the same malaise which had prevented him from sleeping last night was still gnawing at him.

He found Taylor standing on the catwalk grill which paralleled a complex array of more than fifty dials and gauges, studying each of them with a jeweler's eye for the least flaw in the minutest facet of a costly diamond. The chief machinist's mate, Taylor's whip hand over the already harassed Black Gang "snipes," was a Falstaffian tun-of-a-man in soaked dungarees. He stood with splayed legs among the quadruple turbines, proud monarch of the throttle station. Ten minutes after Taylor received his orders, *Shearcross* had advanced from her half-speed 21,100 s.h.p. to almost 30,000. As the arrows on the dial crept clockwise, Prince could hear the forced draft air blowers intensify their whine, keeping the cavernous compartment slightly cooler than Hades itself, though not much.

Taylor led him through the airlock space between the engine and boiler rooms, where a pair of steel doors were never opened simultaneously, lest a flareback from the released ventilation cause a holocaust which would incinerate everyone in the entire department within a matter of seconds.

The boiler room was ruled by another gigantic man, a chief watertender, whose duty was seeing that the requisite amount of Diesel fuel fed into *Shearcross'* sixteen eight-banked furnaces. Through the heat-impervious windows, Prince watched the flames turn from red to pale blue, then to white, as the destroyer revved up. When she finally reached her flank speed apex, nobody would dare look directly into these sight-searing apertures.

Even down here, in this devilish metal cocoon, Prince could feel the ship begin to shudder and her stern to rattle as she edged closer to the thirty-seven knots that Taylor had faithfully promised him.

"Maybe thirty-eight," the gaunt youngster added, "if you'll risk blowing a few gaskets."

Prince viewed him with frank admiration. *Blowing a few gaskets!* That could also mean blowing up a few crewmen in the process if something went drastically wrong with this untested machinery.

"All I'm asking for," he said, "is the best you've got, mister."

"Okay, sir, then we'll shoot for thirty-eight."

"Very well."

Prince clambered back up the ladder from the engineering domain, grateful for the asbestos gloves that Taylor had insisted he wear. Even through their thick material he felt the incredible heat from the iron handrails. How could Taylor, his chiefs and his snipes stand it? Their stolid acceptance of this torturous existence gave him an odd feeling of pride and confidence. *Davidson* had fielded a damned good crew, which he'd never sufficiently appreciated nor granted in his egotistic acceptance of personal credit for their deeds. *Shearcross*, if Samuel Coleridge

Taylor were any criterion, had an equally splendid complement. (He also speculated, irrationally, whether Taylor's parents had been smitten by the poetry of the man who wrote "The Ancient Mariner" when they'd christened their manchild. In a war like this, he told himself saturninely, the chances of any combat mariner reaching an age worthy of being called "ancient" were slender indeed.)

They barreled along at thirty-five knots for about twenty minutes, with the engine-order telegraph locked on flank speed, until, with excruciating slowness, like the hour hand of a clock, the log needle on the dial beside the gyrocompass began to move again. Thirty-six, thirty-seven, thirty-eight knots, by God! Maybe thirty-eight and a bloody half. In landlubber terms, this translated into 44.3 miles per hour. Hell. You could get arrested for speeding in a lot of country-bumpkin towns at that rate.

Prince whistled into the engine-room telegraph. When Taylor answered, he shouted jubilantly, "You've proved your point, Lieutenant. Now let's cut her back to twenty-five before the cops start chasing after us."

"Yes, sir!" Taylor's meager voice held a triumphal overtone. "And nary a gasket blew."

By now it was midmorning. Prince turned to the Beaver. "Reckon you might essay a few rounds of gunfire before we chow-down?"

"Let's do that little thing, milord."

The Beaver ascended the ladder to the main battery director like a clumsy circus bear, while Ensign O'Brien parked himself just below on the unsheltered 40-millimeter director. Both stations were located immediately over the enclosed bridge where Prince, Rodney and Boatswain Hamilton had assumed their places. Around them were clustered the helmsman and his relief, who took over the tedious conn at thirty-minute intervals; the

354

phone-talker, who kept in constant touch with the communications shack, the navigator, the combat information center (CIC) where radar, sonar, radio and visual data were processed; and the signalman, whose duty was to make sure that messages were properly prepared for delivery via blinker light, flag hoist or TBS.

This represented only a skeletal bridge watch. But it would have to suffice, in view of *Shearcross'* curtailed personnel roster. The CIC, Prince knew, was a standing ship's joke. Besides Standish, who doubled in brass as communicator and head of this "brains trust," it was staffed by a yeoman first class and a seaman second, who had hardly begun to learn their complicated trade when a Jap I-boat crippled the destroyer off Cape Esperance. This all-important detail labored in a stuffy compartment below the bridge, aft of Standish's radio room. Once they arrived at Noumea, the CIC would be beefed up, with a combat intelligence team capable of fast evaluation of all the arcane material that filtered in from friend and foe alike, which they would then mark on the big plexiglass status board. Targets and consorts took visible shape on that imitation sea and, through different colors, in the skies above it.

"Sound General Quarters, Mr. Rodney," said Prince.

"Yes, sir."

Rodney motioned to Hamilton, who pressed the GQ button. Because gunnery practice hadn't been expected by the rest of the ship's company until afternoon, Prince reasoned this should provide a nice test of their readiness for instant action after so many arduous weeks on the beach, away from the always unpredictable realities of life at sea.

Gongs rang throughout the ship for about ten seconds, after which the talker intoned through *Shearcross'* loud-speaking intercom: "This is General Quarters. Repeat, General Quarters. All hands go immediately to your battle stations."

Prince listened for the familiar sound of pounding feet, the clatter of leather shoes on ladders, the clang of hatches and weather deck doors being hurriedly closed. He might have had the talker append "This is a drill" to his peremptory order. But he preferred to see how the truncated crew behaved under the stress of presumed emergency conditions. Conceivably they might be required, even in the short time remaining before the ship reached port, to fend off some stalking enemy.

From the various stations—gunnery, torpedo, engineering and damage control—came the readiness reports.

"Tell Commander Monk that he may commence firing whenever he wishes," Prince told the talker.

The word was passed. Almost as if the Beaver had been anticipating this message, all four of the five-inch rifles raised to their maximum elevation, as did the fore-and-aft 40-millimeters and the quartet of twenties. The ten torpedo launchers orbited outward, five pointing directly abeam to starboard, five to port.

Before the seven men on the bridge could brace themselves for the shock, the main battery opened up. The Beaver hadn't even granted them the courtesy of preceding his barrage with the warning buzzer, so that they could stuff cotton into their ears to lessen the shock. Nowhere in the ship's upperworks was immune from the terrific, concussive effect of the blast from these long guns. It was a dirty trick, and the Beaver knew it; but it might also have been a device taken deliberately if a real enemy were to heave into view before the amenities could be observed.

By contrast to *Davidson*'s four-inchers, these larger rifles had an almost apocalyptic authority. Prince could envision himself trapped in a cosmic telephone booth whose doors were slammed tight shut by a capricious giant, or having his feet slapped with a billy club wielded by this same giant, like a New York cop on a Central Park bum. Despite their elevation, the gun muzzles sent a hail of cork particles from the ejected shell fuses whipping aft out of the No. 1 and No. 2 guns through the windshields, which Rodney had wisely lowered before GQ was called. They stung like birdshot. Acrid fumes swept across the bridge, and the muzzle flashes were blinding despite the brightness of the day.

In a lull, Prince yelled to the helmsman, "Come hard right, fella, about forty-five degrees!"

The helmsman twisted around to give him an incredulous glance, apparently to see whether this unfamiliar skipper had gone suddenly crazy, then turned forward again. Prince's set features weren't those of a man bereft of his senses; they simply betokened a stern insistence on instant response to his order.

Shearcross heeled like an America's Cup defender as her knife-sharp prow lurched to starboard.

By now they had shoved cotton wads into their ears, so he didn't much care about the next salvo. Prince merely wanted the Beaver to remember that staying on your toes was a full-time job, after the bearded clown dragged himself off the deck. He grinned wickedly. That should show the bastard that two could play the game of Instant Alertness as well as one.

From where he was standing Prince could hear the Beaver's stentorian bellow through the talker's headset.

"You buggers all right down there?"

"Tell Commander Monk we're fine—just trying to avoid a small floating egg crate."

The talker delivered the message. Then he turned to Prince. "The commander says screw the egg crates, sir, and please don't bother him when he's playing with his toys."

"Inform Commander Monk," said Prince, "that impromptu maneuvers are liable to happen in wartime."

Only one other complaint remained to be recorded. The engine-room tube carried Lieutenant Taylor's plaintive bleat: "Why didn't we get advance notice about the firing? There's soot an inch thick all over the place from the goddamned blowers."

Prince replied, "Sorry about that, mister. We were executing some emergency measures. But we should have warned you to stand clear of the vents." That was true. During her idle weeks *Shearcross'* air pipes had accumulated a thick coating of oily film, which the initial five-inch blast had shaken loose, like foul snow from a slum roof.

After suffering the pangs of the Beaver's monstrous practical joke with his main battery, listening to the Bofors and the Oerlikons was no worse than auditing a bad symphony. Ensign O'Brien raced skillfully through a dummy torpedo run, and then it was lunchtime.

Afterward the weather was sapphire-clear, and, with GQ lifted, the off-duty men lolled around the deck, suntanning themselves. The next forty-eight hours looked like the well-known piece of cake.

Almost 900 miles to the northeast, in his headquarters situated on the second floor of a crumbling French colonial office building, Admiral Halsey was staring at ComSoPac's operational wall chart. He stood with arms folded across his barrel chest, deep in thought, while his chief of staff impatiently awaited the crucial decision which only Halsey could make.

The admiral's attention was riveted on a small, blue-headed pin affixed to the map, far removed from any of the other pins that were clustered around the New Hebrides, south of the impending Solomons battle zone. It lay astride a penciled red line drawn straight as a master archer's arrow flight between Sydney and Noumea.

The pin was *Shearcross.*

Halsey unfolded his arms, jammed his fists into his pockets and announced in a tone of finality, "Very well, Mac, that's the one we divert."

The chief of staff, a tall, gaunt, pock-faced man who was reputed to be something of a genius as well as a strategic madman on occasion, had originally proposed the scheme. But even he was beginning to harbor certain doubts.

"You know who her skipper is, sir?"

"No. What does it matter?" Halsey demanded testily. "Aren't destroyer captains pretty much alike—full of piss and vinegar and rarin' to go?"

"This fellow might be different." The chief of staff approached closer to the chart and scowled at the pin that denoted *Shearcross,* as if he were God Almighty, looking down upon the isolated ship herself. "His name is Prince. Commander Custis Prince. He's the chap who had DesDiv Eleven. Now d'you recollect, Admiral?"

"You mean the three-striper who's supposed to have gotten all fouled up over that tin can that wasn't destroyed in drydock at Surabaya."

"Right."

Halsey meditatively rubbed his jutting jaw. "Hell, by now this man has probably learned his lesson. I'm inclined to give any repentant sinner a second chance. Maybe I'll pull a blooper and need the same sort of break one day."

The chief of staff seemed relieved. The Old Man had, in effect, issued the order. And when you came right down to it, the task they were about to give *Shearcross* could either be a totally innocuous commitment or a suicidal mission. She would have to be regarded as expendable, with her insufficient crew and her dubious skipper. Yet Prince, he recalled from the information he'd requested of ComSouWesPac, didn't strike him as a total minus, not after those rugged scraps off Balikpapan and Bali.

Moreover, as he had conjectured when the tactic first occurred to him, *Shearcross'* very inadequacy as a fighting unit in the days ahead was in her favor, if you could call delegation to such potentially hazardous duty a favor. Rather than subtracting a full-fledged destroyer from ComSoPac's undernourished

359

line-up, he preferred to utilize this reconstructed vessel. He was aware, too, that Prince had chosen a damned capable exec in Lieutenant Michael Rodney and that the veteran British liaison officer, Commander Algernon Monk, was also aboard. Monk's credentials were superb. He would be worth a couple of lesser officers if a showdown developed.

Herding *Shearcross* back to Noumea, fleshing out her crew, seeing that they had minimal training as a cohesive group would consume a hell of a lot more time than the rapidly developing crisis would allow. Thus, had Prince been the lubberliest of lubbers, *Shearcross* unquestionably would have drawn this chore, after all the alternatives were weighed. Yet the chief of staff was glad to have Halsey's imprimatur on the order. It took a load off his own shoulders. Even staff chiefs like their burdens shared, particularly by the Man Upstairs.

What he had proposed for *Shearcross* was by no means a new operational device. Fleets had used it, on various occasions, ever since the advent of radio. Sometimes it worked. Sometimes it failed utterly.

"I'll have the dispatch sent at once, Admiral."

"Good."

After Halsey had gone to his own Spartan office, the chief of staff sat down at the nearest desk and pulled a yellow-lined pad in front of him. With his fountain pen he slowly wrote:

From COMSOPAC
To: Commanding Officer USS *Shearcross*
  You are hereby directed to change course and head toward a point approximately 10 degrees south latitude 158 degrees west. After acknowledging receipt of this message maintain radio silence until you have come within 50 miles of designated station. There-upon you will commence signaling in the clear to simulate presence of a U.S. carrier task force. During this period keep moving about rapidly so that signals will appear to come from numerous units of

such a hypothetical force. Imperative that you reach area by sundown November 11. Continue mission until further notice. Good luck and Godspeed. Halsey.

Ordinarily the chief of staff would not have appended the admiral's name at the end of the dispatch. But he thought that it was deserved, even essential, under the circumstances.

He summoned a Marine orderly.

"Take this to the coding room," he said. "On the double. Tell 'em to label it urgent and top secret."

"Yes, sir."

The Marine saluted, spun on his polished cordovan heel and marched toward the door. As he neared it, the chief of staff had a sudden afterthought.

"Bring that thing back here, Corporal. I've got to make a small addition."

He took the missive. Before the well-wishing sign-off, he inserted: "Regret that no air cover will be feasible."

Silently, he returned the yellow sheet to the orderly, who once more saluted and sped away.

ComSoPac's message reached *Shearcross* one hour later, was decoded on the ECM and delivered to Prince in the wardroom by messenger at 1300, while he was lunching with the off-duty officers. Still fuming at intervals over the nasty trick his frequent cellmate had perpetrated during the gunnery exercise, the Beaver occupied the chair on Prince's right. The skipper presided at the head of the table. Before him, on his left, were Taylor and Franks; beside the Britisher sat Hamilton. All the missing others were at their Condition II stations, which meant that watertight integrity details were standing by, lookouts posted, underwater listening and radar gear operative and half the ship's weaponry ready for prompt use.

"Mr. Standish felt you should see this right away," said the messenger.

Prince accepted the flimsy. With a brief apology to those around him, he read it while they waited, letting their steaks (proudly bestowed by Hamilton as a post-drill reward for every officer and crewman aboard) go cold.

"Dear suffering Christ!" he proclaimed impiously after having perused the dispatch twice to make certain he'd absorbed its full import.

The Beaver knifed into his steak, forked a vast slice into his mouth and demanded between bites, "What gives, old biscuit?"

"Well," said Prince in a purposefully restrained voice, "it's a *billet doux* from Halsey, giving us a brand-new set of orders. We've been waved off Noumea—for special assignment elsewhere."

"What kind, sir?" Franks asked, his tone steadfastly cool, as always.

"It's classified top secret," said Prince, "but since we seem to be the only ship on these immediate seas, and I don't suspect we have any Jap spies aboard with hidden short-wave transmitters, I'll read the whole thing to you gentlemen. Hang on to your hats."

There was a lengthy, unnatural silence when he'd finished reciting ComSoPac's dictum. Even the Beaver laid down his fork and stopped chewing in respectful deference to their dramatically altered goal.

Prince said, "That's how it is. Period. Now let's finish off Mr. Hamilton's elegant viands and go to work. I want a report from every department head within the next two hours, telling me exactly how he intends to operate and what measures he'd take if we run into serious trouble." He gave each of them an individual glance. "Except for a minimal bridge and engine-room watch, I'd like all officers here at fifteen hundred. Savvy?"

They savvied.

To the Beaver he added: "You and I'll join Folkes in the charthouse, along with Rodney, and see what's what with our course change and speed, if we're to meet ComSoPac's schedule."

Both Rodney and Lieutenant Folkes accepted the edict with remarkable aplomb. To the navigator, for the moment, it was simply a matter of switching from one red-penciled straight line to another on his Coral Sea map, thumbtacked to the plotting board. *Shearcross'* noon location was marked by a small x some 200 miles outbound from Sydney. With ruler and dividers, Folkes found the point designated by ComSoPac at 10 degrees south, 158 degrees east, and made another tiny x at that spot, which was virtually due north of them.

"This will put us a hundred and fifty miles west of Guadalcanal," he said, "and five hundred and fifty miles southeast of Rabaul."

Prince nodded approvingly. "That's damned convenient. Halsey 'regrets' we won't have air support. Fine. At least we'll be at the far end of the Nips' aerial run from Rabaul."

"Sorry, sir." Folkes looked personally guilty as he broke the bad news. "But the Japs are reported to have laid down a fighter strip in the Shortlands, off the southern tip of Bougainville. That cuts their distance for possible interception to around two hundred miles."

"So we've inherited new problems," Prince said, making an effort to lighten his tone.

A couple of months ago he would have been caught up in sheer, stark terror at the thought of bringing this undermanned vessel beneath the enemy's very nose. That visceral coldness would have begun playing hob with his gut. And he'd have had to paste a false smile on his face, like a stage-frightened actor, to conceal his true feelings. He still harbored an uneasiness, bordering on fear, as he realized what lay ahead. But this inevitable emotion was accompanied by an almost mystical lifting of his soul, a cleansing sense, that same *katharsis* which he had experienced during his exquisite moment of absolution in *Shearcross'* wardroom when he'd first come aboard.

"How far must we travel from this *x*," Prince inquired, aiming his right forefinger at their approximate present position, "to that *x* up there?"

"About fourteen hundred miles," Folkes answered.

"Give me a safe-speed estimate that will insure our arrival on station as ordered."

Folkes made some rapid computations on a scratch pad. "We've got a little better than fifty hours to work with. To reach that point, with a decent margin to spare, I'd suggest an average of twenty-five knots."

"Very well," said Prince, directing himself to Rodney, "tell Mr. Taylor to prepare for a couple of days at that speed. It'll be rather stiff going, I'm afraid, because we'll have a quartering sea once we advance north. But that can't be helped. Get a reading on fuel, too, will you?"

"Yes, sir."

PART V

12

"Harpooned!"

SHEARCROSS WHEELED BRISKLY from course-045, northeast, to course-355, barely five degrees off true north, heading straight through the heart of the Coral Sea to her solitary rendezvous in the lower end of the island-strewn appurtenance to this larger body known as the Solomon Sea. At the x toward which they were now briskly cruising, the waters were more than 16,000 feet deep. An entire fleet could vanish there without trace. Above it sprawled the New Georgia island group, which the Japs hadn't as yet occupied, and beyond them mighty Bougainville, upon whose menacing appendage, Shortland, they had built their goddamned airfield. Jesus! How these little beggars could dig, thought Prince.

He and the Beaver had retired to his stateroom for a tactical huddle after their charthouse visit.

It was the latter's belief that ComSoPac, in his infinite wisdom, had selected this particular x as the logical place where a carrier task force would choose to launch planes in support of the Allied surface forces in the Slot east of Guadalcanal. Such a contingent would have rounded San Cristobal Island, between the Solomons and the New Hebrides, well beyond the Nips' aerial reconnaissance capability, then swung northwestward.

Prince agreed.

Lying on Prince's bunk, which like all the others had been covered with a flameproof rubber sheet, the Beaver regarded him curiously.

"You don't seem your usual self, old boy," he said. "You act more as if you're secretly high on hashish or something."

"Negative," said Prince. "I've merely found an accommodation with my less than immortal psyche, that's all."

"You mean," asked the Beaver, "the gremlins have evaporated?"

"Almost. I'm still scared shitless. But I've learned to live with it."

"Hell," the Beaver rumbled, "any man who wouldn't be scared shitless on an adventure like this has to be ravin' mad."

"Do *you* have the wind up?" Prince sounded incredulous at the notion that the Britisher's veins contained anything except pure distilled ice water on the eve of possible battle.

"There's a wide difference," said the Beaver, "between getting the wind up and being honestly scared. It's a functional matter. With the wind up, a fellow can behave in a silly fashion. Even dangerously. Whereas contained fright tends to steady a chap so that he does his proper job under stress." He massaged his protuberant belly with an air of complete satisfaction. "Who knows, old cock. Ahab might even discover his great white whale on this expedition."

Prince smiled wanly. "Miracles like that don't happen," he said.

"I wouldn't guarantee a moratorium on miracles, fella. At any rate, I've already made up my mind that every Ahab must have his Ishmael—and I'm yours to command."

"Balls."

"Don't toss it away so lightly. Burn a few candles. Utter a

couple of prayers. Stick pins in a candle carved like *Davidson-maru.*"

"What if our whale showed up with a division of destroyers?" Prince wanted to know, "or a couple of cruisers?"

"That," said the Beaver, "would be damned embarrassing, I'll admit. But judging from ComSoPac's description of this forthcoming squabble, I'd assess the chances of our runnin' into a school of the creatures as being bloody slim. I'm banking on the Nippers having extended their air power pretty thin, too."

"I hope you're right, uncle. Even a pair of tin cans would cause us pain."

Later the Beaver would mystify his gunner's mates by addressing them as Queequeg, Daggoo and Tashtego. But even after he tried to explain their derivation from *Moby Dick,* they still were puzzled. The Limey was an all-right guy, they conceded privately, but queer as a three-dollar bill, to compare Yank gunners with old-time native harpoon wielders.

The wardroom conference lasted less than half an hour. It was a foreordained litany of shortages and solutions, of chewing gum and baling wire to patch together, not sleek *Shearcross* herself, but rather the tight-knit groups of men who might be called upon to take their ship into unequal combat. All this called for extraordinarily bold management and deft footwork.

Item: They must operate the five-inch main battery with eight instead of the requisite eleven ratings and seamen per gun; the 40-millimeters with four in place of the usual six; the 20-millimeters with three, not four. The Beaver wasn't visibly entranced with the prospects of such cutbacks, but he accepted them as inevitable, commenting only that the Crusaders got a damned sight better shake against the Saracen hordes.

Item: Ensign O'Brien was given two men, a gyro-setter and a mount trainer, for each of his five-fish torpedo spreads. Normally there would have been a third, the mount captain; but the young assistant gunnery officer was told he'd have to handle that detail himself. So he just ruffled his mop of blond hair and said he would manage. Somehow.

Item: Lieutenant (jg) Franks' damage-control party was reduced from thirty men to twenty. Rodney, who was calling these unpleasant shots as exec, explained bluntly that *Shearcross* would have to take her lumps if she stumbled into action, relying on her offensive weaponry, trusting to luck that nothing would go radically wrong with her thinly armored interior.

Item: Therefore Sam Taylor's Black Gang would also be chopped by seven snipes, whose new duties would include shell-handling for the big guns and the Bofors. Taylor observed wryly, "At least one bunch of guys will thank you for a reprieve, sir. Inside every boiler-room buckaroo there's a deck hand trying to bust loose." Prince gave the engineer an appreciative nod, then laughed. Coming from this pallid, spectral figure, the twisted epigram which originally allowed that inside every fat man there's a thin one screaming to get out, might have seemed inept. Yet it wasn't. A great many engine-room hands, he knew, wound up in that dismal duty merely because somebody higher up put them there in the first place, when they were fresh from training school, without rhyme or reason. Few volunteered for service in Hades.

Item: Once they arrived on station, there would be no hot meals. In fact, no meals, other than a supply of K-rations for officers and men alike. Cooks, bakers and their hirelings would be reassigned topside. Rodney said, "If you gents find K-ration cheese and minced ham a trifle unpalatable, I commend your attention to the Marines on Guadalcanal, who've been eating this crap ever since August."

Item: The Combat Information Center would be manned by the captain's yeoman and one other rating. One of them would keep his eye on the search radarscope; his mate would relay the Word, soonest, if any strange blips showed up, and relieve him when his eyes gave out.

Item: Lieutenant Standish, the communicator, would stand watch in the radio shack with a single helper. Since they were now on radio silence, the ship wouldn't be transmitting until the start of their decoy messages. If anything bearing on their mission came over the Fox schedule, which was the catch-all long-range system by which ComSoPac sent strictly one-way signals to his far-flung units, Standish would let the bridge know. Otherwise it was strictly a waiting game.

Item: Prince would preside on the bridge. Rodney would go aft to the secondary conn, above the crew's deck shelter, prepared to assume command in case anything happened to those in charge of the primary controls, namely Prince and Hamilton, who would be the permanent JOD.

That was it.

"Any questions?" Rodney asked.

There was none.

"Okay," said the exec. "You fellows start sorting out the details of who's going to do what and send 'em to their new departments. I want a list of all the names and their billets before dinner.

Prince stood up, indicating that the powwow was over, save for one last order.

"We'll have another shoot at oh-eight hundred tomorrow," he said. "And this time, Commander Monk, let's sign a mutual pact to suspend all practical jokes."

The Beaver gravely shook his head. "No tricks, *mon capitaine.*"

On schedule, next morning, *Shearcross* sped through her gunnery and torpedo exercises. Most of the firing, after the initial few rounds, was simulated. Aim. Load. Pull the trigger on an empty weapon. Aim. Load. Pull. And so on, for more than two hours, until the Beaver pronounced his green crews in tolerable shape. This careful hoarding of ammunition was no idle gesture. Because ComSouWesPac had figured *Shearcross'* transit from Sydney to Noumea to be a routine affair, with scant likelihood of more than a chance brush with a sub or wandering Jap patrol plane, he had decreed minimal combat equipment for the voyage.

Prince was appalled to learn from the Beaver that the main battery, all told, had somewhat less than 200 rounds of HE armor-piercing shells available. Firing at maximum rate, that meant they'd exhaust their supply in about three minutes.

"I'd suggest, old cod, that we conserve our ammo even in the event of an engagement," said the Beaver. "Fire only when we see the whites of their eyes."

"Right," Prince said unhappily. "That's all we can do."

As for the smaller automatic rifles, the situation was pretty much the same. Enough for a hit-run attack. Then back to throwing those bloody potatoes.

"There's one bright note, though," the Beaver said.

"Pray tell."

"Since we're so fresh out of civilization, the potatoes are the real McCoy—not dehydrated."

Prince eyed him glumly. "You comfort me no end."

To add to their potential woes, O'Brien finally let it be known that they had precisely ten torpedoes, one for each launcher, which had been emplaced before *Shearcross* left Sydney. O'Brien had begged for more. But ComSouWesPac's ordnance people remained adamant. Halsey was getting the lion's share of materiel at this juncture, so his opposite number in Australia wasn't about to relinquish anything beyond what the letter of the law demanded. Indeed, he'd almost insisted on *Shearcross'* departing with empty tubes, but had relented at the last minute.

As for fuel, Taylor reported that their bunkers held a sufficient quantity for the 1,400-mile northward haul. After they reached the magical point *x,* however, they would have just enough for a slow withdrawal to the south, where, hopefully, *Shearcross* could replenish from a ComSoPac tanker.

The inexplicable joker, of course, was that portion of their orders which read: "Continue mission until further notice." Hell. That could imply several days of steaming around, playing will-o'-the-wisp, and all the while sucking away at their dwindling Diesel oil.

No. Make it a pair of jokers. It was that kind of stacked deck. The second joker was the contingency which even the Beaver, once you penetrated his bravado, admittedly dreaded: an encounter with a sizable foe which would make it necessary for *Shearcross* to maneuver at top speed for hours at a time, either to fight or to flee. With her fuel running low, she would be riding perilously high, her agility impaired and her gunnery subject to the sea's whims, especially if she were caught in a deep wave trough which sent her inclinometer past the sixty-degree mark. Some destroyers had survived more than a seventy-degree roll. But some hadn't.

All during Tuesday and through the daylight hours of Wednesday they held steady at twenty-five knots, meticulously on Folkes' beeline course.

From the Fox circuit, duly relayed by Lieutenant Standish, came news of the incipient battle along the Slot. The lead American transport convoy had been spotted by a seaplane-toting Jap submarine on Tuesday. Whatever slim chance remained for a surprise reinforcement of the 'Canal division went out the porthole fast, so the arriving Marines had to scramble ashore under attack by a dozen Nip dive bombers. Next day, Tuesday, the second echelon of fresh troops was due, shielded by three U.S. heavy cruisers, a pair of antiaircraft lights, eleven destroyers and a couple of minesweepers.

Down from Truk were steaming two enemy battleships, a cruiser and fourteen destroyers. On his plotting board Folkes sought to chart exactly where and when the two armadas, the outgunned Yanks and the Nips, would collide head on. At length he arrived at the conclusion that the major impact would occur sometime in the early-morning hours of Friday the 13th. Prior to that, he opined, there might be a lesser Donnybrook, perhaps late Thursday, if the Japs' advance detail reached the island earlier and started to carry out their basic purpose of obliterating Henderson Field with large-caliber shellfire.

Prince accepted Folkes' estimate at face value, grimly, as he estimated what the timetable meant for *Shearcross*.

Under these circumstances she would have to remain on decoy duty for more than fifty hours, babbling her false intelligence, trying to divert at least a portion of the foe's overwhelming strength from the Slot, or, should the unthinkable happen, actually deterring him from his destructive errand.

Prince, standing on the portside bridge wing, checked his watch. It was slightly after five P.M., and the sun was low on the western horizon, ready, one might think, to dip its fierce red incandescence into the Slot, toward which the contending fleets were steaming so irrevocably. He stared at the sun, now partially obscured by a slight mist, for a few moments before walking through the sparsely populated bridge to the voice tube. There he called for the charthouse.

Folkes answered.

"This is the captain," said Prince. "What's our distance from point *x?*"

"I was just about to tell you, sir. We'll enter the fifty-mile radius in five minutes."

"Very well."

Prince capped the tube with infinite gentleness, as if he wished no harm to any part of his precious command.

Enough spurious short-wave messages to ComSoPac from the "carrier task force," as well as telephonic TBS calls from ship-to-ship within its various mythical components, had been composed in advance of the night's play-acting to last until daybreak. They would transmit them at irregular intervals, in the manner of any hard-working battle group, with every dispatch sent in the clear. Which meant the Japs, overhearing them, wouldn't have to waste a lot of effort in codebreaking, if indeed they could accomplish that difficult feat in the first place. The U.S. Navy had won an awesome reputation (though it was still a closely guarded one) for having cracked the most highly sophisticated Japanese ciphers.

All Standish must do was feed the prepunched tapes through machines which automatically tapped out the Morse signals.

As for the TBS traffic, Prince intended to save it for later, when the Nips presumably would start poking around for the swiftly moving task force. With its low power, talk-between-ships was useful for close-in maneuvers, when ships came within range of each other—that is, no farther apart than the horizon as glimpsed from their high-mast antennae. That might be forty-odd miles. Like a rural party line, TBS could be overheard by anybody equipped with such a radiophone, including the enemy. Once in a while, if a TBS signal bounced off a thick cloud layer, it might be picked up hundreds of miles distant. But this was a rare accident, which chiefly concerned a sender who needed ironclad assurance that only friends would horn in on his open circuit.

The five minutes had now passed.

Prince strolled back to the voice tube to summon the communicator. "We're on target," he said. "Start the tapes rolling."

"Roger, Commander," Standish affirmed.

Then Prince returned to the place he had occupied before his conversation with Folkes, on the bridge wing beside the flag bag, a box in which varicolored signal hoists lay in easily accessible rows, waiting to be clipped to a line and raised to the destroyer's yardarm. It was rather a pity, Prince thought sardonically, that these couldn't be employed, too, along with their electronic gear, in this masquerade party. It was even more of a shame that *Shearcross* wasn't part of a four-ship division so the hoists would have a genuine meaning if they encountered the enemy.

Below him the crew of No. 2 five-incher lolled on the windward ladder of their mount, trying to catch the faint evening breeze, but with singular lack of success. Ten degrees south latitude wasn't renowned for cool evenings. The gun captain sat meditatively chewing cut plug, for the bosun had announced a few moments earlier that the smoking lamp was doused on all weather decks. Occasionally he shifted the position of his earphones. Otherwise he was a dungareed statue, an immovable adjunct to the gun itself, yet prepared to spring into instant action.

Prince glanced up at the director platform. There, with his hairy arms braced against the guardrail, stood the Beaver. His red Gothic beard flamed in the rapidly sea-dipping sun. He, too, looked statuesque, something carved out of impermeable brownstone, but equally as prepared for emergencies as the crewmen on watch at their multitude of guns below him.

A thin silver moon, then a large bright star, followed by a winking trail of smaller luminaries, emerged not far above where the sun had suddenly disappeared. It promised to be a clear, cloudless night. Prince didn't relish the prospect. Had he a choice, he would have selected murk, rain squalls and minimum visibility, knowing that *Shearcross'* modernized radar gave her a distinct advantage over anything the Japs might field at this early stage of the war.

The bastards did have something going in their favor, though, possession of all the incubators wherein bad weather brewed: from Manchuria to the lower Asian mainland. If a storm was pending, they learned about it first and took steps accordingly. Except for their smattering of long-range weather scout planes, plus a few loyal coast watchers who warned of impending gales, the Allies had to take whatever transpired in stoical stride. Meteorologists aboard ship and even back in the major command bases were the subject of constant derision for their guesstimates, because that was about all these tea-leaf readings generally amounted to. They were more often wrong than right.

Prince knew most of the decoy messages by heart. They began with a simple, stouthearted announcement from the fictitious carrier flagship that she had now reached a suitable area for launching.

"Ready with eighty-three planes," radioed the chimerical two-starred admiral of this nonexistent group, "whenever you give us the go-ahead. Assume targets remain the same—all enemy shipping in Guadalcanal region, with emphasis on heavy combat types."

Standish let twenty minutes elapse before he went back on the air.

"Intend to broadcast in the clear," said the non-carrier, "for sake of tactical speed in view of Slot conditions. Find no need to codify dispatches. Pre-sunset reconnaissance failed to show Japs in vicinity. Apparently they are throwing everything your way."

That was wishful thinking at its best, Prince had told himself dourly, as he, Rodney, Standish and the Beaver were composing these signals earlier in the day. Nobody aboard *Shearcross* could envision what lay over the inscrutable horizon, where the starry night met the surging sea, along a definite line that even an untrained eye could discern easily.

The four of them had solemnly agreed that the enemy held three options: to dismiss the messages for what they were, utter nonsense; to accept them as real, but ignore them, since the Japs were too committed to the Slot operation for any meaningful diversion of units capable of taking on such a formidable aggregation; or to send down just enough ships—say, a handful of tin cans—either to sink or drive away this noisy nuisance.

Standish transmitted his third dispatch at 1930, meticulously from point *x,* after which *Shearcross* reversed course briefly, then headed westward for a half hour. This message merely advised ComSoPac and "all task force commanders present" in the Jap-threatened sector that "we still await your orders." The carrier's flight deck had been stacked for immediate launching and the pilots were in their cockpits.

This must have cut it with the Nips.

From the radio shack Standish sent word that his assistant manning the secondary receiver tuned to the enemy's frequency had begun picking up twice the gibberish he'd been monitoring since the fakery began.

"Does anybody aboard speak Japanese?" Prince asked him.

"Negative, sir," Standish answered regretfully.

Prince signaled the yeoman standing guard in CIC through the tube: "I'm sending you another pair of eyes for your radar, Brown. Mr. Folkes will be down there shortly."

"Thank you, sir." The yeoman's voice echoed his relief. "I've got a funny notion we need more of an expert on this damned gadget than just us two fellas."

Folkes expressed no surprise at his removal from navigational chores, after Prince told him they'd play it by ear during the night. Neither islands, reefs nor shoals reared up within 100 miles of them in any direction. Nothing but deep water would pass beneath *Shearcross'* keel, provided she stayed well clear of the New Georgias, north of Guadalcanal, and confined her maneuvering to the south and west.

"That's our plan," said Prince.

"Okay, Commander. In which case I'm ready to take over CIC."

Around midnight a twin-engined search plane passed high above them, unmistakably Japanese from the erratic beat of its engines. The craft returned once, at a lower altitude, but failed to see *Shearcross,* since Prince had ordered the destroyer brought to a halt, thus eliminating the creamy wake that showed in the dim night glow when she was traveling at twenty to twenty-five knots.

Judging from the movement of the director platform overhead, Prince knew that the Beaver had his gunnery radar locked onto the foe and was prepared to open up on the bumbling plane if it ventured close enough to spot them.

"Remember," Prince had the talker inform him, "we don't fire until we see the whites of their eyes."

The Beaver replied that he had this admonition tattooed on his hairy chest.

Pleased that the Nip was now out of earshot and unlikely to return very soon, Prince suddenly felt in a lighter mood.

"Tell Commander Monk," he said, "not to scratch that tattoo off, in case he develops a severe case of tropical heat rash."

For the remainder of the night *Shearcross* quartered about in the vicinity of point *x*, sometimes at flank speed, sometimes hardly moving, while the pretaped messages flashed into the darkening void. At 0400 the sky went totally black, when a mist rose from the sea's surface, leaving those in the destroyer with a sense of complete isolation. The stars had seemed almost friendly. But now their world was infinitesimally small, constricted enough to give a man claustrophobia if he bothered to dwell on it overmuch.

Standish reported that the Japs were getting more verbose than ever, following each of *Shearcross'* illusory transmissions, the latest of which had stated baldly, "We are geared up for a dawn strike. Let us know when needed."

On the Fox circuit he'd heard that a Nip submarine was detected off Lunga Point, near the Marines' landing beach, and that tin cans had been sent to take care of the skulker. "Pistol Pete," the night-raiding bane of the insular garrison's existence, was dropping scattered eggs around the American transports. And, Standish said with more emotion than usual in his voice, coast watchers on New Guinea were telling about flights of Jap Zeros and Bettys en route south from Rabaul.

It was 0535. A baleful sun, the selfsame orb that had sunk so gracefully into the western ocean thirteen hours earlier, was making its crimson presence known in the fog-shrouded east, betokening a day of uncertain weather. Prince, who hadn't left the bridge during the night, tiredly watched the developing crimson gleam. He was grateful for this harbinger of possible storm conditions. As at Balikpapan, during the abortive December air raid that had cost him DesDiv 11's *Travers* and *Gray Eagle,* cloud cover might prove almost as valuable as the air cover which ComSoPac had so irrevocably denied them.

Then at 0545 the voice tube hummed, and Folkes bellowed in a voice that hardly needed amplification: "Blips on the radarscope, Commander! Two of 'em!"

"What's their range?" Prince demanded.

"Maximum, sir. About thirty miles."

"And bearing?"

"Four points off our port bow."

For an instant Prince was assailed by his old traumatic fears. But they quickly dissipated. In their place, surprisingly, came a hitherto unfelt sense of purpose, almost a killing urge, as he buckled down to the exacting task which confronted them.

Shearcross was presently moving at twenty-three knots, straight toward the unknown objects that Folkes had observed on the screen. The helmsman peered around, plainly awaiting an order to reverse course and hightail it to hell out of these uncomfortable environs. With her retooled engines, they could outrace anything in the Jap naval register.

"Veer off fifty degrees," Prince said quietly.

"Fifty degrees?" the helmsman repeated, as if he couldn't believe his own well-trained ears.

"Yes, Peterson. Fifty degrees."

That, the helmsman realized, would take them toward Guadalcanal, diagonally away from the marauders, rather than toward the comparative safety which could only lie due south. With obvious reluctance he swung the huge wheel to the right, until the gyrocompass needle hovered on the desired number.

Prince stepped across the metal deck to the TBS microphone. He picked it up, cradled the instrument in his right hand for a moment, then addressed himself to the phantom task group which had purportedly been divulging its presence all during the night.

"This is Blackjack," he announced, loud and clear, using the code name for which Halsey himself was famous. "We have picked up indications of two enemy units on our radar. As soon as weather and lighting permits, we will dispatch a strike force to intercept them. Meanwhile, all ships prepare for surface action."

Visibility had dropped to less than a mile, Prince noted, so the captains of the approaching vessels would have to interpret his voice message anyway they pleased. It was a long-shot attempt. But it might discourage further probing.

He said to Hamilton, "Take over for a few minutes, mister. I'm going below for a look at those radar pips."

"Yes, sir."

Down in CIC, Folkes was hunched over the 'scope, his beard-stubbled face weirdly illuminated by the faint jade glow from the screen, looking like an alchemist stirring a pot of fool's gold. Prince nudged him on the shoulder, and he stepped aside.

"They're still coming," he said, "and pretty fast."

"Have they changed course to match ours?"

"Yes."

"Then at least one of 'em must also have radar."

Folkes nodded. "Too damned true," he said sorrowfully.

Prince squinted into the circular box. The blips were at the farthest edge of the screen. One of them was larger than the other. Unless the Nip intruders comprised a destroyer and a patrol craft, they'd have to be something bigger: probably a cruiser with a tin-can escort. Their speed of advance, measured on the 'scope, indicated the latter. What, mused Prince, should we do? Stand and fight? Play cat-and-mouse? Or flee? ComSoPac had given him no contingency instructions. On the contrary,

Shearcross' orders were uncompromising: "Continue missio[n] until further notice." It was probable, he thought bleakly, tha[t] Halsey had so many matters of more immediate importance o[n] his mind that he'd even forgotten this lonely decoy duck, sittin[g] out here in the midst of the goddamned Solomon Sea.

Wresting his attention away from the almost hypnotic pair o[f] blips, which shone each time the radar's racing light finge[r] touched their location, Prince said to Folkes, "Call the bridg[e] talker and tell him to ask Commander Monk and Mr. Rodne[y] to come down here, on the double."

"Yes, sir."

Folkes passed the order and then waited calmly for the tw[o] other non-*Shearcross* officers to arrive for what he recognize[d] would be a war council. He wished the ultimate decision woul[d] be made by somebody besides Commander Prince, whose tar[-] nished reputation concerned him deeply, despite his earlier pro[-] testations of loyal support. That recollected vow rang hollowl[y] in his ears, now, like the pious pleading it had been when h[e] first uttered it. In his present harassed state of mind, Folke[s] gloomed, this crazy three-striper was apt to pull anything. O[r] freeze into doing nothing.

Rodney and the Beaver entered CIC simultaneously, thei[r] expressions grave, having met on the gloom-filled foredeck prio[r] to going below. Prince outlined *Shearcross'* predicament in con[-] cise terms. Then he pointed toward the radarscope.

"Catch a look for yourselves."

The Beaver bent over the machine, scanned the translucen[t] screen hurriedly and stood up.

"It would appear that we may have a somewhat unequal due[l] upcoming."

"Depends on what those blips mean," Prince said.

"Cruiser, probably a light type, and a destroyer, I'd venture," said the Beaver.

Rodney didn't hazard an opinion, deferring to his two seniors

But Folkes also leaned toward the cruiser–tin-can theory, because of the enemy's speed and the improbability that the Japs would send out anything less to stalk a putative carrier group.

"At any rate," Prince said stonily, "we'll damned soon know." He raised his wrist watch. "It's oh-six hundred. In another half hour it'll be daylight. And if the surface fog lifts, we should have a nice view of the bastards."

"You sound as if you'd already made up your mind to intercept our heated pursuers," said the Beaver.

"Not positively. But as admiral of this so-called 'task force,' I've called you gentlemen together for a tactical session. It's customary to seek advice from the various flag captains, although," Prince appended unsmilingly, "the admiral reserves the right to veto any motions that run counter to his. He casts the decisive vote. Understood?"

The Beaver, Rodney and Folkes made affirmative gestures while keeping their eyes glued to the 'scope, like gamblers at a crap table waiting for the dice finally to go their way.

"How do you feel, Rodney?"

The exec gave his skipper a nonplussed stare. "Hell, sir, I'm for whatever you order. That's my job, isn't it?'

"Very well. And you, Mr. Folkes?"

The navigator procrastinated. He had no intention of adopting Rodney's slavish acquiescence; and he was neither a coward nor a fool.

"Everything considered," he said slowly, "I'd recommend withdrawing southward, sir, keeping just enough space between ourselves and those two ships to prevent their putting the blitz on us. Maybe by midmorning we'll have a better idea of what we're up against."

"Quite a sound approach," said Prince. "Your turn, Commander."

The Beaver shrugged. "Eventually we've either got to tangle with 'em or retreat. Perhaps I'm too much of a chance-taker.

But I'd opt for coming about and closing on the friggers while the weather's still mucky. This thing—" patting the radarscope reverently—"puts us temporarily in the driver's seat."

"Thanks." Prince's appreciative monosyllable was inclusive "Now let's devote two minutes to silent prayer."

Together they watched the spinning light beam and the briefly emergent pips. It was clear that the Japs were neither gaining nor losing ground. Rather, it seemed that the enemy had adjusted his pace to *Shearcross',* a steady twenty-five knots, as if also waiting for the fog to lift before making a definite move But that mightn't occur for hours. On their present course they would be in the shallow lee of Guadalcanal by early afternoon, with a consequent loss of maneuvering space as well as the increased risk of hostile air attack. Prince knew this could be disastrous. With the odds two to one against them, they'd need all the running room available.

His decision suddenly reached, he said, "We'll combine Mr. Folkes' and Commander Monk's plans, changing to course-one-eighty, but reducing our advance to fifteen knots. Even if we have to hold off for a visual sighting until noon, we'll still be in the clear, with our options wide open."

"You're determined to tangle with the Nips?" Folkes asked dubiously.

"Yes," said Prince, "if it appears we have a dog's chance. Don't forget that our mandate from ComSoPac remains the same."

"Yes, sir," Folkes acknowledged without much conviction.

"Okay. Now back to your stations, gentlemen."

The Beaver rewarded him with an admiring glance. This couldn't have been an easy judgment for Prince. Unquestionably the Japs would be hollering for air support, in anticipation of a scrap, especially if they continued to harbor any off-chance suspicions that there might actually be a Yank carrier group in the vicinity. And the thought of even a hit-run engagement with a cruiser and destroyer, under *Shearcross'* straitened manpower and ammo conditions, was repugnant. Something, by God, had happened to the imperious Prince since he came aboard *Shearcross*.

About an hour before midday the thick surface mist began to lift. Visibility increased with excruciating slowness at first, then more rapidly, until by 1130 the crow's-nest lookout reported to the bridge talker that he now had the two distant ships in sight through his binoculars.

Prince slipped from the captain's chair in which he had been sitting since their CIC conference.

To Hamilton he said, "Take over again, mister. I've got an irresistible urge to climb up there and give those Nips a first-hand peek."

"Yes, sir."

The steel lookout cage was two thirds of the way up *Shearcross'* tall mast, situated below the mattresslike search radar and the smaller gunnery antennae. It was a long, torturous haul for the weary Prince. He reached the crow's nest like a man achieving the crest of Mount Everest with a last, desperate burst of waning strength.

"Jesus," the No. 1 spotter exclaimed to his assistant, "it's the skipper!"

"Or the Abominable Snowman," Prince gasped, holding an upper bar for support while he fought for breath. After a moment he said, "Lend me your glasses, son."

Bracing his elbows on the rail to steady his trembling arms, he focused the long-range binoculars on the two dark objects which by now had measurably closed the gap between their quarry and themselves. Even when Folkes announced from CIC that the Japs were narrowing the range, by perhaps as much as a dozen miles, Prince deliberately held at fifteen knots. Viewed from this altitude, the enemy pair was sharply in prospect, less than twenty miles distant on a sea that was growing bluer and smoother.

Yet there was an aberrational quality about the clearing weather. A trace of mist remained at sea level. Through the binoculars the Japanese vessels seemed to be divided neatly in half, like the layers of a cake, with their gray hulls reflected ghostlike below the dissipating fog line and their upperworks more realistically defined above it.

The bright sunshine turned *Shearcross'* wake into polished nylon, glistening like sheer hose worn by a beautiful, recumbent woman.

For ten minutes Prince kept his glasses trained on the foe. One of the ships was unquestionably an elderly light cruiser of the *Kanju* class, six-inch-gunned, equipped with torpedoes, carrying a crew of almost 500.

The other?

His aching eyes strained to get an accurate fix on this smaller vessel, which was a mile or so in the van of the cruiser. She looked like nothing Prince had ever seen before in the Navy's compendious recognition manuals. But he was staring at her from a bows-on posture. For proper identification he must catch this strange creature in broadside silhouette.

He instructed the lookout, "Telephone down to the bridge. I want a fast ninety-degree turn." Before resuming his vigil, he added with a touch of irony, "Be sure to have 'em alert the gunnery platform and the engine room before making the course change."

"Yes, sir."

The lookout delivered the message, and two minutes later *Shearcross* wheeled briskly to starboard. Behind her, the Japs followed suit, albeit a trifle sluggishly. Their clumsiness, in contrast to his own ship's deft response, gave Prince a briefly pleasurable uplift.

But more important, more to the point, was that in the period it took the enemy to alter course from south to west he had a solid fifteen seconds to observe the *Kanju* cruiser's escort.

For that quarter minute he stared, unbelieving, at the bizarre object which partially filled his circular field of vision. She was tripod-masted, as if a pagoda had been erected on her foredeck, and one of her funnels had been neatly removed. The No. 1 stack slanted aft, thicker at its base than where the plume of black smoke was pouring out of its top, as this strange craft sought to quicken her pace. She was a designer's nightmare, with a straight prow, a long flush deck and a crouching stern which, even at her modest twenty knots, was almost under water.

Unlike the Catalina pilot who had reported catching a momentary glimpse of a similar nautical (or was it surgical?) changeling a fortnight earlier, Prince had ample time to study her. After she finally veered about and was once more on course with *Shearcross,* he extricated himself from the binoculars' neck strap and handed the glasses back to the lookout.

There would be no doubt about it. None whatsoever. By grace of the war gods, Ahab had found his great white whale, many months before he'd dare hope for such a chance meeting.

That outlandish destroyer was *Davidson,* or had been once, flying the colors of Nippon. When you came right down to it, what other earthly use would the Japs have for a tin can that had come back from the grave, as *Davidson* had, with her combat potential so severely curtailed? She couldn't accompany a battle line, certainly, although, as now, she might be pressed into service as bodyguard for a *Kanju*-brand cruiser, whose lineage dated back almost as far as the American four-piper's.

On his way below, Prince stopped off for a quiet word with the Beaver, on the director platform.

"That destroyer," he said without preamble, "is our ex-flagship."

The Beaver accepted the news in typical laconic British fashion, evincing no surprise, offering no comment on the premature miracle of this confrontation.

"It's not beyond the realm of credibility, you know, happening upon yonder bucket-of-bolts," he said. "What better duty for an ancient clunker like *Davidson?"*

"Davidson is going to be our primary target. After that we'll try for the big one."

The Beaver offered no protest at this unorthodox destroyer tactic, even though age-old doctrine required precisely the opposite: ignore the small fry until you'd disposed of the enemy's major units. If, that is, you endured the initial charge. He understood. Had he been in Prince's cordovan jodhpurs, he would have done the same thing, just as unhesitatingly.

Back on the bridge, Prince issued a rapid-fire series of orders. Reverse course. Head directly for the foe. Accelerate from fifteen knots to flank speed. Batten down the hatches. Prepare to engage the enemy.

He hastily wrote a message on the clipboard pad that was fastened to the arm of his chair.

"Take this down to Lieutenant Standish," he said, "and have him get it off—*pronto!"*

"Yes, sir."

It was a brief missive and probably a futile one. But it had to be sent. Addressed to ComSoPac, it recited the essence of their plight in a few uncompromising words: "Intercepted by enemy light cruiser of *Kanju* class and destroyer believed to be former USS *Davidson.* Intend to engage. If opportunity develops would appreciate air support although fully understand your problems. Our location at designated area 158 degrees east, 10 degrees south."

The answer from Halsey's GHQ came back promptly and expectedly: "Glad you understand why air support impossible at this time. Keep us informed. Good hunting."

At that moment Prince felt like Job, deserted by his God, with an almost demented urge to rail against fate. But what else had He said to the supplicant man-of-troubles? "Gird up now thy loins like a man . . ."

What would ensue, Prince felt sure, must of necessity be a short contest. He recalled the Beaver's doleful accounting of their on-hand ammunition. About 200 rounds of five-inch shells. That meant fifty for each rifle, which, if handled deftly by a well-trained crew, could easily expend fifteen to twenty rounds per minute.

Using the talker's headset, he arranged with the Beaver to allow the main battery to fire individually rather than by master control. Sniper shooting, it would be, with fifty-four-pound projectiles.

"I'll tell Number One and Number Two guns to aim low, for the waterline, and the after guns high, for the bridge," said the Briton. "And to make floggin' well sure that every bullet counts."

Prince relinquished the headset to the talker and turned his padded binoculars against the swiftly advancing foe. *Davidson* was still in the lead, but the cruiser was creeping closer, a half mile astern and about 1,000 yards off the converted tin can's port quarter. They had also stepped up their tempo. Prince estimated that *Shearcross* and her two adversaries were roaring together at a rate of better than sixty knots—freight-train speed.

They were only ten miles apart now, a fraction beyond the range of *Shearcross'* five-inch rifles, yet easily within gunshot of the Nip's six-inch weaponry.

Even as the signalman at the telescopic stadimeter sang out the distance, the cruiser let loose a salvo from her forward guns. A quadruple cluster of splashes erupted ahead of *Shearcross,* short, but too close for comfort.

"Tell Commander Monk to hold his fire," Prince called to the white-faced talker, aware as he did so that his admonition was redundant. Even silly, after their chat on the platform. The Beaver knew what to do, and when, without any egregious advice from the bridge wallahs.

"Commander Monk," relayed the talker in a puzzled tone,

"says he hasn't seen any whale's eye-whites yet, so will you kindly stop worrying."

After that response Prince concentrated on his own business, guiding *Shearcross* along a course that would run parallel to the two Jap vessels, while sparing only a fractional part of his mind to wondering how the rest of the ship's company was behaving at this exquisite moment of truth.

Below, above and around him the scene was unalterably set. Its actors were at their accustomed places, waiting for the curtain to rise, ready to enact roles made harshly familiar by repetition—with noise and bloodshed. Overhead, the Beaver's director hummed on its ball bearings as he trained his delicate instruments to pick up any deflection, however minor, in the enemy's position. Rodney was at secondary controls, an accumulation of auxiliary steering gear and levers forward of the No. 3 gun.

Prince remembered the apocryphal saying that you can live through a small eternity in moments like these, facing the possibility of sudden death or mutilation. Someone had also said that elements of your past life rise up and parade past, specter-like. He knew differently. Once committed, you think only of the material readiness of your ship and whether your crew has mustered at their proper stations. These kids had learned much in their woefully short naval lifetime. Even the sight of a bunkroom comrade, alive and cursing at the enemy one instant, then smashed into pulpy unrecognizability the next as a result of a direct hit by a quarter ton of TNT, wouldn't shake them out of their ordered action pattern. They were veterans.

"Nine thousand yards, sir," the man at the stadimeter called tonelessly.

Shearcross and her opponents had halved the intervening distance since the Jap cruiser opened fire. This had taken six minutes, one more than Prince had estimated, because the Nips, for some inexplicable reason, were zigzagging. Probably they expected the brash Yankee to return the *Kanju*-type's erratic salvos, now that *Shearcross* was halfway past the maximum range of her five-inchers. Doubtless they were surprised, even a bit shaken, by the bold tenacity with which their lone assailant held firm, never deviating a split degree from her collision course.

Prince hoped they would keep swerving back and forth. This quixotic pattern was affecting the cruiser's aim. Despite her steady drumbeat of six-inch shells, she'd pinked *Shearcross* only once, a glancing blow on the destroyer's starboard bow that carried away a few feet of guardrail but failed to detonate until it skipped into the sea, well beyond the concussive point. A single near miss had dented some portside plates. He guessed the old cruiser's guns were manually aimed. He fervently hoped so.

"Seven thousand yards, Captain."

The helmsman cast an appealing glance at Prince as the range spotter sang out this latest reading. But Prince shook his head, comprehending exactly what the quartermaster meant— that it was past time to haul ass. *Davidson-maru* and the cruiser were still nicely separated, perhaps 1,000 yards apart. If they remained in that stance, his stratagem might succeed, coming under the big guns, too near for the Jap to launch his Long Lance torpedoes. He doubted they would attempt to edge closer together. They would, he figured, keep well apart, so as to bracket *Shearcross* without endangering each other.

"Six thousand yards!"

A shell burst from the cruiser punctuated the stadimeter man's trumpet call. It caught *Shearcross* squarely amidships, alongside her No. 2 stack. Looking aft from the bridge wing, Prince could see that the blast had carried away a segment of the after-torpedo launchers, which hung like the limp fingers of a fresh corpse across the deck and partially over the destroyer's side.

"Get Mr. O'Brien," he shouted at the talker, "and find out the extent of the damage."

If, he thought, the kid ensign hadn't been wiped out, too. But O'Brien was very much alive, astonishingly cool, after the explosion. Two of their ten precious torpedoes were wrecked, and both the gyro-setter and trainer, who had been astride the quintuple mount, were dead, along with two of the adjacent Bofors detail.

"How about the gun itself?" Prince demanded through the talker.

O'Brien said it seemed to be in fair shape, still operable.

At this, Prince had to force back a guilty feeling. Losing four men was tragic enough; but losing a fifth of his irreplaceable torpedo arsenal, at this moment of onslaught, was a near disaster. To have been deprived of one of the lethal 40-millimeters would have greatly compounded their desperate predicament.

"Reshuffle your crews," Prince had the talker instruct O'Brien. "We'll bring the tin can within torpedo range in a couple of minutes, so we're counting on the automatic guns to keep the cruiser occupied while we get rid of her escort."

O'Brien said the commander needn't worry. They'd make out somehow.

Thrice more, before *Shearcross* could come abreast of the clumsily firing cruiser, they absorbed devastating random blows from the *Kanju*-type. One tore away the destroyer's No. 1 five-inch gun, literally ripping the weapon from its deck fastenings, shattering it to bits, and sweeping the debris overboard, slaughtered crew and all. The second shell tore a sizable hole in the upper end of the No. 2 stack, which was annoying but hardly a matter of grave concern, alongside forfeiture of the rifle, even though *Shearcross'* proud battle flag was blown away by the same explosion. The fourth hit, miraculously a dud, penetrated the superstructure in the vicinity of the wardroom, ricocheted across the steel plating and upended a few mess tables.

Instinctively, as the triple blows hammered down, Prince felt for his sheath knife. This archaic trinket comforted him as a security blanket assuages the subconscious night fears of a small child. Nevertheless he wore it, however disdainfully, like a cutlass in the days of grappling-and-boarding. The Beaver's special whimsy was to strap a .45 Colt automatic around his vast girth, in a waterproof holster, "to shoot sharks with" in the event he was ever forced to abandon ship.

Above *Shearcross,* now, loomed the Japanese cruiser's starboard flank. The *Kanju*s were among the smallest of the Nip light cruisers. But at this instant she displayed all the monstrous attributes of a freight train alongside which a lone automobile was racing on a deserted rural road, under a mackerel sky. Prince could clearly discern the faces of the officers on her navigation bridge and the men who were raising a four-flagged signal hoist.

Davidson (Goddamn it! Why must he still call her that?) promptly acknowledged from her position 1,000 yards distant, slightly ahead of the racing pair. Prince could only guess at what the Jap cruiser captain had ordered. Logic dictated that it was a summons for a torpedo attack by the hermaphroditic tin can, which undoubtedly had been equipped with the Nips' standard oxygen-fueled, twenty-four-inch fish, able to plow across 6,000 yards of turbulent sea with uncanny accuracy at almost fifty knots. The warheads of these behemoths carried twice the payload of the American twenty-one-inch models, more than 1,200 pounds of HE torpex.

Thus, for a variety of drastic reasons, *Shearcross* must make her play now—or never.

The Beaver had already taken *Davidson* under fire with his three remaining five-inch guns. These were thundering away in somewhat random fashion, according to instruction, with emphasis on hits rather than spectacular near misses.

"Inform Mr. O'Brien that I want a full spread of torpedoes

launched immediately at that—at that destroyer!" Prince had to yell into the talker's naked ear, from which the receiver had temporarily been removed, so that he could be heard above the tumult of the gunfire exchange between *Shearcross* and her close-in adversary.

The message was passed.

Within thirty seconds five torpedoes ejected from their barrels, splashed into the blue-green water and plunged toward their target. Prince crossed his fingers and mouthed a wordless prayer that these fish wouldn't dud out on him or explode prematurely. His unhappy experience aboard that very ship toward which they were streaking at forty-five knots had made him a man of little faith in matters involving U.S. torpedoes, whose explosive device was concocted so as to ignite the warhead when the fish entered the presumed victim's magnetic sphere. If all went well, the blast would come at the precise second the torpedo slipped beneath the target's keel. But too frequently all didn't go well, and you wound up holding an empty bag.

If these crapped out, he'd be left with only the three which had survived the *Kanju's* direct hit. There was no telling what that upsetting blow had done to the intricate mechanism of the tubes themselves.

In his preoccupation with the torpedo launch, Prince had paid scant attention to *Shearcross'* hand-to-hand engagement with the Jap cruiser. Nor would he until the spread reached *Davidson,* in about fifty seconds.

Yet, during their parallel race with the larger enemy vessel, both ships had absorbed massive damage. The cruiser's secondary batteries had the advantage of aiming down at *Shearcross,* with a full sweep of her deck, whereas the destroyer had to fire upward and thus had a more constricted field of fire. Nevertheless *Shearcross* was giving her best, perhaps a third of what she took from the Japs, in her return rakes with the 20s and 40s.

That's about all Prince could have expected.

The enemy's bridge was a shambles, pocked with shell holes from the Bofors, and none of the cruisermen dared venture close to the starboard side, nearest the destroyer. But *Shearcross* herself was rapidly being denuded of effective topside personnel. Another of her Oerlikons had gone dead. And there was a strange silence from the overhead gunnery platform, whose constant thrumming had abruptly ceased.

Shearcross' bridge was an abattoir: Warrant Officer Hamilton had been blown into two bloody halves by a medium sized Nip shell; the chief quartermaster had turned over his wheel to the No. 2 man and now lay slumped against the after bulkhead, holding his punctured intestines and repeating, "Christ, O merciful Christ," in a singsong voice. The talker had also been wounded, though not as critically, for he insisted on remaining at his post, knowing there was none to take his place in communicating with the various ship's departments.

Suddenly Prince shouted at the young helmsman, "Spin her hard right, fella!"

Shearcross bowled over, away from the pompomming cruiser, which continued to drive ahead. She pulled rapidly astern, and Prince ordered another course change which brought his ship abreast of the cruiser's stern. This abrupt maneuver gave *Shearcross* a distinct plus, that of crossing the enemy's *T* from the rear, so only the Jap's after weapons could be brought to bear, while the destroyer, as the range opened, could once more utilize her residual trio of five-inch guns.

But *T*-crossing wasn't what had occasioned Prince's action.

Halfway between *Davidson* and *Shearcross* he had caught sight of torpedo wakes, pluming whitely behind the Long Lances which his onetime flagship had finally launched. Four of them. Moving fast and straight. By his quick swing, Prince had taken himself out of their range—and left the cruiser without her shield-and-buckler, namely *Shearcross,* to catch these lethal fish.

Too late, the Japanese captain realized his danger and sough to accelerate, while veering wildly to port.

By now, Prince figured, as this mad drama went on, *Shear cross'* slower torpedoes should have traversed the 1,000 yard to their quarry. He waited. All at once *Davidson* rose high ou of the sea, split cleanly amidships, like the sections of a liftin; drawbridge. Each segment collapsed and sank immediately.

Watching his old command vanish beneath the quiet waters Prince felt no sorrow, no remorse, but only monumental relief a the awesome sight. *Davidson* had never been a handsome wench even in her prime. At the instant of her doom she was an ugl} bitch, a Mongoloid orphan of a ship that deserved to die.

It was only then, after staring for a few seconds at the roilin; spot where *Davidson* had vanished, that Prince could take tim to stride out on the portside bridge wing to see what happene to the Beaver and why his director platform was no longe functional.

Two things were immediately evident: the turretlike directo was an unholy mess from the cruiser's point-blank firing, and the Briton was nowhere in sight.

But a familiar voice, deep-toned and confident, broke the eerie silence that ensued after *Davidson*'s demise. It came from the 40-millimeter tub below the glassless bridge.

"Harpooned, by God, right in the bastard's black guts!"

Prince looked down.

It was the Beaver, perched solidly in the trainer's bucket seat on the Bofors, his feet on the firing treadle, yelling like a man gone berserk. Around him lay the bodies of three of the 40-millimeter's original crew. Only he and the ammo handler were at their nakedly exposed post.

The Beaver had reason to exult again, an instant later, as the *Kanju* was struck by the outermost torpedo of the now defunct *Davidson*'s quadruple spread. Posthumously, the turn-coat destroyer had willed to her onetime foe a Long Lance which pierced the cruiser's after-quarter, exploded with a roar that was audible across the intervening half mile of blue water. The blow sent the Jap vessel staggering off course, until she could be brought under control again by the remnants of her stricken bridge force.

Because the fish had caught her on the farside flank that was hidden from Prince's view, he had no way of telling the grievous extent of the Nip's damage. But it had to be a deep hurt that might have cost her an engine. The cruiser had been traveling at thirty-odd knots when she was hit. Now she visibly slushed down to less than twenty-five, and the first flicker of flames began to show above her No. 3 six-inch gun.

A decision had to be made, a damned tough judgment, whether to pursue the engagement or break it off. *Shearcross* could have withdrawn with full honors, licked her savage wounds and crept back to Noumea. Through good marksmanship and sheerest luck she had demolished a destroyer and helped wreak havoc upon a cruiser of His Imperial Japanese Majesty's navy. What more could really be required of her?

For the time being the cruiser seemed too preoccupied with fighting fires and quenching the influx of water through her breached hull to bother with *Shearcross*. But this lull wouldn't last long. Like all navymen since fleets were invented, the Japs were raised in the tradition of battling to the bitter end, as long as a weapon remained unscathed. Add to this their *bushido* code, the credo of the *samurai* warrior, and you had a combination of elements that meant no quarter given or asked for.

Prince crawled down the ladder from the bridge to the 40-millimeter mount where the Beaver sat like an oversized jockey on a Percheron horse.

"What's the condition of our guns?" he demanded.

"Bad," said the Beaver, "if you want the truth."

"I do."

"Very well. We've had another five-incher knocked out, old

397

boy, and only two of the Oerlikons are shipshape. In short, our gunnery has been reduced by exactly half."

Prince glared aft at the tangled mess of the torpedo launcher in which three fish remained. The odds were astronomic against its being in operable condition.

"We'll fight it out on these lines," he said, unwittingly paraphrasing the dictum of General Ulysses S. Grant at Spottsylvania Court House in the summer of 1864, "for the remainder of the afternoon. After that—well, we just have to wait and see."

Like a pair of punch-drunk pugilists, *Shearcross* and the cruiser began sparring, shortly thereafter, with their major batteries. Because of her superior speed and agility, since the *Kanju*'s torpedoing, the destroyer was able to stay broadside to the foe. Thus both her five-inchers, her Bofors and her two 20 millimeters could be kept in full play. For his part, the Jap captain could respond only with his two rear six-inch guns and a pair of smaller rifles. What he desperately sought, of course, was to fetch his own torpedoes into action. But this was impossible while the wily American clung so tenaciously to his stern.

Salvos from the Nip cruiser, nonetheless, marched relentlessly toward *Shearcross,* each splash coming a hundred yards or so closer. The ships were separated by about four miles. For either of them, this was extraordinarily close range. Finally, too, the Jap gun crews had come awake to their own peril, despite the relative puniness of their opponent, and were taking inordinate care with their aim.

Within minutes, the cruiser had found her mark. *Shearcross* other funnel went first, decapitated, spewing great gouts of superheated steam through what remained of the stack. Another round ripped the destroyer below the waterline, just at the bow, and water began to thunder aft through this jagged aperture, at a rate that was alarmingly heightened by the ship's rapid progress.

Prince reluctantly ordered half speed, then twelve knots, as Lieutenant Franks and his damage controllers strove to stanch the flow.

But it was hopeless. Franks reported that *Shearcross'* watertight integrity was irreparably shattered and that nothing could halt the onrush of seawater toward the engine rooms.

Prince had taken over the headset from the talker, who was sprawled on the deck, too weak to carry on. He asked crisply, "How much time before we lose propulsion?"

There was a muted huddle at the other end of the voice transmission system. Then Franks said, "Ten minutes, give or take a couple."

With an audible sigh Prince instructed him to bring everybody topside, including the Blank Gang, after locking *Shearcross'* on half speed.

He also ordered smoke from the fantail pots. But this was transient protection, the sort you gain while running among the inadequate trees of a sapling forest.

As he did so a near miss from the *Kanju* sent a towering waterspout alongside the destroyer's forecastle which temporarily inundated the entire area, almost drowning the men at their weapons and soaking their ready lockers of small-bore ammunition.

Another shell, exploding prematurely, sent shrapnel through the wide-open bridge. A metallic shard smashed into Prince's right shoulder, stunning him, knocking him to his knees in the slippery pool of Hamilton's glucose blood. He straightened up, wearing the expression of utter disbelief of a man wounded for the first time in battle. After that it was the climactic fifteenth round of a prize fight which the outmatched *Shearcross* could not conceivably have won, unless Jove himself were to strike the Jap cruiser with a lightning bolt from heaven.

On the ropes, scarred, blinded, the destroyer kept slugging. But to little avail.

Despairingly, Prince called for O'Brien. But the assistant gunnery officer didn't answer. A scared rating came on the phone.

"Sir?"

"Who's left back there?"

"Just Roskoff and me. I'm Coles. All the rest are dead."

"Can you make a stab at firing off those three fish?"

Coles paused, then said mournfully, "Jeez, sir, they were blown to smithereens right after the friggin' Nip opened up on us."

"Very well." Prince looked at the helmsman, struggling to keep *Shearcross* on some semblance of a straight course, still abeam of the enemy's scorpion tail. "Stand by to abandon ship."

He himself was feeling the loss of blood from his shoulder wound. But he raised Standish in the radio shack.

"How are we doing, Skipper?"

"Badly," croaked Prince. "We're going down, Herb. And when that water hits the boilers, there'll probably be the goddamnedest explosion you ever heard."

"So we're getting the hell out of here?"

"Correct. Put your code books in the weight bag and bust up the ECM. Then join me here on the bridge. Tell Folkes, too, will you?"

"Yes, sir." Standish hesitated, almost timidly. "Don't you want me to message ComSoPac?"

"Christ, of course! Tell 'em we're abandoning ship at the same position we gave in our previous dispatch. Oh, you might add that we've sunk one dog-dog and damaged a light cruiser. Now maybe they'll send a little aerial help for the clean-up detail."

Maybe. Not right away. Halsey had other crises on his hands at this moment, with a battleship imbroglio about to break loose in the Slot.

Three minutes later, by the bridge chronometer, *Shearcross'* vitals emitted a monstrous roar, heaved, and the destroyer started to settle. Sam Taylor never appeared from below with his snipes, nor did Franks and Ensign de Carlo with their damage-control specialists. They were trapped before they could reach the last ladder still safe from the surging waters.

Remarkably, the *Kanju* also came to a standstill, five miles south, and she had stopped firing at *Shearcross*. Prince assumed dully that she had succumbed temporarily to her internal troubles and was devoting every effort to save her own skin, disregarding the obviously foundering destroyer.

Through the ship's loudspeaker, which continued to function on *Shearcross*' auxiliary power, Prince intoned: "This is the captain speaking. Abandon ship. All hands abandon ship."

On the deck beneath him he could see the Beaver leading a detail to the life rafts which were lashed against the lower reaches of the superstructure. Working frantically, they managed to launch three from the portside, where the sea was already reaching for them, like an animated creature. Each raft could hold twenty-four persons. Seventy-two in all. Plus whoever could don a Mae West jacket and cling to their roped sides. The motor whaleboats had long since been smashed by shellfire.

Prince did not have to leap into the water. It simply came up to meet him, as *Shearcross* slowly turned turtle. But as he stepped from the capsizing bridge, something snakelike wrapped itself around his neck, injured shoulder and waist, tightening like a jungle python, threatening to strangle him before he could struggle free.

It was the destroyer's flag halyards.

In the warm, green, translucent depths, Prince found a curious surcease, a kind of rapture, as he resigned himself to the notion of drowning. Prince thought, too, of Ahab, garroted by the harpoon line which he had cast at the white whale.

Then, in a belated flash, Prince recalled the sheath knife attached to his belt. With his left hand, because his right was now useless, he drew the sharp instrument and hacked away doggedly at the ensnarled ropes.

Wracked by the concussive internal explosions from *Shearcross* as she went down, exhausted by his one-armed struggle to free himself from the quarter-inch hemp line, his pierced shoulder bleeding profusely, Prince surfaced near the life raft occupied by the Beaver and a half dozen seamen. There were no other officers aboard. He'd been under water for less than three minutes. But it had seemed more like three hours. He was amazed to be alive.

They paddled over to Prince, lifted him over its rubbery canvas sides and deposited him, half conscious, on the slatted bottom of the raft, which was at least one quarter awash. The brine stung his wound, bringing him briefly back to his senses.

"I heard gunshots as you were heading my way," Prince muttered. "What happened?"

The Beaver patted his .45 automatic, now replaced in its holster. "As I told you, old cock, I keep this around for bagging sharks. The blood from that nasty pinprick of yours attracted a big bastard, all teeth and dorsal fin, so I indulged in a bit of target practice."

"Commander Monk winged the bugger right between its eyes."

Prince looked at the speaker. It was the junior helmsman, the last person he'd seen before *Shearcross* toppled over. His name, he recalled with an effort, was Barkdale.

"What color were the shark's eyes?" he asked in a pensive tone. "White?"

"More like red, sir, they looked to me."

Prince twisted his head toward the Beaver. "You're on report, mister, for shooting at the wrong color eyes."

"Sometimes," observed the Briton, "one has to disobey even lawful orders in the pursuit of one's bounden duty."

Unable to see over the life raft's rounded gunwale, Prince inquired, almost idly, what the cruiser was doing: heading over to dispose of them with her machine guns, still moving north, or what?

The Beaver said, "I shouldn't worry about our Nip friends. They appear to have troubles of their own without adding to ours. The cruiser's pulling away from us at about six knots, but damned sluggishly, because she's also uncommon low in the water."

Prince accorded him a wan smile. "Good."

"How d'you feel?"

"As if I'd done a decent job," said Prince, "for once in my life."

The Beaver nodded his understanding. "That's not quite what I meant, old boy. But I know what you're driving at. It's your physical condition which concerns me, not being a medical sort. That shoulder's a godawful mess."

"To be honest," Prince admitted, "I feel like hell."

Barkdale doffed his khaki shirt, which had almost been dried by the implacable sun beating down upon the Coral Sea. He began methodically to tear it into narrow strips.

"Here," he said, handing them to the Beaver, "these might do for a bandage."

Together, Barkdale and the Briton awkwardly wrapped Prince's torn shoulder as best they could, after dusting it with sulfa powder from the emergency first-aid stores. Then he requested a drink of water.

Although the seven original occupants had agreed to restrict their ration to a pint daily out of the twenty-gallon supply, in case they had to remain adrift for a protracted period, Prince was allowed to slake his feverish thirst without stint. Later he might have to be rationed also. Everyone aboard knew of classic instances when nautical refugees had drifted for weeks before they were rescued or could reach land. Captain Bligh, cast away from HMS *Bounty* by the mutineers in 1789, had brought his small boat, crowded with seventeen men, 3,600 miles across the southern Pacific in forty-eight days. And only the previous March three downed carrier flyers had spent thirty-four days traversing 1,000 miles in a four-by-eight-foot rubber life raft, catching fish and trapping rainwater in a tarpaulin, until they reached a tropical island's shelter.

Nobody on the Beaver's raft knew which way the prevailing currents flowed. Only Lieutenant Folkes, the navigator, would have possessed that information. And Folkes had gone down with the ship. If they were lucky, they might be carried 100 miles or so southward to Rennell Island, at a few knots per day, or 150 miles westward to Guadalcanal itself. But just being alive, now, someone remarked ironically, might have used up their quotient of luck. Besides, it was the Beaver's vague recollection that the currents swept toward enemy-held territory.

When Prince had finished drinking greedily from the tin cup proffered him by Barkdale, he wanted to hear about the destroyer's other survivors.

"There are some people in both of the rafts nearby," said the Beaver. "Perhaps twenty in all. No more."

"Christ," Prince said, "that means we've lost as many as one hundred and fifty out of *Shearcross'* one hundred and sixty-nine."

"The Japs," the Beaver said stonily, "took a damned sight worse lacing."

"True enough." Prince was quiet for a moment, prey to the pulsating ache from his shoulder. Then: "Is the cruiser still going north?"

"Crawling away like a whipped mongrel."

"Maybe," said Barkdale hopefully, "they'll send planes from Henderson Field to search for us."

"No need for a search," the Beaver told him. "They know

where we are, practically down to the square inch, but they're otherwise occupied, I dare say."

He was right. The greatest surface battle of the war was raging in the Slot, just east of Guadalcanal. It had opened on the night of November 12, when the foe assaulted the U.S. reinforcement transports. It would not conclude until the last thunderous hours of November 14, when American battle wagons and destroyers finally put a powerful Jap task group to flight. Those two days and three nights of murderous action would cost the Nips three battleships, a cruiser, five destroyers and eleven troop-laden transports. Halsey's casualties were destined to be a pair of cruisers and seven destroyers. Two U.S. admirals were marked for death. But that shifting, deadly, unremitting series of engagements would shake the Allies off the defensive in the Solomons for the first time.

Thus the three rafts, lashed together for mutual logistical support, floated for almost five days on the remarkably calm breast of the Coral Sea before help arrived. Each was commanded by an officer, the only two besides Prince and the Beaver who had escaped the debacle. They sometimes moved slightly southwest, sometimes due south, yet never making any appreciable headway, even when the Beaver ordered a jury-rigged sail hoisted on the lead raft, using an oar for a mast and a dozen crudely sewn shirts for a sail. There was no breeze, not enough to stir ripples on the glassy water. And it soon became apparent that wearing a shirt was far more important than using it for this fruitless purpose. Barkdale was lent one at intervals by his mates, since his had been donated for Prince's bandaging. The sun blasted at them from a bronze sky. There was no shelter from its searing rays. You had to endure. Hang on. Pray.

Only once during that entire time were their spirits lifted. A signalman 2nd class, in one of the rafts, suddenly leaped up from the emergency short-wave radio receiver to which he'd been paying industrious attention and danced a precarious jig on the slatted floor. It was early on the morning following the day *Shearcross* had been sunk.

"They got the frigger!" he yelled. "They blew her to smithereens!"

Propped against the side of his raft, leaning on his left elbow, Prince stared at the youngster.

"What frigger?"

"The frigging *Kanju* frigger," shouted the signalman. "Four Marine dive bombers just sent her to kingdom come!"

"Good," Prince said contentedly. "That puts a period on the unfinished sentence." He closed his eyes for a moment against the blinding light. "And we know ComSoPac got our last message."

On the afternoon of the 15th, when the sun began its agonizingly slow descent toward the western horizon, a Navy Catalina sighted them. It landed on the still serene surface and taxied close to the clustered trio of rafts.

The pilot shouted through his open cockpit window, "How are you guys holding out?"

The Beaver answered for them all.

"Not too goddamned well, Lieutenant. We've got a few chaps here who need medical attention badly—and soon."

"Okay," the pilot said. "Can you bring yourselves alongside?"

"Yes."

Clumsily, still in a group, the rafts were paddled across the intervening twenty yards to the flying boat. A pair of brawny airmen stood at the main hatch, ready to hoist aboard the wounded—first Prince, then seven others, all enlisted men.

When they were safely inside the cabin, the pilot called out, "There'll be a tin can along to get the rest of you. It's scheduled for about midnight. So at twenty-three hundred fire a parachute flare every fifteen minutes. And don't worry about any Japs in the neighborhood. There aren't any."

A carton of flares was passed along to the boats.

Prince had been placed near a gunport so that he could gaze down at the congregated life rafts. His face blackened and bloated from the pitiless sun, the Beaver grinned at him.

"See you in Noumea, old cock," he bellowed as the PBY revved its twin engines, preparatory to taking off.

Lieutenant Rodney looked up, also grinning. He waved. Prince waved back. Then the Catalina began moving faster, lifted heavily because of the lack of head wind, and within a few minutes the life rafts were out of sight.

Plugging away at her 196-mile-an-hour top speed, the PBY took five hours to reach the landlocked harbor of Noumea, New Caledonia. They could have gone to Espiritu Santo, in the New Hebrides, and saved half the time. But the Old Man—Halsey— had decreed that *Shearcross'* wounded, and later the others, were to be brought to his headquarters for whatever austere R-and-R the French colonial town offered.

The ancient craft made a bumpish landing, despite the placidity of the bay, an aberration for which the pilot later apologized, blaming the tricky cross currents of winds bouncing off the hills north of the town and the quick darkness. She puttered alongside the Ile Nou, a desolate, rocky islet that once housed the French felons who, like Australia's earliest foreign arrivals, ultimately came to rule their own Purgatory. Ile Nou was now a seaplane repair base.

From the beginning, Prince comprehended, ComSoPac was determined to accord him the VIP treatment.

Although he wanted to walk unassisted, the pharmacist's mate aboard the PBY, who had dressed his wound after pronouncing it incipiently gangrenous and therefore nothing to be screwed around with, told the officers meeting them at the ramp that the commander should be taken to the boat in a stretcher. Prince didn't argue. He felt weak, dizzy, and the hole in his shoulder had begun to hurt like hell again after the pharmacist's ministrations. Previously he had merely felt numb, still in a state of shock, during most of the five days they had drifted in the raft.

Halsey's chief of staff accompanied the welcoming party, having arrived in ComSoPac's four-starred barge, which would ferry Prince to Noumea, four miles away.

He said the admiral would visit Prince next morning at MOB 5. This was a mobile hospital, situated among the lush palms of a former copra plantation, near a cinematic beach called Anse Vata. Only a ten-minute drive from downtown, Anse Vata was much esteemed by both officers and enlisted men as a splendid place to drink stateside beer, when available, and to romp with their dates, which were somewhat less available, the French being overly protective of their female offspring and the supply of American nurses being deplorably short.

Through the windows of the dun-colored military ambulance which met the barge at the wharf and took him to MOB 5, Prince caught fleeting glimpses of disused pillboxes, originally erected by the Vichyites who were quickly overthrown by the Free French in the autumn of 1940; the deserted bandstand in a leafy park, where *"La Marseillaise"* was last played in mid-1941, when the Americans took over virtual rule of the island, despite protests of the colonials; the crumbling Catholic cathedral; the sidewalk kiosks that sold bootlegged GI edibles; and the malodorous open sewers, thinly disguised as gutters, which paralleled the cracked sidewalks.

None of these things stood out very clearly. Noumea's street lighting, vestigial at best, had only recently been permitted to operate. But now the blackout had been lifted. The Japs, all hands agreed, would never again be in a position to strike at New Caledonia.

Inevitably, witnessing these sights, hearing the night sounds, inhaling the odor of human offal, Prince was reminded of Surabaya.

He slept soundly for the first time in days, a morphine-induced slumber, and didn't awaken until almost noon. A horse-faced Navy nurse was at his bedside when he opened his eyes in the hospital tent, brooding down at him as if she had been willing him back to consciousness, so that she could start her regimen of blood-sampling, injections, X rays and, for good measure, forcing upon him an assortment of unknown capsules and pills.

Prince suffered her businesslike attentions in stolid silence. Afterward he ate a breakfast of sliced pineapple, two soft-boiled eggs, toast and weak tea, prepared English style, with milk and sugar. He still felt hungry. But the equinish nurse said this was all his digestive system could absorb for the nonce, since he had been practically starving for the better part of a week.

When Prince finished and the tray was removed, she asked whether the commander would like to see the mail that had been accumulating against his arrival.

"Mail?" he echoed incredulously.

"Yes," said the nurse, "honest-to-God airmail letters. We're on a regular run from San Francisco and Honolulu nowadays. You'd be surprised. It only takes six days from the Coast."

She departed but returned quickly, bearing a packet tied with string, which she snipped loose with her surgical scissors. The letters cascaded upon Prince's bed. Obviously, Fleet Post Office, San Francisco, had finally gotten off its duff and back into the business of tracking down lost souls in the Pacific wilderness.

"Read them in good health," said the nurse.

Prince's tentmate, a blond young naval pilot who wore his wings on his pajama tops (to impress the nurses, he confided later), made an observation. Until now Prince had been only vaguely aware of a second patient in the boxy little canvas-walled room.

"I beg your pardon?" Prince apologized, not having heard what the man said.

"By God, sir, you sure as hell hit the jackpot!"

The flyboy had a Southern accent. His leg was in a plaster cast, which had been pulleyed upward, in the manner of a railroad semaphore signal.

"Looks like it." Prince smiled feebly. "But I've been rather out of touch."

"Lots of girl friends?" the pilot asked with undisguised envy.

Prince scanned the array of letters. "Mostly from dear old mom," he said, leaning forward to gather them up.

MaMa's unmistakable lavender-scented outpourings were laid aside, in a neat pile, for perusal when he felt strong enough to withstand her scribbled chatter. There were eight letters from Province Beach. Count 'em. Eight. Most had reached him promptly, owing to the fact that MaMa knew that he was joining ComSoPac.

One of the remaining five concerned his failure to respond to Uncle Sam's official appeal for a war-bond deduction from his salary. Another was an advice from a San Francisco hotel that in March 1941 he'd failed to pay for the final luncheon he had consumed before catching the Clipper for Manila, because this item (they regretted to inform him) was relayed too late from the grill to the cashier for inclusion in his reckoning; so would he kindly remit the $1.75 at his earliest convenience. Prince glanced at the postmark. It had taken somewhat longer than the nurse's joyously proclaimed six days to reach him. Eighteen months was more like it. The third missive, a postcard, was an offer from a used-car dealer in Newport, Rhode Island, to buy the 1940 Chevy he'd bought to drive during his War College tour. Elapsed time: nineteen months.

Then, very slowly, very gingerly, he picked up the last two letters. They were exceedingly crumpled, stained, bearing marks of far more rigorous travel than any of the other eleven. From their appearance they might have been delivered by meteorite from outer space.

The first bore the inscription "Santo Tomas Internment Camp,

Manila, P.I." on its upper left corner. The second had been sent from a smudged address which he could make out only after a great deal of study: "Civilian Prisoner Center, Madura Island, N.E.I." Each carried the Red Cross seal of authorization.

He opened the Manila letter.

It was from Gwyneth Dean. *"Mon plus chèr Prince,"* it began, in her precise, elegant, familiar hand, "you are the second person to whom I have written from this dreadful place, after my parents, naturally . . ."

His eyes wandered down the single page of ruled paper, which had been torn from a note pad, catching chance phrases.

"All this has to conclude one day, of course, and perhaps we shall see each other again. I devoutly hope so, dearest Prince."

He wondered why Gwyneth had strayed at this point from the diplomatic French which she'd used in her salutation. But it was an unkind whimsy. Poor, lost, damned Gwyneth, bewailing her dismal existence inside the guarded walls of Santo Tomas University, along with 3,300 other men, women and children. Food was miserable. There were no martinis. But the boredom was worst of all, after the gay parties they'd enjoyed before this terrible war broke out.

At the bottom of the page, in tiny printed characters because she had almost run out of space, Gwyneth penned: "I have had time to think about us and I've come to the inescapable conclusion that we deserve, and therefore need, each other. Please write me. And think occasionally of those marvelous times we had together."

For a moment Prince lay back against the propped-up pillows, staring at the peaked canvas ceiling, pondering Gwyneth's final words. She was probably right. They *did* deserve each other: he the 14-karat bastard, she the 14-karat bitch. Yet their prewar kind of bastardy and bitchery weren't enough, any more, to glue them together. It had been rather fun, he supposed, jousting with Gwyneth, matching her at their sly games. But that was long ago, in another country; and besides, the wench was dead. Or might as well be, so far as he was now concerned.

Finally, with fingers which he could not keep from trembling, he tore open the other letter.

Saskia's penciled note was equally brief. Nowhere in it did she mention her troubles in the Japanese prison cantonment on the bleak island off Surabaya, except to say that "life is endurable here." She spoke only of their short, happy moments in the interim before the enemy invaded Java and of the future.

With these few sentences as preamble, Saskia wrote: "It may have been due to the excitement, the turmoil which sometimes causes a premature birth, but our Princeling was born a month early, on October 3. Do you remember the night he was conceived? Do you still want me?"

Prince remembered.

How could he forget that noxious officers' club shantyroom which had served as their nuptial chamber, even though they were married only in their own minds, rather than before some stern-faced Dutch Reformist preacher? What had he told her when she had whispered that the thought of bearing his child gave her great pleasure? And what had he replied when she said they would be reunited, Prince, Saskia and the child, after the war ended?

"Christ," he'd said, "I'd want you, anytime, anywhere, and always."

Deliberately, then, he picked up Gwyneth Dean's letter and crumpled it into a small, tight ball, which he dropped into the wastebasket beside his bed. He reread Saskia's note, twice, before placing it among the rudimentary toilet articles that had been provided him in the adjacent cabinet drawer.

One hour after MOB 5's noonday meal there was a tremendous hubbub outside, near the graveled entrance, as ComSoPac arrived in his sedan. Behind him came another, smaller car, carrying the Beaver and Rodney. Halsey typically hadn't bothered to alert the hospital staff to his coming, so the doctor-in-command had less than two minutes to whistle up sideboys, get somebody to blow something raucously appropriate on a bugle and escort the great man to his destination.

The admiral was at his gruffest, most satirical best as he strode across the planked floor to greet Prince.

"Commander," he barked in the sort of voice usually reserved for captain's mast, "I've come out here to make you a little present—and offer you a job when you recover."

Prince visibly gulped, but he found himself unable to respond, so Halsey continued: "It gives me great pleasure to award you this Navy Cross for valor. I'm no good at reading citations out loud. They sound so goddamned silly, not at all like the things they're trying to describe. You can memorize this nonsense after I leave."

"Thank you, sir," Prince managed.

Then the admiral beckoned to Rodney and the Beaver.

"Hand me those other boxes," he told his aide, a handsome, not too young lieutenant who was (Prince correctly surmised) a reservist. Non-regulars were getting more of such billets these days, freeing line officers for combatant duty.

To Lieutenant Michael Rodney, USN, went the Silver Star for gallantry in the night of action of Bali, plus a gold palm representing a second Star for the recent engagement involving USS *Shearcross*.

To Commander Algernon Monk, RN, was given the Legion of Merit for a series of brave deeds beginning with Balikpapan, along with a Purple Heart.

Prince forgot the Old Man's presence long enough to remark in a startled tone, "Good God, man, I didn't know you'd been wounded!"

"It was in a place which a gentleman doesn't generally expose,

413

matey," said the Beaver. "In the ruddy buttocks, if you're really curious." He grimaced. "At any event, my sainted mother will be pleased, for, as you recall, she's always been intrigued by Purple Hearts."

Halsey's face exploded into the charismatic ear-to-ear smile which so delighted his subordinates, however humble, and the newspaper correspondents who covered ComSoPac.

"Try not to let it happen again."

"I shall see to it," promised the Beaver, "that I never turn my back to the enemy, even to reload a forty-millimeter gun."

"Now," said the admiral, "you officers may leave. I crave a few private words with the commander."

After the others had gone, Halsey sat at the foot of Prince's bed. The flyboy in the adjacent cot was asleep, as he had been during the entire impromptu ceremony; so it was just the four-starred admiral and the bemused three-striper, confronting each other across a narrow expanse of navy blanket.

"I mentioned new duty for you a bit earlier," said Halsey.

"Yes, sir."

"You've got two choices. I could use you on my operations staff, here at Noumea, considering the experience you've had." Prince did not respond immediately, waiting for the admiral to proceed with his alternative proposal. "Or you can have command of a destroyer squadron we're patching together out of some bits and pieces of this week's battle survivors." He paused, studying Prince closely, as if attempting to gauge his innermost feelings. "It'll be rugged duty, Commander, because we're just starting along the long road back. First we've got to clean up the Solomons. Then some island-hopping before we hit the Philippines. And after that the Jap homeland itself." Halsey's grin flashed once more. "You know, young fella, I've a secret ambition—to ride the Emperor's white horse. And, by God, I'm going to do it one day, too!"

But Prince had heard nothing that followed the Old Man's

mention of the Philippines. For that was where his heart lay, where he had to go, where he was willing to die, if need be, to help liberate the captured archipelago.

"Would this squadron be part of the Philippines invasion, sir?"

"Of course," said the admiral. "As part of my fleet."

"In that case, sir, I'll take it—with thanks for your confidence in me."

"Good!" Halsey rose nimbly from the bed. "I was hoping you'd see it my way."

"Your way, sir?" asked Prince in a wondering tone.

"Certainly." The admiral delved into the inner breast pocket of his immaculate Eisenhower-style jacket. "Here are your orders. Signed, sealed and delivered personally by ComSoPac. We'll allow you exactly two weeks to get back on your feet."

"Make that one week, sir."

Halsey extended his right hand and gave Prince's left palm a powerful squeeze.

"Very well. One week, provided the medics approve. Report to me when you've been declared in all respects ready to proceed on duty assigned."

"Yes, sir."

Prince watched the admiral's sturdy back disappear through the tent flap. Then he reached over and picked Saskia's letter out of the drawer. He read it for the fifth time.

One thing was goddamned certain. No son of his would ever be named Custis Hensley Morgan Prince, *Junior.*

PRINCE, Custis Hensley Morgan, retired naval officer, ambassador; b. Province Beach, Va., Nov. 12, 1906; s. Julian K. and Cornelia (Hensley) P.; B.S., U.S. Naval Acad., 1927; grad. Naval War College, 1941; m. Saskia van Dekker, Dec. 8, 1945; children—Custis H.M., Jr., Cornelia Dekker, Peter Monk. Commd. ensign USN 1927, advanced through grades to admiral, 1960; officer U.S.S. *Texas;* staff, 11th Naval Dist., San Diego; aide, Comdr. U.S. Asiatic Fleet; comdg. officer Destroyer Division 11, Destroyer Squadron 24, U.S.S. *Moline* (heavy cruiser); successively assigned staffs Comdr. U.S. 3rd Fleet, Supreme Allied Comdr., Europe; chief of staff, then comdr., U.S. 6th Fleet; chief of naval operations; ret. 1966; ambassador to The Netherlands, 1967-69. Director various corps. Decorated Distinguished Service Medal, Navy Cross with oak leaf cluster, Legion of Merit, Purple Heart, Presidential Unit Citation (United States); Order of Oranje-Nassau (The Netherlands); Order Brit. Empire; comdr. Legion of Honor (France). Mem. Council Fgn. Relations; Clubs: Potomac Yacht, Burning Tree, Metropolitan (Washington). Home: Watergate West, Washington, D.C.